BURIAL *of the* DEAD

ALSO BY MICHAEL HOGAN

Man Out of Time

This is a work of fiction. All of the characters, organizations, and events portrayed in this novel are either products of the author's imagination or are used fictitiously.

THOMAS DUNNE BOOKS.
An imprint of St. Martin's Press.

BURIAL OF THE DEAD. Copyright © 2008 by Michael Hogan. All rights reserved. Printed in the United States of America. For information, address St. Martin's Press, 175 Fifth Avenue, New York, N.Y. 10010.

www.thomasdunnebooks.com
www.minotaurbooks.com

Library of Congress Cataloging-in-Publication Data

Hogan, Michael, 1950–
    Burial of the dead / Michael Hogan.—1st ed.
        p.   cm.
    ISBN-13: 978-0-312-36729-9
    ISBN-10: 0-312-36729-5
    1. Rich people—Death—Fiction.   2. Inheritance and succession—Fiction
3. Connecticut—Fiction.   I. Title.

PS3608.O4826 B87 2008
813'.6—dc22

                                                                2008018100

First Edition: August 2008

10   9   8   7   6   5   4   3   2   1

BURIAL
of the DEAD

———◆———

MICHAEL HOGAN

THOMAS DUNNE BOOKS
ST. MARTIN'S MINOTAUR 🐾 NEW YORK

To Lisa, my wife and my love,
and
to John and Helen, may they rest in peace

ACKNOWLEDGMENTS

I thank Adam Chromy of Artists and Artisans. He's brilliant, industrious, honest, committed, and successful. He's a good friend and the best agent any writer could hope for.

I thank John Parsley, the editor who took a rough and unfinished manuscript, saw something in it, and wouldn't give up on it or on me until the manuscript became the book you're about to read.

I thank Ruth Adams, who shares her life with us and whose kind support afforded me the time to write this book.

I thank Steve Foley and Doug Harvey for their friendship and company. See you Friday—same time, same place.

Well I know that snobbery is a common charge that may be leveled against recluse and busy man alike. And the former, by their choice of a quiet life, acquire an extra stigma: they are deficient in energy and spirit. . . . So I . . . but this unexpected blow which has befallen me has broken my heart.

— EURIPIDES

BURIAL *of the* DEAD

EMMA KOST O'NEAL

Dear Manny,

I have much to tell you and one favor to ask, so I have chosen this means of communication, not to make this more formal than it need be—an intimate conversation between a niece and her great-aunt—but because I'm now an elderly woman who is getting older all the time, and given the current state of my memory, particularly my short-term memory, I am no longer assured of my ability to tell you everything I need to tell you in the detail it deserves.

You don't know this, but I was diagnosed with Alzheimer's disease a few years ago, and although the diagnosis is troubling, it has also had the laudable effect of focusing my mind on certain matters at hand. The failings one can expect with old age are a given for which I thought I could prepare myself, and, until now, I have been fortunate that the progress of the disease, at least in my case, has been slow. However, during the past few months I have experienced several troubling episodes that were of a different stripe than mere forgetfulness. As the disease progresses, more rapidly now, the diagnosis is not unlike what it was for the late President Reagan when he informed the country of his illness. Perhaps, like the president, I too will live several years more. Only God knows such things and I have tried to trust Him for the better part of my life and, all things considered, have found my trust not to have been misplaced. At the very least I do believe this—that we should expect to exert no more control over the date of our departure than we did over the date of our arrival.

A few weeks ago I met with Robert Sullivan to inform him of my health. As you might already know, Tommy, my husband and love, your great-uncle, hired Robert over thirty years ago. Your uncle was a man's man and an Irishman in more ways than one and he believed in hiring Irish whenever he could. We were unable to have children of our own and one of your uncle's weaknesses was to confer special status on certain young fellows he'd taken under his wing. *Suffice it to say that your uncle would invite young Bobby Sullivan to join him and his other men friends on weekends at Punter's Pond, where they liked to hunt and fish and drink some, I suppose, telling tales (the Irish love to talk) around the fireplace. I am not saying that Mr. Sullivan was a surrogate son, at least not as far as I was concerned. However, on many occasions he did receive the benefit of the doubt when things went wrong and perhaps undue praise when things went right. As you can probably tell I was never as taken with young Sullivan as my husband was, and when Tommy died I considered making some changes. And yet people who've been at something for a long time tend to have ways of attaching themselves to so many strands of a business that on balance it's often easier to remain with the status quo than to upset the apple cart. Today I wonder about my choices and decisions after Tommy died. Had I had the energy grief stole from me, then perhaps today things would be different and certain things would be unnecessary.*

Manny, when your great-uncle died of cancer I was devastated. We had our ups and downs, as will any marriage, but I loved him so, you cannot believe, and to this day I sometimes forget that he's not off at the lodge for a long weekend, fishing on Punter's Pond, about to come through the back door with his muddy boots and the fish he'd caught and cleaned, with his big smile, so optimistic he was, always, he told me it kept him alive during the war where he saw real action and was a hero.

I am rambling some. I admit. Memories can do that to me. Like a boat that slips away from the dock.

So now, back to business.

How can I say this other than to simply state it: Manny, sometimes I worry. I worry about you and about this mortuary and about the estate I inherited from my family, the Kosts. I worry about what will happen to all of this when I am no longer here, or before that time when I am no longer capable of managing affairs. I worry because until you arrived and made my every day more pleasurable than I can say, I was resigned to leaving the business to Mr. Sullivan and the bulk of my estate to the Kost-O'Neal Trust. But now that you're here, I find that I not only have a grandniece but I also have an heir—and I have given much thought to what that means for me and my interests, financial and otherwise.

Truth be told, and I pray you keep this confidential until I am able to meet with Mr. Stevens, my attorney, I have never wholly trusted Mr. Sullivan. For my husband's sake I never raised too many questions concerning his employment; however, I believed then and I believe now that for whatever reason I was able to see what my husband could not see, he having been blinded by his desire for a son.

Please do not think that I have evidence of wrongdoing on Mr. Sullivan's part. I don't. Not in the sense of hard evidence, the kind one would provide in a court of law. My objections, hesitations, are purely subjective and as such difficult to maintain in the absence of evidence. Nonetheless, I do have my reasons. A woman's intuition can be a powerful thing, and as I told Tommy, the Irish have not cornered the market on things metaphysical (we English have always had our fey brethren), and during my life I came to rely more and more on a sixth sense to help me chart my course in this world.

As I alluded to already, after a long internal debate, I have decided to meet with my attorney, Mr. Cal Stevens, to address these concerns. This afternoon I telephoned his office and spoke with his clerk, Ann Dillon, a lovely young woman, and have made an appointment for the first Monday in October.

My dear Manny, since the morning you walked up my front steps and I saw you through the lace curtains hanging in the bay windows, my life has been unduly rewarded with rich memories of my favorite sister, who was your grandmother. The way you look and act and carry yourself, your manners are the manners of my sister, whom I loved more than any other. I am so grateful that you found me and felt that you could come here and perhaps find a home here. I love you, Manny, and feel strongly that the fruits of Tommy's hard work and the little that remains of our family's past should pass within the family.

Therefore, I am writing to inform you that I wish to change my last will and testament so that my interest in the O'Neal Funeral Home will pass to you as well as any remaining interest I have in what was left to me by my family. The estate is a significant one, at least as regards money and material concerns. If you manage it well, you will never have to worry about such things again. I want that for you. And more than anything I do not want this gift to be a weight or hindrance to a happy life—I want you to use this inheritance as an aid in living a happy life. Over time you will find that wealth guarantees nothing—it only assists us in traveling whatever road we choose. Be a good steward of God's many gifts. Invest wisely and do not let mistrust or suspicion rule your heart or your mind. And above all be grateful, not to me, but to Life itself for its many wonders. If I knew then what I know now, I would have been more grateful. If I knew then what I know now, I would have taken more risks, would have loved more people, been kinder to more strangers. I would have smiled more, enjoyed simple pleasures, all the time realizing that true joy resides in those things that lie under the surface of glitter, tradition, pedigree, inordinate propriety, the rituals we employ to obtain identity, which, in the extreme, can smother us and keep us from knowing one another. All my life I was kind but not because my heart was warm, but because kindness was a duty to be performed. Manny, warm your heart first and then let kindness flow from there.

Finally, Manny, your great-aunt cannot finish such a long letter without putting her nose where it does not belong. I am talking about Matthew Wyman. As you know Matthew came to work here on the recommendation of my driver, Billy James, who happens to be a friend of Matthew's brother. I knew nothing about Matthew when he first arrived and yet I felt that there might be a great deal to know about this person. His books, his use of language, and his manner of conversation—in short, his charm—have all worked to support my first impression that Mr. Wyman is more than an educated and intelligent person—he is a serious person who's been disappointed in life, perhaps by life, and has turned inward, I believe, to protect himself. If he is at all fragile now it is not because he is not strong; it is because he is healing from some trauma unknown to me. I suspect you have feelings for Matthew and far from dissuading you, please accept these observations as my endorsement in this.

Yes, I am meddling where I do not belong. Forgive me. And yet because I wish you happiness in your life, because I will leave you my estate and business, because you are my relative and heir, allow me to say that if you and Matthew find your way to grow closer, more intimate, even to marry, I would be in favor of it and would rest easy knowing that you had given your heart to a good man.

I will close now. This letter will be filed with my papers and after probate will further explain the reasons behind my decision to change my will. When you read it, I will be gone. Please don't be sad about my passing. I had a wonderful life, filled with much good and just enough bad to help me appreciate the good all the more. I loved deeply and was loved in return. God is good, Manny, and everything is a gift.

Love,
Emma

EMMA KOST O'NEAL, 70, daughter of the late Terrance and Elizabeth Leffingwell Kost of Old Lyme and Wethersfield, died at her home on Sunday, September 29. Mrs. O'Neal was the granddaughter of Earl G. Kost, prominent merchant, financier, and philanthropist and founder of the Kost retail empire extant throughout North America and the United Kingdom.

Mrs. O'Neal attended Ms. Porter's in Farmington, Connecticut, and later matriculated to Mount Holyoke College, South Hadley, Massachusetts, where she studied English literature and composition and graduated magna cum laude.

In 1954 she married Thomas (Tommy) O'Neal of West Hartford on Mr. O'Neal's return from distinguished duty in the Korean Conflict, for which he was awarded the Bronze Star. Mr. O'Neal owned and operated the O'Neal Funeral Home on Asylum Avenue, Hartford, and on his death in 1987 the operation and business of the mortuary fell to the capable hands of the deceased, Emma Kost O'Neal. Mrs. O'Neal is survived by a grandniece, Emmanuelle (Manny) Whitman.

Calling hours will be 2:00 P.M. and 7:00 P.M., Tuesday and Wednesday at the O'Neal Funeral Home. The funeral will be held at Saint Richard's Episcopal Church, Thursday at 11:00 A.M., Wethersfield. Mourners are urged to make donations to the Kost-O'Neal Charitable Trust established by Mrs. Kost O'Neal in 1970 to shelter, feed, and clothe children in several third-world countries.

MIDWINTER SPRING

Midwinter spring is its own season

— *T. S. ELIOT*

Early that year when the sun was warm enough to melt the snow that had fallen all winter, Manny and Matthew lived in a house near the road that ran behind Punter's Pond, about seven miles from the town where there was nothing but a store, a post office, a diner, and a movie theater. No one traveled on the road except the couple who lived in the farmhouse on the other side of the pond and the guy with the beard who drove his truck by their house every morning heading west and returned every night heading east. They didn't know where he lived and even though they'd waved to him a few times, he'd never waved back. It was different with the couple in the farmhouse. They seemed friendly. Both waved back. She had spaces between her teeth. He was missing one hand.

The house Manny and Matt lived in was bigger than they needed. Mr. O'Neal, the late widow's late husband, had built it in the early sixties because he wanted a place in the country where he and his friends could hunt, fish, and drink. Mr. O'Neal had read a little Hemingway at Yale and that had been enough to get things started, and appetite had been enough to keep things going. Mrs. O'Neal's family owned the property on Punter's Pond, and she gave her husband the land and the money to hire a firm from Avon to build a lodge like Hemingway's home in Idaho.

Didn't he shoot himself in Idaho? Mrs. O'Neal once asked her husband, and Tommy O'Neal had grumbled some kind of answer, unintelligible but for the message hidden within the words to forget about Hemingway because he wanted his lodge and Hemingway's late-life psychosis wasn't about to screw it up.

The place had a big kitchen with a mudroom and pantry for dry goods and canned goods, and a second pantry with two refrigerators and a freezer. There was a huge room with a bar, a piano, and a fireplace and a TV room with an old hi-fi and shelves for books from Mrs. O'Neal's library. There were smaller rooms in the front, one with bay windows, two oversized bedrooms in the back, and stairs to more rooms on the second floor.

Manny slept downstairs and Matthew slept upstairs.

This was new for them. They'd been lovers—sweethearts made dewy with that film of sentiment and diamond-fury particular to early romance, noting dates, times of day, and out-of-the-way places, affording them a significance that happenstance and coincidence rarely confer.

And then it happened. Mrs. O'Neal died and Manny changed. Bobby Sullivan pulled one of his tricks, and Manny and Matt moved to Punter's Pond to wait out the storm in separate beds. Matt wrote it off to grief or preoccupation with Bobby Sullivan trying to take over the family business. Stress can do many things to people—let alone lovers—and Matt felt some grief, too. Mrs. O'Neal had been good to him. He'd miss her, but he missed Manny more. Even though they lived under the same roof, even though they brushed arms passing each other in the pantry or by the kitchen sink, even though they sat within a whisper's breath of each other before the fireplace, they weren't close, and when he watched her move about, eyes down, intent, dour, acknowledging him with a nod and busy eyes, he felt like he was lost in black space watching a satellite pass by—an impossible proximity in an infinite field, so close that proximity itself argued for joinder, even after it had moved on, leaving a shadow of false anticipation and then a grudge, a tear in the worldly fabric, another one of God's small cruelties.

One night, sitting before the fire, Matthew told Manny he missed her.

I'm right here, she said too quickly, flippant, defensive.

I know, he said and would have said more, but he didn't know how to whisper and shout at the same time.

The week before it happened, an unseasonably mild day, Matthew was walking by the edge of the pond and stepped in a patch of loose soil covered by yellow grass. His foot sank until the mud rose over the top of his boot. The mud was cold and thick and hardened as he tried to free himself. In the distance the sound of an engine shook the movement of geese flying over water. He turned to the sound of the engine and sank deeper in the soil and marsh as gelid as peat and became wedged between two objects, one of which was sharp and hard.

He called out. There was no answer—only the sound of the engine now idling behind a row of fir trees. He called again and pulled at the muscles stretched taut behind his knee. The engine stopped. A door opened. From behind the trees somebody moved. Matt called a third time but whoever was standing there didn't answer. Then he heard the door open, the engine start, accelerate, and fade down the road. After that he cursed his neighbors, the strange couple and the guy who never waved back.

He was stuck there for about an hour before he could free himself, digging away at the soil around his leg, taking care not to sink farther with wasted movement, working his leg back and forth until it slipped free with a sucking sound and he fell backward across a mound of dirt and old snow.

He limped to the road and sat on a large rock and rested until the sweat dried under his sweater. He was about to start back to the house when a car stopped and the woman with the spaces between her teeth rolled down her window.

Enjoying the lovely scenery, she said, her curious smile stretched across her face like a mistake.

Were you parked here a while ago? Matt asked.

A while ago?

And he told her how he'd been stuck. He said: My foot got stuck; there was somebody walking around back here, and I called out and they didn't answer.

That's terrible, she said, being stuck like that. And you say there was a person here who wouldn't help.

Yes, he said, calm now, trying to smile, trying to move it along.

Is your foot all right?

A little strain or muscle pull. He rubbed it and made sure not to grimace. Nothing serious, he said.

You live down the road in the O'Neal house, she said.

I do.

And your wife—I take it she's your wife—she's such a lovely-looking woman.

Thank you, he said. I'll be sure to tell her.

Let me give you a ride home, she said. You don't want to go walking on that bad foot.

I'm fine. Really. The exercise will do it good. Keep it loose so it doesn't tighten up.

Suit yourself, she said, and she started the car and turned again.

Mr. Brando and I—I'm Lilly Brando by the way—we were thinking how maybe you and your wife might like to come to dinner some night.

Well, that's nice of you, Mrs. Brando. I'll have to ask Manny.

That's just fine, she said. What say you ask Manny for Saturday night. Mr. Brando goes hunting on Saturdays, but when he gets back we can cook up something real good like maybe rabbit.

Rabbit, Matt said, his smile beginning to fade, never having eaten rabbit, wondering whether people should eat rabbit.

Thank you, Mrs. Brando. I'll ask Manny and maybe we can plan for that.

You just plan to be there, she said. Come anytime after dark, which is about half past six these days, what with the days getting longer, halfway to halfway to summer I always say this time of year. So anytime after dark then, Mister . . . ?

Wyman, Matt said. Matt Wyman.

And your wife's Manny. What a fine name. Well, that sounds fine, Mr. Wyman. Matt.

I'll bring something to drink, he said.

Oh, no, no, no, she said softly, as if sharing a secret. Mr. Brando, you see, Mr. Brando don't allow no liquor at all.

Certainly, Mrs. Brando. No liquor at all.

On Saturday afternoon Matt sat at the piano in the living room and drank coffee and touched a random white key, striking a note or two and then a chord. Manny'd gone into town to pick up the mail. They'd had a hell of a fight. Manny didn't want to go to the Brandos, and she didn't like the idea of being mistaken for Matt's wife.

What the hell are we going to do at the Brandos? she asked.

We'll talk, Matt said.

Talk? And what are we going to talk about?

Hunting, he said.

Hunting, she said.

And Mrs. Brando will show you how to cook rabbit.

Rabbit! she yelled.

Rabbit, he said.

And with that she put on the parka she'd bought at Bloomingdale's that fall and the small woolen cap that made her look European, said she was a long way from being anybody's wife, slammed her way out the back door, and throttled the Chevy down the road to town.

When she returned it was almost dark and they passed each other in the kitchen. Matt glanced through the mail on the table. There was an envelope from Bobby Sullivan, a letter from his father, and one of Manny's magazines. In the bedroom he heard her slam two bureau drawers and something hit the floor.

Jesus, she said, and he called to her and walked to her bedroom. She was sitting on the edge of the bed, her legs tucked up, her shoulders shaking as she cried. On the floor lay one of the sculptures he'd made for her. It was an angel kneeling, hands in prayer. He sat down next to her and put his arms around her, and for the first time in weeks she fell into his arms.

I'll call the Brandos, he said. We don't have to go.

No, she said. It's all right.

I know things are hard right now. But they'll get better.

It's all right, she said. We'll stay here as long as we have to, and she ran her hand along the center of his back as he leaned over and picked up the pieces of hardened clay.

In Hartford, when people asked Matt Wyman what he did for work, he didn't tell them he was a handyman or a janitor or a yardboy, even though that's what they paid him for at the funeral home. He'd tell them that he was a sculptor, because there weren't many sculptors left—at least not the kind of sculptor who knew how to swing a mallet and inhale marble dust. Matt figured these days it's a bunch of bricks on a museum floor and iron workers scavenging dump sites, would-be metaphysical poets, trying to yoke disparate objects in a Hegelian search for metaphor, all the time blackmailing people into liking it. He'd say: Carve me one hand that looks like a hand—four fingers, a palm, and an opposable thumb and then we can talk about the abstract stuff. But the time for that argument had past. The post-postmodernist guys said they stood on the shoulders of giants, but what they didn't say was that for a giant to qualify as a giant the giant had to be dead, and Matthew knew they disdained artists such as himself—artists who found representational forms in stone and had the audacity to carve them while they were still alive.

Granted there was little call for Saint Teresa of Avila swooning in Spanish heat, taking an arrow dipped in God to a heart of marble made soft by grace. Granted it was the rare counterreformative Jesuit patron who sought to build a Bernini chapel in the place where the first wife once parked her Porsche. Granted Matt hadn't sold even one piece of work but had carved and starved and grown bitter, stubborn, refusing to take up the welder's trade, to scavenge dead autos, to Dumpster dive for the crockery that might underwrite a house in the Hamptons. And granted Matthew Wyman had been driven out, or drove himself out (some say crazy), from the cities and towns where a kind of cynicism promised long life and had made his home in the shelter of huge rocks in a cemetery on the outskirts of a mill town in the foothills of the Berkshires. And granted it was among monuments to the dead that he found what he was looking for: angels weeping, pietàs, crucified Lords, Moses, tablets, pediments, and columns, because only among the dead did the Renaissance thrive. And then one night in a rainstorm, while sitting on a blanket of pine needles under a blue tarp over a wide crevice where field mice ran freely, Matthew Wyman realized that artists and artisans had carved the beautiful stones set throughout the acres of the lush cemetery lawn, that somebody had paid them for their efforts and that maybe, someday soon, he, too, would find work as a sculptor in a stone garden carving monuments for the dead.

On Saturday night Manny was sitting at the kitchen table with a sketch pad and a pen. She was writing page after page, and when Matthew entered the kitchen to tell her it was time to go, she raised her elbow to cover the page. Matthew respected Manny's privacy. He'd encouraged her in her attempts at writing stories and poems and what she called correspondence, letters to and from imaginary lovers, written during a time of crisis.

I'll warm up the car then, Matthew said, and he started for the back door by the mudroom.

Matt started Manny's car and waited as she started down the back steps, one hand on the railing, the other hand holding her cane. She wore the parka, a sweater, a heavy skirt that fell to midcalf, and the boots that gave her legs shape and heft. She sat in the passenger seat and stared at her image in the window, lifting a strand of hair from her forehead.

Do I look all right? she asked.

You look fine, he said, and he touched her shoulder and started the car and drove a short distance around the pond.

I think it happened over there, he said, slowing the car, pointing to the row of fir trees near the place where he'd caught his foot.

And there was a car nearby?

I heard an engine stop and a door open.

Who was it? she asked.

I don't know, he said. They were crouching behind the trees.

Man or woman?

Man, I think.

But you didn't see his face.

No. I mean, the trees were in the way and I was pretty shook up. I'd never fallen into a sinkhole before. It was like what quicksand must be like.

That's odd, she said. Somebody not willing to help. Then she leaned over and patted his thigh.

They drove halfway around Punter's Pond, and the road narrowed and became a dirt road with round rocks lit up by the headlights like shorn gravestones in a dirt field. There was no light except for the headlights and it rose and fell in quivering movements. About three miles past the place where Matt had fallen, the road widened without tar or macadam and became level and turned to the right. The Brandos' house, lit up and still, sat on a small rise overlooking the water.

Manny and Matthew got out of the car and walked over the gravel to the back of the house where Mrs. Brando stood, a silhouette in a screen door. They passed a small shed with two poles set in the ground. Lines ran between the shed and the poles, and dead rabbits hung by their hind legs, moving slightly in the wind.

Dinner, Matt whispered, but Manny didn't think it was funny and turned away from it.

At the back door Mrs. Brando's features were hidden in the shadow cast by the light behind her. Matt recognized her voice as she called them a lovely couple and invited them inside.

Come in, come in, she said, now Mr. Brando's just upstairs cleaning up from today, but he'll be right down, Matt and Manny. And how nice, Manny, I mean how really nice it is to finally meet you.

Mrs. Brando was shorter than Matt had expected. Her arms were heavy and full and tapered to loose folds of skin at the elbows. She pressed her hand over the top of her hair, patting it down, as if that were the first step toward making everything go just right.

Manny's smile was genuine, and in one of those surprise interminglings of personalities that don't appear compatible until the two people get together and some unexpected chemistry takes over and one person warms to the other, she seemed to like Mrs. Brando and relaxed because of it.

Let me take your coats, Mrs. Brando said, and let's all sit in the living room.

In the living room the vertical hold on the TV needed adjustment as the accordion player on the Lawrence Welk rerun continued to spin, bottom to top. On a coffee table there was an aluminum tray with an inlaid photo of an Olympic ice skater from the sixties holding a bottle of Coke. Four bottles of ginger beer stood on the tray with a box of crackers, some cheese spread, and an empty plate.

Mrs. Brando turned off the TV and the dog in the corner picked up and lowered his head, as if to say hello, though not making any great effort to do so.

Ol' Truck is a tired dog tonight, Mrs. Brando said, and the dog, on hearing his name, picked himself up, crossed the room, and rubbed his nose between the cuffs of Matt's pants.

Truck likes you, Matt. You must have rabbit smell on you.

Matt rubbed Truck under his chin, the loose folds of dog skin full in his fingers.

Good dog, he said.

How did Truck get his name? Manny asked.

Now that was a story, Mrs. Brando said. Poor Truck here was the only one of the litter of Mr. Fuchs's dogs that survived 'cause that fool dog had her pups in midwinter in the back of Fuchs's truck, and Mr. Brando and I, see—we've known Fuchs for sometime now—not long, but long enough—and we knew he wouldn't care nothin' for something he didn't think he'd need, and, well, we knew he didn't need old Truck here, so, 'stead of lettin' Truck fend for himself like all the rest, Mr. Brando and I took him in and called him what else but Truck.

As she spoke the sound of footfalls preceded Mr. Brando down the stairs and into the room.

Now here we are, Mrs. Brando said, introducing her husband who shook Matt's hand with his left hand and nodded to Manny, uncertain whether he should extend his only hand to another man's wife.

Mr. Brando was older than his wife. His skin was pocked and drawn inward around his mouth in one of those unforgiving Jefferson Davis frowns. His thick hair, as dark and gray as burnt steel, was damp and brushed back from his narrow forehead. He rubbed his face with his forearm and Matt noticed again the hook shining at the end of his sleeve.

See Truck's taken a good smell of you, Mr. Wyman.

He's a good dog, Matt said, trying to be pleasant.

Good for shit half the time, he said, 'scuze my French, Mrs. Wyman. Dog can't trap for nothin' since he got his leg caught last year. Damn dog's gone trap-shy on me, is what he's done.

Mrs. Brando opened the bottles of ginger beer and passed them around. She offered Manny some crackers and Manny took one but declined the cheese and sipped her drink from the brown bottle. Matt took some crackers, scraped some cheese over them, and set them on the plate. Mr. Brando swallowed his ginger beer in three long swallows, set the bottle on the figure skater, said nothing, and stared straight ahead. Mrs. Brando watched her husband. His behavior concerned her, but she didn't want to say anything for fear it would only make him worse. So she avoided the problem, excused herself, and left for the kitchen, saying she had to check on dinner. The silence that followed was heavy and unpleasant, the kind of silence where those prone to talking can't find a thing to say and those who are comfortable not talking get a kick out of torturing the others. Finally Manny spoke.

I used to spend summers on a farm, she said, in Wisconsin with a friend's family, and their neighbor did some trapping, but I don't remember him using his dog to help him.

Mr. Brando looked at Manny and then at Matt.

I might set down close to one hundred traps, he said. Now I am not saying I can't remember where each and every one of them is, but I gotta be damn sure I don't forget none, either, and Truck here, halfhound, half-mutt that he is, with his sense of smell, he can find each and every one of them things set down over three, four miles a' land, and that's why I use him, or used to use him before he went trap-shy on me. Now I'm not certain of nothin' with him. He see a trap now he might as well go the other way as not. There's never no telling with him no more, and I know I still got traps out there ready to snap at anything that gets too close, and that dog ain't helpin' me at all.

Sounds like a lot of traps out there, Matt said, trying to sound impressed, no more convincing than when he complimented the dog.

You wanna see my traps, Mr. Wyman?

Matt looked at Manny who raised her eyebrows as if to say, You're in it now, Big Boy, and nodded her head because it would be the neighborly thing to do.

Yes, Matt said. Yes, I think I would.

See my traps, Mr. Brando said, and you can call me Lyle, and he smiled for the first time and then forced a laugh through teeth stained yellow with tobacco, coffee, or chew.

Lyle and Matt walked to the shed. Lyle carried a flashlight and the beam swept the ground in a wide arc. Feathered spears of ice formed on the surface of puddles. Matt's breath was white vapor and the cold was damp, cutting, and made him shiver.

Still feels like winter, Matt said.

It ain't spring yet, Lyle said.

Midwinter spring, Matt said.

What?

Nothing, Matt said.

In the shed Lyle shined the light on a string hanging from the ceiling. He pulled the string and the dull light of a yellow bulb threw a bronze glow over the small interior. Hanging from floor to ceiling on every wall, filling almost every conceivable place in the cramped shed, were the open jaws of black traps—as if the shed were the burial tomb of hundreds of sharp-toothed fish stripped to their skeletal jaws.

These here are my traps, Lyle said.

Matt stared at the bizarre scene and smelled the odor of decay.

Whaddya think? Lyle asked.

Pretty fucking impressive, Matt said, not knowing what to say, using the expletive in a failed attempt to accomplish something.

Lyle looked at Matt and didn't smile. He didn't say another word.

And then, without warning, with one move of his arm, his hook pulled the string and they stood in the darkness before Matt heard him turn, open the door, and leave the shed.

The table was set, and Lilly hummed a tune as she ladled portions of stew into four brown bowls. Manny was sitting at the table when Lyle and Matt entered the kitchen. Manny caught Matt's eye and said something with her lips and then took out her pill box, opened it, and took two pills. Lilly continued to hum and Lyle took his seat and tore some bread from the loaf in the bread basket.

Sit down, he said to Matt, and Lilly placed the bowls of stew before them.

Lyle, she said, taking her seat, Manny tells me that Matt here is an artist who carves statues for cemeteries.

I don't care much for cemeteries, Lyle said.

Yes, you do, Lyle . . .

I don't care for them, either, Matt said, trying to regain some balance if not respect. I was just one of those kids you hear about—like when the other kids were outside playing ball I was in art museums staring at things.

What's that got to do with cemeteries, Lyle said.

Long story, Matt said.

Long stories are for girls, Lyle said.

Lyle! Mrs. Brando said. Now, please.

This stew is wonderful, Manny said.

Thank you, dear, Mrs. Brando said. My Lyle always catches the best rabbit for stew. No better trapper 'round these parts far as I am concerned.

Fuchs is better, Lyle said, serious, not lifting his head.

Fuchs, Lilly said, exasperated. I don't think that man's any good at all. He's just no good is what he is.

Then Lyle turned to Matt and spoke as if he were the only person in the room: Don't go wavin' at Fuchs no more, he said. Matt was taken back with this. He and Manny looked at each other, and Mrs. Brando interrupted.

Lyle, she said, did you know that one time Manny lived in New York City?

Lyle grunted and continued to eat.

Too many people, he said.

So whatever brought you two to Punter's Pond? Mrs. Brando asked.

Actually I'm from New York, Manny said. I lived in Manhattan most of my life. It used to be easier than it is now. Now it's a hard city unless you have a lot of money—hard because if you want to live there you have to make more money every year just to keep up with the way you lived the year before. I just got tired of it: Up in the morning, off to work, lunch at my desk, home from work, sometimes not till midnight, and home wasn't much of a home after my mom passed.

So you moved to West Hartford then? Lilly asked.

I did, Manny said. I had family there, my great-aunt, and that's where I met Matt.

So why'd you come here? Lyle asked, meaning Punter's Pond.

Well, Manny said, hesitating some, the hesitation saying more than she wanted.

'Nother long story? Lyle asked.

I needed a rest, Matt said.

Rest from what? Lyle asked.

From life, Matt said.

Rest from life means you're dead, Lyle said.

After dinner Lyle excused himself, saying he had to get up early. Lilly poured three cups of coffee and served oatmeal cookies. Matt and Manny drank the coffee, and Manny told Lilly stories about life in Manhattan. Manny's face brightened with fond memories. She said she missed New York and that maybe someday she'd move back there.

Overhead Lyle walked the floor, pacing, waiting, pacing.

That man, Lilly said, as she offered Matt and Manny more coffee.

Did you and Lyle have children? Manny asked.

The question stopped Lilly midstep till she recovered and put the pot back on the stove. Children? she asked.

I was just curious—I'm sorry . . .

No, no, dear, that's fine. Just haven't been asked that in a while, is all. But Mr. Brando and I, well, no, we didn't have children.

My aunt didn't, either, Manny said.

Your aunt?

Yes, Emma—Emma Kost.

Oh, of course, the house where you're staying.

The thing is, Manny said, when she died I think I was her only living relative, and I was just her great-niece.

That is something, Lilly said, though when you live a long time, outlive others, I mean, though I thought your aunt—your great-aunt—had a child. Of course, I'm talking many years ago now.

Manny moved in her chair. What? she asked with effort to keep her voice calm. I mean I don't think Aunt Emma ever had a child. At least, I . . .

No, I know, I know, dear, it was all so long ago, and it was none of my business, of course, I never should have said a word . . .

But you heard she had a baby. Back then.

No, it's just that there was talk around the lake, seeing as the Kost family was so wealthy and all, they tended to draw everyone's attention, and you know how it was back then, things like that—that kind of gossip, I mean—well, things were kept inside the family and . . . Lilly sat back and waved her hand in front of her face, red with blush. Well, now, she said, haven't I said too much this evening?

No, Manny said, not at all, but what did you hear about my Aunt Emma?

Now see and look what I've done, Lilly said. I've gone and upset you and that was the last thing I wanted.

It's okay, Lilly, really.

All I remember, Lilly said, and I was just a young girl then, but all I heard was gossip, not even gossip, more like somebody telling somebody she went away for a while, and that was it, and back in those days when a young woman went away for a while it usually meant—well, you know—or else, like during the polio epidemic, it could mean that maybe a person had gotten that. For some reason people felt they had to keep polio as quiet as being pregnant-like.

Manny sat back in her chair, raised one leg, and relaxed it again. Matthew grabbed her hand and squeezed. It was time to leave.

Well, you know, I have to get up early tomorrow, too, Matthew said, looking around the room, as if he hadn't heard a thing about Emma Kost or the twice-told gossip about Emma going away for a while.

Manny stood and shook Lilly's hand, and Lilly got their coats, and everybody said good night and that they'd have to do this again sometime.

Manny and Matt were halfway to the car when Lilly called out Matt's name.

He turned.

Yes, Lilly?

I know what you mean about being tired, Matt. So you give yourself a good rest now.

Matt stood there, looked at Manny, looked down, and then waved to Lilly Brando.

Outside the air smelled of snow. When they reached the car Matt turned to wave again, but it wasn't necessary. The back door was closed and the house was dark.

On the drive back to the lodge Matt held the steering wheel with one hand and lit a cigarette with the other and offered Manny a smoke and then threw his out the window after Manny got angry about it, saying he'd promised to give them up for Lent.

I picked up the mail today, she said.

I know.

I saw the letter from Bobby Sullivan.

Hard to miss, he said.

Addressed to you.

Yes.

So what's this letter all about? she asked.

It's not a letter.

It isn't.

No.

Then what is it, Matt?

I haven't opened it yet.

What is it?

Money.

Money for what?

Bobby's paying me to keep quiet.

About what?

About the plastic bag that was over your aunt's head.

I don't understand.

There was an insurance policy.

So?

If it was a suicide, the insurance company won't pay.

So you're helping Bobby Sullivan get the insurance money? And you're lying to do it?

I'm trying to help you, Manny.

How does helping Bobby Sullivan help me?

The money won't go to him. It'll go to the company your uncle set up.

But you're giving him an alibi. And if I can't prove he did it, I'll get nothing.

You really think he did it.

We both know he did it.

I don't know that.

Of course he did, and I'm not going to let him get away with it. She was my aunt and she wanted me to have everything.

Let's not worry about it tonight.

And then this talk about a baby, I mean what the hell is that?

Nothing, I'm sure, Matthew said. If there'd been—you know—you can bet more people than Lilly Brando would know about it.

It's not fair, she said, and she stared through her reflection in the window to the place where the fir trees stood black and still against the sky.

That night Matt couldn't sleep so he sat in the rocker by the bay window in the front room. Manny had drunk two glasses of brandy to calm her nerves and had retired to the back bedroom, where she slept soundly. Matt smoked cigarettes and thought about Bobby Sullivan and Manny's great-aunt and the phone bill from September for Manny's cell that he kept in his wallet. He thought about Mrs. Brando and her efforts to entertain guests with a husband who was antisocial and rude. He thought about the brandy in the tea cupboard off the kitchen. He thought about it for a long time, but he didn't want to drink again, so he just sat there, not rocking for the noise it would make. From the bedroom he heard Manny breathe deep clear breaths, and in between he listened for the silence that had settled over the house until a sound disturbed his thoughts and the silence and the steady lovely movement of Manny's breathing. Outside from down the road a car or truck approached the house heading east, and the light from its headlights ran up and over the yellow shades and white curtains. It touched and covered everything as if to swallow him, and having swallowed him, passed by, leaving him in the darkness that falls between two seasons.

CY PRES

cy pres—(see *pray* also *si*). *[Law French "as near as"] The equitable doctrine under which a court reforms a written instrument with a gift to charity as closely to the donor's intention as possible, so that the gift does not fail.*

Cf. DOCTRINE OF APPROXIMATION.

—*BLACK'S LAW DICTIONARY*

THE BROTHER

Brian Wyman, stout, pearly white, made jolly with the intermittent blush of rosacea, closes the door to the narrow passage with the steam pipes, the concrete, and the wires—a kind of closet aside the morgue, one of the hospital's internecine corridors leading nowhere, unused except for the storage of glass slides with tissues and cells from dead people. Two years before, one of the administrators upstairs had asked: Who wants to make an office out of a crawl space? Brian Wyman had said he did, and since he'd already made ten thousand requests, entreaties, and mild admonitions for some kind of space he could call his own, the hospital, on the say-so of Coop Johnson, chairman of the board of trustees, gave it to him, this space, which was more an absence of space, an unknown, overlooked area squeezed between the formal squares and rectangles drawn on blueprints designating function and use. It was the best the big boys were going to do for Brian Wyman, a professional good guy and diener for the morgue, and they said he could make an office out of it as long as he didn't disturb the scaffold with the cardboard boxes of slides enumerated in some code for deadly diseases like a twelve-tone scale of mortality.

So Brian installed a surplus desk from a vacated board room, a phone from laundry, two lamps from Goodwill, supplies from Staples, a picture of his second wife, Carol, and a small picture of his mother. This would be his first and only office in a career spanning decades, the place from which he'd monitor the comings and goings of pathologists, interns, maintenance men, mortuary people, and the young residents from Yale and UConn who rotated through the place three times a year, the same ones he didn't trust or like, the privileged students with the eager faces, upturned and plugged nostrils, white knuckles, ambition, and dreams (which, of course, were his dreams) of bright lawns and white houses in wealthy suburbs outside Hartford.

And his office was also the place where he counseled newly sober drunks before the meetings on Wednesday nights. Most of the pigeons from the program who made their way through the morgue were nervous as hell when they knocked on his door, not so much about picking up a drink, as about what they might see in a hospital morgue as they imagined the big guy, Brian Wyman, dressed in a blood-stained smock and one of those cylindrical paper hats, standing like a careless butcher over the eviscerated body of some poor soul who'd passed from natural causes or the autopsy itself. But Brian was careful about that. He never made an appointment for the same time Pathology scheduled an autopsy, and when he couldn't avoid the conflict, he'd meet the new guy or girl in the cafeteria on the second floor, where he held court most afternoons and where everyone knew his name.

It's a Wednesday afternoon, and Brian tosses his wallet on the desk and starts to rearrange his credit cards, the necessary designations of identity and purchasing power in a society that demands so much of both. The phone rings; he checks the LED. It's the same number that rings every night, and he thinks how his mother won't let this go. He thinks: Did I screw up Matthew's life? Am I supposed to make everything right for him, the privileged one, the spoiled one, the brother who'd always be a boy? Hadn't he been spoiled his whole life? Hadn't he gotten everything he wanted: sleepaway camp, private schools, college, ski trips, island hopping, the fucking guitars he never learned how to play, the art lessons, all that useless, fem-bullshit the old man paid for, holding his purse strings like a dying man in a desert holding water bags for himself, untying them only for the prince who'd tested well because he wasn't dyslexic and letters didn't dance around the page when he read, but fell in place so he could pencil scratch the innards of pale brackets on stupid tests from New Jersey?

"Fuck him," Brian thinks, remembering the time he found Matt, disheveled and homeless, off his meds, living in a cemetery near their hometown. Off his meds, Brian thinks, well, you mess with the bull, you get the horns. At the very least his fuckups weren't my fault and they shouldn't be my responsibility, either.

After seven rings, Brian picks up the phone, knowing it'll only get worse if he doesn't answer, that it'll ruin his night because he'll know she's out there, waiting with something he's got to deal with until she says what she wants to say, asks what she wants to ask, all the time detailing her disappointment in her youngest son, Matthew, the flawed prince, and her abiding love for Brian, her first and favorite, flavoring the whole thing with generous dollops of regret over her husband's inadequacies.

He picks up the phone. Pleasantries come and go, and Brian answers the first question: "I don't know what happened, Ma, all I know is she died in her sleep. Matt found her in her bed."

"And what was Matt doing in her bedroom?"

"Church," Brian says. "He and the old lady's niece drove her to church on Sundays."

"What do you mean 'old lady'?" she says, not liking the term, thinking that's what Brian calls her when she's not around.

"Mrs. O'Neal," he says. "I've told you all about this."

"Don't tell me what I've been told," she says. "And even if I have read the papers, I think you can take the time to tell your mother what she needs to know." So he tells her again about the trouble at the O'Neal Funeral Home and how his brother, Matt, who'd worked there as a handyman had left town with the niece to hide out in a house on a pond somewhere in the Berkshires.

"And why are they hiding out? What's this 'hiding out' business?" And he tells her how the police are still investigating Mrs. O'Neal's death. The whole story's secondhand, because he gets it from Billy James, a friend from the program, who drove for the mortuary and got Matt the job in the first place.

"Matt and the girl just wanted to get away," Brian says.

"What's her name again?"

"Manny. She's Mrs. O'Neal's niece or something."

"Manny? What kind of a name is Manny? That's a man's name. Don't tell me I raised a homo on top of everything else."

"No, Ma. She's a girl. You know how it is with these WASPS. They get a few bucks and start naming their kids after breakfast cereals."

"So she's the niece?"

"Yeah, she's the niece. Great-niece I think." He pauses. "Look, Ma, if I already told you this stuff, why are we going over it again?"

"We're going over it again because your father's worried some of this could show up in the papers. He doesn't want anybody to find out."

"Find out what? The old lady died. It was already in the papers."

"He doesn't care about that," she says. "What he cares about is whether the family name will end up in the papers."

"Whose family name?"

"Our family name," she says.

"Our family name," Brian says, tossing a pencil over his shoulder.

"So how's Matthew involved again?"

"He and Manny went to the house . . ."

"Whose house?"

"Mrs. O'Neal's house. They went there that Sunday morning. Manny can't climb stairs so—"

"And why can't she climb stairs?"

"I don't know, something with her back or hip, anyway she stays downstairs while Matt goes upstairs to see if Mrs. O'Neal's ready."

"For church."

"Right. For church."

"And Mrs. O'Neal just allowed Matthew upstairs like that?"

"She wasn't allowing anything. She was dead."

"You know what I mean."

"Billy told me she liked Matthew. I mean she was fond of him, trusted him, even wanted him and Manny to hook up. You know. So I guess he thought it was okay. Billy said they were worried."

"And who's Billy?"

"The driver. Mrs. O'Neal's driver."

"He's your friend?"

"From the program."

"So what happened next?" she asks.

"Matt goes upstairs and calls for her and there's no answer and he's thinking how something isn't right so he knocks on her bedroom door. He goes: 'Mrs. O'Neal are you in there?' and there's nothing. No sound. But he knew she was in there and he wondered: Should I open the door or not?"

"And he did."

"I guess, after he called down to Manny and asked if he should."

"And that's when he found her."

"That's when he found her."

"He was the first one to find her."

"He was."

"Of course that must have shaken him."

"I'm sure it did."

"So what's going on, Brian? There's got to be more to this."

"I don't know, Ma. I really don't. Mrs. O'Neal had a ton of money and the police are asking questions. After that I don't know."

"Did Matt kill her?"

"No . . . I mean . . . Jesus, Ma, I don't know!"

"What did the death certificate say? Wasn't there a coroner or something?"

"Frawley?"

"Is he the coroner?"

"Yeah, Doc Frawley. He's about 102. I've heard he'll sign anything for his friends and all of these guys are buddies from Tommy O'Neal's time."

"Well, this is just wonderful."

"It is what it is, Ma."

"And Matthew's involved. Did he lie to the police? Because if he lied to the police that's a crime, too."

"I don't know, Ma. He doesn't talk to me."

"Well, somebody's paying somebody," she says. "It doesn't take a genius to figure that out," and Brian hears the familiar tone of the shrewd, street-smart woman who's been around the block, who understands the little black markets of subterfuge people engage in, who's capable of gleaning the stories within stories, never articulated, but read daily by those in the know.

"Look, Ma," Brian says, "the cops got nothin' to go on except think-ing things aren't the way they seem."

"What about the body?"

"They're a funeral home, Ma. Where do you think the body is?"

"Cremated?"

"Cremated. Like I said, word is the police are stuck, but won't let it drop."

"But Matthew lied to the police . . ." she says.

"We don't know that, Ma."

"Well, the whole thing's got me very worried and it's driving your fa-ther nuts around here."

Brian half-listens now as he rearranges papers on his desk, straighten-ing them corner to corner, edge to edge, seeking order in another sphere. He moves the photo of his mother to the back of the desk, pulls an ash-tray from behind three books, dusty, battered, never opened. He centers the desk calendar with the vocabulary builder—a different word for each day of the year. Yesterday's word was *moiety* and he tears the sheet, certain that moiety's got something to do with guys who aren't priests. Then he lights a cigarette from the pack in the top drawer, inhales, and waits for his mother to stop talking. The nicotine touches his system with an enforcing calm and the exhalation of small tensions ever ready to pop like shingles down his arms, across his back, over his shoulders. Worry is his inner storm, the runaway fears of nothing specific and everything in general.

Then he thinks how his mother loves him and has never loved Matt, how his father loves Matt and has never loved him, how the two broth-ers have become enemies, chained to each other, pitted against one an-other by parents who've chosen sibling rivalry as the medium to express their frustrations with one another. He thinks: So this is my family. He thinks: No wonder I drank.

There's a knock on the doorjamb and Brian looks up. Louis LaPorta, a cop and one of the new guys who's still debating with himself whether he's a drunk or not, waves three fingers at Brian. Brian cradles the phone and motions for LaPorta to take a seat.

"I gotta go, Ma," Brian says.

"You have to keep me informed," she says.

"I will, Ma."

"And how are you, my number one boy."

"I'm fine, Ma."

"And Carol's treating you right?"

"Good, Ma."

"Did you get the recipe I sent for the vanilla tarts?"

"Yes, Ma."

"Did you make them yet?"

"Made them for Mr. Johnson."

"You should have been a chef, Brian. You have a gift. I don't know why your father couldn't accept that."

"I gotta go, Ma."

"All right then, and you're sure Matthew didn't kill her?"

"He didn't, Ma."

"Because if that ever got back here, we'd have to move. What would people think?"

"I think people think about themselves, Ma."

"Easy for you to say."

"Bye, Ma."

"Good-bye, Brian."

Brian hangs up the phone and breathes.

"Am I interrupting something?" LaPorta asks.

"No, no," Brian says. "And how have you been doing?"

"I can't complain," LaPorta says.

"Did you drink today?"

"Not yet."

"So you're doing great, then."

"If you say so."

"That was my mother. She's crazy."

"You hear from our friend?" LaPorta asks.

"Not yet," Brian says. "I figure next week he'll settle up."

LaPorta says nothing, looks at the three hardbound books standing at the back of Brian's desk. "*War and Peace*," he says. "Three copies."

"Yeah, well," Brian says. "Sometimes I like to read."

"Guess so," LaPorta says.

BILLY THE DRIVER

Billy the Driver sits in the '64 Bonneville he's been working on forever, a huge thing from GM's glory days, sitting on blocks in the backyard of his house. His face is streaked with sweat and oil and he rubs his hands with a rag made black, blue, purple with the residue of oil, petrol, dirt, and time. He's one of those quiet men who look like they've no need to talk, who consider conversation a kind of womanly weakness. But that's not the way it is. Billy talks all the time, mostly in his head, usually to himself. But the chatter's ongoing, and if anybody had told Billy he was a quiet man, he would have disagreed—at least to himself.

Iron Brian Wyman, the Big Dog, stops by Billy's place and hovers under the hood like a surgeon resecting a clogged artery while Billy grabs another can of club soda from the cooler on the front seat. He pops it, drinks half, and offers the can to the Iron Man. Brian declines, pulling back from the engine, ducking, then standing straight again, grabbing a chair off the untended lawn and dropping it next to the Bonneville's open door. He tells Billy his old man had one of these "Queen Marys" back when Jimmy Carter was president and that he could barely drive it, the car being so wide it was hard to gauge where the passenger side of the hood ended. He asks Billy if he ever tried to parallel one of these bad boys, and Billy says driving's his lifework, his calling, his vocation, as in passion, the word all the movie stars have been using lately.

"So what in hell happened?" Brian asks, the question coming from nowhere, catching Billy out of step so that he almost coughs on the tickle of cold carbonated water.

"What are you saying, Boss?"

"You know what I'm saying, Bill. There's what happened and what really happened, and I want to know what really happened."

"I told you, Brian. I told you what really happened—at least what I saw of it, and to be honest I don't like thinking about it all that much."

Brian Wyman makes a church and steeple with his fat fingers, looks at the dirty ground, and shakes his head with empathy, compassion, a tinge of sadness shared between men.

"I know you did, Billy. I know, but the old lady's calling me every day and I've told her all I know, and she's got a rat-trap mind when it comes to ferreting out whatever she thinks she needs to protect herself and the old man."

"I don't know what to say, Brian."

"What happened when the cops took you downtown?"

"Not much."

"They interview you?"

"Sure did."

"How'd that go?"

"Went fine," Billy says. "I told you."

"How'd it go for my brother?"

"I don't know," Billy says. "I guess it went okay. They didn't keep him or nothing."

"Yeah."

"He's gone to ground, huh?"

"I don't know where he is," Brian says.

"Well, the Professor, he's as smart as he is crazy, and she'll make up for the part of him that's got no common sense at all."

"You mean that Manny girl?"

"I do."

Billy and Brian work on the car for another hour, not talking, the silence of busy men. After that Brian wipes his hands on a rag and says he's got to get home. "Carol's got tickets for the Bushnell."

"What's playing?" Billy asks.

"Into the Woods," Brian says.

"*Into the Woods,*" Billy says. "What is it, a horror show?"

"I think," Brian says.

After Brian leaves, after Billy finishes with the car, washes up, and makes himself some beans and franks, after he begs off speaking at a Saturday night meeting in Windsor Locks, he takes a notebook he bought in the back-to-school section of a Walgreen's and a mechanical pencil with the 0.9 lead, sits in a chair with a lamp and the curtains drawn, grabs his Walkman from a side table and inserts the cassette he recorded the night he returned from the police station. He fumbles with the recorder, checks the cassette again, hits playback, and listens to his voice through the speakers:

They lined us up in a corridor downstairs with those halogen lights that buzz and make you look pale blue and nauseous going gray with a kind of pallor that tells you before you get started that whatever's about to go down isn't going to be good. A lot of guys are scared of cops, not because they're guilty of something criminal, but because they remember the time when they were kids in high school and ran wild with mischief, like the time Louis Brown stole a bag of briquettes off the front steps of Stale Joe's grocery store and ran over the tops of parked cars, dropping the black pellets like rabbit turds until we got to some girl's house he had a crush on, where Louis stuck a garden hose through the top of a basement window shaped like a letter box and turned it on. Cop car happened to drive by just then and Louis ran and got away with it, and I was stuck there, as if somebody had soldered the soles of my sneakers to the black driveway, once again putting me in the wrong place at the wrong time, which seems to be one of those recurring stories in my life, and I walked right up to the cop who looked old to me then, but probably wasn't more than a kid himself, and I thank Jesus he was a brother, and with my hands in front of me I told him to put the cuffs on me because I must have been guilty of something given the way we'd been running wild that year, though I wasn't guilty of flooding a basement, but of hanging around with guys who did things like that and a million other things and always got away with them, not counting the things we did in our bedrooms, like I did in my bedroom in the house in Ansonia where my grandmother raised me—which is why, all things considered, I think I've felt guilty about a lot of things for a long time for nothing more than just being human and alive in the wrong place when something heavy's going down and I have to dance and shuffle and dummy down to give myself the time I need to figure the whole thing out.

So today then, this cop, Officer David Talmadge, brought out chairs from the back room and lined them along the wall and told us to sit and wait until Detective Moraski called us into the interrogation room, which I imagined before I got there had to be dark and dull, depressing like the room on Law & Order with the two-way mirror in the wall and the army surplus furniture, the metal table with room left over on all sides so the good cop can lounge against a wall while the bad cop paces and swoops in like a fucking vulture for the kill shot, putting his face in mine, scaring the shit out of me, till I confess to the garden hose and Stale Joe's briquettes and the shit that went on in my room after school when I was a kid.

The Professor, which is the name we gave Brian's brother, was sitting two chairs down from me, saying nothing as usual, at least not to me, probably because even though I know his brother pretty good, the only person the Professor talked to was Mrs. O'Neal's niece, who'd fooled him and Mrs. O'Neal, too, though she never fooled me or Mr. Sullivan with her little-lost-girl act with that bum leg of hers. My own thinking about her I had to keep to myself since the old lady wouldn't have put up with it, probably would have called it blasphemy and fired me on the spot if she'd imagined even a little of what I thought about little, lost Emmanuelle, since there was precious little or lost about her from where I stood. Regardless of any of that, the Professor figured he'd seen a good thing come along— which is to say the girl's good looking enough, can't take that away from her—especially when the old lady went out of her way at the St. Patrick's Day party to introduce the two of them, as in: Mr. Professor, I've been watching you since Billy, my chauffeur, brought you around and I've noticed that you have more than a touch of learning and class, the kind you're born with and can't pick up on the fly, even in a place like Connecticut, and you're not too bad looking when you smile, perhaps you'd like to meet my late sister's granddaughter, which makes her my grandniece. As you can see, she's had some problems to deal with in her life, being an orphan passed around from home to home till she had the courage and the good sense to find me here, and I have every intention of taking care of her so she'll never have to worry about the details of things like food, shelter, and clothing that can distract a pretty girl and make her old and cunning before her time. What Mrs. O'Neal did not know was that the train had already left the station on that one: Manny Whitman's as cunning as they come, and the Professor, with his nose in a book, standing by a wall of books for all he was worth with that superior thing he's got about himself (as if I don't know how crazy he is and will be again if he stops taking those pills he takes every day, living in a fucking cemetery like that fucking mad man in the Bible), he saw a good thing coming down the road and he picked up on it so as to make sure he snagged the inside track respecting Mrs. O'Neal's fortune.

Iron Brian had warned me about the Professor, saying he was a piece of work—a college boy with more diplomas than a man could need, let alone want, after his name as if the spelling he was given at baptism weren't enough to convey how important he thinks he is. And Brian said every year the Professor spent in school was paid for by the old man who resented the cost but loved the diplomas, all of which only made the kid an expert about nothing useful—didn't even know how to drive a car, though I tried to teach him and almost told him to forget about it because he was nearly hopeless behind the wheel.

Detective Moraski took the Professor first, and when he stood up and put his hand out to shake hands, Moraski just looked at him like there was something wrong with him because he wasn't going to get all friendly with anybody till he got a better picture of what had happened with Mrs. O'Neal.

The tape ends with a coughing fit and Billy saying he needs a glass of water and that when he gets a chance he'll pick up where he left off and tape the rest of what he knows about how Mrs. O'Neal exited this world. Then there's a click and Billy pushes the recorder across the table, stares at it, remembers Iron Brian, his big round head, his thick fingers and troubled eyes—troubled because Brian knows there's more to the story as Billy knows there more to the story in the way that stories can swallow other stories.

Billy's known Brian Wyman for years, from before the time Billy got sober, when Billy was the one who picked up the bodies from the hospital and drove them back to the house where Bobby Sullivan's crew got them ready. Billy was hitting it pretty fair back then, though nobody knew it, not really, since he sipped all the time and was sensitive to the amount of liquor in his blood, like B. B. King pricking his finger five times a day. Then there was the accident in the North End with the coffin flying out the back of the hearse, smashing the curb, the body falling on the sidewalk, and the mother with her kids screaming till the police came and had to call reinforcements to keep the neighborhood from rioting, after which they had their own way of measuring how much liquor was in Billy's blood. Billy knows he would have lost everything if Brian Wyman hadn't stood up for him in front of a judge who was another "Friend of Bill's," taking Billy under his wing, making him go to meetings, especially in the beginning when a pigeon's supposed to go to ninety meetings in ninety days, making Billy call him every day, just to check in, just to say hi, just to keep the wires alive by which Billy maintained contact with a world outside of himself at a time when he thought he might die inside.

So Billy feels indebted and wishes there were more he could tell Brian, but there isn't much to tell. He figures Matthew must have done okay with Moraski because no noise came from behind the door of the interrogation room, and when Matthew left the room he looked pretty calm, out of touch really, walking down the hall to the double doors with the broken exit sign.

Billy looks about his own room now with the drawn curtains, the Zenith TV, photos from his army days. He daydreams and thinks of nothing, hesitant, suspended in that warm unknowing before duty or desire, until resolute, as if coming awake at the wheel of a car after having driven a long way perfectly, he leans over the side table, picks up the recorder, flips the cassette and begins again:

And what do I know, really, when you come to think about it. I'm just Billy, the driver, the kind of guy people in the know don't feel the need to communicate with, let alone share all kinds of information with, which is another way of saying I might be the kind of person who learns over time how to watch and listen when people don't think I'm watching or listening, that I'm the kind of person who knows more about what's going on than people might think.

It was Sunday morning and nobody had told me that Matt and Emmanuelle were going to take Mrs. O'Neal to the Episcopal church, which was her real church, since Mrs. O'Neal had a list of churches her husband, Tommy, had left her, so that just like he'd done, she'd go to a different church each Sunday until she'd been to all of them and then start all over again with the Episcopal church first. Tommy had always said that going to different churches every week was a way to get more business for the mortuary than if they stuck to the same church every week. Back in the eighties I'd drive Tommy everywhere on Sundays—all over town and the suburbs—Baptist, Lutheran, Presbyterian, Congregational, Methodist, Church of Christ, of course the cathedral since he was Irish, though I don't think he was Catholic to begin with, and then sometimes out in tobacco country with those little out of the way places, white buildings hardly bigger than a doll's house with a sign saying: THE ONE AND ONLY FIRST TEMPLE OF JESUS CHRIST CRUCIFIED AND RISEN WITH SIGNS FOLLOWING, and all the rest of it that goes along with services in a place like that. One Sunday afternoon we drove farther than we'd done before and stepped into a place like that and the people inside, white and black, looked at me and Tommy O'Neal as if we were aliens, which to them, I guess, we were, though to be honest, as far as being aliens you'd have had to have seen this crowd to believe it. Sure, they were poor people, and I got nothing against poor people for being poor. And they were tobacco workers, probably migrants, and the men had the leathery look of being outside too much, with the narrow eyes, most of them with narrow heads with everything pinched too close together, like they were in constant pain, like the constant hum you hear at airports, and most of them had beards or stubble and the women with that hardness that's in their blood from families who lived hard lives, never safe, not really, giving them that edge, that worried look always on the faces of people not accustomed to comfort, let alone pleasure. Up front there was this little guy with a water head and cracked eyes, too bright, crazy-like, who spun back and forth across the stage, spouting gibberish I couldn't make out, though it seemed to make sense to the others when they went forward and drank some kind of bug juice, after which some of the older boys picked up copperheads from a crate, and Mr. O'Neal and I stood there, our backs against the back wall, till Mr. O'Neal told me to go on up there and drink the bug juice and pick up a snake and I said, "Mr. O'Neal, you don't pay me enough to drive you this far on a Sunday morning, let alone kill myself with these crazy fuckers," and the old man laughed out loud, and we left that place and drove back to West Hartford where we stopped off at one of his favorite bars and drank beer for the afternoon, while he entertained Mr. Sullivan and his friends with stories about the people who drank poison and kissed snakes. After that, most Sundays, near dinnertime, I'd drive him home to his wife who was better than most with the tut tut tut bullshit, and then I'd drive into town to one of my places where the brothers didn't give a shit how much I drank as long as I paid up every week and didn't kill anybody.

So that Sunday morning in September was a normal Sunday morning as far as I knew. I was sober. I'd read my Big Book and the daily lesson and the calendar was on my closet door. I was supposed to drive Mrs. O'Neal to the Baptist church, having just gone to the Episcopal church the week before. So I drove over there in plenty of time, since she was punctual and didn't like people who were late, and when I drove up to the house I knew right away something wasn't right. First, there was a cop car parked in the street, parked haphazard like as if the cop hadn't had the time to park it right. Second, there was Emmanuelle's car, the BMW the old lady had given her outright some weeks before, and then, half on the sidewalk, half on the curb by the driveway, was Bobby Sullivan's car, and that was strange because since Mr. O'Neal died twenty years ago Bobby Sullivan's never been around on Sundays at all.

I got out of Mrs. O'Neal's Mercedes, the one I'm in charge of all the time, the one I maintain, keep clean, all of that, the one she told me to drive every Sunday, calling it her church car, and I knew, looking over the front lawn and the cars parked every which way that whatever was going on had to be some serious shit. I walked up the front steps. The front door was open a little and I went in and Manny was sitting there with her back to me, those shoulders of hers, you can't mistake them, as if she'd been some kind of bodybuilder one time, though I know she's never been no athlete, and she didn't turn around, though she knew somebody was there, and I could see the tissues in her hand as she wiped her eyes, though when I saw her face to face, there were no tears and she wasn't really crying with teardrops and a runny nose but in that high-pitched whine, half-pleading, half-exhausted, slain in the spirit whine, blackmailing me, manipulating me so I wouldn't say what I was thinking because she was supposed to be in too much pain to hear it. So I asked her, "What's going on?" And she had this phony, choppy, gurgle voice with the hiccups, catching her breath, and she says, "My aunt" (meaning her great-aunt, though she always said aunt as if to emphasize they were closer than they really were), and as soon as I heard her say, "My aunt," I ran up the stairs even as she was telling me to stay downstairs because the right people were already up there taking care of everything.

I got to the second floor and turned and looked down the corridor to Mrs. O'Neal's bedroom. The door was open and I could see the Professor and Bobby Sullivan and some cop and they were having a fucking war, and I couldn't see Mrs. O'Neal, but you couldn't miss what was happening, and then everybody took a breather, probably waiting to see if anybody was mad enough to go to the next level and pull guns or not. Matthew was standing between the cop and Bobby, trying to calm things down, and I still couldn't see Mrs. O'Neal, though by that time I knew she must be dead, because these guys weren't putting on a show for her entertainment. Then Bobby Sullivan saw me, and he shouted, "What the fuck are you doin' here? Get the fuck outta here!" And he slammed the bedroom door and I heard Matt say, "This whole thing's outta control," and then Bobby shouted something about a million dollars and for the cop, LaPorta, to call Doc Frawley because the old bastard would sign whatever Bobby Sullivan told him to sign. That's when I figured it was time for me to get the hell out of there, so I walked down the steps to the first floor where Manny was fooling with her cell phone, not using it, just holding it, and I asked her how Mrs. O'Neal had died, and she shook her head and wouldn't answer me, wiping her eyes with her thumb and forefinger, waving me away with her other hand.

I liked Mrs. O'Neal as much as any employee. I was just a driver after all—a chauffeur on her fancy days. She was always good to me and kept me on when other bosses would have let me go. I know I don't know half the story of what went on in her bedroom, though I can imagine a few things given the way they felt the need to make sure I didn't come any closer. I know whatever went down wasn't completely honest and that they were fighting over how they'd change what really happened into what they wanted people to think had happened.

At the police station, the afternoon me and the Professor got interrogated, it was almost dinnertime before Officer Talmadge opened the door again. Matt was long gone, not having looked left or right, passing me without a word, not because he was being stuck-up, but because his mind was so far away from where he was walking that it was going to take a while before he caught up with himself. I even said to him: "Hey, Matthew, you be careful out there," because I know when a guy's that far out of his mind he's as likely to walk into traffic as not. Then he surprised me, the Professor did. He stopped and looked back down the hallway to where I was sitting and he said, "You're a good man, Billy James, and there's no reason you should be caught up in this." And that was just what he said as he went down the corridor to the door with the broken exit sign and left the building in the rain.

Talmadge held the door for me when I entered the interrogation room that wasn't as ugly as I'd thought it'd be. It didn't even have a two-way mirror. I listened to Detective Moraski say he had a few questions that shouldn't take more than a few minutes, after which I'd be free to go, and they'd be grateful for whatever I'd be able to tell them. Needless to say, for everybody's benefit, and mostly for my own, I told the truth, but I didn't tell them much. After all, old people die of natural causes all the time. And we should know. I mean, we're funeral people; it's our business.

TRANSCRIPT

Portions of taped interview of Robert Sullivan (RS) by Detective Mark Moraski (MM) and Officer David Talmadge (DT)—4:30 P.M. Wednesday, October 9— Signatures and attestation waived for reproduction

RS: So, Dave, you remember those guys? Where did they come from? Avon? No. Farmington?

DT: I think Farmington. That was one hell of a night.

RS: You remember that guy? What was his name? I think it was Smitty. Motherfucker must have been six ten. What a fuckin' madman. Remember what he was drinking? All the time what was he drinking?

DT. Came in a jug . . .

RS: Colt 45?

MM: They still brew that stuff?

RS: I don't know. Maybe they got their own microbrewery.

MM: Doubt that.

RS: Nothing micro about Colt 45.

DT: Yeah.

MM: So, Bobby, you know why you're here.

RS: I think I do.

MM: We're just trying to wrap up a few loose ends.

RS: [overlapping] Whatever I can do . . .

MM: With regard to Mrs. O'Neal's death.

RS: OK.

MM: If you don't mind I'd like to tape the interview. Lot cheaper than having a court reporter.

RS: Is this thing running?

MM: It is.

RS: No problem, though maybe I should apologize to Smitty. [distorted—too close to mike] Meant nothing by it, big guy. [laughter]

MM: So, Bob, just what is your position with the mortuary.

RS: Well, I guess I'm the boss.

MM: You're a mortician.

RS: I am.

MM: But there are other morticians on staff?

RS: Yeah, sure, there's Larry and Greg.

MM: Full names?

RS: Oh, uh, Larry Trembly and Greg Rashford. Larry's about thirty. He's from New Haven. Been there about four years, and Greg's a young guy, Troy, New York. Little German kid in his twenties. Shaved head. All spick-and-span. Davie, you'd get a kick out of this kid. Just came on board last year.

MM: So your duties at the place are more administrative than actually doing the, uh . . .

RS: Right. I haven't done the day-to-day embalming for some time now, though every now and then they'll call me in on a face reconstruction. Larry's very good with the artistic stuff, but if it's a really bad car accident, burn victim, whatever, they'll call me in and I'll do that or help Larry with it.

MM: Are you a partner in the business, I mean in the legal sense of the word—or maybe I should ask, do you know how the place is organized. Is it a corporation, a partnership?

RS: It's a corporation. Tommy O'Neal set it up years ago. He and Mrs. O'Neal were the only shareholders and they made me an officer, and after Tommy passed I became a director.

MM: You're an officer?

RS: Yeah. Vice president.

MM: And a member of the board of directors?

RS: Yeah. Board of directors. After Tommy passed. Mrs. O'Neal and I are the only two.

MM: Are you a shareholder?

RS: I don't know.

MM: What do you mean you don't know?

RS: I wasn't when she was alive, and I don't know what her will says, so . . . guess I won't know till they read it. The will.

MM: But she must have talked about this. I mean she must have indicated whether the shares would go to you or to some-body else.

RS: Yeah, we talked about it. Not much, but she let on a few things as she got older. And, yes, I expect to inherit the place. I mean the stock shares. What are they? Certificates? I don't know. Kind of complicated. Why I never became a lawyer.

DT: I hear ya.

[laughter]

MM: They do make a living.

RS: Don't they?

DT: License to freakin' steal if you ask me.

[laughter]

RS: Mark, didn't you go to law school?

MM: Long time ago.

DT: One of the honest ones.

RS: Quick! Clone him!

[laughter]

MM: So, back to this dry bullshit . . .

RS: Okay.

MM: Did you have any indication before Sunday, I mean before Mrs. O'Neal died, that she had any intention whatsoever of changing her will?

RS: What?

MM: Before she died, did Mrs. O'Neal give you . . .

RS: [overlapping] No, no, no—I heard the question. I mean I un-derstand what you're asking me . . . But no. None whatso-ever. I was like a son to her. She wasn't about to change that. I don't think.

MM: You've been there a long time.

RS: Thirty years, or more. I, uh, I was a kid when Tommy hired me. And he liked me. One time said I was like the son he never had.

MM: And Mrs. O'Neal . . .

RS: [overlapping] And she liked me, too. They both did, and I liked them. Him more than her, but both of them.

MM: Okay, then, you expect, I mean your frame of mind as we sit here today is that you expect to inherit the place.

RS: Yes, I do. Of course, nobody knows the future, but as far as I've been led to believe, I expect it'll come to me.

MM: So the O'Neal Funeral Home. As a business—I take it it's a healthy business. Does well. Am I right?

RS: We do very well.

MM: I expect you do.

DT: Best funeral house in town. Everybody knows that.

RS: Tommy built a beautiful place.

DT: He was a firecracker, that guy.

MM: Yes, he was fun.

DT: You knew him, Mark?

MM: Met him once. When I was a kid. I'm thinking more about the stories I heard over the years.

DT: Guy was a legend.

RS: Like a father to me.

MM: Now, Bobby, you know Billy James.

RS: Of course. Billy's been there as long as me. Longer even.

MM: And his job?

RS: You know, he's the driver. Always drives the number one car. Chauffeured Mrs. O'Neal when she needed a ride.

MM: Okay, Bob, just to clarify. I might know the answers to some of these questions, but I have to ask them anyway. We have to make a record here. You understand.

RS: Whatever—I mean, yeah, I understand.

MM: Does he have a schedule—scheduled hours to work?

RS: Who? Billy?

MM: Billy.

RS: It's not nine to five, but it's never been that way. Hasn't had to be. He's always there when we need him.

MM: But what about a conflict.

RS: Conflict?

MM: Scheduling conflict. I mean what if there was a funeral and Mrs. O'Neal needed a ride someplace else at the same time. How'd you work that out?

RS: Whatever Mrs. O'Neal wanted, that was that. No conflict. I don't think it ever happened that way. At least not that I can remember, but if it had, whatever Mrs. O'Neal wanted that was it.

MM: So was there a funeral scheduled for Monday morning? The morning after Mrs. O'Neal died.

RS: I—uh—let me think. No, I don't think there was. We had two wakes that day, I know, but I don't think we had a funeral scheduled.

MM: So, if there was no funeral scheduled, then Billy would have been free to drive Mrs. O'Neal if she'd asked him.

RS: I guess, yeah, of course. I mean he was free whenever she asked him. That was the way it was.

MM: And would Billy have told you, you know, to keep the scheduling clear.

RS: Told me what?

MM: Was it his practice to notify you whenever Mrs. O'Neal asked him to chauffeur her?

RS: Yeah, I guess, I mean he wouldn't not tell me. But it wasn't that formal. Didn't have to be. We're not that formalized around there, but usually he'd let me know what was up.

MM: And when he told you he was driving Mrs. O'Neal someplace would he also tell you where they were going?

RS: Maybe, yeah, sometimes, like—Hey, Boss, I gotta bring the boss out to Lord & Taylor's. I gotta bring the boss downtown. He calls everybody boss . . .

DT: Didn't call me boss.

RS: Davie, when did you talk with him?

DT: What?

RS: When did you talk with Billy?

MM: Let's move it along, okay? I got to get home for my daughter's birthday.

RS: Okay, then.

MM: Now, Bob, do you know a woman named Ann Dillon?

RS: I do.

MM: How do you know her?

RS: She's—uh—what do they call them, a clerk or something for Mrs. O'Neal's lawyer.

MM: A paralegal?

RS: Yeah, that's the word. She's that for Cal Stevens.

MM: And Cal Stevens is Mrs. O'Neal's lawyer?

RS: Cal Stevens, that's the guy.

MM: And Mrs. Dillon works for him.

RS: She does, and I think she's single. Miss Dillon. Ms. Dillon.

MM: Okay, Ms. Dillon, then.

RS: Pretty woman.

MM: Now, Bob, the next couple of questions will wrap this up, so I don't want them to offend you because—

RS: Offend me?

MM: Sometimes the questions we ask can be very direct.

RS: [overlapping] C'mon, Mark. We go back, don't we? A little bit, anyway. Davie and I, we go way back . . .

DT: Them freakin' nuns.

RS: Don't remind me.

[laughter]

MM: No, Bob, what I'm saying is if the questions seem too personal or direct I just want you to know up front it's because we got a job to do here and I have to do it.

RS: Mark, just ask. Okay? You got a birthday party to go to and I got a wake to take care of. How about that—birth and death?

DT: Ain't that the beginning and the end of it. For all of us.

RS: I hear ya.

MM: Bob, concerning that Monday morning, the morning after Mrs. O'Neal died, did Billy James tell you that he'd been scheduled to drive her on that day, that Monday morning, to her lawyer's office.

RS: Billy never said a word to me about that.

MM: Did Ann Dillon ever call you or inform you in any way that Mrs. O'Neal—

RS: [overlapping] Absolutely not, no way.

MM: [continuing question]—that Mrs. O'Neal had been scheduled to meet with her attorney on the morning after she died?

RS: I said no.

MM: So you've had no information whatsoever from any source that Mrs. O'Neal intended to meet with her lawyer—

RS: [overlapping] No.

MM: For the purpose of changing her will?

RS: Are you serious?

MM: I am.

RS: No. No way. And I'll tell you something else, there is no way that woman would ever change her will. Once she put her hand to something that was it.

MM: Even if circumstances changed?

RS: What circumstances?

MM: You tell me.

RS: You can forget that. And it'd have to be one hell of a circumstance.

MM: Okay, then. The next few questions have to do with the Sunday morning you found Mrs. O'Neal's body.

RS: All right.

MM: How did you learn that Mrs. O'Neal was dead?

RS: That nut job, what's his name, Billy's friend, uh—Wyman, Matthew Wyman, he called me.

MM: Who's Matthew Wyman?

RS: He's a handyman, janitor-type guy. We hired him as a favor to Billy . . .

MM: And Billy is the driver.

RS: Right. Actually it was a favor for a friend of Billy's, the kid's brother. The kid was having a few problems, the brother asked Billy, Billy asked Mrs. O'Neal, and that was that.

MM: Why do you call him a nut job?

RS: Nut job, fruitcake, whatever.

MM: Okay, why?

RS: I don't know. I just got no patience for some of these kids. All they do is contemplate their fucking navels and can't get out of their own way.

MM: So you don't like Matthew Wyman.

RS: Like? Don't like? I dunno. Maybe respect is the word. I don't respect kids who get a leg up and then call themselves crazy when all they are is too lazy to get their hands dirty.

MM: Was Wyman lazy in his job at the mortuary?

RS: No. Not really. I mean I'm not directly responsible for what the handyman does. That's Billy's job. So I don't know. Billy said he was okay, and the old lady liked him.

MM: The old lady?

RS: Mrs. O'Neal. She said he was a lost soul. Brought out her maternal instincts, I guess. I'm just saying he didn't impress me.

MM: But he was a handyman.

RS: Janitor, yard guy, whatever.

MM: So it was the handyman, janitor, yard guy who called you.

RS: That's right.

MM: You keep saying he's a kid, but he's older than that, isn't he? I mean, he's older than your average student.

RS: I was thinking in the way that some men are men and some men are boys.

DT: Got that right.

RS: [overlapping] Men take care of men; men put up with boys.

MM: But wasn't Matthew Wyman at your apartment the night of Mrs. O'Neal's funeral?

RS: Yeah, he came by, we had a few drinks.

MM: Seems strange then . . .

RS: What?

MM: Well, here's this kid you don't like, or respect, and yet he's the one who stops by for drinks the night after you bury Mrs. O'Neal, the woman who's been like a mother to you—who loved you like a son.

RS: What are you getting at?

MM: Doesn't it seem a little odd that of all the people you're friendly with and who knew Mrs. O'Neal that you chose to share your grief with a person you don't even like?

RS: Share my grief? We were sharing a jug. I'm Irish, for Christ's sake, that's what we do at funerals.

MM: But why drink with a kid you don't even like? There's got to be some reason.

RS: Then obviously you haven't been drunk in a while.

MM: Guess not.

RS: When you're drinking like that, you don't give a shit if you're drinking with some fucking towel-head suicide bomber.

DT: Them guys don't drink.

RS: Maybe they should.

MM: All right, then, maybe I'm looking for something that isn't there. It just struck me as odd.

RS: Look, Mark, let me lay it out for you: After the funeral everybody went back to the O'Neal house. Everybody, and I mean everybody, pounded them pretty good that afternoon, and this kid was pounding them, too, so somewhere along the line I said, hey kid, let's go back to my place and open another jug. It was as simple as that.

MM: Let's back up a sec to that Sunday morning: Matthew Wyman called you that Sunday morning.

RS: The morning she died.

MM: Correct.

RS: Yes, Matthew Wyman called me.

MM: And what did he say?

RS: He said the old lady was dead and I should get over there right away, which I did.

MM: Did he describe the manner of death?

RS: Manner of death?

MM: Yeah, did he describe how she looked or anything out of the ordinary.

RS: I guess she looked dead.

MM: Didn't it seem strange to you that this handyman who'd been employed at the place just a short time should be the person who discovered the body? In Mrs. O'Neal's bedroom?

RS: Yes and no. What you don't know is that he was fucking the old lady's niece.

MM: Who?

RS: Manny Whitman. Emmanuelle Whitman. She's—what is it—a niece or great-niece of Mrs. O'Neal's. She showed up a couple of years ago and wormed her way into the place.

MM: Wormed her way?

RS: Yeah, you know, she inserted herself. Where she don't belong, if you ask me, but that's not for me to say. She was blood and Mrs. O'Neal took to her, and Mrs. O'Neal always made up her own mind about people—blood or not.

MM: So you're not friendly toward Manny Whitman.

RS: Not particularly. I'm polite. What do they call it? Professional. That's it. I'm professional. Let's leave it at that.

MM: So what does Manny have to do with Matthew Wyman being the person who called you that Sunday morning? [pause] Let me ask that again: How did Matthew Wyman's relationship with Manny land him in Mrs. O'Neal's bedroom the morning she died?

RS: They were both there, at the house. Something about they were going to drive her to church.

MM: Wasn't that Billy's job?

RS: Yeah, it was, but I'm guessing this was more a social thing. Maybe they'd go with her and then go out for brunch or something.

MM: So, Manny and Matthew were an item? Going together?

RS: He was fucking her. Yeah, I guess that's an item.

DT: She's not bad looking.

RS: Get your eyes checked.

MM: So who was at the house when you arrived?

RS: Mrs. O'Neal's house?

MM: Yes.

RS: You know, uh, this Matthew kid, Manny was downstairs, and Louie came right after.

MM: Officer LaPorta?

RS: Yes, Louis LaPorta. You know I've known him as Louie since we were kids. Meant no disrespect.

DT: None taken.

MM: So it was you, Officer LaPorta, and Matt Wyman.

RS: Upstairs, yeah. Manny was downstairs.

MM: Why was Manny downstairs?

RS: I don't know. Her choice. She's got a bad leg. Uses a cane. Maybe that's why she didn't climb the stairs.

MM: And what was the condition of Mrs. O'Neal's body?

RS: Dead. Believe me, I know dead.

MM: I guess you do, which . . . okay—I'll just ask—you're something of an expert at this sort of thing. Looking at the body, did you draw any conclusions or form any opinions as to the cause of death?

RS: I did.

MM: And what is your opinion, Mr. Sullivan?

RS: Natural causes. She had a good run; she was seventy. Not ancient, but she smoked, and at that age a person can go to sleep and not wake up. It's a peaceful death. She must have said a lot of prayers to Saint Joseph during her life.

MM: Saint Joseph?

RS: Patron saint of peaceful deaths.

MM: I didn't know that.

RS: He died in his sleep. At least that's the legend. Funeral homes got to know this stuff.

DT: I thought he was the one who could sell your house.

RS: That's another legend.

DT: Worked for my sister. Buried the statue, two days later, sold.

MM: And who called Doc Frawley?

RS: Louis LaPorta. He called him.

MM: And he came right over?

RS: Pretty soon, maybe a half hour.

[pause—rustle of papers]

RS: Are we pretty much done here?

MM: I think so, Bob. Let me look over my notes here.

[pause]

MM: Okay, Bob, I think we're done for now.

RS: For now?

MM: Hey. We're just getting things together, Bob. If we don't do it, you know the insurance company's got their own people, and they're a hell of a lot worse than we are.

DT: Talk about your proct-o-scope.

RS: Nice image, Dave.

DT: Hey, we're the Insurance Capital of the World.

RS: Don't remind me.

DT: I hear ya'.

RS: So what's the insurance company got to bitch about?

MM: There's a policy, right? Life insurance?

RS: Yeah.

MM: On Mrs. O'Neal's life, I mean.

RS: Yeah.

MM: Well, the insurance company's as confused as everybody else about the way she died.

RS: Confused? What the hell is there to be confused about? She died in her sleep. Natural causes. Look at the freakin' death certificate.

MM: The one Doc Frawley signed.

RS: Of course, the one he signed.

MM: There are still questions, Bob.

RS: What questions? Didn't you see the death certificate? Natural causes. Old age. Finis. Kaput. It happens every freakin' day of the week. Believe me, I know.

MM: I'm sure you do. Talk about ancient. How old is Doc Frawley now?

DT: He treated my grandmother for Christ's sake.

RS: I don't know how old he is.

DT: Talk about a guy who liked to drink.

MM: You've worked with him forever, I bet.

RS: Long enough. He's the coroner. What am I supposed to do?

DT: Easy, Bobby. This whole thing's just routine. No need to get excited.

RS: Yeah, right. Just sort of threw me there. I hate those fucking insurance companies. Take your money in a heartbeat; always looking for a way not to pay up.

MM: They're checking out a suicide thing here.

RS: Suicide?

MM: That's right.

RS: Now that is total bullshit. No way that old lady killed herself.

MM: And we happen to think the same, Bob. No way she killed herself—

RS: [interrupting] Suicide?

MM: That's what they think, but what do you expect them to think?

DT: Thanks, Bobby. Always good to see you.

MM: Yeah, thanks for coming in, Bob. We'll be in touch.

STATEMENT OF MANNY WHITMAN
* *

My name is Emmanuelle Whitman. I am known as Manny Whitman. I am twenty-nine years old. My permanent residence is at 312 Oak Avenue, West Hartford, Connecticut. However, for the past several months I have been living in a lodge on Punter's Pond. Mrs. Emma Kost O'Neal was my great-aunt. At the request of Detective Mark Moraski I am writing this statement regarding what I know about the circumstances surrounding my great-aunt's death and events that occurred before and after she died. I am cooperating with the police investigation into my aunt Emma's death because I believe that she was murdered, and for reasons which will become clear, I believe that Robert Sullivan committed that murder.

At the memorial service my aunt's lawyer, Mr. Cal Stevens, and his assistant, Ann Dillon, offered their condolences. Mr. Stevens was a friend of my aunt's and he was saddened by her death. I'm guessing he's in his late seventies. He's a tall, thin man with horn-rimmed glasses. He always wears a bow tie, white shirt, a real patrician. I think he went to Yale Law and comes from an old and well-respected family. Ann Dillon is probably a little older than me and she's definitely the brains of that outfit. After we shook hands she asked to see me in private because there was something she wanted to discuss.

We settled in a side room where Billy James had made a fire. I'd been crying all day and I must have looked tired and worn-out. She said a memorial service probably wasn't the best time or place to discuss legal matters, but Mr. Stevens asked if I wouldn't mind, since there were things about the estate I needed to know sooner rather than later.

So I listened. At first she spoke in a stilted, overly formal way, as if she were trying out for a part, and this is what she thought lawyers were supposed to sound like. I told her to relax and start again. I said, "Please, Ms. Dillon, I understand your concerns, so just tell me whatever it is as if you were speaking to a friend. That way it'll be easier for both of us." At first I thought maybe I'd offended her, but then she relaxed a little.

She told me that the week before they'd received a letter at the firm from my aunt addressed to me. It was sealed with directions not to be delivered or opened until after her death.

I told her I didn't know anything about a letter.

She said my Aunt Emma had also sent a second letter to Mr. Stevens, and that this letter outlined instructions as to how she wanted to change her will.

This was the first I'd heard of my aunt's will, let alone her desire to change it.

She said the letter to Mr. Stevens informed him that according to the instructions in Aunt Emma's letter to me, Aunt Emma wanted to make me the sole beneficiary of her estate. She instructed Mr. Stevens to draw up the necessary papers and that she'd be in on Monday—which turned out to be the day after she died—to sign everything.

I was dumbfounded.

Then Ann Dillon handed me the letter from my aunt. I read it and started to cry again. Ann Dillon stood up and leaned over and put her arms around me and comforted me until I could stop crying.

I asked her what it all meant, since my aunt was dead, since she'd died before she had a chance to sign anything.

Ann Dillon told me that that was where things got complicated. She told me she'd been working on a legal memorandum for Mr. Stevens to analyze all the legal issues as to how the property should pass in accordance with Connecticut law.

I told her I wasn't expecting anything. I told her how much I would miss Aunt Emma. That was when she took my hands in hers and leaned in very close and looked around the room to make sure nobody was listening in on our conversation. Then she told me that Aunt Emma had made her appointment to see Mr. Stevens last Tuesday. She told me that she had called my aunt last Friday to confirm her appointment. She told me that the problem was that when she called my aunt on Friday, she'd been unable to reach her by phone. She said a man had answered the phone and that she spoke with him. She told him who she was and why she was calling. The man said, "You're telling me the old lady's got an appointment with her lawyer for Monday." Ann Dillon said, yes, that she was just calling to confirm. Then the man said—and I think this is significant—he said, "What's she meeting with him for?" And Ann said she couldn't talk about that because it was privileged information. And he said, "It doesn't have anything to do with that crazy niece of hers, does it?" That's when Ann Dillon hung up the phone.

I believe that the man on the phone was Robert Sullivan. I think that phone call triggered a chain of events that brings me to today and my efforts to write all of this down in this statement.

After the memorial service everyone went back to my aunt's house. It's a mansion, but there were so many well-wishers the place was crowded. I'd had it catered and there were open bars all over the place. Throughout the afternoon Matthew Wyman stood at the bar near the front staircase. I watched him early on and was certain that he was only drinking soda. He and I had reached an understanding about drinking alcohol.

The bartender poured him several Cokes, I could see that, but then, I don't know when, late afternoon, five or six, I noticed that he'd become very outgoing with other people in the room. He was laughing and talking in a loud voice. Right away, I knew something was wrong. Matthew is not outgoing or loud. So I asked him if he was all right and that offended him. At that point I smelled alcohol on his breath.

He said, "I'm fine, Manny, what's the problem with you? Can't I enjoy myself ever?" And I just walked away. I had guests. I wasn't going to deal with it then. As the night wore on I saw Bobby Sullivan, another drinker, sidle up to Matthew, pouring him drinks after I'd told the bartender to cut Matthew off. Matthew never liked Bobby Sullivan, never trusted him, and yet there they were, like old-time buddies, long-lost friends, getting sloshed together.

Sometime after that, as the other guests were leaving, I saw Matthew and Robert Sullivan leave together.

The next morning, the morning after the funeral, I received a phone call from Detective Moraski, who asked to see me later that day because they were investigating my aunt's death.

When Detective Moraski interviewed me, he asked me to draft a statement that he could place in the file concerning the investigation. This is my second draft of that statement.

Sometime after that I told Matthew Wyman that we should move to my late uncle's lodge on Punter's Pond. Matthew was down on himself and full of remorse for what had happened, and I couldn't just abandon him. Also, I have a bad leg from a childhood illness and thought maybe I'd need a man out there to help me with things in the country. Our relationship had changed, but I still had feelings for Matthew and wanted to get away where we could think about what had happened without having to worry about Bobby Sullivan on a day-to-day basis. During this time I was in close contact with Ann Dillon, who was very cooperative and helpful answering my questions about my aunt's estate. The long and short of it was that as long as my aunt's death was under investigation, the probate of the estate was on hold.

Matthew and I lived at Punter's Pond when things began to unravel after Matthew received a sealed envelope from Bobby Sullivan. I happened to see it because that day—it was a Saturday—we'd had a fight over something and I'd gone into town instead of Matt to pick up the mail. When I asked him what was in the envelope, he didn't hesitate to tell me that it was money from Bobby Sullivan. He said Bobby Sullivan was paying him to say my aunt had died from natural causes when she'd died with a plastic bag over her head. I asked him why he was helping Bobby Sullivan. And he tried to convince me that he was doing it to help me. He said that the insurance policy my Uncle Tom had taken out on my aunt over fifty years ago was now worth multimillions. I guess they'd just kept upping it over the years, or it was like an annuity, compound interest or something. I don't know those kind of details, other than what he said. The point was that if the insurance company thought it was suicide they wouldn't pay. But if my aunt had died from natural causes they would. It was pretty complicated for me to understand, complicated enough that I didn't like it, any of it, because whenever anybody gets involved with Bobby Sullivan I know they end up having to lie for him while he gets away with everything.

BURIAL of the DEAD

Matthew didn't open the envelope until the next day. We'd gone out to dinner the night before and had gotten home late. But the next morning at the breakfast table he opened the envelope expecting whatever. The point is the money wasn't there. There was only a twenty-dollar bill and a note from Bobby Sullivan saying the funeral home was not in the business of keeping alcoholics on the payroll and that the enclosed money was payment in full for Matthew's last week of work and that Matthew had been fired for cause. That's when Matthew lost it. Not right away, though. He sat in the front room most of the day, sulking, feeling sorry for himself. I tried to make him snap out of it, but he wouldn't. He said he'd only done what he thought was right to protect me. And then around 5:00 or 6:00 in the afternoon, he threw a fit like I'd never seen before and grabbed the keys to the Chevy and left for town. I said, "You don't even have a license. Where the hell are you going? Get back here!" And stuff like that—but he was gone.

Later on, Ann Dillon told me what had happened at the lawyer's office. I guess Matthew had gone to the mortuary first and nobody was there. My guess is the next morning Larry or Greg told him Sullivan was at Mr. Stevens's office, which is where he was. My guess is after that Matthew went to Mr. Stevens's office and caused a scene. All I know is that after that he had a kind of breakdown and that his family had him committed to some hospital for psychiatric problems. I liked Matthew. He's a good person deep down, but I can't spend my life with a person who's got so many problems. And even though my aunt's letter wished for something else, I think she'd understand why I've broken up with him.

This is my statement, made this _____ day of _____. It is the truth to the best of my ability, so help me God.

By:_____

MEMORANDUM

* *

MEMO TO FILE:

On Monday of this past week, Matthew Wyman, employee of the O'Neal Funeral Home, entered this office at about 10:15 A.M. and threatened my paralegal, Ms. Ann Dillon, screaming that if he was not allowed to see Mr. Robert Sullivan [O'Neal Funeral Home, employee of late Emma Kost O'Neal, Client No. P10054], he would do damage to the office and possible bodily damage to my clerk, myself, and Mr. Sullivan. The man was intoxicated and out of control.

Ms. Dillon immediately telephoned Building Security.

At the time of Mr. Wyman's arrival, I was in the back conference room with said Mr. Sullivan, discussing with him several issues that have arisen as a consequence of the investigation into Mrs. O'Neal's death and that investigation's impact on the probate of the will of the late Emma Kost O'Neal. The door to the conference room was closed and we heard nothing of the commotion up front. Suffice it to say Ms. Dillon handled the matter with the same dispatch characteristic of all her work at the firm.

Again, for the record, Mr. Wyman was intoxicated.

Evidence of this: Ms. Dillon asserts that Mr. Wyman stumbled about, slurred his words, and smelled of alcohol.

On notification of Building Security in his presence, Mr. Wyman said he wasn't going to "f–k with that bullshit" and stormed out of the firm. When security arrived ten minutes later they stated that they had not run into Mr. Wyman on his apparent exit of the building. After some minutes during which I and Ms. Dillon spoke with Security Officers Talvacchia and Green, we filed a formal written report with Building Security and forwarded said report to the firm's counsel, Mr. Abe Schoen, Esq., with a copy to the local police.

Discussions ensued as to the benefits of obtaining a restraining order against Mr. Wyman and said discussion resulted in no immediate action taken at this time.

Ms. Dillon was shaken by the incident. I offered her the afternoon off for rest and recuperation. Ms. Dillon declined my offer and worked throughout the day.

Cal William Stevens, Esq.

DEPARTMENT OF FAMILY SERVICES
Division of Adoption and Foster Family Placement

Dear Mr. Deacon Leavitt,

This Division of the Department of Family Services is in receipt of your letter, dated July 7, addressed to Mr. Trent E. Malloy, Commissioner. Please be advised that Commissioner Malloy retired his position with the department several years ago and matters heretofore directed to Mr. Malloy's attention have been redirected to the current Commissioner, Mr. Joseph Forte, by way of Mr. Anatole Smith, the current Assistant Director of the Department of Family Services for the State of Connecticut.

For your information and records, a review of your file notes that your adoption identification number is C-09-28647-A287. Please use this number on any further correspondence.

The substance of your letter presents your request to obtain the identity of your biological parents. The request is recognized by legislation passed and signed into law, amended as of 1981, and to be acceded to on your achievement of the age of majority, which as of the date of your adoption was determined to be twenty-one (21) years in the State of Connecticut. Your file indicates that you are currently past the age of majority and therefore well within the terms of State Statute 35-098-80 of the Connecticut Civil Code governing the release of the identity of biological parents on request properly made in accordance with the statute's requirements.

However, with reference to the instant matter before us, I must inform you that as eager as this Office remains to comply with requests such as your own, a careful reading of the Statute by the Office of the Attorney General, Thomas Somers, Jr., Esq., Attorney General, informs this Department that we are disallowed from releasing the requested information because a similar request for the said identities was made some years ago in accordance with the terms of the Statute, as then amended, by your adoptive parents. At that time this Office under the auspices and authority of Commissioner Malloy did in fact convey to your adoptive parents the information requested.

Please know that such requests, when made by the adoptive parents, place this Department on constructive notice that the information in question has been disseminated to all interested parties in accordance with the wishes of the adoptive parents, thereby removing further disclosure from the jurisdiction of this Office. Please also know that although this Department is compelled to refuse your request at this time, you are entitled to appeal this ruling to the State's Administrative Law Courts. Contact information and forms to institute such an appeal are included in this package for your convenience.

The Department acknowledges and recognizes the importance of these matters and remains willing to assist you with any future questions you might have regarding this matter.

Yours very truly,
Lori Masterson, Paralegal

TRANSCRIPT OF NOTES:

* *

DETECTIVE MARK MORASKI

Re: *Emma Kost O'Neal*

DEATH/homicide/suicide/natural causes ??
Vic: 70, rich, widow. Emma K O'Neal
Husband was Tommy O. Man about town, drinker, party man, war hero
(Korea—Bronze star), skirt chaser, Yale.

Emma K O—heiress of Kost retail fortune. Bought, financed, and supported Tommy's funeral biz.

Also estab Kost-O'Neal Charitable Trust Foundation. Knew Audrey Hepburn. Did good work in 3rd World countries and Soviet bloc post breakup.

Bad news: Trust has been mismanaged for years by elderly college
acquaintance—Attny Calvin Stevens.

(NB: see Ann Dillon, law school classmate, now paralegal for C. Stevens)

This is the 2nd official investigation
(cold case file) (6 mos. Sept.–Apr.)
Case reopened at instigation/specific request of Cal Stevens by way of DA
James Reis (as per AG Somers)

C. Stevens pestered the AG's office. (Thomas Somers Jr.) (check family
connection: Stevens and Somers)—law firm? Stevens & Somers?

Cal Stevens accuses Bobby Sullivan, discounts coroner's findings.

Accusations re: Bobby Sullivan, also made by Manny Whitman, victim's great-niece.

Concerns about Sullivan taking under the will. Shares in funeral biz he's managed for years. (Motive?) Insurance? Key man policy. High 7 figures.

Check following:
Sullivan and Tommy O'Neal; "father/son" relationship
Sullivan and Emma K O; strained relations
Sullivan and Manny Whitman; "enemies"
Sullivan and Matthew Wyman (Manny W's boyfriend); ??? kid's a question mark
Sullivan and Louis LaPorta, Officer; boyhood friends?? Age difference. They "go back."

Talmadge is balking at assignment, pain in the ass (boyhood friend of B. Sullivan).

Talmadge and I drive to State Hospital to interview Matthew Wyman. 2nd time. Questions re: night of murder, dinner at Cal Stevens' house, birthday party for Emma Kost O'Neal.

   Obtain roster of all present.
      Cal Stevens;
      Emma Kost;
      Matt Wyman;
      Yale Doc?;
      Deacon Leavitt;
      Coop Johnson;
      Ann Dillon

Why was *Manny Whitman absent??*

And who is *Deacon Leavitt*, aka the Amazing Levon? What was he doing there? Why was he there?

2nd interview: Matthew Wyman—

State Hospital: run-down industrial area near Meriton, Wyman's home-town.

Dr. Lehman, Wyman's doctor/shrink advises against (prohibits) interview of Wyman at this time. Dr. L states that MW has had a significant break brought on by trauma associated with some unknown event experienced in recent past. Source of trauma—either unknown to Dr. L or protected by Doc/Patient privilege. Occurred at Mrs. O'Neal's house on Punter's Pond.

Dr. Lehman's assistant—Dr. Martha Wurtzel (sp?)—pretty blond exchange student from Fribourg—accent—German? French?—Swiss—

After Dr. Lehman leaves room she buttonholes me: Says Matthew Wyman is a genius. Talented, troubled, but not mad. Breaks off when Dr. Lehman returns to escort us out of building.

Call next week re: Matthew Wyman's progress.

Talmadge: "Fucking place ain't a hospital; it's a fuckin' cinder block."
Wyman's parents have spared no cost for his well-being—not.
What is family situation? Relevant to this case? Probably not.
See: brother—Brian Wyman.

Wyman spends most days in crafts room. Unresponsive. Works in silence with clay, etc. In first interview at station identified himself as a sculptor/artist.

Talmadge to set up morning interview with Bobby Sullivan—tomorrow, or day after.

MRS. LILLY BRANDO

Halfway to halfway to summer I'd say when I was a girl and it was this time of year. The night I came down here after the Wyman couple came for dinner was very cold, bitter cold really for this time of year, though maybe I just feel it more now. Even Mr. Brando said, when I told him what I was up to, he said: Lilly, what's wrong with you? You can bring that back later in the week, and I said: You saw the trouble she has walking with that hip out of joint and the limp she has. She must have bad pain with that, and she'll need her pills, and he reminded me that we didn't have her pills, but what she'd left behind was a pill box and even then it was empty. So I said: Never you mind, Lyle, I will bring it back and be done with it; after all, Mr. Brando, it's the neighborly thing to do. After which he made some noise about neighbors and how he didn't consider those two neighbors, and that even if he had, the best you can expect from neighbors is trouble, their trouble, which soon becomes your trouble. And I said: It's not right you should feel that way about people, Lyle. Some people are good and good to be around, too, and he didn't answer me, but just looked at me with those eyes of his I've known since we were kids, and I can see through them and know he's nowhere near as hard as he would like people to think, that he's just shy in the way he can't admit he's shy, thinking it would mean he's weak, and the more times he tries to hide it the worse it gets because there's always somebody you've got to deal with or talk to and when you haven't let yourself talk to anybody besides your wife for too long a time, it gets hard to be social, which was the problem that Saturday night when Mr. Wyman and his wife came for dinner.

Now, thinking about it, yes, I suppose I was curious about the O'Neal house, too, about seeing the inside of it, and curiosity being what it is, a kind of itch that only gets worse for the scratching, until you see what you were looking for and then wonder why you were so curious in the first place. But I did want to see what the Wymans had done, if anything, to the inside of that place. It's been such a long time since anybody's lived there or even used it, all boarded up, though I remember the parties that Mr. O'Neal used to throw with his friends and the women, I do not know where they all came from, all I know is they weren't from around here (New York City or New Haven, I guess) with the way they looked, all dolled up, and the cars they came in with the big fins and the colors like nobody around here would ever use, not wanting to stand out and be made the butt of conversation or ridicule.

A long time ago, when I wasn't twenty yet and already engaged to Lyle, not pregnant like the way some of the other girls would hook a man, no matter what his parents accused me of at the time, Lyle told me (yes, he could be romantic then) he told me he'd get us invited to one of Mr. O'Neal's Saturday night parties and we'd have a good time, the two of us, because there's never been much around these parts in the way of fun—in fact people round here don't even use the word all that much, as in talking about having fun, saying instead that they're resting or doing nothing—fun being nothing more than not working. But when you're young like we were you have so much energy, and the energy gives you such a hunger for everything, you're liable to do things you shouldn't, or would think better of if you were older, and it was the times, too, when boys didn't have to worry about fighting a war yet, though that came a little later on, and they worked on their cars and listened to Elvis and the Everly Brothers and then those others with all the hair that smoked cigarettes and drank beer, depending of course on what church you went to on a Sunday morning, and I'd never (believe me, I am telling the truth here) I'd never gone to a party in my life, at least not a dress-up party for adults, the kind where you have to get yourself ready for it, and I told Lyle that I didn't even have a new dress, and he pulled this box from under his bed and laid it open on the bed for me to see, and there it was, a beautiful blue dress his sister had made for me.

We are going to that party, he said. And I said: But we're not even invited. I don't know how we can just go up there and walk in when we're not invited. And he said: Lilly, now you listen to me, Punter's Pond is our lake and the land around it is our land. The fish they hook are our fish, the animals they shoot are ours, too. We grew up here, our families laid claim to this place long before these people even knew it existed, and I don't care what papers they got, what banks they got, what money they got in their wallets. Fact is when all is said and done they're the ones who should be inviting us.

So some weeks went by and it was almost Christmas and Mr. O'Neal rolled into town with his caravan of people, all driving those big GM cars with the fins out to there and Lyle came by and said: Lilly, you get yourself ready, because we are going to dance tonight. But I don't know how to dance, Lyle, I said, and he said, Oh yes, you do Lilly. Oh yes, you do. And we walked around the lake to get there and by the time we got there I was more concerned about what the dust on the road had done to the shoes I'd painted sky blue, same as the dress, and of course the closer we got to the place, the more nervous I got about going there at all, doing something I'd never done before, taking myself someplace where I knew, despite whatever Lyle said, I did not belong.

I waited off the porch next to some laurel bushes that looked dark blue in the moonlight while Lyle walked up the steps and knocked on the front door. Across the porch and through bay windows I could see shadows of people moving about and I could hear the laughter and a piano and every now and then a shout and more laughter. Somebody called for Tommy and then somebody called for Bobby and there was a woman's voice, like a screech it was, uncomfortable to hear. Point being whatever the noise was in there, it was too much for them to hear Lyle knocking, so after a while he took his hand with this ring he'd made from some kind of lug nut on his car and smacked it against the window, so hard I thought he might break it, because it made a loud cracking sound, and the party inside quieted down for a moment, and this young woman opened the door. And wasn't she a sight, all dressed in red with these heels that must have been impossible to balance on, though somehow she could do it, and a red dress cut so you could see where her breasts went their separate ways, and her hair, not so much permed as wavy and swept up, the color of a copper penny, and her lips made double wide with lipstick, which I'm sure was red though it looked black from where I was standing.

Lyle introduced us and she said: What do you two kids want? And Lyle said we came down here special like a welcome wagon to invite them all to Punter's Pond, and he swept his arm backward saying, this place, where we live. And she laughed one of those phony laughs, condescending like, and she said: And you want to invite us? which was when Mr. O'Neal came to the door, looking so spiffy with his hair watered down, brushed back, and he said: Howdy, boy, thanks for stopping by, but we're not buying any tonight. And Lyle said: I'm not here to sell you something, Mr. O'Neal, we're just here to say welcome and it looks like you're having a fine party in there, and my girl and I, going to be married come summer, we love to dance after all.

That's when Mr. O'Neal sort of figured out what was going on, meaning what Lyle was talking about, and he looked over Lyle's shoulder and down to where I was standing and he said: You're not from the sheriff's office, are you, son? Oh no, Mr. O'Neal, we are not. And Tommy O'Neal said: Because I paid the sheriff, I don't want anybody around here thinking I did not pay that man. I did, and there's no way I would disrespect the local authorities. So who are you again? he asked, And where do you come from? And the girl with the red dress said: They came here to invite you to Punter's Pond, but if you ask me they just want to come in and drink your booze. And she put her arm around Mr. O'Neal's neck and kissed him on the cheek and almost fell off one of her shoes and right then and there I knew there was no way that man was going to let us inside his house, and he said to Lyle: Now look here, boy, and it was calling Lyle a boy that made Lyle so angry, but he kept on, he said: Boy, I want to thank you for your very kind welcome to this lovely place, but as you can see I have guests and I must see to them. Perhaps another time we can get together, you and me and your lovely lady friend there, and he looked at me and with that look I knew too much about this man, Mr. Thomas O'Neal, and I hoped Lyle would turn around and walk down the steps. But Lyle felt different about it, probably because I was all dressed up in the blue dress he'd paid his sister to make for me, and I could tell Lyle didn't so much want to be invited to Mr. O'Neal's party as much as he wanted just to get us inside, to be able to say he'd done what he'd set out to do, to let the city folk know that when all is said and done, no matter what they think they own, no matter what fences they put up to keep themselves in and the rest of us out, this is our land, and we live here, and we have always lived here, and we will never leave this place except by passing over when our children and their children will live here.

Well, Mr. O'Neal was no fool. And he was no weakling, either. I could see he was a stocky guy, not fat, but muscular like Irishmen can be when they come from heavy lifters, and he sent the girl in the red dress inside and stepped out onto the porch and lowered his voice, whispering-like to Lyle. All I heard was: Look, kid, and I watched him as he tried to put his arm around Lyle's shoulder, not knowing Lyle never allowed nobody to touch him ever since his accident, no matter what the circumstance, except maybe me, and Lyle pulled away, violent-like, and Mr. O'Neal raised his voice and said: No! Now that's it. Enough is enough. This is my house and these are my friends and you are not invited into my house, so please take your girlfriend and leave, and I even saw him take a few dollar bills from his pocket, thinking maybe he might shove them into Lyle's shirt pocket, though he soon decided against that.

I can't say that what happened that night was the thing that made Lyle the way he became, I mean the way he is today. But I will say that what happened that night changed Lyle, because it was after that night he got into trapping in a way that didn't make much sense or even seem healthy with all of his traps, hundreds sometimes, and the miles he'd walk just to set them down and give himself a sense of space that was his. At least that's what I thought was going on in his mind, somehow certain that Lyle's traps have everything to do with outsiders, all those people who come from someplace else. All of which is a long way around to say why Lyle did not want me to go back to the O'Neal house, even to do the neighborly thing of returning the pill box Manny had left on our kitchen table. Of course returning the pill box was an excuse, but it was the kind of excuse that gave me enough to stand on so I could get stubborn about it, which is a good thing to get with Lyle every now and then or else he'll just take you over whole.

So, I went there after dark on Monday night. I drove and I parked on the road some distance away and walked up to the front door. The curtains in the bay windows were drawn back and the shades were up and inside the light was bronze and flickered from a fire in the fireplace and I could see Manny dancing, or maybe I should say trying to dance with her bad leg and hip and all, whatever her medical problem is, using her cane with a lion's head like Fred Astaire in one of his movies, half her clothes on, half her clothes off, and there was somebody else with her, and I figured it had to be her husband, Matt, though I couldn't say for certain, since I could not see him. Manny was doing all the talking, saying: Don't you understand? He'll never back up his story now. And she said that several times, doing this little hop each time, which is when I banged on the door and Manny grabbed at her front, covering up like, and came to the window and pulled back the lace curtain with a face that said: Who dare interrupt me? and for the first time I heard the other person's voice, certain only that it wasn't Matthew Wyman's voice. Then there was some more delay till Manny opened the door and made nice like: Oh, Mrs. Brando, how good to see you again, I was just telling Matthew what a wonderful time I had visiting you and your husband, and when she said that I knew she was full of it, so I asked: Is Matthew around? And she faltered some and said: Yes, yes, why yes, he is, though he's upstairs in his bedroom right now, sleeping, and Manny's no fool, either, and we both knew neither one of us was buying it, and that no matter what she was saying, her eyes were saying: Look, lady, I'm lying through my teeth, and I know you know I'm lying, and I don't care because what's going on here is none of your business, so why don't you just get on out of here, which is when I handed over the pill box, reminding her that she'd left it behind. She thanked me, what else could she say, but she didn't waste any time closing the door. So I stepped off the porch and started up the road, back to the car, when I heard him. The sound was so weak I thought it might be an injured cat, because it was almost a whine and there was so much pain in it, it hurt me just to hear it, and I moved a little closer off the road into the brush and he was barely talking, coughing like, though when he did make words he asked for help, which made me all the more determined to find him, and I did find him, lying there, all pulled up, knees to his chest, gasping for air, and I almost yelled out because right there on the ground next to him was one of Lyle's traps, jaws open, ready to snap, always ready to snap (though, at least Matthew'd been fortunate enough not to have stepped into it), and I stepped away and asked him if he was all right, but I could see he wasn't, and it was more than sad, looking at him lying there like that, unable to breathe or get up on his own, and it made me wonder just what could have happened in that house to make Matthew Wyman so sick as to end up like this.

SERENITY

And his name is Levon; and he shall be a good man.

— BERNIE TAUPIN

I

Peace falls like rain through trees, the descent of spirits, the ripple click of leaves, the silence that is not silence, the advent of late summer, shadows gone blue.

A concession to place:

The patient named Matthew, who calls himself Levon, sits in a room with three windows and oversees the descent of all that falls away to green water, the crater lake without beginning or end, so deep.

A concession to time:

The patient named Matthew, who calls himself Levon, having read the name, having heard the name, having stolen the name, sits in the room with three windows, at night, balmy summer, late summer, cricket summer, when mosquitoes rise up in a mist and look for blood, sending out sentries, scouts, pilot fish, agents that are determined, focused, programmed, genetic, as innocent as soldiers, not so much in need as fully formed, a state of being, their brief reconnaissance, until the bastard finds him and Levon hears the hum about the ear, the light, the sting, the draw, the gorge.

Some nights, heavy with drugs, Levon sits at the desk with the light on thinking of some band of twenty-year-old cowboys, too young for legal, pounding it like mad men in a bower of mesh and wire in Reno while country girls thick in the hips do that two-step with their Jack Spratt rope 'em boys, lean as jerky, all the time dreaming (this patient named Matthew who calls himself Levon, who pulls the name over himself like a blanket on a cold night), all the time watching, not seeing the little bastard from stagnant water circle, dive, thrust, parry, and perch on alien legs no more than the fiber of translucence, a shadow of dust on his wrist, unmoving, a cone of yellow light. Only then the fat face of his flat thumb presses the winged thing to a kind of nothingness, the way stains are nothing, too diffuse, though present still in an inch of space on his wrist and thumb. He thinks by way of breakdown how some perfect surgeon with the nanoskill of an alien in some perfect future will rebuild atoms, molecules, cells and remake the bug from a grass stain but never guarantee flight, instinct, let alone will. Something else, more easily intuited but hardly known, is necessary for that, and when he tells the doctor this, the doctor says: You may have found your way back, Matthew, though it's not the way I would have prescribed, being a man of science, as enlightened as Diderot, with my immense and unshakable belief in the perfectibility of happenstance.

A concession to time and place:

Weeks on and the medication takes hold like a rock climber hanging by white fingertips, about to get one leg up, over an impossible edge, hoping wind from the other side won't throw him down.

Weeks on and one night in a cottage on the hill above the lodge, the fields, the cabins, the cottages, the huts, the infinite lake is summer cool, but only this night and only for one night. News of rain unceasing, floods, earthquakes, rolling triggers throughout Connecticut arrives three weeks late and fills the inmates with the dread they'd reserved once for themselves, for the entertainment of love, the accommodation of loss, the celebrity of death's neighbor or spouse.

Stella from Bristol, the elfin widow, born of Puritan blood, older than revolution, pampered, wise, willful, seeks New London on shortwave and tells Levon that trouble isn't relegated to this gated community of crazies, that her children once took the Grand Tour and barely survived an audience with Fuseli when tongues of fire spun like tornadoes through Rome.

Such is the heart of a romantic, she says, and Levon escorts her to her cottage where she sleeps for two weeks in August.

Levon's radio, the one he borrowed from Molly, the cook, is silent, too. Nothing crackles or deigns to grace the air between Hartford and this clinic, this mountain, this sanitarium, this place where one whose sight has been sullied by crimes or dirty games can hope to have his mind raked clean with the spark of flame in a sea of oxygen.

A concession to memory:

Levon's crisis: With letter in hand, he left Manny and Punter's Pond for Hartford. He drove the Chevy. Anger born of betrayal moved him. He couldn't find the Mick who was hiding or gone. His key worked so he slept in the morgue, dolorous with the scent of formaldehyde, the sheen of decay, the walls and cabinets replete with the shadows of jaws.

Then morning, past dawn, and Greg from Troy woke him with a start, complained bitterly, the new employee having been told whom to hate, so fresh faced and eager to do it SS right, Herr Obergrupenfuhrer, Herr Sturmbanfuhrer, Herr Motherfucker, and not one chip of compassion in the beady little Herr Himmler eyes with the lenses layered, bisecting everything, sheep and goats, good and bad, white and black, us and them, the living and the dead he pumps with fluids to purchase just enough immortality before the grave for one matinee and two shows of mannequins on parade.

Greg from Troy shouts: Get the fuck out of here, dialing Larry on speed dial, punching intercoms and buttons, turning keys, locking it all up, notifying Officer LaPorta and the Feds, wondering what the drunk might steal from a mortuary's heart: a hose, scissors, a scalpel, a spatula, a spade, a milk glass of rouge?

Where's Sullivan? Levon asks when Larry from New Haven enters the room and lets it slip, he's at Cal Stevens's office, the lawyer, and Greg, hating him for saying it, beside himself with secrets and the failure to keep secrets, fumbles about, complaining about Matthew Wyman and the storms far away that threaten to drown Connecticut.

Then Larry, the moderate, the mezzanine of all seats, the boy in the middle, as calm as the sea in irons when water is saturated with salt, when the equilibrium of wisdom settles like serenity, says: What's wrong, Matt? Easy, Greg! What's going on here? What letter are you talking about, Matt?

But Matthew, who calls himself Levon, was gone by then, up the stairs, over white tiles and Persian rugs, through oak-wood doors, and outside to cower under the insult of too much sun burning off the damp air of the cold jungle, Hartford in April.

A concession to progress:

It's late summer, not high summer, and the heat is a comfort. Dr. Ley delegates group to his assistant, Claude from Zurich, and Levon, certain of his own election, convinced of his failings, bristles under the healing guidance of one more Calvinist.

A concession to insight:

His mother starved him and now he is a glutton. His mother starved him and now he starves himself. She starved him, and one afternoon in the big chairs on the deck this side of the lodge overlooking the lake he tells Stella his secret of how he was too young for such thoughts, but old enough to think them, unbidden, troublesome, when he placed himself in a world of all sensation without filters or avenues of discriminate entry, saying he watched the girl, who was one year older than himself, who was petite and feminine, who wore the best clothes, having come from construction money, Italian and Irish, when she walked down the corridor at noon, returning from lunch with her friends, the sight of her making him feel small, insignificant, powerless, unable to move or speak, knowing he'd never meet her, wondering what difference it would make if he did, feeling the beginning of a space that can never be filled, pierced with the sweet pain of an arrow dipped in the most profound unknowing, making a broken thing that can never be made whole, the birth of the human within himself. And he knew it would take more than sex or love or bodies becoming one, more than biblical myth, praise, esteem, or creature comforts to heal any of this, to return to Eden, to progress to heaven, because there is no cure for the other—another one of God's little cruelties.

11

The patient who calls himself Levon leaves his cottage just after dawn and walks down the macadam trail to the parking lot with the foreign cars and the camp's vans. He approaches Sammy Raymond, the camp's driver, who, with cotton rag, bucket, brushes, and soapy competence, buffs the hump of one failed hood.

"Hey, Boss," Sammy Raymond says.

"Hey," Levon says.

"Up early this morning."

"They give me pills for that."

"You take them pills, Boss, cuz they can't get to crazy less they go through sober."

The small rim of black on rose and Perugino's sky above flat water deeper than Black Forest green is still in the morning air, gentle breeze, sun dipping solemn tips of firs.

"We drivin' today," Sammy Raymond says.

"Where to?"

"The mall. Dr. Ley says he gonna take Second House and teach them girls how to shop again."

"What's that got to do with anything?"

"Doc says ain't nobody gonna get called crazy if they buy enough stuff."

"Guess so," Levon says, going along, allowing the cliché of wisdom to wash over him with an ordained and old voice hewn from fire, iron, earth, the refining kiln, the shriving wind, passing all thought and grammar, deleting all subterfuge, emitting one syllable insights.

"God bless us this good day," Sammy says, desirous of life, benefits,

91

and a prescription card. "Now, Dr. Ley's got Molly cookin' good food this morning."

"She can cook," Levon says.

"She come with problems; when she leave here she'll cook for the president."

"I guess."

"Today I order up her dead-man-walkin' breakfast, all buttered up with biscuits, bacon and eggs and pancakes, two stacks of toast with jam, them potatoes fried, juices, all kinds, dependin' what fruit you care for, and a pot of Jamaican Blue Mountain. Now c'mon, Boss, and I got you to thank for all of that."

"Me?"

"Not just you, but everybody here, cuz you pay the Doc so much for a bed. I'd never get food like that if he wasn't fleecin' somebody."

"I'm not paying a dime," Levon says. "Truth is I don't even know how I got here."

"You tellin' me you don't know."

"That's right."

"This here's Serenity Lake, Boss. Finest, deepest, purest crater lake in the world. That's reason why Doc can charge so much, cuz it's more than a clinic; it's like one of them mountain retreats for rich folk."

"So what are you?" Levon asks, "Patient, inmate, worker, rich folk?"

"All the above 'cept the rich folk," Sammy Raymond says. "I just please the boss till I get sick of all the step-and-fetch-it, then he does his little magic, puts my head right so as I'll give up the deep dark ones, secrets I didn't think I'd tell anyone, black murderous secrets, and then he's got me again, after which I got no choice but to do what he says, since the only freedom you're gonna find round here is not giving a shit or killing every bastard who knows too much about your business."

"That's a problem," Levon says, and he thinks about the first three meetings with Dr. Ley after enough of the medication had saturated his blood and calmed the brass band in his head, made the ego shine competent and the lowly id pass so far away he considered becoming a Republican.

"I see you worry some," Sammy says, snapping the rag once, twice, three times. "Must be you still got some secrets you don't want nobody to know, which are them self-same little stones in the river bed Dr. Ley pans for every day, or, failing that, I figure now you feeling better, maybe you got some rabbit in you."

"Rabbit?"

"You know, Luke, itchin' to run-rabbit," and Sammy casts his thumb over his shoulder to the low glass building designed by some out-of-fashion architect from Fairfield. "And daydreamin's nothin', either," Sammy says. "It's just your subconscious on recess, and Dr. Ley don't allow no recess 'round here."

"Go figure," Levon says, knowing the way through sober's got about forty stops on the local line of self-revelation and the desire not to get better greets you at every one.

"So what was it, my brother?" Sammy asks. "Wife, family, job, money, gamblin', drugs? You can tell me, Boss. I know 'em all; I seen 'em all. Drove 'em every one."

"I got to go," Levon says.

"Why you change your name, then?" Sammy asks. "I know you're no Levon."

"How do you know that?"

"Cuz there ain't one white Levon in all Connecticut last time I looked."

"We're not in Connecticut."

"But that's where you from."

"Don't matter what my name is," Levon says. "Don't matter where I come from, either. Not much matters once they think you're nuts and somebody else has to pay for it."

Sammy Raymond puckers his lips, bright pink and deep blue, a portrait of impoverished dignity.

"Hell, Boss, I know that, but that don't mean you can talk that way 'round here. You talk that way 'round here to Dr. Ley and you'll end up no better 'an me—full time daredevil flunky for a bunch of frauds with money."

III

Levon enters Dr. Ley's office with the long glass walls and mirrors, so empty, sharp, and clean, devoted to function, a place for thinking about thinking, for parsing dreams, naming symbols, shaving feelings, a cold place, arrogant with expertise and the curse of new beginnings.

Dr. Ley moves behind the glass top desk, peripatetic, pacing from one side of the office to the other, from glass wall to mirror and back, hovering at times, then moving again. He says to Levon: "Your equation is wrong." He says that success is not immoral, that it's a measure of how well certain tasks are performed in accord with certain rules to obtain a certain result. He tells Levon that his mistake has been to drape the whole process with a self-indulgent concern for morality, which "is like pouring molasses over the inner workings of a watch."

Levon says nothing.

Dr. Ley says: "You've been injected with a strain of religion, endemic to America, a catechism that means nothing of what it says, except to require absolute obedience—a catechism that extols poverty in return for promissory notes that never come due. You've been fooled, Matthew, or Levon, or whatever you call yourself. You've been sold a bill of goods, and your father never took you aside to let you in on the secret, which is to be polite but not to take it all so seriously. There's a lot of wiggle room in the Baltimore Catechism."

The phone rings. Dr. Ley crosses the room and picks it up. Levon listens as Dr. Ley tells someone to purchase a thousand puts as per the information in the morning's fax. He hangs up the phone. Levon notes the absence of small talk.

"You're depressed," Dr. Ley says. "I assume that's why you're here. Alcohol or whatever has been your medication. No surprise there. Society approved of it till late midcentury when all those drunk drivers ruined it for the rest of us. Now they'd prefer you watch more TV, live vicariously, virtually, sell your soul to some sports team. Dress up like a fool on Sundays. Cheer for something that won't harm the state, which of course is not the state."

Levon thinks about the Yankees and the Red Sox. He's seen photos of men dressed like dogs in Cleveland, like pigs in D.C.

"You're depressed because you feel the world's treated you badly, and your brother's paying me a fortune so I can tell you it's all true and commiserate with you and say the world is unfair, which I would do if I were a quack and intended to drop you back into the world as fucked up as the day you got here. Because the inescapable fact that most wounded people can't seem to accept is that the world isn't unfair, Matthew. It just is—like nature, like the weather, like the ocean. It doesn't care about you one way or the other." And he tells Levon that although he'd been well trained in certain bookish pursuits, he'd been hamstrung with notions of good and evil, of ethics and law, of choice and consequence, of punishment, exile, and separation.

"What are laws?" the doctor asks. "A call to honor? Hardly. It's the minimum. You can fuck a million people a million ways and never come close to breaking any law. And what about ethics? A lot of pretty thoughts cast in the subjunctive mode without consequence: You should do this; you should do that—or else. Or else what? Or else nothing, except maybe a book deal and an hour with Barbara Walters. And as for good and evil? Really. It's a medieval concept employed to keep people paying, quiet, and dumb. Why do you think the Church stands at the right hand of royalty? Because if the minister can scare the shit out of the congregation on Sunday, they're less likely to toss the king out on his ass on Monday. In the end the Church is little more than a state's cost-effective police force.

"So, were you fucked? Absolutely, but not in the way you think. You were fucked because you were sent on a bear hunt with one bow and no arrows in your quiver, while your competition carried AK-47s, a map, a compass, and a bottle of bear smell."

Levon looks out the window. Across a narrow bridge over a creek that runs to the lake, past a fountain and a stone garden, Molly carries crates of milk cartons to the storage area. Stella sits on the deck overlooking the lake, swatting flies, talking to Marta, Dr. Ley's blond wife, who rubs her young legs with tanning lotion.

After a while Levon looks at the doctor who's moved on to some other matter on his Blackberry.

"So, that's it?" Levon asks.

"That's it, Matthew."

"Thanks," Levon says, and he leaves Dr. Ley's little Bauhaus.

IV

The sight of Marta standing near the boathouse on a dock over water, about to dive and swim, causes Levon to miss his supper and walk the grounds till midnight—a mild relapse, or perhaps more.

Owl light on old roads, a nether region of the jungle's pallet, and Levon, the plagiarist, writing someone else's story, throws pebbles at the failed lattice and green glass darkened for private night. This is the untoward toward, a capsule of sleep, a momentary romance, a memory of airwaves brushing the long hair of careless youth when he believed he'd been carved from white marble, the perfect slope of muscle, the incalculable calculus of beauty, an epic hero, languid on waking, turning with the long lingering somnambulant breadth of his shoulders, and again his hand scoops the smallest bean, a wedge shot ricochets off the bay window, and he calls her name.

Marta comes to the window, the blond woman he watches from a distance, the married woman who watches Levon from a distance. She looks about and then pulls the shade. He thinks: perhaps another time in a world where men fly, breathe without air, move within themselves till all movement stops, having learned that time is not space and cannot be traversed but requires the utter stillness beyond patience of one seeking passage back.

V

Levon walks slowly across the recreation field. He's tall, slim, broad-shouldered, and walks with the easy athletic grace of a champion swimmer or center fielder. He doesn't look left or right, his baseball cap pulled down, framing the high forehead, emphasizing the straight nose, the strong jaw, the sensuous lips. With the cap, he's handsome; with his height, grace, and style, he's superior; with the attitude, he's irresistible. He imagines how all must look upon him and wonder at the far end of worldly possibilities, at the perfectible image of an almost perfect specimen.

At the far end of the field past the main lodge, Levon looks for Molly Knox, the cook. After dinner Levon usually finds her sitting on the deck of the small cabin she's made her own, resting in a lawn chair with a glass of iced tea, sometimes staring at nothing, sometimes looking through pines to the lake below.

Levon remembers the first time he met Molly in the storage room behind the dining hall where cans of food stood like pillars from floor to ceiling. He told her he liked her meals, but she sobbed and almost cried, saying: "Three meals and, except for you, just now, not one compliment, not one thank-you, not one smile. Three meals and, except for you, all I heard was one complaint from the anorexic who's probably not the best judge of institutional cuisine." Levon took her hand and kissed the back of it and thanked her again. Then Molly told him how when Marta Ley had hired her in March, she'd imagined a life lived among the universally challenged at a compound of lodges, cabins, huts, a quaint Tyrolean village set on the side of a hill overlooking a crater lake, as a task that might exercise her faith, call upon her tired grace, satisfy her desire to be needed, to matter, to count, to replenish her ever-diminishing reservoir of goodwill. "But work is work," she said, "and never as gratifying on Monday as it looks on the Friday afternoon they hire you."

"Molly?" Levon calls in a whisper, and his voice rises like damp humidity giving way to the undercool of twilight.

"Molly?" he calls again and Molly lowers her legs from the yellow banister and leans forward and looks over the railing to the grass below.

"Levon," she says, with a warmth that transforms the heat and humidity to the feel of blankets on an October night when love wraps itself within itself. "What are you doing down there?" she asks, and with three movements—arms, legs, all muscle, tense and relaxed, the effort of a gymnast half his age—Levon levitates and vaults the railing and stands beside her.

"For you," he says and from a backpack he takes out a small angel, kneeling on one knee, holding a pillar, perhaps a flame, waiting by the tomb, waiting on the dead Lord to live again.

Molly holds it in her chapped hands. "Levon," she says, "how beautiful," and she asks him to sit.

He declines and leans against the railing, legs thin, denim pants nearly pegged over brown pointy boots.

"You remind me of a country singer tonight," she says.

"I remind a lot of people of a lot of things," he says.

"Well, tonight I'd say a cowboy or one of those line men for the county, because of the cap."

"Yeah, well," Levon says, "I never wanted to wear one of those Spin-and-Marty hats."

"Spin and who?"

"All-hat-no-cattle hats."

Molly leans back in her chair. "You did this," she says, holding the angel before her.

"It's nothin'," he says. "I thought you might like it."

"Nothing!" she says, an exclamation and protest. "This is beautiful," but Levon's smart enough to know the clay sculpture, baked and hardened in the camp's only kiln, is flawed. He knows in the way his mind's eye works overtime to correct the lines of the too-thick arm, a misplaced muscle, the failure of the three-quarter view. He knows in the way he wants to take it from her and set it on the railing in the only position where everything falls into place, where mistakes are hidden by point of view.

"No, Levon, now don't you minimize your talent. That's the best part of you, the part that shouldn't be covered up."

Levon says the aw-shucks-cowboy thanks, acting and then unable to act as the cowboy's shy unease overlaps some discomfort resident within, so that as two tones of synchronous waves resonate and shiver with simultaneity, he momentarily dissembles downward, a man falling through trees, reaching out, grabbing air until he finds the lost rebel's inarticulate mumble.

"Would you like some tea?" he asks.

"I've got some, Levon, right here. Maybe I can get you some."

"I like to make it," he says. "The way you boil the water, pour it through the pot, soak the leaves, let it steep."

"I'm fine, Levon, but let me get you some," and she starts to get up and he touches her arm to let her know he's fine—fine again now—because the invisible blanket's pulled up again, tucked snug, the way it should be, the world having returned to its proper place, spinning without motion or dissembling wind.

"So what made you come here?" Levon asks as he pulls a lawn chair across the deck, sets it next to her, and sits with his legs straight out, a triangle of space between his belt, his back, and the seat.

"Well, you know, Levon, I was married and then I was divorced and I was living with my mother in Middletown."

"I guess those are good reasons," Levon says.

"It's a job, and I needed a job."

"I know," he says, his hand resting for the briefest touch of light fingers on her forearm, as if to say he does know in ways she can only guess, having been gifted with the second sight of the half-crazed manic-depressive with pieces of his soul in hell and sometimes in flight toward heaven.

"I've never hurt a living thing," he says, "except once, and that's the worst thing I ever did."

"It's all right, Levon."

"My father worries about me," he says. "There was this trouble in Hartford where somebody killed an old woman and I was the first one to find the body and my father's worried it will get into the papers and ruin his reputation."

Molly says nothing. Now she touches Levon's arm.

"My mother asked my brother if I'd killed the old lady."

"Why would she think that?"

"If she thought I was capable of murder it'd probably be a step up in her estimation."

"In her estimation of?"

"In her estimation of me."

"I see."

"In my family it's like: Men are capable of murder, boys aren't."

"You're not close then."

"No."

"But who was the woman who was killed?"

"Mrs. O'Neal from Hartford. She was a good woman. Good to me, anyway."

"And you were the first one to find her?"

"Second, really. Found her with a plastic bag over her head. There was this guy who was going to pay me a lot of money to say there wasn't any bag."

"Why?"

"Because the bag made it look like suicide and he wanted the insurance money."

"Do you think he killed her?"

"Most everybody else does. I don't know."

"Maybe she did commit suicide."

"A few people think so, but I don't. Then again, what do I know? I'm sick, right?"

"Are you? I think you're one of the healthy ones, doctors included. Time will come very soon, you'll be leaving here."

"Soon enough," he says, "but not too soon. They only let you go when you want to stay, and they keep you as long as you want to leave."

"Levon, they only let you go when you can't pay anymore."

"Yeah."

"Your family must have money to pay for this."

"They keep saying my brother's paying. I don't know where he got the money."

Overhead the Magritte sky remains cerulean blue as the pine trees grow black and the sloping lawn devolves to green and umber. From across the lake the sound of children singing carries over water. It's a show tune. Something Levon's heard before, something fantastic, something of legends, myths, fairy tales.

"Are you going to go?" Molly asks.

"Where?"

"Across the lake."

"What for?"

"The camp's putting on a musical. It's one of those summer stock camps for kids."

"A musical?"

"Yes. Summer theater."

"How are people getting there?"

"Dr. Ley will be driving one van. Sammy will drive the other."

"Do those kids know we're coming?"

"I would think so."

"To think they'll be all dressed up with makeup and then here come the crazies."

Molly leans back and sips more tea. Her arms are full and heavy, and Levon imagines that maybe, for a moment, she can feel the weight that bears on him, the weight of the not-quite-sane, the fatigue of keeping things at bay, of saying enough but never too much for fear the dam will break and everything will be washed away. He thinks of floods out west where rivers overflow their banks and the reticence of cowboys. He thinks of God's flood and wonders if it happened because God had said too much, shared too much, couldn't contain the pain of creating this whole thing.

"Dr. Ley's all for entertainment," Molly says.

"I guess he is," Levon says, hat beak down again, the cowboy's jaw in shadow.

"I heard that last year he had this troop here from some circus."

"Great," Levon says, and the word is flat and careless as he leans back and his profile goes even with the horizon—the line of his aquiline nose, the delicate nostrils, the beautiful eyelashes, the round lips.

Across the lake the singing continues and the words finally take shape as they repeat "Into the woods," until a crescendo ends the last rehearsal before the show.

Levon imagines the excitement of little girls running about back-stage, little girls who've been told they're talented and worthy and valuable, looking for bangles and baubles and the lipstick they'll wear, the wigs and cloaks and charcoal sticks they'll use to make themselves old before their time.

Then Levon asks Molly about her former husband, Tommy, the sport, long gone now, having moved on to some job someplace else—a traveling man from the beginning, a salesman from another century, in love with the rails and the smiles and the handshakes, the ever present all-consuming need to make friends of strangers, to make his environment safe, to co-opt the unknown, to ease the world and its terrors with a story, a joke, a drink in a smoky bar.

"Everybody called him a pistol," she says, "and he relished the notoriety, the sense that people wouldn't forget him."

"He was a professional good guy," Levon says, "like my brother, a back slapping oral autobiographer, a prince, himself, his very self."

"All of that," Molly says, "and a shit at home," and Levon thinks about the arrival of others, members of his own family, who approached with the weight of darkness descending when fatigue, his fatigue, would fill the house with a kind of smoke ("devil's fog," he called it), because they were alone with one another without governors or restraints— because there were no strangers around to be wooed and won.

"He never hit me," she says, "but he was cruel, calling me names, re-minding me that none of my diets worked, that I was a thick-legged peasant from the old sod with no wit or grace or earthy wisdom to make up for it."

Molly sets the glass of iced tea on the armrest and sighs. Levon opens his eyes and looks at her.

"I'm sorry, Molly."

"It ain't nothin', cowboy."

"Don't sound like nothing."

"But it is," she says, "just a few memories I should forget."

"Easier said than done," Levon says. "If it weren't for my memory I'd be totally useless. On the other hand, I'm halfway to useless because my memory's so good. I can't forget a thing, and more than remember, I have to feel it all over again, which is to say it stops being a memory and becomes a story factory, after which I start remembering things that never happened. And none of that's too good."

Molly says nothing.

"Dr. Ley says you're a vegetarian," Levon says.

"I am," she says.

"What made you do that?" he asks.

"It wasn't a big thing."

"What was it?"

"My ex."

"Tommy again."

"Yep."

"So how did Tommy make you give up meat?"

"He didn't make me," she says.

"You know what I mean, missy."

"It was Thanksgiving and we visited his family in northern Michigan. The part that's not part of the mitten. Way the hell up there."

"Okay."

"We flew out there and I met his folks and they lived in a doublewide right near the woods, and I mean real woods, like get-lost-in-the-woods woods, and they were nice enough, didn't like to talk, though, and his father was a hunter, not for sport, but for the food they ate, and that year he hadn't shot a turkey—I don't even know if they got turkeys up there—but they had all these rabbits. Hundreds of them in these cages . . ."

Levon takes his thumb and tips his cap. He says: "They wanted you to eat rabbit for Thanksgiving meal."

"That was it," she says.

"Least you got a good reason, then. Sounds like the rabbits were good and maybe your husband wasn't so good."

She leans over and pats his arm. "It's okay, Levon."

"You know, my name's not Levon," he says.

"I know," she says.

"It's Matthew. Matt. Matt Helm."

"Like Dean Martin."

"Just like him."

VI

On Saturdays Dr. Ley and Marta invite guests to put on wide-brimmed hats, clam-diggers, and camp T-shirts and go sailing on Dr. Ley's boat.

It's a good size Cape Codder and seats six comfortably. Marta works the rudder and Dr. Ley works the sails.

This week two brothers and a dark-eyed woman from some Persian royal family exiled to Georgetown join the doctor and his wife. They arrive in a limousine with a driver in his fifties, white, overweight, obsequious, humorless.

Levon watches them from the kitchen window, while Molly cleans up after lunch. Levon looks and looks again. "Jesus," he says.

"What is it?" Molly asks.

"I know those guys," Levon says, as he watches the younger brother, the harmless one, Little Drew, who appears to have a soft spot for the black-eyed princess with features Levantine and Swiss accounts from the Peacock Throne. They pass by, and Levon listens as they talk money all the way down the flagstones to the docks below the lodge to the slope and the brown deck with half tires bunting wood. He listens as their voices dissolve in the sound of water lapping the docks and the webs of water spiders, the dust of crayfish, the last swarm of flies, and the impossibility of unseen life.

Dr. Ley follows with Marta and Tom, the older brother, impossibly handsome, walking arm in arm, making the kind of small talk that requires first-person plurals and a tolerance for an excessive pride in toys.

Levon stands under a tree by stone steps and watches as Little Drew, Sweet Drew, educated now in the ways of snobbery, helps the princess out on a floating dock rolling some beneath their feet, minor quakes, one-point Richters as plates of water rub against and over themselves.

The chauffeur follows carrying a camera, a book, a bucket of sunscreen in brown tubes, and a gym bag slung over his shoulder. His face is red, splotchy, sweating. He's about to have a heart attack. Levon asks if he can help. The guy looks at him, says, "Indigestion," and continues on.

In the boat Dr. Ley helps the others to their seats in the bobbing stern and then looks over the boom with the white sail shedding itself like the liquefaction of clothes about his brown legs, too thin for his body. He looks up the hill, sees Levon and calls out, asking him if he'll work harder next week. Levon says nothing. The two brothers look up the grassy slope and see Levon standing there. They remember him, too, not well, not fondly, and Levon continues to stand there, staring them down, envious, small, trying for the rebel pose of inarticulate ennui. He debates whether giving the finger is over the top, decides it is, and maintains his line.

The doctor pushes away from the dock, and as Marta steers the boat out into the lake, Levon sees Marta's yellow hair in the patch of sunlight that opens and closes with admonitions of a front and summer storms. Dr. Ley pulls the lines taut and points out something to his guests and then leans his body over the side before the wind catches canvas and pushes them away, about to disappear in a fog bank halfway across the lake.

Levon watches the whole thing and thinks about Little Drew, Sweet Drew, the little brother who can't afford to be arrogant, who hopes others will like him, especially the older brother, the desired one, the chosen one, the one made perfect, without need of humor, as dull as Apollo, solid, no gas or water weight, no seepage, straight goods, square business, Atticus-integrity, a closed-lipped superiority, the perfect company's company man, one of the good ones.

Levon watches from the shore and then steps onto the deck and sits next to Stella who predicts something more interesting than weather will ferry the boat to the island of dead trees and abandoned homes midmile past the summer theater camp, and Levon asks her what she means. She tells him to remember the storm the night he returned to a cabin by a lake. She tells him to remember what he saw in the glow of candles and the heartsick of betrayal, the loss of love that was never love, the pain that is with him still and will be with him, forever resident in his furious chest.

And far out over still water, no scallop, no sound, but the little lap and suck, past a bank of clouds the bow turns and turns again. Dr. Ley stands visible waving his arms, a kind of greeting or drowning as the pale afternoon made white and blue with the last squeeze of humidity, the cascade of cold air falling, and Stella turns to Levon and says, "They're not patients."

"I know," Levon says. "I know them."

"How do you know them?" Stella asks.

"The older one, we went to the same college. Then he transferred."

"They say he's very successful."

"I'm sure he is."

"They say he'll be president someday."

"I'm sure he will."

"What was he like?"

"He was successful."

"You weren't friends."

"No."

"Did you think he was better than you?"

"Stella, what kind of a question is that?"

"Well, did you?"

Levon turns to the wide window and the reflection of the lake. Then he looks at Stella. He says, "Stella, if I say yes, you'll think I'm a loser and have no respect for me. If I say no, you'll think I'm an envious loser and have no respect for me."

"So you did, then."

"Did what?"

"Think he was better than you."

"I guess."

"Levon," she says, "you worry too much about everything, but especially about love, about giving it, about receiving it," and she tells him about a young man who ruined his life for want of her love.

"What are you talking about?"

"There was this young man, and I loved him, and then I didn't love him, and it ruined his life."

"It did?"

"Most certainly."

"How did that happen?"

"First of all, we were young. In college. He played in a band. Saxophone, a horn player. They were the big thing back then, like guitarists were later on. And it was the week before Christmas. I was supposed to go to Yale for the weekend, but there'd been a storm and I couldn't go. So I stayed in the dorm, and there was a party on Friday night and his combo played. They weren't very good. Not good at all, but when he looked at me and held my eyes for more than ten seconds, something happened. They took a break and he sat by himself off to the side and asked me to join him. We sat there and I told him I had a serious boyfriend at Yale, and he said he figured as much since I was so pretty. And that got my attention. Levon, don't ever think pretty girls don't like compliments."

"They do?"

"Of course they do. And yes, sometimes they're perverse and want what they can't have and take criticism like catnip wanting more, but when all is said and done, pretty girls like to be told they're pretty, and I was both."

"Both?"

"I was pretty, and I was told I was pretty."

"I see."

"After the holidays and winter break I returned to my college. He wrote to me, and I wrote back, and he invited me to his school one Saturday night and said we wouldn't even call it a date if I'd be more comfortable with that."

Stella pauses and looks out over the lake. Her lips move without sound. Levon watches her and then says her name.

"Stella?"

"Yes, Levon."

"You went to visit him. On a Saturday night."

"Yes, I did. And we met in the student center. I was standing by a banister near a stairwell and watched him run up the stairs to meet me."

She pauses again.

"So tell me what happened," Levon says, and when she speaks, she stares at the water where the fog bank settles like a line between the here and there.

"Levon," she says, "I don't know if this has ever happened to you. I suspect it has, and I'll do my best to describe it."

"What?" Levon asks.

"Well, it's like this, or it was like this: You see, Levon, most of my life, most of our lives, we live on the surface of something like a shell, and life there is average, routine, settled, sometimes good, sometimes not so good, but nothing too extreme. The day-in, day-out sort of thing. And living like that we become gray, and if we live like that long enough, we disappear into our surroundings, having negotiated our deal with life—with the fact of being alive. We agree to put in our time, to expect less each year, to grow as old as health and circumstance permit, and life, for the most part, agrees to sustain us. Yes, we'll suffer some losses, some deaths, health problems, money problems, but on the whole life will sustain us, and we'll value longevity over everything."

"Sounds bleak."

"And, I suppose it is, unless something comes along to knock you out of it."

"Like what?"

"Like what happened to me that Saturday night."

"So, what happened?"

"After we sat in the cafeteria drinking sodas, after his friends stopped by, one after the other, to tell me how brilliant this young man was, after he'd charmed me with his wit and his air of self-sufficiency, after we'd gone back to his room and I lay with him on his narrow bed, and after we looked through one another and saw something quite wonderful and felt something wonderful, the shell on which I'd lived my life gave way and I fell to a deeper, better world that enlivened every part of me, that resonated with things I'd heard about and knew about in the abstract, like words, but had never experienced, a feeling that I was more real than I thought I was, that there was a world that was more real than the one I'd lived in, and in that moment of falling, my life was full of something that defies description, but is what I think people mean when they talk about the truth."

"You fell in love with him."

"I fell all right."

"Why didn't you stay with him?"

"Because he was terrible in bed, and my boyfriend at Yale was a bull who made me scream, and I didn't want to give that up."

Levon looks to the rim of black trees at the end of the lake. A small cloud the size of a full moon rises up from the book of Kings, like a dollop of air in a honey jar, and begins to spread under a darkening sky.

"And now you're here," Levon says. "Do you regret your choice?"

"What choice?"

"For sex over soul."

"When you're young you think sex is soul. The boy was intelligent, sensitive. Those were his gifts."

"So then you chose sex over sensitivity and intelligence."

"Don't get sentimental on me, Levon. I regret nothing."

"You say it ruined his life."

"It did."

"What happened to him?"

"He became his opposite. He went from self-sufficient to self-destructive. He became foolish, religious, sentimental, weak, addicted, a failure. He grew fat and lost his hair. He went from job to job. For a while he was homeless, destitute. I'd heard he died, and then I heard he was alive. I don't know where he is now. It's been such a long time."

"And you think he fell apart because you chose not to love him after you'd fallen in love with him."

"I know that."

"How can you be so certain?"

"You, Levon, of all people, should know the answer to that."

"Should I?"

"She withheld her love and you became a glutton; she withheld her love and you starved yourself. What you don't know is that she withheld her love so you could go to hell in this life and not the next."

The clouds become a ceiling of steel, solid with rolls of light. At the horizon a ribbon of yellow forecasts trouble. The sailboats on the water move over water like hydroplanes, spinnaker fast before the wind, sometimes listing to port, scooping water when the black water turns on itself.

The first funnel forms in the distance and looks like a thread of floss spinning into the water where it widens and becomes blue. The second funnel forms to the side and overtakes the first and threatens the island of dead trees two miles away. The third funnel's longer and wider than the other two and moves over water toward the camp across the lake where children struggle to get out of the water. A bolt of lightning almost strikes a counselor sitting in a tower, shouting orders through a bullhorn. It all happens so fast, and yet the utter impossibility of a present suspended in time allows the unreal movement of nature to slow itself sufficiently for eyes trained upon the proximity of death to see that only death happens in its ordained cycle.

Stella tries to stand, but the wind catches her and it's Matthew who grabs her arm, so thin, nothing but a bird's bone, and he helps her to the back door and the kitchen. From there he crosses the floor to the wide window and looks out on black water and the waves knocking sailboats against one another as another funnel forms and moves toward the lodge, raising a flood of water with the sound of a train over old tracks laid through a suburb of average homes, and he knows what it is to be damaged in the dense air of love withheld and to stand defiant in the face of it, and Molly grabs him from behind and pulls him away as the window bursts inward and showers the room with bits of glass like so many jewels tossed aside in a world of other values, once known to Matthew, now hidden in the blindness of sanity.

VII

Levon leans against the van, takes a hit from Sammy's joint, looks over his shoulder, and hands it back.

It's Friday afternoon, bright and hot, and from across the parking lot of pressed gravel Levon watches as Dr. Ley leads a group of women from the building they call the Second House down the macadam trail to the vans parked side by side.

The women are young except for Virginia from Moosup, who's over sixty, and Caroline from Bedford, who's over fifty. The others are in their twenties or thirties. All have problems. Most are addicts, two or three have eating disorders, and some are just nuts. But they look good and keep themselves better than most. All of them come from money and their families' money has been the floor, the backup, the net, the sense of something ever found as they lose themselves from time to time.

At the bottom of the trail Dr. Ley meets his assistant, Claude, and the girls are a football field away as Sammy sucks the last little bit from the brown paper dissolving between his fingers.

"Motherfucker," Sammy Raymond says, "that shit's good as ganja."

"It's good," Levon says. "Don't know if it's that good."

"Fuck me, it's not that good."

"Fuck you, then," Levon says, and the two of them do that shoulder-shiver laugh people do at wakes and funerals when the minister lies about the dead.

"We better scrub this," Sammy says, and he drops the roach and twists the heel of his boot. The breeze off the lake blows the smoke away, but the aroma hangs in the air and a couple of the women recognize it and start to laugh behind their hands. Dr. Ley smells it, too, but he doesn't let on. He figures it's Sammy. It's always Sammy, but the place needs Sammy so Dr. Ley lets many things go until things build up and then he'll throw a fit over a pot with a crust of dried tomato sauce about the rim, screaming that he spent too much money on a dishwasher to stack dirty crockery in his kitchen.

"Are we ready, Sammy?" Dr. Ley calls from the far end of the lot.

"I'm ready if you are." Sammy shouts.

"Are the ladies ready?" Dr. Ley asks, and the women don't answer but look at one another and whisper.

"I guess we're ready," Dr. Ley says.

Sammy talks to Levon without looking at him so Dr. Ley won't pick up on it. He says, "You know, Levon, I've seen more bullshit than most, but I see him marchin' those ladies down the hill, and I know the world's upside down, like a negative of the real picture, and the sin of it is he's the only one making money because of it."

"You're right," Levon says, because it's the easiest thing to say.

"Oh, please don't say that, Levon. Please don't say I'm right."

"Why not?"

"Cuz you tell a person he's right and same time you best be measuring him for a box and a grave."

"You're right again, Sammy."

"So now I'm dead two times. What's up, Levon, you got it in for me or what?" And they laugh again and the women board the vans for the musical at the camp on the other side of the lake.

"Coming with us, Matthew?" Dr. Ley asks, and Levon ignores him.

"Matthew?" Dr. Ley asks. And then, "Levon?"

"I'm right here, Dr. Ley. No need to shout. I'm crazy, not deaf."

"Joining us tonight?"

"I don't think so."

"Significant," Dr. Ley says.

"Is it?" Levon says.

"Given the production, I believe it is."

"I'm blocking, Dr. Ley."

"You said it, Levon, not me."

Sammy pinches Levon's upper arm, rolls his eyes, says something in that small, bubbly voice that should be singing jazz someplace, steps up into the van, and starts the procession down the dirt road to the paved road that rings the lake.

Levon walks down the slope to the lawn that gives way to a stone wall where the lake's dark enough in part to catch the reflection of harbor lights, bright enough in part to reflect the almost light of the twilight sky.

The heat and the light and the smell of water, soil, summer grass remind him of his childhood when his father sent him to sleepaway camp, where he made friends and learned how to swim and stood up to a bully and then cried for having hurt the kid in a fight he didn't set out to fight. He remembers the summer when he was old enough to work and get paid for it, when he became a counselor and lost his virginity with a local girl who worked in the kitchen and drank coffee in the morning and seemed older for that and for other reasons. He remembers another kid from a family of lawyers who was a day counselor who arrived every morning in one of his father's limousines and was as handsome as Bobby Kennedy and was a snob and made the old guys feel inadequate and then safe as they gave him more and more responsibility, because he looked so darn capable. He thinks how a lot of men who look capable have made life hell for a lot of people, and he thinks how looks are as important as people swear they're not.

Levon was young and full of juice then, that summer, when he learned that the girl from his hometown, the girl he'd never met, the girl who'd entered his heart and mind with the axiomatic interplay of desire and disappointment, lived with her family in a huge cottage on the same lake, and every night he'd think about walking around the lake, into the woods to the far side where she lived, until one day he saw her on a road by the camp with the kid who looked so capable, a handsome couple, perfect in the way their looks complemented each other, walking arm in arm, her shoulders rounded, head down, as easy and serious as newfound love, the way her hair fell and that kind of laughter that acts as a barrier and moat, because she'd waited on a young man with perfect hair, brown, thick, falling in a wave, right to left, dipping like a wedge of water over his forehead and his velvet eyes.

And these thoughts lap against the shores of memory with the twilight and the warmth and the dark image of deep water, pure, spring fed, and cold, and Levon knows this is the point where the charade of his illness would end, if he could stop his mind from the avenging realities of age, fatigue, and abuse, of dreams shattered without a poignant soundtrack to woo the sweater girls who require tragedy in the way they require eyeliner as a handy tool to afford depth and volume to comfortably flat lives, wanting nothing of pain unless it be mediated through somebody else's vice, or of some false promise of timely denouement, their very selves, safe again in daddy's study with warm lights, a fire, a crystal decanter, and the soap-star haze of the almost real.

"Levon?"

He hears his name and looks up the hill to the lodge and past that to Molly's cabin where the lights are off and a barely audible thread of music from a radio floats overhead like a moth through trees.

"Levon?" This time the voice is louder, more distinct, not Molly's voice, but a whisper promising something mysterious if not forbidden.

"I'm here," Levon says, thinking of Samuel, called, waking, sleeping, and called again how many times before the Lord touched him and, like Elijah, made him mad with prophecy.

"Didn't go with the others?" Marta asks, and she stands next to him, dressed in light summer khaki, made bright in the darkness, as her hair is bright in the darkness, long, thick, blond, almost turned under.

"Can't you say hello?" she asks, noting the silence; and Levon looks at her, knowing that he's intrigued her since the day he arrived, being sober, but fragile, given to suicidal ideation, given to a hopelessness that was vague and attractive in its refusal to accept the unacceptable, having deemed the smallest, most insignificant things as unacceptable, affording them a significance normal people miss and never question. So many times Levon heard Sammy say, "Don't tell me I'm right," and when Sammy said it he'd think of Marta's marriage to the doctor who was older, and how he, Levon, was old, too, but in a different way, being one of those rare men who seem young in the way genius and mental illness can make a person seem young. He thinks that, perhaps, in another time they might have lived in a room at the top of a second set of stairs, that he might have been famous in Paris with a wife and a child, cheap wine, baguettes, and beer. But he'd been born in this time with its fetish for health and an abhorrence of illness as something to be pitied, but not forgiven, a time when behind every visible defect there's a sentimental saint, a yellow ribbon and a boot full of money, while behind every mental disease is a program and an unforgivable sin. He thinks how Marta, too, is prone to black nights, married to an Austrian who drowns patients in medication and the ameliorating benefits of fresh air, good food, and abstinence, and he believes that Marta wants to leave the doctor and marry him every time she calls him Levon, every time she sees him, eye to eye, brilliant in shared frailties, holy in their cells, perhaps someday ravenous in bed.

"I didn't want to go," Levon says. "I don't like being driven in a van like a schoolboy. We a pay fortune to get better; they humiliate the shit out of us and then they get pissed because we're not better, which is something they don't want as long as we can pay."

"Who are they?" she asks.

"You married them," he says.

"I see," she says, leaning against the tower, her hands palms down on the short deck, supporting herself, her fingers about to touch his.

Levon looks at her, the profile white against dark lawn and the over-rush of night. She is beautiful, foreign, more alive and passionate than the cynical party girl she might have become had she been born in Boston during the last year of this aging empire's tired bow. He asks himself whether he can lose himself and fall through a thin and banal floor of security and routine. He notes the way her eyes slope downward in a kind of perpetual sadness, the finer line, the elegant articulation of something that eludes him—that resides just beyond the border between the here and there.

"Levon?"

"Yes?"

"Here," she says before the silence between them and the small sounds of nature make her rude with expectation, and she hands him a key and tells him that next Friday Dr. Ley will be traveling to give a talk at a symposium, that he won't be back until Sunday night after midnight.

She says, "When the place is shut down and everyone is sleeping, I'll be upstairs in my bedroom, waiting."

Levon takes the key and rubs his thumb over the brass points. He puts the key in his pocket and his arm around Marta's shoulder and pulls her to himself, smelling the soap smell of cleanliness, the Swiss woman, Marta Wurtzel Ley, who bathes three times a day in a cove half a mile away. He feels the soft cotton of her white shirt. He feels her and she is petite, small boned, a woman for autumn and the indoors, and she puts her arms around his waist, reckless, unrepentant, caring nothing for onlookers or small-minded Pharisees watching from balconies and windows, seeking out points of contention and leverage. She married an old doctor, but she never really married him, not in the way she holds her fragile man, so sturdy and strong under his denim shirt, so tall, languid, cool, his eyes so blue.

"I am without hope," she says and kisses his chest, the denim full with man smell, and he holds her closer than he thought possible, thinking of her and then of the other woman, the woman he never met, known only in a dream when she asked him to help her clean her room, to meet her mother whose name was Muffy, to be there for a moment so she could string another bead of disappointment on the bracelet she'd made of him.

"And I am lost," he says, to the darkness and the water and the sound of applause tumbling slowly over water from the other side of the lake where children are lost, too, having broken rules, having ignored their parents' wise and reasonable admonitions not to go into the woods.

VIII

Word spreads like bacillus on the backs of rats, and when Levon's summoned he's in the long, low cabin reserved for crafts, his hands in clay, listening to the Allman Brothers on one of the boom boxes Molly smuggled inside, while Stella and Virginia throw beads at one another.

Sammy calls from outside, "Levon, the Doc wants to see you."

Levon withdraws his hands, holds them in front of his face, and then dips them in a pot of water on the shelf by the open window.

Sammy shouts again, "Levon, you hear me?"

Levon dries his hands, comes to the doorway.

"What is it, Sammy?"

"Doc Ley sent me over. He wants to see you."

"About what?" Levon asks, and Stella joins Levon in the doorway.

"Make him wait," she says. "Patience is a virtue, too."

"He's all excited 'bout somethin'," Sammy says. "Will you just come, so I don't get my ass in a sling?"

"Don't go," Stella says.

"He better go," Virginia says, standing behind Levon.

"I'll go," Levon says. "I just like a little reconnaissance before this sort of thing."

"You and that freakin' Renaissance you always talkin' about," Sammy says.

"Ain't it awful," Levon says, leaving the crafts cabin, stepping down the stairs, joining Sammy, patting him on the back. "C'mon now, Sammy. You see everything around here. What's going on with the Doc?"

"Truth?" Sammy says.

"Truth," Levon says.

"Your brother's here."

Levon stops and stands there. The color drains from his face, white as marble, and the sun strikes with a force that could put him down. He stops and starts again, his legs unsteady, his feet seeking some purchase on pressed gravel.

"You okay, Levon?"

"I'm okay, Sammy," and they cross the field to the doctor's office.

Sammy leaves Levon at the foot of the steps. Levon ascends the steps like King Charles I. He reaches the porch with the door and looks about for his brother's car and can't find it parked among the fancy cars in the lot. He looks again, shrugs his shoulders, enters the office.

The first thing he sees is what he always sees when he enters the office—Doctor Ley standing behind his glass-top desk, a German tank commander, a Rommel toady, despised by his men, as gay as Rohm, Herr Ley, half German matron with teats like Wagner's grandkid.

And the second thing he sees is the back of the head of the man in the visitor's seat—smaller, more narrow than his brother's head.

"Here he is, then." Doctor Ley says. "Matthew, your brother," introducing Levon to someone who's not his brother.

The man in the chair stands and turns. "Hello, Matt," Bobby Sullivan says, extending his hand for a brotherly handshake.

Doctor Ley leaves the two "brothers" to talk in private, suggesting they walk around the camp and enjoy the fresh air, the cool winds off the water. Bobby Sullivan steps from behind a birch tree and skips a flat stone down the bank toward the lake.

"So, Matthew," he says, not certain what to say after that.

"I expected you to show up sooner or later," Matthew says as they walk through the wooded area on the land side of the lodge. "And call me Levon."

"Levon? Why?"

"It's my name for now."

"Whatever you say, Mr. Levon . . ."

"Just Levon."

"Okay, then, I guess you know why I'm here."

"To beg me not to tell the cops you killed Mrs. O'Neal."

"I didn't kill her."

"You didn't?"

"No. I didn't."

"And to think I expected you to say you did."

"Matthew . . ."

"Levon . . ."

"Levon, I think you've got me all wrong."

"You're not the guy who doesn't hire drunks, right?"

"What are you talking about?"

"I'm talking about the letter you sent me with the twenty dollars. You wrote, 'I'm not in the habit of hiring drunks,' or something like that."

"What letter are you talking about?"

"Let's forget about it, okay? But it was your letter that kicked off this nightmare."

"Matthew, I mean, Levon, I never sent you a letter."

"Right, and I'm not crazy."

Sullivan, troubled, eyebrows pinched, a question on his face, walks ahead of Levon over the parking lot toward the macadam trail.

"Levon, you don't know Manny like I do."

"I know her better than you do."

"You think you do, but you don't."

Matthew picks up a pole, a broom handle cut at the base. He drags it through the ground at his feet. He tries to make a word. He thinks of the adulteress. He thinks of letting her go.

"Levon," Bobby Sullivan says, "you've got to believe me. Yes, I'm a drunk. Yes, I'm a prick. Yes, I break most of the rules, and I'm not a good person. But I didn't murder that woman. Now maybe I tried to scam an insurance company, but if you feel for those bastards, then you are crazy."

"I went along," Levon says, "but you fucked me."

"I didn't send you any letter, but I bet I know who did."

"Manny."

"You said it."

"No way. Manny and I were close."

"Think what you want about Manny, Levon, the only thing that's important now is that I didn't kill Mrs. O'Neal. I'm being set up. Manny's doing it, and she's got it all worked out so I'll go away, and she'll take everything."

"That's what her aunt wanted."

"Are you shitting me?"

"There's a letter," Levon says.

"Oh, right—another letter."

"There is."

"I know all about that letter. And it's bullshit, too."

"So, you're saying Manny killed her aunt."

"I'm not saying that. As much as I'd like to. I don't know who killed her. Fact is, I thought she committed suicide. That's how I got fucked up in this whole thing."

"So who killed her then, because no way she killed herself."

"I said I don't know," Bobby Sullivan says. "For all I know you did."

"Now that is not a statement designed to elicit a cooperative response."

Sullivan breaks a minor smile. "Look, Levon, if you want to tell them about the bag, go ahead—fuck the insurance money. I can handle fraud. But don't tell them you think I did it."

"Tell who?"

"You know who. Moraski and Talmadge."

"Moraski and who?"

"Talmadge. The detectives. They interrogated you; they interrogated me; they interrogated everybody."

"If they ask me again, I'll tell them the truth," Levon says. "There was a bag, and if it wasn't suicide, somebody must have killed her."

"But it wasn't me," Sullivan says.

"So you say."

"I had no motive."

"She was going to change her will. That's a motive. She was going to leave everything to Manny. There's a motive."

"How do you know that?" Sullivan asks. "That fucking letter?"

"From Mrs. O'Neal to Manny. Yeah, that fucking letter."

"And how do you know the old lady wrote that letter, Matthew— Levon, because I definitely knew Mrs. O'Neal better than you, and I know what that woman would let herself put down on paper, let alone to some girl out of the blue she didn't even trust."

"She didn't trust Manny?"

"Are you shitting me?"

"No."

"You can't be this naïve."

"She wrote that letter."

"That wasn't a letter. That was War and fucking Peace, for Christ's sake, and no way Mrs. O'Neal was going to write War and fucking Peace to anybody about a loving husband who played around as much as Tommy O'Neal. She would have divorced the motherfucker if he hadn't been dying of cancer."

"No way."

"Levon, Mrs. O'Neal was a Yankee dragon, and if she couldn't take it with her, she wasn't going. All that 'Tommy, my love,' and 'life is a gift' bullshit? I read that. And it's bullshit, Levon. Bullshit."

From up the hill voices and laughter disturb them.

"I'm out of here," Sullivan says. "Look, I've been dealing with this quack, Dr. Ley. Thing is I've paid for you through the weekend. Then you're out of here, too."

"You've been paying for this?"

"That's right, and I didn't fuck you with any insurance money, either. It should come as no surprise they haven't paid off yet. But think about this, it's in your interest that I don't go away for something I did not do."

The voices grow louder. It's Marta in lederhosen with a few of the women.

Levon looks up the hill, stares at Marta, and waves. When he turns again, Bobby Sullivan's already gone.

IX

And this is Levon's room: A rectilinear space, van Gogh in Arles, a bed, a red blanket, a desk, a floor that recedes to infinity, his difficulties with perspective. No fire, no fireplace, a window, a lamp, two candles, a mug, and a chair. The chair's broken. One night he leaned back like Bruce Lee, his chi focused at T5, all weight, all force, all newtons, and the chair cracked, splintered, broke. Now Bruce Lee sits on a makeshift stool.

She invited him for midnight. Saturday night. Late summer. In a lodge by a lake. When Doctor Ley would be away.

He leaves his room and stands on his porch.

The patients are asleep, each in his own miniature cottage along the hills and down the slope.

From inside, through a screen door, his alarm, the small black one with the little chick cheep, rings at 11:45. He set it this morning thinking otherwise he might fall asleep and miss the whole thing.

Outside, the cabins are visible in the dark.

He walks down the hill, across the parking lot, past the kitchen, and stops before the back door of the main lodge.

Overhead more music. A pale sound. Singer-songwriter stuff. Mild, almost soft. He wonders if Molly's watching. She's always watching; she thinks she's a cop. When they found her she was passed out with a jug lying under her bed with a police scanner clutched to her chest. He gave her an angel and touched her arm.

He takes out the key and tries to place it in the lock. It doesn't fit. He tries again. The misfit key sticks and makes noise, an unlikely scratch. He thinks he's been betrayed. Tested and failed. He waits for searchlights and whistles and horns and German shepherds, barking, frothing, teeth bared, straining, the bulging fur of brown necks against leather, jaws, torque, teeth, and the black coats, the arrogance of power.

The cascading anger comes to rest with the white pebbles of an avalanche resting over some quiet Swiss village.

He looks about and then walks the perimeter of the huge house. The windows are tall and wide with heavy drapes pulled tight. The glow of nightlights soak the fabric. He hears the sound of the smallest outboard on the water a mile away. He looks up to the second floor and beyond that to the gables set on either side of a third window, a black square.

He makes the final turn and crosses the wide deck where Dr. Ley fires up the grill on Sunday afternoons and feeds the patients picnic food. He's kindly on Sundays. Children, church, and kitchen. Kinder, kirche, kuche. KKK. Twelve steps to Munich and the eagle's nest. But Levon knows the whole story about Dr. Ley and his wife; about how he treated her years ago and how he loves her small Swiss body, the contours and curves of an entirely self-sufficient being; about how he loves her mean spirit, the many methods of rejection, the betrayals, the affairs, the way she flirts with the young men, in his presence, on Sundays on the deck, at picnics with the funnels of steam and smoke and the sizzle and the smell of meat and the bowls of chips and the trash cans filled with ice.

"She's got a mature woman's hands," Levon thinks, "the length of her fingers, the shape of her thumb, the impervious declamation of those long nails. And with those hands she knows how to hurt the doctor, by touching somebody else, flashing her eyes as if to say, 'See, Herr Doctor? Can you see what I'm doing? Can you see what I've done?'"

Far away a dog barks.

The wind falls through the trees.

Levon stands in front of the front door. He places the key in the lock and the pressure's enough to open the open door. Marta steps down the last three steps of the staircase, crosses the floor, and sits in a chair in the center of the room. She wears a hand-knit sweater, the kind made with needles made for giant fingers. It falls below her knees. She's crying and she holds tissues in her hand.

"What is it?" he asks.

And she doesn't answer, but only cries.

"What is it?" he asks again, and she looks at him as if he were an addendum, a footnote, an inconsequential member of the cast, a bit player whose presence must be acknowledged, but doesn't matter. Something far more important than a midnight rendezvous has taken place—is taking place, even as he stands there, something of moment, something serious.

"Marta, please," he says, "tell me what's happened," and he kneels before her, taking her hands in his, watching her eyes as she looks away, as if he could be anybody, as if the real story resides elsewhere, in some parallel reality, and all of this is unnecessary, though deserving of something like the politeness of manners, the rituals of arm's length transactions.

"Is someone upstairs?" he asks. "Is there something wrong upstairs?" And the two of them look toward the stairs, and she can only mumble words through the contractions and contortions of muscles, gasping for breath, weeping real tears as the world spins away and loss is more than a falling, but a closure, a burial.

He stands; her hands drop to her side. He crosses the room where the cherry banister ends with a pedestal with the head of a lion. He takes three steps, and only then, with the name he stole from another, a name that now sounds false, that no longer seems necessary or appropriate, does he turn to her, below him now, looking down, her hands over her face, crying without tears.

"What happened, Marta?"

She says nothing.

"Please, tell me, what happened here?"

She's silent.

"Who, Marta?"

He climbs the stairs. One step to the second floor.

"Manny," he slips, confusing ghosts and the flight of shadows, stepping to the second floor, which is dark except for a vertical line of light from behind a door, nearly closed at the far end of the hallway.

"Manny," he says again, and the game he's been playing to protect himself in a shroud of make-believe and memories seen through the gauzy veils of personal mythology fall away like scales, translucent and dry, and Matthew—not Levon, but Matthew, now—remembers the body of a woman lying on a bed in her bedroom in a house in West Hartford. An unusual passing, he thought then, and thinks now, with Manny's cruelties, with Sullivan's scramble to free himself, to benefit, to receive what he believes to be his, with his brother's many betrayals and his mother's blind refusal to love, all of it as crooked and contradictory as the primordial lie, as old as death itself, resting like the timeless serpent coiled at the center of all betrayal, all murder, all greed, all pride, all power, all sin. . . .

He looks down on her for the last time (for her time is overdrawn) as this sylvan charade, this illusion of woods, water, and passions, now lingers on the cusp of dissolution, and she looks up at him and watches him, her mouth moving, speaking silent words. He can't read lips, but he thinks she's telling him that she loves him, that she had nothing to do with crimes of the heart, that whatever waits behind the door at the end of the hallway is just another one of those things we struggle with—each of us, in the silence of our rooms, as we try to make our way, to perform the task set before us, to achieve a desired result, the mathematics of success, to live out the unconscious impulses drafted like directives in the mysterious alphabet of genes and chemistry, inherited, neither sought nor desired, but there, controlling and ultimately doomed, conscious of shame, guilt, an ending or perhaps the end.

PLOTS

———◆———

— ❖ —

Brian Wyman leans against the fridge, waits for the blast from the kettle on the stove. There's the little rumble, a kind of rush, it builds, fades with a puff of steam, begins again, and whistles. He twists the dial, the flame disappears, the boiling sound goes quiet. He picks up the kettle, pours water in two mugs. The old man only buys instant coffee, so Brian will drink tea.

He places one mug before his mother and takes one for himself.

She thanks him without a word, just a nod, dips her spoon, moves the bag in hot water, catches it, presses it, moves it again. It's 5:00 a.m. Neither she nor Brian is fully awake.

There were snow showers overnight and the windows are damp with it. Sometimes it snows in April. They expect it to rain on the weekend.

"I don't see why we have to go," she says.

Brian reminds her that they've put it off three times, and there's a question about what insurance will cover if they refuse to meet with Matthew's doctor.

Overhead Brian hears footsteps, his father walking down the long hall. His mother hears the footsteps, too. She looks up, makes a face, looks down.

"I guess he's not gonna come," Brian says.

"Of course he's not," she says. "He leaves the dirty work for me."

"It won't be that bad, Ma. I've talked to the guy. He's a nice guy, very calm like."

"I just don't know why we have to go," she says, and Brian sips his tea, adding sugar, stirring it, adding more milk, stirring that, looking out the window as a blue light begins to settle like fog over the wet lawn.

They arrive early. The hospital's psychiatric ward is a low, flat building standing in a field fronting a back road with a gas station, a fast-food joint, and an abandoned bowling alley.

"It's always me," the mother says, sitting in the passenger seat, bundled in a cloth coat, refusing to move, refusing to look directly at anyone or anything, as if her eyes had turned inward and grown opaque. Brian knows the look. He's seen it forever. It's the look she prepares for a world that's fucked her, oppressed her, hurt her, disappointed her, made her crazy—the look that can give way to one of her episodes, or make her catatonic, rife with a kind of anxiety that can't find release and freezes inside of her, paralyzing her, making her small, brittle, silent.

"It'll be all right, Ma. The doc said he'd see us whenever we got here. He said it'll take an hour at most."

"Do we have to see Matthew, too?"

"No. The doc said he's still pretty doped up."

"At least I don't have to go through that then, having to listen to him blame me for everything. As if I caused all of this. It's such an embarrassment, and do you think your father might help with any of this?"

"He can't handle stuff like this, Ma. It's too much for him."

"And it's not for me? What do you think that whole town thinks of us now? My family had a name in that town, and I've got a son who's been committed. Committed!" She spits the word. "We did not set out to raise a crazy person. I told him from before high school to be normal in this world. Nobody wants anybody to get too smart for themselves. It's not much better than being too stupid. The world's not made for left-handed people. Too smart or too stupid—either way it's trouble, and then doctors get involved and you end up in a place like this. Sometimes I think it would have been better if he'd been retarded. At least then people would say how sad or whatever, but they don't say how sad when your son's crazy. They don't say anything. They try to ignore it. But they don't ignore you. They look at you and they can't hide it. They know and you know they know and it's awful.

"Do you know your father's not gone to one Elks meeting since all of this started? Not one Knights of Columbus meeting. Not one Rotarian lunch. He won't show his face except to drive to work and hide in the teacher's lounge. Hiding! And I'm the one! I'm the one who has to wait behind when the doctor touches my elbow so he can give me the bad news."

"I know," Brian says, trying to make his voice as smooth as a stone in a river bed, offering no resistance as the flood of indignation and hurt runs over everything. His mother cries now, though not really, because she never really cries. Instead it's a kind of damp chirp, like a hurt bird, held in, restrained, evidence of wrongs greater than tears, evidence that whatever's killing her can't be let out because it would cascade and destroy her with unforgiving indictments and end-of-the-world scenarios. She's warned Brian since he was a kid: Cry and they've got you. Cry and you're somebody's slave. Cry and you're not so much dead as barely alive, just enough to feel the fear that's been waiting forever at the edge of the small circumference of the small circle of your small life.

After a while, she catches her breath and settles again. Brian asks: "Are you okay?" She shakes her head and looks at Brian, her first born, her favorite, a fleeting look, though her eyes meet his eyes, and she offers him the love she's always given him, keeping him, at least this one person, close to her—this protective and strong man, a real man, not afraid of work, sweat, or dirt, the type of man who can hold his own in a bar, drink a lot, and keep his date safe, too, a rough-edged man of common sense, never lost in thought, unafraid to call bullshit what it is, a man who's never needed books or education to get himself situated in this world, a man capable of some awful things, crimes even, but wouldn't embarrass her the way Matthew has. She thinks how Brian's mischievous and Matthew's malicious, how Brian's good natured and Matthew's dark, how Brian likes people and Matthew doesn't, how Brian's funny like a comedian on a variety show and Matthew's wit is like a searchlight seeking out weakness so that the best a person can hope for is that the light shines someplace else. She gave birth to two boys and only one is her son—truly. The other was a mistake, an autumnal baby conceived in some drunken holiday mood, conceived with no more forethought or desire than asking for another round at closing. And this is where it's all come to, she thinks, a flat box of cinder blocks standing on a plane of frozen grass on a Monday morning in April.

"What day is it?" she asks Brian.

"Day or date?"

"Day."

"It's Monday, Ma."

"World hasn't been the same for a long time," she says. "Not for a long time."

The doors open. The entrance to the ward is dark. The lights are off and no one's sitting at the reception desk. Brian steps past the semi-circle of pressed wood, cheap paneling, and looks down two corridors extending out like spokes on a wheel with squares of light at the end.

"Why did he want us here so early if he wasn't even . . ." she starts.

"Please, Ma," Brian says. "Let's just sit over there." He points to a couch and chairs with frayed upholstery set in a small alcove by the front door.

She drops her arms in angry surrender and walks across the scuffed floor when Doctor Lehman greets them from behind.

"Good morning," he says.

Brian and the doctor have spoken on the phone. They shake hands.

Dr. Lehman looks different than the impression Mrs. Wyman had made of him. She'd pictured a big man, a German burgher with blond-white hair, oversized shoulders, and a kind of womanly softness sometimes present in men with overly large features. But Dr. Lehman's a short man, thin with a dark complexion and handsome in the way small men can possess features so compact and articulate they achieve a fine detail and balance larger men rarely possess.

They shake hands, and the doctor asks the Wymans to accompany him down one of the dark corridors to a meeting room. "I'm glad you could make it today," he says. "I know my secretary's tried to schedule something before this, but it seems our schedules haven't been able to mesh." He pauses, looking from Brian to Mrs. Wyman. "Now you're Matthew's mother?"

"I am."

"And you're . . . ?"

"I'm Brian. Matt's brother."

"You're his brother?"

"Yep."

"His only brother?"

"As far as I know."

"Is there a problem, Doctor?" Mrs. Wyman asks.

"No, I'm just a little confused is all . . ."

"It's early enough to confuse anybody," Mrs. Wyman says.

"And where is Mr. Wyman?" Dr. Lehman asks.

"He couldn't make it," Mrs. Wyman says. "He has to give a presentation at the teacher's conference."

"I see. All right, maybe that explains things . . ."

"Explains what?" Mrs. Wyman asks.

"Nothing," Dr. Lehman says. "And it is awfully early."

"Sure is," Brian says.

"So, Mr. Wyman's a teacher then," Dr. Lehman says.

"He is."

"And what does he teach?"

"Accounting. High school."

"I see, an accountant. I'm afraid I've never been that good with numbers. Most of my colleagues hire accountants; I've yet to need one—then again I don't know how to golf—I hope neither of those factors impugn my reputation as a doctor." He waits for a reaction, but the Wymans miss the humor.

They enter a small sitting room with more state government furniture. Mrs. Wyman sits bolt upright in a chair, legs crossed at the ankles, a posture cast in iron.

Brian stands near the doorway, not knowing whether he should join the meeting or not. Then he relents and takes a seat next to his mother.

Dr. Lehman checks his beeper, fumbles in one of his pockets. "Now please," he says, "let me assure you that this won't take long." He pulls up a chair and sits down. "I know this isn't the easiest thing for any family member on a Monday morning, but it is necessary for

Matthew's welfare that I meet with you to discuss his progress and obtain some background information that might help in his treatment."

Brian and his mother look straight ahead and say nothing.

"First, let me begin with a diagnosis. As I am sure you've been told before, Matthew appears to suffer from a form of manic depression, bipolar disorder, with episodes of severe clinical depression. Without treatment and medication, he develops tendencies toward mild paranoia. On occasion the mental anguish associated with all of this has resulted in apparent breaks with his immediate reality, the here and now, for lack of a better term, the normal world, and this dissociation has driven him inward to an interior world of his own making. The first break, as I understand it, might have happened in his teens, brought on by any number of complexes and conflicts associated with adolescence. I suspect that at the time it was masked by a kind of adolescent rebellion and reticence, though I do have some notes concerning migraines."

"He was always complaining about headaches," Mrs. Wyman says.

"After that," Dr. Lehman continues, "the most significant development is the well-documented break that occurred approximately one year ago when he took up residence in a shelter he constructed in a cemetery near his home."

"Hillside Cemetery," Brian says. "I'm the one who found him. Actually the cops found him after a complaint, but I'm the one who got him and brought him home."

Dr. Lehman refers to his notes: "At that time Matthew was placed under the care of a Doctor Bradford?"

"That's right," Mrs. Wyman says. "He's our family doctor. He said Matthew had an overactive imagination, which isn't unusual with a person as bright as Matthew's supposed to be."

"Yes, indeed, and he is bright; however, perhaps to his detriment. It seems that undue attention has been placed on Matthew's intelligence as being the cause of his mental illness. What I'm saying is because Matthew is intelligent I'm afraid some of his problems have been too easily explained away with the 'smart but crazy' cliché. Now we have tested Matthew several times, and he tests within a well-established classification. He is very bright, but that, in and of itself, is not considered abnormal. I say this because if we continue to place the responsibility for Matthew's illness at the doorstep of some extraordinary gift, it might serve to absolve us from looking more deeply into the traumas or the biochemistry underlying his condition."

"He's troubled," Mrs. Wyman says. "We never agreed to calling it 'mental illness.' His father won't hear of it, and I won't, either. We have neighbors and people who know us where we live, and we're not about to start calling things 'mental illness.' They're problems, and that's all they are."

Dr. Lehman sits back and flips a few pages on his clipboard. Brian notices the stains on the doctor's white coat, the beaten down brown Hush Puppies, the wide flare to the double-knit pants. He thinks about the doctors at the hospital and how they wouldn't be caught dead wearing clothes like this.

"I agree, Mrs. Wyman, that we shouldn't get caught up in language or terms. Certainly Matthew is troubled—has problems—which is why I want to look at those traumas which might have contributed to his condition. Now, as a boy or teenager—"

Mrs. Wyman interrupts: "He had a normal life. A privileged life, really. He never wanted for anything. His father saw to that."

"All right, now did he attend summer camp?"

"Every summer," Mrs. Wyman says, "for several years. His father wanted him to go away for the summer to learn how to swim and all the rest of it. It cost us quite a bit of money, even with the discount we received from that Dr. Somebody—Brian, do you remember his name? He ran the place."

"I think it was Late or Laid or something. Lay, that was it."

"He wasn't a medical doctor," Mrs. Wyman says, "just one of the other kind. I think he was a famous coach or teacher or principal out of Hartford. He gave other teachers a break on the price. I wasn't in favor of it, though. The camp, I mean. After all, my Brian worked every summer, delivering papers and then did heavy work, construction work, a man's work, but Mr. Wyman didn't want that for Matthew. 'He'll meet people,' he said."

"It seems this camp experience was quite significant in his adolescent years."

"Was it?" Mrs. Wyman asks. "I wouldn't know. I thought he enjoyed himself."

"I'm not saying he didn't, but when one of the therapists asked him to work in the crafts room—it was an exercise in self-expression—he built this enormous diorama of this waterfront aquatic camp with decks and cabins and a lodge and everything. It was really quite marvelous."

"He's good with the artsy stuff," Brian says.

"Well, this was a little better than just 'artsy stuff,'" Doctor Lehman says, as he lifts two yellow stickums and asks, "Now, did Matthew ever catch his foot in a trap?"

"A what?" Brian asks.

"A trap, like a bear trap, with the semicircular jaws and the teeth."

"No," Mrs. Wyman says. "Of course not."

"You saying a 'bear trap'?" Brian asks.

"Yes, you see, because the first few weeks here Matthew was adamant that the reason he'd been admitted in the first place was because he'd been caught in one of Brando's traps. Now, except for the asthma, which we treated right away, there wasn't any evidence of injury, so I've been curious about the image and the name—Brando's traps."

"That never happened to him," Mrs. Wyman says, "least not that I know of, but Matthew was always one to exaggerate the least little bit of pain. He cried as a baby and complained after that, always dying from whatever. He tried to play football like his brother here, though I don't think he lasted more than a week once they put the pads on."

Dr. Lehman makes a note. "Recently he's been very concerned about a former employer, an elderly woman in Hartford?"

"That's Mrs. O'Neal," Brian says. "She died. Matt liked her, said she was a good woman. I never met her, but I knew of her because my friend works at the same place, and he said she was a good woman who'd taken an interest in my brother."

"An interest?"

"You know, like he was a 'lost soul' and she felt bad for him and knew he was smart."

"Okay then, getting back to his time in high school, right around the time he started getting the migraines, do either of you remember anything that could have happened, something or someone he might have seen, perhaps a classmate, a teacher, whatever, that caused him undue anxiety."

Mrs. Wyman stares at the doctor and says nothing. She looks at Brian who shrugs his shoulders.

"I'm not surprised," Dr. Lehman says, "these events, when they do occur, can be so incidental as to be all but invisible to everybody but the person in question. For them they're nothing short of a kind of epiphany—sometimes for good, sometimes not."

"What's an epiphany?" Mrs. Wyman asks. "You mean a religious thing?"

"In a way," Dr. Lehman says. "What I mean is some event or happenstance, sight, sound, impresses itself so deeply on a person's subconscious that it overshadows everything else. To you or me or anybody other than Matthew it doesn't require a second thought, and wouldn't make sense if it did, but for Matthew it becomes a big part of his life, conscious and unconscious."

"You mean something weird?" Brian asks. "Because he is strange."

"Not exactly," Dr. Lehman says, "though if the imprint, the expression of the imprint, is repressed long enough it can gather a kind of power and come out in what you might call strange behavior, interests, obsessions. Addiction's often a problem, too, because it can medicate the anxiety associated with the underlying problem. At least for a while. In any event, it's been a source of trouble for him, contributed to his depressions and, when he was younger, the mania."

"He met a girl in college," Brian says. "It didn't work out though. After that he started to drink."

"Whatever happened in college probably echoed something that happened before."

"She was wealthy," Brian says. "That's all he ever told me about her. He's always had a thing about girls with money."

"Matthew never shared his thoughts about girls with me," Mrs. Wyman says. "I was just happy to hear he liked girls. And I think he does, doesn't he, doctor?"

"Matthew likes most people," Dr. Lehman says, "I'm afraid some of his problems stem from what he thinks other people think of him."

"I think people think about themselves," Brian says.

"Which is why you're going home today and Matthew isn't."

"How much longer is he going to stay here?" Mrs. Wyman asks.

"I don't know," Dr. Lehman says. "He's made some progress. I think the meds have finally kicked in to help with the depression, but he's still fragile. One good sign is that after he made that model of the campsite, he got very excited about getting back to his artwork, the sculptures and whatnot. He's been working with clay, and he's made some very nice things."

"What are you talking about?" Mrs. Wyman asks. "What's this about artwork?"

"Your son is a talented artist, Mrs. Wyman. I'm sure you know that."

"He might fool around with that sort of thing, but his father and I never encouraged it. It's not a man's thing, after all. If he's got the brains all the teachers say he has, then he should have gone to law school or even medical school like you—but we never agreed to Matthew being an artist."

"Just like you never agreed to his 'mental illness.'"

"That's right, Dr. Lehman. Matthew has problems."

"Do your love your son?" Dr. Lehman asks in a pleasant voice, so soft the question hangs like a bauble of air in the air between them.

"Of course I do," she says. "I don't know what I'd do without my Brian."

"I was asking about Matthew."

"Oh, well, yes, Doctor, I love him, too, if you must know."

"Frankly, Mrs. Wyman, Matthew's the one who needs to know."

The blood flushes the woman's face. She stares at the doctor with dark eyes. The silence almost hurts. "Matthew's family," Brian says, slurring the verb. "But it doesn't mean we have to fall all over each other. We're not like that."

The door opens and a small blonde with perfect skin and hazel eyes enters the room. She's wearing a white coat with a name tag, and she carries a clipboard stuffed with papers.

"I'm sorry to interrupt, Doctor," she says with an inflected English reminiscent of another language spoken in another country.

"Yes, Dr. Wurtzel, we're almost done here."

"I just have these papers from the weekend," she says, and she hands two blue forms to Dr. Lehman. "Molly said you'd want to see them right away."

"Thank you, Martha."

Brian stares at the woman. She's gorgeous and foreign and her smile is open and pure and seductive.

"Hello," she says to Brian and Mrs. Wyman.

"Hello," Brian says.

"This is Martha Wurtzel," Dr. Lehman says. "She's here for the next year with an exchange program from Fribourg."

"Germany," Brian says.

"Switzerland," Martha says.

"Martha's spent some time with Matthew, too," Dr. Lehman says. "These are the Wymans, Martha."

"You should be very proud of Matthew," Martha says.

"Why?" Mrs. Wyman asks.

"He's a very talented man, a very wonderful artist."

"I see," Mrs. Wyman says.

"I'm his older brother," Brian says.

Martha Wurtzel nods in reply as Dr. Lehman initials and hands back the two blue forms. He thanks Martha and she leaves the room, Brian watching her as she goes.

"Are we finished, then?" Mrs. Wyman asks.

"I think so," Dr. Lehman says. "Thank you both for coming today. Matthew will be here a while longer, perhaps through the end of the year. We're beginning to see some improvement with a new combination of meds, and I expect in time he'll be highly functional."

"He'll go back to school," Mrs. Wyman says.

"And maybe he will," Dr. Lehman says. "I only want him to choose a course in life that will make him happy and fulfilled. What more can a doctor want for his patient?"

Dr. Lehman stands at the large tinted window in the front of the hospital wing and watches Brian help his mother to the Pontiac parked in the middle of the lot. They reach the car and Brian helps her into the passenger seat and with his forearm wipes the morning dew off the windshield. Then he gets in behind the wheel, starts the car, and drives slowly out of the lot to the main road.

The receptionist arrives through a back entrance and greets the doctor with a question, wondering if he's been up all night worrying about his patients.

"No," he says. "No, Molly, I slept pretty well last night."

"I never had insomnia," she says, "but I hear it's terrible."

"It can be," Dr. Lehman says. "And how was your weekend?"

"Pretty good," she says. "Tommy was away on a trip, but then he came home Saturday night and we had some friends over for dinner."

"Did Tommy cook?"

"Of course, as always. Braved the chill and grilled the chicken."

"It's been a cold April so far."

"Not too cold for Tommy. He loves a party."

"Nothing wrong with that," Dr. Lehman says as he begins to leave.

"Dr. Lehman," Molly calls to him. "Did Martha bring you the H-17 forms?"

"Yes, she did."

"And we had a discharge over the weekend."

"Who was that?"

"One of Dr. Lefler's patients."

"Okay."

"And Mrs. Johnson died Friday night."

"Dr. Morrisey's Mrs. Johnson?"

"That's right."

"They do all the paperwork on Saturday?"

"They did. The funeral home picked up the body Saturday morning."

"So it goes," Dr. Lehman says.

"What do you want housekeeping to do about the empty bed on two?" she asks.

"On two?"

"Two-oh-nine," she says.

"I didn't think we had an empty bed on two. Isn't that Matthew's room?"

"I don't know," she says. "I'll check."

"Two-oh-nine," Dr. Lehman says, and his beeper goes off and the day begins again with questions and confusion.

Officer Talmadge is flat-out, fuck-you pissed. He sits in Moraski's car with the newspaper and the sports section and Sunday's scores and wonders where he'll get the money to pay Gemelli who runs everything out of his head. As the wise guy said: You bet; you lose; you pay. Fuck you, where's my money. Talmadge is also pissed with Moraski—pissed they're still jerking each other off over this old woman who lived longer than his parents and who died with enough money to buy half of Hartford twice. He picks up the Styrofoam cup with the Donut-Wholes label and curses the chief or the commissioner or the mayor or whoever it was who laid their hands on Moraski's head, making him a detective before he was due, as if he were some kind of quota prize, some kind of one-armed, transgender, queer Nigerian Jew, jumping him ahead of other guys who deserved it more. He's got no gut for this, Talmadge says to himself, thinking how Moraski's got no instinct, no sense of people, let alone any feel for the street. He's not a bad guy, Talmadge thinks, but when they make an okay guy a detective and the guy's not up to the job, all you get is one of those check-off-the-boxes guys who thinks he can get things done without having to get his hands dirty. The old lady was old, Talmadge says to himself, and Doc Frawley signed off on it. Let them read the will and get on with it because good people are getting shot up every day. Drugs are flooding the streets. Kids who used to watch cartoons are shooting each other with automatic weapons, and nobody's doing a thing about it, especially if the best Moraski can do is harass Sully with useless bullshit.

Talmadge tosses the paper on the dash; it slides to the floor. He kicks it and sips the last bit of coffee sloshing over the bottom of his cup. Outside across the street three black kids stand huddled against the April chill. They've got the baggy pants with the crotch hanging down to their knees, the football parkas, the stocking caps. They're talking, though nobody would know it, mouths barely moving, not needing to move, talking nonetheless, and Talmadge can't imagine what they're talking about unless it's about him, the white cop sitting in the unmarked car in a bad neighborhood, sticking his white nose where it does not belong, checking them out, watching them, watching the neighborhood, fucking up their business, scaring off the assholes who come in from the suburbs for a little baggy of this, a little slip of that. Talmadge tries to imagine the sound of their voices when they speak English that's not English anymore, lyrical and tough sounds, punctuated in a perpetual shorthand, repetitive, insular, a kind of descriptive genius, as threatening as it is accurate and unknowable. Those fuckers are up to no good, Talmadge thinks, the prejudice cascading like temper, and he is wondering how long Moraski's going to take when the dirty glass door to Harry's bodega opens from the inside and Moraski appears with a brown paper bag and a newspaper, standing there, his be-all-you-can-be buzz cut, blond and flat, shining in the sun.

Moraski passes the black kids and one kid makes a move. Talmadge, with the instinct of a kind of cop no longer valued, reaches for the gun under his jacket until the picture develops and the scene clarifies and one kid holds out a cup and a second kid reads something from a yellow sheet of paper. Moraski stops, listens, waits. The kid reading the paper finishes and Moraski says something and hands the third kid his package so he can get his wallet. Then Moraski takes out a few bills, stuffs them in the cup, pats one kid on the shoulder, says something else, laughing, all four of them laughing.

"What was that all about?" Talmadge asks as Moraski gets in the car and sets the coffee on the seat.

"They're collecting for a youth center; that Bishop Ravezzi's behind it."

"He's the communist," Talmadge says.

"Whatever he is, he's doing some good for these kids."

"You gave them money?"

"Sure I did. Maybe you should, too."

Talmadge looks at Moraski like he's nuts, like he's so freaking naïve he doesn't know he just gave it up for three kids who don't give a shit about youth centers or communist bishops.

"You trust those kids?" Talmadge asks.

"Yeah, I do."

"You don't think they just scammed you."

"Talmadge," Moraski says, as he takes a large coffee from the bag, lifts the lid, and sips. "Now you bet with a bookie named Gepetto . . ."

"Gemelli."

"Whatever—three times a week during football season and I don't know how many times with basketball."

"What about it?"

"You trust this Gemelli guy?"

"Yeah."

"You don't think maybe after all this time somebody's not taking you for a ride?"

Talmadge kicks at the paper by his feet. "Fuck me," he says.

"Anyway, those kids got something going tonight."

"I bet," Talmadge says.

"Some kind of daredevil show their group's putting on."

"For what?"

"Raise money. They got bungee jumping, some human fly, and this other guy who's been on TV."

"Too cold for that sort of thing."

"Warm front's coming through this afternoon. Anyway, kids don't care about that. They want to see some guy levitate."

"What do you mean, 'levitate'?"

"Just what I said. They say they hired this guy who's getting famous because he can do all kinds of things, like that guy on TV."

"And he's gonna levitate."

"That's what they said."

"Levitate this," Talmadge says.

They drive toward Waterbury and north to Litchfield. The scenery changes. There are hills and fields and farmhouses, always in the distance, always alone. The trees have leaves again and the ones that don't are beginning to sprout green-and-yellow blossoms.

"People don't know how pretty this state is," Moraski says, and Talmadge grunts, sick of Moraski, hating the chief again for having assigned him this temp duty till Koegel, Moraski's permanent butt-boy gets out of the hospital with one less kidney.

"Just what the fuck did he do?" Talmadge asks.

"Who?"

"Your partner, Koegel?"

"What do you mean?"

"You're tellin' me he gave away a kidney?"

"Yeah. His brother needed a kidney. Koegel was a match. No big deal."

"Are you shitting me?" Talmadge says, the edge, the voice catching Moraski off guard.

"No, I'm not shitting you," Moraski says, with his own edge. "He did it for his brother."

"No fucking way," Talmadge mutters.

"What are you saying? 'No fucking way.' You'd do it for your brother."

"I don't have a brother."

"You got a sister?"

"I got a sister."

"So your sister needs a kidney and you're a match, you're not going to give it to her?"

"No fucking way," Talmadge says.

"I don't believe it," Moraski says.

"You ever meet my sister?" Talmadge asks.

"No."

"Well, she's got a brain that don't work and there's no fucking way I'm giving her half of my brain, either."

"How much you lose this week?" Moraski asks.

"Fuck me," Talmadge says, and he looks out the window over the round side of a hill covered with trees and some bare branches.

They drive for half an hour and Moraski talks about how everybody's forgotten about Homeland Security and how incompetent the Feds are, even with the recent memos coming out of the New York office about chatter and threats and the kind of trouble that's been sitting out there, waiting, behind veils, talked about like hard weather that's always a day away. Talmadge ignores the whole thing, changing the subject, not giv-ing a shit. "So where is this place?" he asks.

"Outside of Torrington," Moraski says.

"Torrington? What the hell is Torrington? I thought we were going to Litchfield."

"Torrington's next door."

"Jesus Christ," Talmadge says. "I knew he did some shit; I just didn't know he did it at the end of the fucking world."

They drive up the Naugatuck Valley, the river on their left, some-times visible, mostly hidden. It's a poor valley with old and abandoned mills and factories where each town once manufactured its own thing: hats, brass, clocks, rubber, ball bearings, needles, and pins. But modern technology passed by all of that. Now the factories are empty and the money men won't gentrify factories when there aren't enough yuppies to buy the condos. Only quaint little Litchfield retains a name conso-nant with New England charm with its bare white church, the austere beauty of a place founded by people suspicious of any beauty other than God's.

Moraski gets lost and they can't find the hospital, so they stop at two gas stations before they get directions that make sense. The roads twist, turn, descend, and ascend over and around hills. After they miss a turn, they backtrack and drive down a country road, newly paved, barely wide enough for two lanes of traffic. The hospital's a combination of two buildings, one, old and yellow, an impressive block of permanence, the other, a low building, sixties modern, United Nations–ugly, functional.

They get out of the car and cross the lot. They enter the main door of the large building and ask the receptionist if Mr. Robert Sullivan's on the premises. She checks a daybook, and Moraski leans over and reads it upside down and sees Sullivan's name.

"He's the puppy man," the receptionist says.

"The what?" Moraski asks.

"He's in Lounge B with some kids."

Moraski and Talmadge walk down a corridor and come to an open area where about twenty kids sit on couches, in wheelchairs, some with IV drips, some with bandanas wrapped around their bald heads, some pale with sickly blue shadows under their eyes, some emaciated, some swollen with drugs, all of them smiling, most of them laughing as best they can. Bobby Sullivan's standing in the center of the room in a ring of several dog carriers, opening them, closing them, passing puppies around for the kids to hold and pet and play with.

"What the fuck?" Talmadge whispers. "I knew he did some charity stuff, but I didn't know he did this."

The puppies are painfully, effortlessly cute, and the kids hold them and some of them get down on the floor and let the dogs roll around, nibbling each other's fur, paws in the air, lying on their backs, loving the petting and the attention.

Bobby Sullivan makes sure every kid gets some time with at least one of the dogs. His face is bright and he laughs from time to time and his eyes are warm and the kids, who've got a collective sixth sense about good people and frauds, take to him the same way they take to the puppies.

Moraski steps back into the corridor's shadow and watches the whole thing from a distance. He doesn't want to disturb this.

After a while Sullivan asks the nurse's aide to fill some bowls from the sack of dog food set against the wall. The candy striper takes several bowls stacked on a table, picks up the sack of treats, and steps back as the puppies go crazy jumping around her legs. The kids love it and Bobby Sullivan tells them he'll be back in a few minutes and leaves Lounge B to meet Moraski and Talmadge.

"I didn't know you guys wanted to see me," Sullivan says. "We could have met in Hartford. I got to be back for a funeral at eleven o'clock."

"How long you been doing this?" Moraski asks.

"Doing what?"

"With the kids, the dogs."

"Long enough," Sullivan says.

"It's a good thing, Bobby," Talmadge says. "It's a good thing."

"Yeah, well, so what do you two want?" Sullivan asks.

Moraski shuffles his feet. The kids and the dogs have touched him, softened him. When he talks his voice is low and inquisitive. "It's like this," he says. "I'm not saying a guy who cares about sick kids like you do can't get himself in trouble, but let's just say we want to work with you on this thing. All I ask is that you tell us the truth."

"I didn't commit a crime," Bobby says.

"But you lied to us," Moraski says. "You said she died of natural causes."

"She did."

"And you paid LaPorta and that Wyman kid to go along with the story."

"I fired that kid. I paid him twenty bucks severance."

"And LaPorta?"

"That's crazy. Davie, you know LaPorta. LaPorta's a good cop."

"Always has been," Talmadge says.

"We got a witness who says different," Moraski says. "And what about Doc Frawley?"

"What about him?"

"Frawley's overdue for the dog track," Talmadge says.

"What's that got to do with me?" Sullivan asks.

"You had him sign off and then cremated the old lady before anybody could get a better look," Moraski says.

"This is bullshit," Sullivan whispers. "Since when is it up to me to call in a second opinion just because Frawley drinks too much."

"C'mon, Bobby," Talmadge says. "We got to follow up on this."

"On what?"

"We know the old lady was going to change her will," Moraski says.

"Then you know more than I do, Mark. And who told you all of this? The niece? Manny? I told you about her. The girl lies when her lips move."

"It wasn't the niece," Moraski says.

"Then it must have been the tooth fairy."

"At the very least you tried to defraud the insurance company. They don't pay on suicide."

Bobby Sullivan looks from Moraski to Talmadge. Laughter explodes from the lounge, and Bobby turns to see what's happening. A kid leaves the lounge and stands next to Bobby, his fingers touching his pant leg. The three men look at the kid and all of them change.

"What is it, Josh?" Bobby says.

"Are you coming back inside?" Josh asks.

"Just give me a second," Bobby Sullivan says. "I just got to say good-bye to my friends here."

"Why don't you guys come in, too?" Josh asks.

Talmadge coughs; Moraski says they have to get back to work. "Maybe some other time," Moraski says, but Josh heads back into the lounge without a word. He knows Moraski's full of it, and there's no need to waste time with an adult who's full of it.

After Josh is gone, Sullivan gets real close to Moraski. He's not afraid of this guy, and he wants Moraski to know it. He says, "You come all the way out here to accuse me of something, and I'm telling you you're looking at the wrong person. I worked at that place my whole adult life and maybe the old lady and I didn't always see eye to eye, but I didn't touch her, and I can tell you she did not kill herself. Now if you're getting a different story from someplace else, well, I guess that's your problem."

The laughter continues in the lounge. Bobby Sullivan leaves the corridor and picks up one of the puppies waiting for him at the doorway.

Talmadge and Moraski watch the show for a few minutes and then walk back down the corridor, through the main doors, and outside to the car for the drive to Hartford.

"What do you think?" Moraski asks.

"I think the lady lived a long life and we got better things to do."

Moraski's cell beeps. He notes the incoming number. "What the hell?" he says.

"What?" Talmadge asks.

"A-t-t-n-g-e-n," Moraski spells, answering the phone. "Hello . . . Yeah, that's ours . . . Me and Dave Talmadge . . . I can't say we are . . . Ten o'clock . . . We'll be there."

"What's up?" Talmadge asks.

"You know this guy Somers?"

"The attorney general?"

"Yeah. The guy who wants to be governor."

"He announce yet?" Talmadge asks.

"I don't know."

"So, what about him?"

"That was his brother, Andrew Somers. He wants to see us."

"What for?"

"I guess he thinks the old lady could have lived a little longer."

"So what's this all about?" Talmadge asks Moraski as they park in the lot behind the Capitol.

"Don't know," Moraski says.

"But the attorney general called?"

"His brother made the call."

"You can bet they're joined at the hip."

"Are they?"

"I don't know. They think they're the fuckin' Kennedys."

They get out of the car. Moraski looks overhead, a solid haze, the kind of sky that often gives way to blue sky and sunlight.

They take the elevator to the attorney general's office where Andrew Somers, the A.G.'s younger brother and chief of staff, meets them and ushers them to an anteroom to brief them before the real meeting begins.

"Thanks for coming," he says, "and call me Drew," a little guy, so heady in the reflected light of power he raises manners to a grand calling, the manners of a military man, informed by false modesty. "I'm afraid we have a problem," Drew says, "and my brother hopes you can help us achieve some kind of resolution."

"What problem?" Talmadge asks.

"Mrs. O'Neal."

"The old lady," Talmadge says. "The only problem with her is that she won't go away and the whole thing's a waste of time."

"Let's just say there've been phone calls."

"Who's making phone calls?" Moraski asks.

"I needn't go into names or identities."

153

"Insurance company doesn't know whether they should pay out or not. Somebody's clock is tickin'," Moraski says.

"That's your guess, not mine, Detective."

"We've been closing in on a guy," Talmadge says.

"But I'm not so sure," Moraski says. "And neither is my partner here."

"Temporary partner."

"You're talking about Bobby Sullivan," Drew says.

Moraski says nothing; Talmadge grimaces.

"We're not uninformed," Drew says, looking about the small room. There's a pot of coffee and cups on a side table. Drew hurries over, as if he's forgotten his manners, and asks if they'd like a cup. Talmadge says yes; Moraski says no. Drew does the honors, and Moraski notes the crisp white shirt, newly pressed, the club tie, the casual elegance, and thought of a prep school and the ease of unconscious, unearned, and very real superiority. Moraski thinks if he were tougher, he'd play the roll of the streetwise Bogart and allow a kind of thirties noir style, world-weary and unimpressed, to protect him from the toxins of envy and insecurity. But Moraski's not that tough, not since law school, not since before law school. He's an ambitious second-generation immigrant, Polish and very Catholic, insecure, prone to airs, and, in this room, vulnerable. He grows small as Drew moves about, serving Talmadge, checking the time, utterly secure. Then he denies the feelings, fighting with himself, and he grows smaller and hopes to gather himself, to obtain some leverage, some height, some weight before he meets the older brother.

"My brother's got the coroner and the D.A. with him," Drew says.

"Frawley?" Talmadge asks.

"Right."

"And what's his name? The D.A.?" Talmadge asks.

"Jimmy Reis," Drew says.

"That's right," Moraski says.

"Jesus," Talmadge says.

"You have a problem with Jimmy Reis?" Drew asks.

"Never mind," Talmadge says, looking away.

"It's been what—seven months? We just want an update on what's going on," Drew says.

"Sullivan had the motive," Talmadge says.

"Motive, means . . . What's the other one?" Drew asks.

"Opportunity," Moraski says. "Watch *Law & Order* tonight. They're big on opportunity."

"What?" Drew asks.

"Nothing," Moraski says.

"No, what, Detective?"

"Nothing."

The door opens and a pretty woman with black eyes, black hair, a dark complexion, looks to Drew. "He's ready," she says, pulling back, closing the door.

Drew stands, sets his coffee cup down as the lamp on the end table flickers, goes bright, dark, and then light again.

"What's up with that?" Talmadge asks.

Drew ignores the question, looks to Moraski. "Just tell the attorney general whatever he needs to know," he says, and Moraski follows him out of the room.

"Hey, I got a question," Talmadge says.

"What?"

"How'd you get Doc Frawley out of bed so early?"

Drew looks at his watch. "It's after ten," he says.

"Yeah, how'd you get Doc Frawley out of bed so early?"

The attorney general's office is huge. The money the government saved on the cheap furniture and bad lighting littered throughout the lower realms of state service obviously made its way to the coffers of several subcontractors for the attorney general's fancy woodwork, the carpet, the paneling, the lamps, the furniture, the desk.

The attorney general himself, Thomas Somers Jr., Esq., sits at his desk and stands when his brother and the others enter. He's a fine-featured man, half-woman-Brit-handsome, the kind of handsome that makes school girls gossip and middle-aged men uneasy—like a movie star playing a serious role, a marriage of celebrity and power.

Talmadge crosses the room to shake the man's hand, and Moraski follows, eyes lowered as if to ward off the full impact of staring into the sun. It takes a moment for the officer and the detective to take in the whole room, but then they see Doc Frawley at the far end of a couch under a painting of some colonial barrister in a nineteenth-century courtroom.

"Hey, Doc," Talmadge says, and Doc Frawley shifts about, scattered movement, unable to stand.

"Don't get up," Moraski says as he shakes the coroner's hand.

A door set in a side wall opens and Jimmy Reis, the D.A., emerges from the attorney general's private bathroom.

"C-Coffee," Reis says, his high voice prone to stutter. "G-Goes right th-th-through me."

Somers takes a call as his assistant, the well-dressed black-eyed woman, enters with papers for his signature.

D.A. Reis talks with Drew, and Doc Frawley talks to himself. Even with the imposed propriety of protocol and the sense of moment inferred from the setting, the office takes on a disturbing, pedestrian buzz. "Yes, Bishop," the attorney general says, "I'll do what I can to attend. . . . A daredevil . . . The Amazing Who? . . . That does sound exciting. . . . Yes, sir, you are doing wonderful things for those kids." And the attorney general hangs up the phone and looks about the room. He doesn't talk and the buzz subsides.

"What do we have?" he says, brusque, active, rhetorical, as if he's about to roll up his sleeves and toss a football at Doc Frawley. "I've read a file on this. Sounds like we've got an old woman who died seven months ago and nobody knows whether she killed herself or was done in for reasons we'll get to."

Doc Frawley comes alive. He's been around long enough to know a cover-your-ass moment. "If I may," he begins, "when I got there, to Mrs. O'Neal's, there was nothing out of the ordinary, nothing untoward, no evidence whatsoever of any kind of wrongdoing. Mrs. Kost O'Neal was elderly. I examined her and stand by my findings."

"Exactly, Doc," the attorney general says. "This office has no quarrel with you. We're well aware of your years of service and your expertise. If there is a problem, it was covered up before you got there. Now, this Sullivan character . . ."

"Bobby Sullivan," Talmadge says.

"He's running the show over there at the funeral home, and Jimmy Reis here should have been able to indict him before they buried the victim."

"They cremated her," Doc Frawley says. "That's part of the problem."

"And these two haven't given me what I need," Reis says.

Moraski feels the circle close. He's entered a sound stage without benefit of a script.

"What does it take to indict somebody in this state?" the attorney general asks, moving now behind his desk, pacing, but not really, the movement tempered by a certain self-conscious review, the now-it's-time-to-pace pacing of an actor incapable of losing himself in his role.

"It takes evidence," Moraski says, and saying it out loud is like pulling a pin on a grenade.

"Evidence!" Somers explodes, turning on Moraski, stepping across the room, pointing a finger. "Exactly, Detective Moraski, evidence, and in this case I can only wonder why you and your partner here have failed to act—"

"We haven't failed—" Moraski says.

"You have failed to gather the evidence Jimmy Reis needs to do his job."

"I'm r-ready to go," Reis says. "But I g-got to have something here."

"Why is everybody so sure Sullivan's guilty?" Moraski asks.

"I've seen the file," Somers says. "I read the letter to her niece. I've met with Cal Stevens. I know what Mrs. O'Neal was prepared to do. And I know enough about that drunk, Sullivan, to put a few things together."

"He does some good in the community," Moraski says.

"So did John Wayne Gacy," Talmadge says, moving, changing sides, saving himself.

"So tell me, Detective Moraski, you don't think Sullivan's our man," Reis says.

"I don't," Moraski says.

"Then who the hell else was around there that morning?" Somers asks.

"Well, there was—"

And Somers interrupts: "I mean who was around who also has a motive." He walks away and stops by the window as if an electric current has shocked him to stillness. The room is silent. He turns to Moraski. "Who?" he shouts.

Moraski names the other people who were there that Sunday morning.

"Forget the niece," Somers says.

"Forget the niece? Why do you want to forget the niece?" Moraski asks.

"Because she only made out if her aunt lived."

"And she made out if the aunt died," Moraski says.

"But only if the old lady had changed her will," Talmadge says.

"Was the niece in the will?" Somers asks.

"No, but . . . ," Moraski says.

"But what?"

"Mrs. O'Neal had every intention of changing her will," Moraski says.

"And how do you know that?"

"There was a letter," Talmadge says. "From the aunt to the niece."

"A letter," Somers says.

"Letters are useless," Reis says.

"I just think it's too soon to forget the niece," Moraski says.

"All right, then, Detective Moraski, don't forget the niece. You can keep her on your list; just don't keep her at the top of your list. Now, who was the other person you named?"

"LaPorta," Talmadge says.

"Not the cop, there was another name."

"Wyman," Moraski says.

"That's it."

"Matthew Wyman," Talmadge says.

"Describe him."

Talmadge does a credible job.

"Do you know him?" Reis asks.

"I'm not sure," the attorney general says, "but if it's who I think it is, then you guys better go back to square one and look at this whole thing again."

Moraski and Talmadge trade glances. Moraski thinks, "The attorney general's fingering Matthew Wyman?" Moraski thinks, "No way."

Doc Frawley's oblivious. He's covered his ass. He'll stop off at Harry's on the way back to the morgue.

D.A. Reis stands, leans forward, leans back, body language designed to look involved, concerned, on board, with just the right suck-up nod to the boss to close the deal.

"What are you saying?" Moraski asks the attorney general.

"Never mind what I'm saying. I think I've said enough, and I think I've made myself very clear."

The dark-eyed woman enters again and whispers in the attorney general's ear. He bends to hear, a blank quizzical expression on his face. "Turn on CNN," he says, and Jimmy Reis crosses the room to the flatscreen TV.

The phone rings and the attorney general picks it up and turns to the wall and says he just got the news.

D.A. Reis fumbles with the remote and finally gets a cable news channel.

There's been a small explosion in a Manhattan subway, cause unconfirmed but suspicious.

"Terrorists?" Somers says into the phone.

"Here we go again," Reis says, and the newscaster from Atlanta reads more copy.

The attorney general puts his hand over the phone and nods to his brother.

Drew stands and moves his arms in a half-wheel scooping motion to direct everyone out of the office. The meeting's over.

Outside the state capitol, under a Romanesque arch under a plastered and Elizabethan front, D.A. Reis, apoplectic, yells at Doc Frawley, calling him incompetent, too old, and a fool. Doc Frawley, a Kutuzov, well schooled in the art of defense, with wisdom gleaned from years of survival, just walks across the lot to his car, refusing to listen to one more ambitious son of a bitch blame his problems on somebody else. Reis continues to screech, his voice cracking once before the stutter begins, hanging on the *F*, reciting the phoneme three times before speaking the name.

On the other side of another pillar, Moraski turns to Drew who stands in shirtsleeves in the mild wind. Moraski asks Drew what his brother *really* wants, and Drew tells the detective that the attorney general had made himself very clear.

"Like hell he did," Moraski says.

"He wants this case solved, and he wants more focus on the guy who found the body."

"You're not serious," Talmadge says.

"We can't make things up just because your brother doesn't like somebody," Moraski says.

"We know this Wyman guy," Drew says.

"So what?" Moraski says.

"My brother's got his reasons," Drew says.

"So what?" Talmadge says.

"We'll follow every lead," Moraski says, uncertain as to the number and intent of the several agendas, hidden and apparent. "Now who's been making all these phone calls?"

"What phone calls?" Drew asks.

"The ones that got us here in the first place," Moraski says, and Reis joins them and interrupts with his own piss and moan.

"Why is that man still employed?" Reis asks, face gone pale, skin drawn, eyes all bugged out, pointing to Frawley, who's halfway across the lot.

"Forget him," Drew says. "We have to get this thing wrapped up so my brother can get about his campaign."

"So that's it," Moraski says.

"What are you saying, Detective?" D.A. Reis asks.

"And what are you bucking for?" Talmadge asks Reis.

"F-F-Fuck you," Reis says, though the impact is dulled with a hitch on consonants that won't let go.

"Look," Moraski says. "I don't know what this is all about. I don't know what phone calls got made to make your brother butt his tiny little head into our business, but we'll investigate every lead and when we have something, you'll be the first to know."

"Remember who you're talking about, Detective," Drew says. "My brother's the attorney general."

"Your brother's an arrogant rich boy who's gotten a long way on papers and a head of hair. I took it from him this morning, but I won't take it from you." Again, Moraski notices the white shirt, the club tie, the disdain. He turns and starts across the lot to the car. Talmadge looks at Drew, at Reis, shrugs his shoulders and follows. Drew calls out to Moraski, something about doing his job. Reis calls out with the "me, too" thing, saying he expects a full report on his desk on Wednesday morning. Moraski debates whether he should raise his arm and give them the finger. But he thinks better of it, controls himself, and opens the door. Talmadge gets in on the passenger side. The two of them breathe air that fogs the window. They say nothing. Moraski starts the car. Talmadge looks at him, and Moraski slams the wheel with the palms of his hands.

"John Wayne Gacy?" he says.

"Tiny little head?" Talmadge says.

"I think we should split up this afternoon," Moraski says.

"Thank God for that," Talmadge says.

"You can thank whoever the hell you want," Moraski says.

Billy the Driver's in the backyard with Darren and Orpheus. They're sitting at a card table with coffee cans wrapped in orange paper filled with change and bills. They're counting the money spread over the table, the coins in small stacks, the bills pressed down.

"Not too bad," Billy says, and Orph says Teddy went with Brown and Dom to work the malls for the afternoon.

"How much this guy gonna cost us?" Darren asks, and Billy says it depends on what kind of daredevil he turns out to be.

"He was on TV," Orph says. "Motherfucker starts flying around Atlantic City with some brothers right there, watchin'; they see this shit and they freak right the fuck out."

"He can levitate?" Billy asks. "I mean you're tellin' me this guy defies the laws of gravity."

"Saw it on TV," Orph says. "Then again they coulda had wires and made 'em invisible with some special-x Superman bullshit."

"Dom says he ain't gonna fly tonight," Darren says.

"Motherfucker better fly, what the fuck we payin' him for," Orph says.

"Dom says he's gonna do this other thing where they bury him alive."

"Get out," Billy says. "I put out the flyers sayin' this guy's gonna fly."

"Maybe they gonna bury him and then he's gonna fly," Darren says.

"Tell you right now," Orph says, "this motherfucker cancelled twice and we get him on a Monday night—he better fuckin' fly."

"It's still a holiday," Darren says.

"It ain't no fuckin' holiday," Orph says.

"Sure it is," Darren says.

"Then it's one of them bullshit no-mail-today holidays, not like it's Thanksgivin' or nothin'."

"It's local," Billy says. "Something about the Charter Oak."

"I thought it was Veterans Day," Darren says.

"That's November," Billy says.

"You're a veteran," Darren says.

"Don't remind me," Billy says.

"Those Vietnam motherfuckers," Orph says, "Now those motherfuckers were crazy."

"You know, Orpheus," Billy says, "I could do one of those college boy drinkin' games with you."

"What the fuck you talkin' 'bout, Billy?"

"What I'm talkin' about is every time you say fuck or motherfucker, person playin' the game's gotta take a drink. Swear to God, five minutes into the game those college boys'll be drunk on their ass."

"Fuck me," Orph says.

"Jesus," Billy says. "Enough, already."

Orpheus and Darren get serious till Billy leaves the table, then they do the high-five bullshit and laugh about the old guy who treats them okay.

Billy walks by the fence and down the driveway and sees the Buick parked at the curb. He walks around the front of the house. Detective Moraski's standing on the front porch, ringing the doorbell.

"Morning, Detective," Billy says.

Moraski looks over the banister. "Hey, Billy, I'm glad you're home."

"They got you workin' on Veterans Day."

"Veterans Day? It isn't Veterans Day."

"I know, I was just funnin' with the boys back there. We're gettin' ready for tonight."

"You working with the bishop?"

"Sorta. We figure better on board than off the side watchin' things go by."

"You know, when I was a kid they called it Armistice Day."

"Sorry?"

"Veterans Day. They called it Armistice Day."

"Oh, right, I remember that—Armistice Day," Billy says.

"Eleven, eleven, eleven," Moraski says.

"Yes, sir," Billy says.

"You a vet, Billy?"

"Nam, two tours."

"Two?"

"Yes, sir."

"Marines?"

"Army."

"God bless you, Bill," and he notices the chain around Billy's neck with a small cross and a little gold charm in the shape of the Vietnam Memorial.

"Thank you, sir. Two tours was more than enough."

"I bet," Moraski says. "Mind if I sit a minute?"

"Be my guest," Billy says, joining him on the front steps.

"A little chill this morning, but it's warming up nice."

"Yes, sir, it sure is. So what can I do for you, Detective?"

"I'm looking for Matthew Wyman."

"Okay."

"Any idea where he is?"

"No, sir. Last I heard he was in a hospital, least that's what his brother told me."

"I called out there," Moraski says. "They say he broke out over the weekend. They think he hitched a ride with whoever picked up a Mrs. Johnson, a woman who died over the weekend and was taken to the O'Neal Funeral Home."

"That was me," Billy says.

"So?"

"So what?" Billy says.

"You gave Matthew a ride back here?"

"I just picked up a body and delivered it to O'Neal's."

"And you didn't see Matthew Wyman."

"No, sir."

Moraski leans back and picks at his front teeth with a toothpick.

The April sun lays a sheen of almost white, barely perceptible by sight, that registers as some element of air changing from cool and hard to mild and soft, like the sky opening up after a long season of metal clouds and the weight of impending storms. It's there, beyond a veil, this seasonal affectation, and more than anything else it speaks of that bittersweet turn of a world at birth, about to wake, too young to acknowledge its bold cycles.

Moraski waits for this every spring, like a memory from his childhood, and though he's unable to articulate what it is, he feels it when it happens. And this year it happens, unbidden, unexpected, as he looks over Billy's front yard with the new grass and the gray grass and the broken pavement of a worn sidewalk.

"You from here?" Moraski asks Billy.

"Pardon me?"

"You grow up in Connecticut? New England?"

"Grew up in Ansonia."

"Family from there?"

"Family was from St. Louis. My father moved here to go to dental school."

"Father's a dentist?"

"He was."

"That's great."

"I guess it was."

"Parents still alive?"

"No, sir. Both passed. Long time ago."

"Sorry."

"Thank you, sir."

Moraski pauses. Looks across the street to another house, not unlike Billy's—same size, same color. An old woman brushes old leaves off the porch with a broom. She looks over her shoulder, sees Billy, and waves. Billy waves back.

"Tell me something," Moraski says. "How well do you know Matt Wyman?"

"I know him; we were acquainted, ya know, worked at the same place."

"What did you think of him?'

"How do you mean, Detective?"

"I mean what kind of person is he. Did you like him?"

"I liked him okay. I got him the job as a favor to his brother."

"How did you do that?"

"I just introduced him to Mrs. O'Neal, and he took it from there."

"I heard he's pretty smart."

"Book smart, all right."

"You call him the Professor."

"I used to. I meant it friendly-like."

"Do you think he had anything to do with Mrs. O'Neal?"

"Dyin' you mean?"

"Yeah, dying."

"No, though I'm not surprised you're askin'."

"Why is that?"

"It's like this, Detective, I mean the world is like this: There are all kinds of people out there and there are some bad people, I mean really bad people, and most times they get away with all of it, and more often than not they tend to do pretty good for themselves."

Moraski sits forward, breaks the toothpick, puts the pieces in his pocket.

"Matthew like that?" he asks.

"No, sir. Not at all. People like the Professor are the exact opposite, like the balance on the other side. Matthew Wyman's not bad at all, but people like him, they do one little thing wrong they'll pay for it their whole lives, and that's when they're not payin' for somethin' they didn't even do. There were guys like that in Vietnam—fresh-faced good boys and you just knew they were gonna catch it and you stayed away from them so you wouldn't catch it, too. Call it bad luck, karma, coincidence, bein' naïve, foolish, call it whatever—fact is the world says the Professor's gonna pay, guilty or not—doesn't matter—he's the one's gonna pay."

Moraski nods. "It's a mystery," he says. "Some people are just fucked from the get-go. And some people walk on water. No wonder people got to believe in a better life than this. Most people want things to be fair."

"Now, you're givin' me one of those I-have-a-dream speeches, Detective. Now don't be settin' me up with one of those I-have-a-dream
speeches."

Moraski wants to say something about what it feels like to be let
down, to be disappointed, when he sees the flyer sticking out of Billy's
shirt pocket. Block letters spell: THE AMAZING LEVON.

"The Amazing what?" Moraski asks.

"Sorry?"

"The flyer there. In your pocket."

Billy takes it, spreads it on his knee.

"The Amazing Levon," he says. "Cat's suppose to be able to levitate
or some such thing."

"He's the daredevil you guys got for your show tonight."

"Bishop got him. Bishop Ravezzi's wife knows Eddie Davis, the guy's
manager. Guy's supposed to be able to do all kinds of weird things."

"Like what?"

"I don't know—talk with dead people. They bury him alive sometimes; he does card tricks, you know, the usual stuff."

"Levitating sure isn't usual."

"No, but I think that's the hook to get you in the door."

"So the bishop's wife knows his manager?"

"That's what they told me."

"I didn't know bishops could have wives."

"He's a Protestant bishop."

"And this Amazing Leon, he really does come off the ground?"

"Levon," Billy says. "They say he can, though they're supposed to
bury him alive tonight. You should come on down, Detective. We're
trying to get people to show up."

He hands Moraski the flyer. Moraski holds it up, folds it, puts it in
his pocket, and stands up.

"I'll do what I can, Billy. I'm all for helping out when I can."

He puts his hand out to shake Billy's hand. After some hesitation
Billy offers his hand, and Moraski feels the limp handshake, looking
Billy in the eye, trying to send the same little signals white men send
white men to say something about trust and respect. Billy sees it, he

knows all the white-on-white signals, and he doesn't hold it against the guy for trying.

Moraski walks across the lawn to his car, and Billy enters the house and walks through the front room, the second room, the dining room, and then the kitchen where he opens the door to the basement. He walks downstairs into the darkness where one light hangs from the ceiling. At the far end of the basement there's a room with a cot and an outlet and a lamp and a radio, a desk and a chair. The radio's on, and Matthew Wyman's sitting on the cot.

"What's going on?" Billy asks.

"Just this dirty bomb stuff out of New York."

"That guy, Moraski, was just here," Billy says.

"What did he want?"

"He wanted to talk to you. Figured I was the one who gave you a ride this weekend."

"I guess I can't blame him," Matthew says. "Especially since I'm the only one who knows what really happened."

"So, they're causin' trouble in New York, then," Billy says.

"Looks that way," Matthew says.

"World hasn't been the same for a long time," Billy says.

"Not for a long time," Matthew says.

"Won't be for a longer time, neither."

The church is packed, lit up, high church, extra holy with the smells and bells. Officer Talmadge sits in the back and waits. He doesn't know who died, whose remains are lying cold, pumped and waxed in the bronze coffin between the candles and the honor guard with two bishops on the altar, two governors in the first pew, but the send-off argues for somebody important, rich, or both.

Talmadge listens to the Episcopal priest drone on, an affected accent with clips and curlicues, and he listens to the mourners' sad little whimpers, choked-back tears. He figures Brits are more reserved than wealthy Irish and remembers that when he was an altar boy at Assumption Elementary he served funerals every week and could tell the old-world nationality of the deceased just by listening to the way the mourners mourned. Wealthy Irish were reserved, trying to pass as Brits, worker Irish were sad with a belligerent edge and the ubiquitous out-lyer, everintoxicated, capable of a shout or two. Brit-Catholics were rare and silent. Italians were effusive, big on flowers, sometimes wild, but never belligerent. Puerto Ricans let loose, as did the Lebanese. The blacks were the best at keeping it real, mourning as an art form, and Asians could surprise you, go either way and all the way from silence to jumping on the coffin. The rest of the northern Europeans, Germans, Scandinavians, some French, were either in the wrong church or hardly there at all, as if funerals were an inefficiency, an homage to outdated and bourgeois thoughts about death and dying, as if they had better things to do.

The funeral ends with a little kid in a white surplus and red cassock swinging the thurible with the incense rising and the bells ringing and some woman overhead singing with the organ.

Bobby Sullivan's crew flanks the casket and moves it down the aisle. Sullivan follows and sees Talmadge standing in the pew. Sullivan nods. Talmadge says, "Outside," and follows Sullivan to the door and down the steps as the mourners follow. Talmadge sees a governor, a senator, two reps, several execs from insurance companies, and a gaggle of those old doddering guys who smell of pedigree, Yale, secrecy, and power.

Sullivan moves to the side and greets Talmadge with a nod.

"Who the fuck died?" Talmadge asks.

"This guy's wife. Mrs. Johnson."

"Then who's Mr. Johnson?"

"Coop Johnson, the insurance exec. Backroom sort of guy. Pulls a lot of strings everywhere."

"So that's why all the pols are here."

"That's it."

"Those guys look like professionals," Talmadge says, and he points to a phalanx of six-foot-tall guys dressed in identical black suits, with identical buzz cuts and little phone wires in their ears.

"Secret Service," Sullivan says.

"Get outta here."

"See that woman over there?" Sullivan asks.

"What about her?" Talmadge asks, as he looks at a fairly attractive, fairly petite, but otherwise nondescript middle-aged woman in a nice suit.

"She look familiar to you?"

"She looks like a high-priced real estate broker."

"She's the Speaker of the House."

"What house?"

"The House."

"Of Representatives? In D.C.?"

"You got it," Sully says.

"Holy shit," Talmadge says. "So why the Secret Service?"

"She's third in line for the presidency."

"And the trouble in New York," Talmadge says, feeling a little stupid, slow to put things together.

"They'd be here, trouble or not," Sullivan says, and when he turns to look at her again, Cal Stevens, the attorney, tall, elderly, stately, and pissed, separates from the crowd and walks up to Bobby Sullivan and blocks his view.

"Mr. Stevens," Bobby says. "How are you?"

"You've been a client of mine, Mr. Sullivan, though not a client of my choosing."

"What do you mean?"

"In your position as the last remaining officer and director of the Kost O'Neal Funeral Home Corporation, I've done my duty to represent you and the corporation in the wake of Emma's death."

"Okay," Bobby says. "I got no complaints. You're a good lawyer."

"What I am is not in issue, Mr. Sullivan. But what you are is in issue."

"What are you saying?"

"I'm saying I no longer wish to represent the man who killed Emma Kost."

"Well, I'm sure that'll upset whoever that is, Mr. Stevens."

"Don't get cute with me, sir. You can consider our attorney-client relationship at an end as of now."

Sullivan turns to Talmadge who's been standing there the whole time. "Can he do that?" Sullivan asks. "Doesn't he need some kind of order from the court or something?"

"I have it right here, Mr. Sullivan, my motion and the order of the court, granted and signed by Judge Nash." Cal Stevens hands copies to Bobby Sullivan. Bobby takes them, looks at them, folds them in a roll, and stuffs them in his pocket.

"Mr. Stevens," Bobby says, but Cal Stevens turns and disappears into the crowd gathered on the church steps.

Talmadge and Sullivan move down the sidewalk near the line of black cars where Sullivan watches his men do their work, precisely, a choreography made more elegant with the beefy men in their black topcoats, velvet collars, the elusive and faint aroma of mouthwash and aftershave.

"Now what the fuck was that all about?" Sullivan asks Talmadge.

"He's a crank," Talmadge says. "Everybody knows he's a crank."

"I don't like being accused, though."

"I'm sure you don't, which is why I'm here. So, can you get away for a few?"

"I should go to the cemetery."

"Got somebody who can handle it for you?"

"Give me a second."

Sullivan walks to the front limo, says a few words to the driver who points to a limo in the back. Sullivan walks down the line of cars and grabs a young kid with a shaved head and wire rim glasses. He says a few words and the kid stands at attention, almost salutes, a little soldier. After that Sullivan walks back to Talmadge and says, "Let's get out of here."

They go to a breakfast diner that used to be a bar. It's empty except for one guy at the counter drinking coffee. Talmadge orders two cups and a bear claw for himself. They sit in a booth in the back. Talmadge sees that Sullivan looks beat-up, exhausted. He says, "How you holdin' up, Bobby?" and Sullivan doesn't answer but looks into his coffee cup.

"Just how official is this visit?" Sullivan asks. "Are we friends here or what?"

"We're always friends, Sully. I hope you know that."

"Where's your twin brother?"

"Moraski?"

"Yeah."

"He's probably home lickin' his wounds."

"What happened?"

"The attorney general sort of kicked his ass this morning."

"What's the attorney general got to do with anything? Jesus Christ, this thing's become one royal pain in the ass."

"And he's running for governor, too."

"Jesus," Sullivan says.

They drink their coffee. Talmadge eats the bear claw, brushing the glaze flakes from the front of his coat. Sullivan stares out the front window, his eyes bloodshot, his skin pale.

"So, are you okay, Bobby?" Talmadge asks. "I'm worried about you."

Sullivan comes to, returns from wherever. He looks at Talmadge and gathers himself. "Let me ask you a question," he says.

"Go ahead."

"If I were to ask you to remember something, nothing in particular, but just something—what's the first thing that comes to mind?"

"I don't know. Time I got shot. Time I won the trifecta. Day I got divorced—thank you, God."

"You know what I remember?" Bobby asks.

"What?"

"I remember my kid."

"Pat, yeah."

"I remember the day he was born, the day he learned how to ride a bike, the day his mother and I split up and he couldn't stop crying. I remember how sick he got. I remember the pain he was in before he died. That's what I remember."

"Those were hard times, Bobby."

"They were," Bobby Sullivan says, "and because they're with me, all the time, I drink a little, I try to do some good things, things I don't come by as easy as some other people. Every now and then I even try to think about somebody other than myself."

"You're a good man, Bobby. I've always said that."

"Fuck that," Sullivan says, "I only bring it up because I want you and Moraski to know that I don't give a shit. You fuckers can do what you want with that asshole D.A. and the attorney general and the Grand Jury and everybody else. I don't give a shit. Pat's gone, and nothing can hurt me more than that. Nothing and nobody."

Talmadge sits back. His cup's empty. He looks around but the place doesn't have table service. He debates getting two more and doesn't. He figures it's better to have this out with Bobby now.

"Bobby, between you and me, now. Just you and me. We've known each other since we were in first grade with that witch. We were altar boys for Christ's sake. We stole things together. We got laid in the same car on the same night, for Christ's sake, different girls, of course . . ."

"Thanks for remembering," Bobby Sullivan says.

"So, now tell me, Bobby, and I mean me, not Moraski, not the D.A., not anybody else, just me—tell me what the fuck happened with the old lady."

Bobby looks at Talmadge and the part of him that knows how to survive thinks about making something up, about telling Talmadge what he wants to hear so Talmadge can tell Moraski and they can close the case and leave him alone.

"I was home in bed," he says. "I was hung over. I'd finished off a fifth the night before. The phone rang. It was Matthew Wyman. He told me to get over to Mrs. O'Neal's house. He told me she was dead. I got there about a half hour later. It was only nine thirty, maybe nine forty-five. Manny's sitting downstairs. She's got this wide open look on her face, and after it sinks in that I'm going upstairs, her face changes and there's nothing but hatred. So much hatred it pisses me off. But I don't give a shit. I run up the stairs and turn down the corridor and enter the bedroom. Matthew's sitting on a chair by a vanity table. He's got a plastic bag in his hand and the second he sees me he stuffs it in his back pocket. Mrs. O'Neal is lying there. She's dead. And that's it. I called La-Porta. He came over. He called Frawley. Frawley examined her, signed off on it, and that was it."

"Matthew Wyman had a plastic bag in his hand."

"That's right, and he stuffed it in his back pocket."

"Did you tell Moraski?"

"No fuckin' way and I'll tell you why. I got to run this funeral home now, and truth be told, it's nowhere near as healthy as you might think, at least not like the way I brag about it, and if the corporation doesn't get the insurance money on her life, all I got is a monster debt that will bury me and everybody else involved, so there's no way I want people thinking she committed suicide."

"And that's it," Talmadge says.

"That's it. Now maybe I've committed a little fraud with the insurance company, and that's still a maybe, given that we both know there's no way Emma Kost O'Neal killed herself, which means somebody killed her, and Matt Wyman had the plastic bag in his hand, for Christ's sake."

"What about Billy, the driver? He said he walked in on a fight."

"I don't know where he gets that. He was there. Came a bit later. I saw him when he got to the top of the stairs. I told him to leave us alone, to get out of there, that we didn't need another person crowding the place. Maybe that's what he's thinking about."

"So what do you think is going on?" Talmadge asks. "You think this Wyman character's trying to set you up?"

"Pretty fuckin' obvious," Sullivan says. "I mean how did you guys even hear about a bag?"

"We got a tip."

"From who?"

"I don't know. Moraski took the call."

"Man or woman?"

"I don't know, Bobby." Talmadge takes a deep breath, coughs once, reaches across the table, and touches Sullivan's coat sleeve. "You think maybe Wyman killed her before you got there?"

"He could have, and it'd make sense, given what I saw, but truth is I don't think so. Yeah, okay, maybe he took the bag off her head, but I think somebody else killed her, and my guess is it was his girlfriend."

"Manny Whitman."

"She's a fraud, con artist. Great-niece, my ass."

"I don't know about her. That's Moraski's side of the street. What I do know is the A.G. hates this Wyman kid."

"Why?"

"I don't know why."

"I mean how does he even know him? Tom Somers and Matthew Wyman? It's not like those two would run in the same circles."

"I don't know where it comes from, but Somers hates him. And he wants to fuck with him. He all but told Moraski and me to arrest him."

"Well, that's Somers's business."

"No, it's your business."

"What do you mean, my business?"

"What if the kid got loaded with you after the funeral, what if it loosened his tongue, what if he had to get something off his chest, what if you asked him about that plastic bag, what if he—you know . . ."

"Confessed?"

"Yeah, confessed."

"But he didn't."

"I don't give a shit what he said," Talmadge says. "I give a shit about gettin' you out of this thing."

Bobby Sullivan pulls his arm back. "You want me to finger Matthew Wyman. You want me to say he did it."

"No, what I want you to say is that Matthew Wyman told you he did it. For Christ's sake Bobby, just tell 'em that and get yourself free of this thing once and for all. Because I'll tell you right now, Moraski doesn't think you did anything. And that asshole Reis is a coward. He'll only do what the attorney general tells him, and that pretty boy don't give a shit about you."

"This is bullshit," Bobby Sullivan says, looking out the front window again.

"Think about it, Bobby, please."

Talmadge stands and asks if Bobby wants another cup of coffee. Bobby declines. Talmadge looks at his watch and says he better take off. He says, "Think about this, Bobby; I mean it."

"I'm going over there," Bobby says.

"Over where?"

"To her house. Mrs. O'Neal's house."

"What for?"

"I've got to find something, something that'll convince me the kid did it, or the girl did it, then I can say whatever the fuck you want me to say."

"Don't do it, Bobby. Don't make it more complicated than it is."

"I'll make it simple," Bobby says. "I got keys. Property's still part of the corporation."

Talmadge looks at him, shrugs his shoulders, sighs, and leaves.

Bobby Sullivan waits and, without reason, forgetting his troubles, he thinks about the phone call he's supposed to make to the shelter to order up a few more puppies for Sunday. Then he thinks about his kid, Pat, and about his wife who lives in Oregon now. He puts a dollar under his cup, stands up, brushes his topcoat's black-velvet collar, and leaves the diner.

Clive the Bartender's one of those shifty guys in his thirties who looks like the shifty kid from high school who pretended to know a lot about drugs, booze, cigarettes, pool, and fake ID's. He sits on a stool, reads a paper, fumbles with an old radio, and, when called upon, serves some old guys.

When the old guys hear Clive's midlands accent they talk about Normandy and Montgomery and how the Yanks and the Limeys got along in '44. They ask Clive to put the TV on so they can see what's happening in New York and argue over Homeland Security and how the president's over his head, screwing up worse than LBJ (who at least gave a shit about people). They leave after two rounds talking about "dirty bombs" and how New York's dirty enough, and Clive turns off the TV, and the place is empty until the cop comes in.

The cop's not a drinker. He orders one draft and drinks slowly. He doesn't make small talk; he doesn't like to be bothered.

The front door opens with the percussive wind, and the good-looking lady with the limp and the cane with the lion's head enters and sits next to the cop. She calls the cop Louis. That's how Clive knows the cop's name. They've been meeting like this on Monday afternoons. She never stays long and after she leaves Officer Louis orders one for the road, drinks half, and leaves. At first Clive figured it was an affair, but then some things happened and he changed his mind about that. It's not an affair; it's something else. They're planning something, trying to solve a problem, negotiating something—something that's got to be taken care of.

LaPorta calls to Clive, orders a club soda for the lady. Clive shoots a glass with the soda pump and sets it on the bar for Manny.

"Thank you, Clive," Manny says, and Clive offers up a short smile, feeling dismissed.

"Clive," Manny says, calling him back.

"Yes, mum."

"Where do you come from over there?"

"Family was from Liverpool, mum, but I was packed off to the midlands early on. South of York. Worked on my uncle's farm, went to school there for the reading, writing, and figures."

"Liverpool's famous," Manny says.

"My grandparents knew the Starkeys," Clive says. "In the Dingle."

"The Starkeys?"

"Ringo's folks. Fear they must be all gone now."

LaPorta listens to the back and forth but he doesn't pick up on it. He just stares at his beer and moves his lips every now and then.

"I bet you could make some money with that," Manny says.

"With what, mum?"

"Being from Liverpool, knowing a Beatle's family. People are making money off them left and right these days. Memorabilia, eBay. All that sort of thing."

" 'Fraid not, mum, I was out of Liddypool by the time I was seven. I didn't know anybody. Couldn't even tell you what the place looks like."

"That's the easy part," she says. "They got maps and books for that. You've got the accent. That's what will sell it."

"Maybe so," Clive says, looking at her face—the face of an American beauty from a hundred years ago, the kind of face he's seen on posters in pharmacies extolling the virtues of a cough medicine sold at the turn of the century, a face from a time when young women had half the rights and twice the cunning.

LaPorta looks up from his glass, looks at Clive, looks at Manny, and then looks at his glass again. Clive figures LaPorta wants to get on with it, and all this talk about Liverpool is holding him up.

"Can I freshen you up, Constable?" Clive asks LaPorta, and LaPorta shakes his head. Then Clive picks up the newspaper from the bar, snaps it open, moves a few feet down the bar, stands behind the broadsheet, pretends to read, and listens.

"Have you thought things over?" Manny asks LaPorta.

"I've been thinking," he says.

"You know I can help you."

"You think I need help?"

"If you lied for Bobby Sullivan you're going to need a lot of help."

"What makes you think I lied?"

"You told me you did."

"I lie all the time," LaPorta says. "It's a family trait."

"Detective Moraski's zeroing in on this."

"Moraski's a dickhead."

"He knows who killed her."

"He knows squat."

"He knows Sullivan killed her."

"She killed herself."

"There's no way she killed herself."

"There's no way Bobby killed her."

"Well, I can see we're no further along than we were a week ago."

From behind the paper, Clive's eyes go cloudy, focus on nothing.

"I can help you out," Manny says to LaPorta.

"You told me."

"I tell Moraski you got there an hour later than you did, and you're out of it. Whatever they did, they did before you got there. All of a sudden what you're telling Moraski's the truth, because an hour later there was no bag."

"You think your boyfriend and Bobby Sullivan were in it together?"

"Pretty obvious to me. And he's not my boyfriend, and Sullivan did double-cross him."

"Where do you get this stuff?"

"You saw the bag," she says.

"I never saw a bag," LaPorta says.

"And that's what you told Moraski, and that's why Sullivan paid you off. What I'm saying is I can make that lie true just by changing the time you got there. All you have to do is drop a word or two that'll keep Moraski on Sullivan."

LaPorta fingers his mug. He looks at Clive. The broadsheet's upside down. It takes a moment to register. He turns to Manny.

"But then you got to deal with Billy." LaPorta says.

"The driver?"

"Yeah, when did he get there? He saw me in the bedroom."

"Forget Billy. Nobody listens to him."

"What's in this for you?" LaPorta asks.

"Don't get me started," she says.

The phone behind the bar rings and Clive folds the paper and picks up the phone. It's his cousin from Bridgeport. He tells Clive the trip to Manhattan's been cancelled. Clive can't get rid of him fast enough, and when he turns and looks down the bar, the girl with the limp is out the door, and LaPorta's sitting there, not moving.

"Call me Thursday," Clive says into the phone and waits for LaPorta to touch the rim of his mug. The silence grows heavy as Clive realizes he's staring at the cop, waiting because he thinks the cop's got a routine, that it'll go the way it's gone before. But LaPorta doesn't make a move. He just stares at his glass.

Clive sets the house phone under the bar. " 'Nother?" he asks La-Porta, trying for the nonchalance, the easy sale, the good guy bartender who knows how to keep a proper place.

"Another what?" LaPorta asks, looking at Clive, his eyes taking on a light and depth they didn't have before—knowing eyes, capable of threats, trouble, violence.

"I thought maybe you'd care for another beer," Clive says, the voice high, the words tumbling too fast.

"What were you reading?" LaPorta asks.

"Sorry?"

"I said what were you reading?" and LaPorta nods to the newspaper folded on the bar.

"Oh, that," Clive says. "Just the paper."

"What part of the paper?" LaPorta asks.

"Basketball scores, mate. And I got to tell you, the way they play it over here, it's like these guys are superhuman."

"You always read upside down?" LaPorta says.

"What? Sorry, I guess you've got me at a disadvantage."

"Shut the fuck up," LaPorta says, standing, reaching in his pocket for a quarter, tossing it on the bar.

"What I meant was . . ." Clive begins.

LaPorta watches the lacy, phony faggot fall apart, caught in the act, scared, about to be punished.

"Listen to me," LaPorta says. "You see how empty this place is."

"Yes, sir."

"That's why I come in here. I like privacy."

"Quite understandable, Officer."

"And privacy means I don't like people listening in on my business."

"I'm sorry if it seemed that way, sir; it seems that I've suddenly gone deaf and dumb."

LaPorta stares at the guy. Clive turns to go about his business and La-Porta leaves the place.

Some time passes. Clive uses the restroom where he dampens a paper towel and rubs his forehead and wipes his eyes, leaning into the mirror, pulling back his thick black hair.

"Jesus Christ, Almighty," he says to the mirror as he wipes his hands and returns to the bar.

The place is still empty. He stands behind the bar, stretches once, wipes his forehead with his forearm sleeve, picks up the phone from under the counter. He dials. It rings. A man at the end of the line picks up.

"Mr. Johnson," Clive says.

"Who's this?"

"I'm supposed to talk with Mr. Johnson."

"Mr. Johnson's attending his wife's funeral."

"I'll call later."

"Wait. Is this Clive?"

"Yes."

"Mr. Johnson said you'd be calling on this line. He asked me to take a message."

"I don't know, I . . ."

"It's his wife's funeral, Clive. Now what's the message?"

"I'm just checking in."

"Go ahead then."

"He was in again."

"Officer LaPorta?"

"Yes, and the woman."

"Ms. Whitman."

"Yes, the one who uses the cane."

"Manny Whitman. So?"

"She's still after him to finger Sullivan for the murder. And LaPorta's getting a little freakish about all of it. He knows I've been eavesdropping. He's not a total idiot."

"We don't think so, either."

"But I can tell you one thing."

"We're paying you for that and more, Clive."

"Those two don't agree on anything. She says there was a bag; he says there wasn't. She says Sullivan killed the old lady; he says she just up and died."

"From natural causes."

"That's right—natural causes."

"So?"

"My point is neither one of them thinks she killed herself."

"And this concerns you how, Clive?"

"Doesn't concern me, but I thought the deal was that the insurance company would have to pay out unless they can prove it's a suicide."

"That's correct. The policy doesn't cover suicide."

"All right then, that's what I'm saying—what I'm saying is these two, this Manny Whitman and Officer LaPorta won't be any help to Mr. Johnson because neither one's saying suicide. Like I said, she's saying murder, he's saying natural causes."

"And none of this is for you to worry about, Clive."

"I'm not worried; I'm just trying to help out is all."

"And Mr. Johnson will appreciate that, but for now he just wants summaries of what they say."

"Okay."

"Is the taping system working?"

"No reason to think otherwise."

"Didn't you check it?"

"No, I called you first. Like Mr. Johnson told me."

"You know the procedure for delivery then."

"Yes."

"We'll send somebody by about ten. You'll be there then?"

"Yes."

"He'll have a book."

"*War and Peace?*"

"It's fat enough, don't you think?"

"It is for the small cassettes."

"Anything else then, Clive?"

"No. That's it."

"Thank you, Clive. Mr. Johnson will be pleased, and when Mr. Tolstoy arrives he'll have an envelope for you."

The conversation ends. Clive turns to the mirror behind the bar. He feels the low level warmth of self-satisfaction that always accompanies thoughts of payday. He remembers what he owes all over town. He remembers the bet with Gemelli. He says, "Good day, guv'nor," the way he's heard it in those old fog-and-darkness movies. He's never been to England. He's never liked the Beatles. He read a book and that was it. He could give a shit. He lives in a town of whores like himself, a town where people pay good money to people who know how to listen. And Clive knows how to listen.

In downtown Hartford, in the football building, in an interior office of Cal Stevens's one-lawyer firm, with a MoMA print of Monet's *Water Lilies* on the wall and open blinds on the reception area, Ann Dillon, paralegal, office manager, sits at her desk, littered with papers and files. She clears a space to set down a legal pad, to draw lines, boxes, abbreviations, symbols, runes, the essential etchings of abstract plots. She reviews the memo-to-self she drafted that morning. She makes notes:

Mrs. O'Neal dies:
1. Natural causes—Sullivan will take all under the will, including insurance $'s
2. Suicide—Sullivan will take all under the will, but no insurance $'s
3. (a) Murder (if Sullivan did it)—
   (i) Sullivan's out, insurance pays, and EITHER Manny takes all ("cy pres") by terms of "letter" from Mrs. O'Neal to Manny OR
   (ii) Kost-O'Neal Charitable Trust takes all under the will, plus insurance monies.
   (b) Murder (if anybody other than Sullivan did it)—
   (i) Sullivan will take all, plus ins. $'s (see Natural Causes, above)

She circles 3 (a) (ii), underlines "Charitable Trust takes all," and digs through a pile of papers on the right-hand corner of her desk. She remembers an image of paper and hi-toned script: CHARITABLE TRUST. She digs, a lawyer's dig, strata of substance and time, clients remembered and forgotten, the perpetual "gotta-get-to-that" notion of things, things to be done, the mild anxiety of deadlines or the easy confidence of competence.

She finds it under an advance sheet from CCH and an opinion from the tax court. It's a copy of the document that established the Kost-O'Neal Charitable Trust. She scans the title page and reads the paragraph designating Cal Stevens as trustee. She flips the yellow pages of her legal pad and begins to draft a document to amend the trust. She's decided to make herself the trustee, and she knows how to do it. She starts and stops. She'll need a form book—*How to Designate a New Trustee*. Will it require an election, a vote of the board? Is there a board? If so, who's on it? How many votes to amend the trust? What will it take? How many documents will she have to place in front of Mr. Stevens for the signature that counts? One? Two? Or several in one of those marathon end-of-the-day moments when Stevens's Mont Blanc scratches his initials wherever she tells him to scratch his name—as if he were somebody important, scratching, writing, turning around to hand out another pen to an imaginary row of dignitaries standing by his side.

Manny, she thinks. Always Manny. And what kind of document will it take to keep the favorite great-niece in her place after Ann becomes trustee? How many votes will it take to amend Manny's career path? She wonders: How will I profit if Manny succeeds in setting up Sullivan and then convinces the Probate Court to give her everything? I'll keep her close to set up Sullivan, Ann says to herself, and then, when the time comes, I'll out her for the fraud she is.

The front door opens a crack and the tip of an umbrella points to the floor followed by the polished round toe of one black shoe. There's a little fumble; the door opens all the way, and attorney Cal W. Stevens, Esq., enters his firm.

Ann watches him through the blinds of her interior window. Then she stands and greets him in the reception area.

"Good afternoon, Mr. Stevens."

She adheres to the little formalities he appreciates, manners as a kind of code, beneficial to the proper placement of boundaries, a bulwark against unwanted and unpredictable emotions.

"Good morning, Ann. Afternoon, whatever."

He shakes his umbrella and places it in the umbrella stand, takes off his coat, and hangs it in the small closet.

"I'm sure it was a grand funeral," Ann says, anticipating Stevens's response to the question she didn't ask.

"Quite marvelous, really," Cal Stevens says, "as far as funerals go, of course. They're sad affairs and nothing can change that, though an outpouring of affection and remembrance provides some comfort."

"For those left behind," Ann says.

"For those left behind," Cal says. "I once heard a chaplain say, 'Concerning our prayers for the dead, if the deceased is in heaven, he doesn't need them; if the deceased is in hell, they can't help him; if the deceased is in purgatory, he was a Catholic and nothing can help him.'"

"Harsh, but true enough."

"And what is truth?" Cal Stevens asks no one, musing now, the Cambridge don, the wizened old master, a purveyor of clichés and the fruits of rote memory.

Ann asks, "Did you speak with Mr. Johnson?"

"Just as I was leaving."

"How's he doing?"

"Holding up, holding up," the last words failing some. "There's a small reception at his place tonight for his close friends."

"Are you going?"

"I was invited, but I don't know."

"You look tired, Mr. Stevens."

"Pardon me?" the head bobs, a tall bird sniffing some challenge.

"You look tired," Ann says again. And Mr. Stevens grunts, bobs the head, lets it drop to his chest, struggles to defend himself against the proffered sympathy of a pretty young woman, only to surrender, to pause, to straighten, to move forward, to take on the burden of self, once again.

"I want you to expunge all the addenda and juvenalia from the Kost-O'Neal file. 'Addenda' and 'juvenalia' are my words for crap."

"I know, Mr. Stevens, and you're referring to the corporation's file?"

"Yes, anything to do with Mr. Sullivan. I formally fired him today. He's no longer a client of this firm. I told him I would not represent the man who killed Emma."

"You said that? I mean, Mr. Stevens, you're so direct, it's refreshing."

"I know what I know, and if the courts around here worked on behalf of Hartford's good people, we'd have a lot less to worry about."

"Yes, sir."

"It makes a person appreciate the need to take things in hand sometimes. To make the big gesture, so to speak. To leave your mark."

"Yes, sir, I think I know what you mean."

"I was quite a boxer at Yale, Miss Dillon."

"Yes, sir."

"They made light of me, I know, but none of them wanted to go too far. They knew about my jab and the left hook."

"Yes, sir."

"I'm not unacquainted with violence, Miss Dillon. People might think we're a lacy bunch, but we'll fight like wildcats. You can ask the Germans about that."

"Yes, Mr. Stevens."

"But I pray God, He keep me civil and my soul calm during this time of tempestuous emotions."

"Yes, sir, I understand."

"I don't want to do what I should not, and yet I'm not sure what I should or should not do. I think old Saint Paul wrote something about that."

There's a pause and silence as Ann and Stevens just stand there, neither knowing what to say after the Old Yankee's unexpected proclamations.

Finally he asks, "Anything I should know about?"

"Sir?"

"With firm business."

"All's quiet," Ann says.

"Did young Somers call?"

"The attorney general?"

"Yes."

"No, sir. I mean I spoke with him last night, but that was, you know, a personal call."

"I spoke with him yesterday about this—about Emma."

"Yes, sir, I know."

"I told him what I think, but he doesn't take it very seriously. I'm afraid he has his sights set on somebody else, which is to say he's taken an interest in a person who shouldn't be of any interest."

"He's hard to read, sir. In many ways."

"Handsome young man. Very capable. Now, you two have been going together for some time now."

"Yes, sir."

"Well, you tell him to pop the question and stop fooling around."

"I'll be sure to tell him," Ann says.

"His father and I were partners, you know."

"Yes, sir, I know."

"His father and I and Coop Johnson, we all roomed together at Yale."

"Yes, sir."

Mr. Stevens starts toward the corridor and his office, stops short as if he's forgotten something, turns and collapses in a wingback chair, and rubs his eyes.

Ann steps back. "Are you all right, Mr. Stevens?"

He drops his hand and looks away.

"Mr. Stevens?"

"Ann."

"Yes, Mr. Stevens."

"When I spoke with young Somers about this yesterday, I told him that Sullivan killed Emma, because I know it as surely as I know anything."

"Yes, sir."

"I can't prove it. I have no evidence other than motive, but it's like intuition."

"Yes, sir."

Cal Stevens continues to rub his eyes. Then he looks around the room, taking in the furniture and a painting of a whaling ship on the far wall by the entrance.

"You know, Ann, I never married."

"No, sir."

"Bachelor all these years."

"Yes, sir."

"A person should marry for love."

"I agree."

"Did you know that when I was in college I formed a small combo to play at weekend get-togethers?"

"No, Mr. Stevens, I didn't know. You were a boxer and a musician?"

"Better boxer, but I played the piano. Wasn't very good, and back then the girls went for horn players."

"Mr. Stevens," Ann laughs. "What a surprise. I'm sure the women found you very attractive."

"Some did. One in particular."

"What happened?" Ann asks, and Mr. Stevens looks up from the chair, a stern expression, a failure of sorts.

"I'm sorry," Ann says, gathering up the silence. "It's none of my business."

"No," Mr. Stevens says, as if catching his breath, a coming to, a sense of where he is and what memory means. "It's all right. I was daydreaming, I think. What happened was she was engaged to a friend, and when that fell apart for one very sad reason, she married a bounder, a rogue was what he was."

"A bad boy?"

"I suppose."

"Some women like men like that."

"Yes, they seem to."

"Yes," Ann says, debating whether she should say something about dreams and disappointments, something worn and overused, something to help her back to her office.

"After her, I allowed myself to fail," Stevens says.

"That's not true," Ann says, finding her place in the script again, even as it writes itself. "You've been very successful."

"No, Ann," Stevens says, "I look at Coop Johnson and old Somers— now they've been successful."

"No more than you, Mr. Stevens. And you were the one who gave Somers his opportunity."

"Thank you, Ann, but that was my father's money, and I'm in no mood to feel better." He stands with shoulders drawn up. He catches his breath, not certain where he should go, what he should do, as if the memory of this woman from long ago has disturbed the most basic parameters of time, space, desire, and duty.

Finally he walks down the short corridor to his office with the large window overlooking the city.

Ann returns to her office and fumbles with papers, stacking them, moving them, as if tidiness were sufficient to solve so many problems. She reviews the handwritten first draft of the amendment to the trust. The language substitutes Ann Dillon for Cal Stevens as trustee. She stacks and places words the way she stacks and places paper, moving them about, as if tidiness were sufficient.

Mark Moraski was a marine, and his wife was Miss Cobb County—one of the last. They'd met at the pageant when Mark's platoon had been dragged into honor guard duty. Mark fell for the soft blond southern girl who knew how to flirt, and she fell for the marine with the brush cut, the jaw, and the blue-gray eyes. It was a brief courtship, shorter engagement; they got married with one on the way.

Years later up north in the cold weather that depressed her and the two children, Mrs. Moraski grew tired and plump and lost her looks, let her hair go brown, then red-brown with a wash she picked up from a hairdresser who believed in big hair as a matter of conscience.

Mark went to law school and worked days. The marriage was tough; law school got him out of the house longer, later. He did fair to average. Sometimes the rigidity of military thought bumped up against the incongruities, inconsistencies of an adversarial system overseen by some Greek goddess with a blindfold. Ninety percent of law school is an unresolved shade of gray. Marines are a lot of things, but rarely unresolved, rarely gray.

By second year he'd made some friends. He wasn't a party boy like the younger guys. He wasn't a politician or some feeble kid in search of an identity. He was a married cop who wanted to be a detective with a leg up on the D.A.

He met Ann Dillon second year in Domestic Relations, taught by a tall guy from Texas who had a habit of leaving his roller-ball tip down in his dress shirts, creating small pools of blue at the bottom of his shirt pocket.

Mark was attracted to Ann and noted the many differences between her and his wife. His mother had said, "Breeding will out." As regards

Ann Dillon, it had—even though acknowledging the hard fact would offend his wife, let alone the democratic ideals of the politically correct, ideals that reside light years beyond and above the all-too-human propensity for rewarding or penalizing appearance.

At the pageant, in full bloom, at the beach and in town afterward, Mark's wife had been more brilliant than stunning, a flame, a shock of beauty, which in her youth was capable of masking all the work that went into the presentation. On the other hand Ann Dillon did nothing to look the way she looked, and although she wouldn't blind a guy with shining overstatement, she was long-time, long-term beautiful, another carrier of another generation's pleasant burden.

Mark and Ann talked during breaks. She had little good to say about the students her age, especially the guys who were on the make and loud and bright in ways that were more offensive than attractive. She liked Mark because he was older, quiet, steady, circumspect, married, and almost handsome in a jarhead sort of way.

Any school's a closed system, and students see enough of one another to see through one another soon enough. Over time all the masks, charades, and postures fall away with the relentless wearing of time's tendency toward truth. Cool students become assholes; quiet students grow wise. Benefit inures to introverts. Extroverts rise, shine, and flame out. But Ann liked Mark and he liked her, and (as far as he was concerned) only some vague sense of honor, culled not from the Marines Corps or any church sodality, but from a father and grandfather from the old country who wouldn't stand for anything as tawdry as an affair, kept the whole thing aboveboard and, for all of that, enduring.

Years after they graduated, years after Mark became a detective and Ann (who had had some trouble with the bar exam) chose to run Cal Stevens's office, Mark stayed in touch with her. There'd be the surprise telephone call, short conversations, a cup of coffee during the day in bright lights and public. And now he had a reason to see her again.

He made the call early in the week. They agreed upon a dark, private, cozy restaurant.

That afternoon his kids fought over the TV, complained about a ruined dinner (one of Miss Cobb County's new recipes), and Mark left the house, sucking air, about to yell nonsense, holding himself together, thinking about Ann Dillon, about how much he needed to be with a pretty woman and, for a short time, not to trouble himself with the consequences of decisions made at a time when he didn't know better, when he should have known better.

The restaurant's bar is set off, quiet with heavy, dark wood, the leather and the fire in a small fireplace. Few people from town drink there.

Mark arrives and waits for his eyes to adjust when he sees her in a booth in an alcove on the far side of the room. A small table lamp brushes light from below. He bends over, kisses her on the cheek, takes the seat across from her.

Her fingers touch the round base of a glass of white wine. A waitress in colonial dress stops by. Mark orders bourbon and water. The waitress curtsies and leaves. Mark and Ann talk about nothing, some old times, some recent times, like birds circling, waiting to light.

"I've missed you," he says.

"I've missed you, too," she says, and the words carry nothing, all surface. He tells himself he hoped for nothing more.

"Thanks for helping me with this," he says.

"I'm as curious as you," she says. "Do you have the letter?"

Mark hands her a copy of Mrs. O'Neal's letter to Manny Whitman.

She reads the first few words out loud: "Dear Manny, I have much to tell you and one favor to ask . . ." Then she reads the rest in silence. When she finishes the letter she looks over her shoulder. "Miss?" she calls, and a second waitress in the white cotton and crinoline and black pleated puritan skirt stops by. "This gentleman ordered a bourbon and water."

The second waitress mumbles an apology, curtsies, leaves.

"You have to be more assertive," she says.

"I'm assertive all day," Mark says.

She folds the letter and hands it back to him.

"What do you think?" he asks.

"It reads like a person's idea of how an elderly, cultured, wealthy woman from the last century would write."

"It reads phony?"

"I think so."

"And you've never seen this letter before?"

"Never," she says.

"Could Manny have written a letter like this?"

"She's smart enough. Maybe that's the problem. The letter reads too smart—too studied."

"I thought so, too," Moraski says.

"You checked the signature?"

"Emma signed her name with a slash."

"Artsy."

"Just a line with a hook. Handwriting guy said inconclusive."

"Was it typed on Mrs. O'Neal's computer?" Ann asks.

"Generic LaserJet, but Manny had access to her aunt's office."

"So, do you have a theory about all of this?"

"I've been working on one."

"Well?"

The second waitress returns with a tall glass of bourbon on the rocks.

"He ordered bourbon and water," Ann says.

"It's okay," Moraski says, and the waitress tells him the drink's on the house, curtsies, and leaves again.

"I hope your theory's assertive," Ann says.

"Can theories be assertive?" Moraski asks.

"I don't know. $E=MC^2$ was a declaration of sorts."

Moraski nods. "I think Mrs. O'Neal had no intention of changing her will. I think the Manny letter's a fake. I think Manny knew she was out, and as a last ditch attempt to get something out of her aunt, wrote this letter, waited for her aunt to die, planted a plastic bag, tipped us off—all to set up Sullivan."

Ann asks if Manny's smart enough for such a scheme.

"I don't know," Moraski says, leaning back in the booth, trying to relax. "Smart can be naïve or devious. I think she's a little devious."

"The major flaw is the waiting-on-her-aunt-to-die part. She had no control over when, where, how, unless she did it, and I don't think she did that."

"So much for my flawed, albeit assertive theory."

"Isn't there something like Occam's razor?"

"I always picture a barber when I hear that."

"No, it's another theory. It says: What's most likely is most likely—something like that."

"What's most likely . . ." Mark Moraski says, failing to finish the thought.

"Sullivan."

"What about him?"

"I'd vote for him, in the bedroom, with the plastic bag."

"You would?"

"Yes, I would."

"Why?"

"Manny's letter is a fake, but Mrs. O'Neal did make an appointment to meet with Mr. Stevens that Monday. I did call the prior Friday to confirm, and Sullivan did answer the phone and had the nerve to ask if this was about her crazy niece. That's your motive, means was easy enough—just a trip to the local dry cleaners, and, as for opportunity, you can bet he has keys to that house."

"Jesus, I don't know."

"What don't you know?"

"Sullivan, I don't know him. Tell me what you know about him."

"Divorced, had a son, kid died from cancer. Broke the guy's heart. Tore up the marriage. He drank and continues to drink. Sort of lost his way for a while. Got involved in some shady deals with some friends in Atlantic City. Lucky to get out of it alive, if he is out of it. Mrs. O'Neal couldn't stand him, but she had no choice but to keep him on after Tommy died. She knew what I know."

"What's that?"

"That he's not a good man, if that word means anything to anybody these days."

"He's not?"

"He's been in the office several times. Mr. Stevens puts him off as much as he can, but sooner or later he has to meet with him. Talk about relentless."

"Assertive?"

"Very."

"But why is he bad, what's he done?"

Ann Dillon fingers the stem of her glass. "It's hard to say. He's devious. He knows how to cover himself. That craziness in Atlantic City cost Mrs. O'Neal a small fortune to take care of, and Bobby Sullivan wasn't exactly grateful, took no responsibility for it. Blamed everybody else. Other than that, at least around this town, he doesn't leave much behind. It's funny, though—I'm certain he's no good, but then when you ask for specifics, I don't make the strongest case. Maybe that's the way it is with bad people. Part of what makes them bad is their talent for covering themselves. So, I guess I have to fall back on Mrs. O'Neal's assessment and my own intuition."

"You think he's capable of murder?"

"I do."

"Really?"

"Sometimes you meet a person, you shake their hand, you look in their eyes. Afterward you want to take a shower. You know you've come up against something, and your first instinct is to get away. That's how I always felt with him."

"Okay."

"It's like a self-protective sense, beware of danger."

"I figure he's a greedy, horny, drunk in a nice suit," Moraski says, "but more than that? Murderer? I don't know."

"I can only tell you what I think, what I feel," she says. "And greed skews everything. It's amazing what people can be capable of."

"I do know that."

"I think Sullivan did it," she says, "and Manny knew she was over unless she came up with something to muddy the waters—hence, the Dear Manny thing you just put in your pocket."

"So you think the letter's a forgery?"

"Absolutely. Manny wants to nail Sullivan and then tell the probate judge she should get everything, being next of kin, just like the letter says."

"Will a court do that?"

"I don't know. There is a will, but the court can act in equity, analogize a *cy pres* argument. Poor little orphan Manny can argue that her aunt's letter was the last statement of her intentions regarding the estate. A judge might listen to that."

"Now we're in bar-exam territory," Moraski says.

"Please," Ann says, "don't remind me."

"I mean it's complicated."

"It is."

"So, who gets everything if Manny can't convince the court?"

"Mrs. O'Neal's charitable trust. Kids in third world countries. Cal Stevens has run that for years."

"Your boss, the lawyer."

"Lawyers always win in the end, Mark. We both know that."

Moraski drinks the bourbon, leans back, stretches, and tries for nonchalant cool.

Ann's not unaware of things, of subtext, of motives within motives. She knows Mark Moraski has feelings for her. She can see how hard he tries to hide them with his forced and world-weary slap of the arm on the table, as if he were a Komodo lizard lazing in the sun.

"I guess I better get going," she says.

"So soon?"

"I've got a dinner date."

"Really? Okay then. Who are you seeing these days?"

"Just another lawyer."

"Talk about incest," he says.

"Tell me about it," she says with the pale levity of a quip designed to bring all conversation to a close, and Mark Moraski reminds himself that the little fantasies he unwraps at his peril shine only in a nonexistent world.

Ann stands by the side of the booth. She places her hand on Moraski's shoulder to tell him to stay down, to wait, to give her time to leave. She says good-bye with a "good to see you" wrap-around, pats his shoulder, and starts toward the swinging doors, passing the second wait-ress as she goes.

"Another, sir?" the waitress asks Moraski.

Moraski looks at his glass. He feels remarkably empty, somehow di-minished in stature. "What happened?" he asks himself, wondering why any of this should bother him—even as it bothers him.

"Just the check," he says.

"Yes, sir," she says and curtsies.

Moraski stops her.

"Sir?"

"Tell me something. Why do you curtsy every time?"

"It's part of the job. The boss says it gives the place an old-time fla-vor."

"You don't mind doing it every time?"

"I'll tell you what—if it helped with tips I'd stand on my head."

She leaves.

Moraski pushes the glass over the tabletop. He fingers the beads of water. A wave washes over him. He sits straight and breathes deeply. "I'm assertive all day," he says to himself, and the waitress stops by with the white slip of paper detailing how much the drinks cost—how much he owes.

Ann Dillon drives back into town and parks under the Hilton. She takes an elevator to the lobby, walks by check-in, presses twelve, and waits. Doors open, doors close, doors open. She reads the sign with the arrows, turns to the right, counting down door numbers. Then she stops, knocks on the door, and hears a brush of movement. She waits. No time to think. Only time to do this. Her heart beats, one thought about to fly away. The door opens and doubt, hesitation, inhibitions dissolve to a quickening, a heat. She steps into the room and they embrace. Manny Whitman kisses her on the lips and, with arms extended, grabbing air, they close the door for privacy.

The women back step to the bed. They lie on the quilt with patterns from Versailles. Manny with the bad hip and the weak leg rolls once to make room. She takes Ann in her arms and brushes back her brown hair.

"I've missed you," Manny says, and they hold each other in the almost dark. Manny sobs a little, as she always sobs when lying with Ann, as if passion tinged with the sadness of impermanence is something to be mourned.

"Don't," Ann says, and Manny buries her face in Ann's arms, trying to hold her breath, not to stop crying, but to stop time.

They lay there for a long time, soft hands, strong hands, caressing, touching. Then Ann raises one arm and turns her wrist. "We haven't much time," she says, and Manny looks into Ann's eyes, searching for something, seeking a depth born of warmth and the intimate knowledge of one another.

"What is it?" Ann asks.

"I don't know," Manny says. "Nothing."

"You look so worried."

"No, I'm not worried."

Ann holds her again and they kiss and then separate again.

"You never told me about Matthew," Manny says.

"What about him?"

"About the day he showed up at your office."

"That was weeks ago—when he was looking for Bobby Sullivan."

"Was he out of control?"

"Not at all," Ann says. "He was very polite. Seemed to have a little trouble breathing is all. Said he has asthma."

"He wasn't drunk or crazy or anything?"

"No, he wasn't."

"Your memo convinced me he was."

"I only wrote what you told me."

"You had Cal sign it."

"I did."

"You can make him sign anything."

"He trusts me," Ann says, "like a daughter."

"I figured he would be, though," Manny says.

"Who'd be? What?"

"I figured Matthew would be out of control," and she struggles to roll across the bed, drops her feet to the floor, and sits upright. Ann watches her from behind, the broad shoulders, her white neck visible with her hair caught up in a tortoise-shell clip.

"You know his family had him committed," Manny says.

"I know," Ann says.

"He was never stable, not really."

"Did he find out about us?"

"I don't think so," Manny says.

"Growing up, I always thought his family had money," Ann says. "I thought they'd send him off to some fancy clinic."

"To take the waters?"

"Yeah, to take the waters," Ann says.

"How nineteenth century."

"Don't people take waters anymore?"

"I don't think so," Manny says, looking at Ann, then turning to bend, reach, and slip on her shoes. "How well did you know his family?" she asks.

"Matthew's?"

"Yes."

"I didn't know Matthew existed," Ann says. "I knew his father. He was a teacher at the high school. The mother was invisible. Never saw her, though it was her side of the family that had some money, property, whatever. Her family had a big house on a pond where kids skated in the winter. It was nice there."

"What did he teach?"

"Who?"

"Matthew's father."

"Accounting."

"Did you have him?"

"Not in class, just for study hall."

"Was he, you know, nuts?"

"The guy was an accountant. He was Mr. Normal. Seemed like a nice enough guy."

"I knew Matthew would go off again," Manny says.

"Well, he must have if they had him committed."

"I thought he'd get drunk and stay in Hartford. He was building up to it after he heard from Bobby Sullivan. That's what set him off in the first place."

Manny stands and looks into the mirror, checks for smudges and powder, draws a line with one finger over her eyebrow.

"I'm sick of this color," she says.

"What color?"

"My hair color—this Junior League frosty blond color."

"Then change it."

"I will, though I don't know if I'm ready for the natural look."

"What look is that?"

"Red."

"Red's beautiful."

"Not my red. I've got that bright, bright red from my mother—the original redhead."

"That can be very attractive."

"You think so?"

"I do."

"Well, we'll see," she says, and she grabs the cane with the lion's head, takes three steps, and stops. "Aren't you hungry?" she asks.

"I don't have time," Ann says. "I have to pick up Mr. Stevens at a reception." She stands, smooths her suede skirt, and brushes the front of her sweater. "The one at Mr. Johnson's. He buried his wife today. It's for close friends and family."

Ann walks across the room and leans into the wide mirror. She says, "But I'm a little confused, Manny."

"About what?"

"What's this about Matthew hearing from Bobby Sullivan? What's that about?"

"It was just a note that said Matthew was fired."

"So that's what upset him?"

"Yes, and that Sullivan was supposed to have paid him money."

"What for?" Ann asks, concerned now.

"To keep quiet."

"About what?"

"About the way he found my aunt."

"Wait a minute," Ann says, irritated, confused. "Are you saying Matthew lied for Bobby Sullivan?"

"He did."

"About the way your aunt died?"

"Yes."

"What did he say?"

"He said there was no plastic bag. You know, that she'd just died."

"Why?" Ann shouts. "Why in the world would he do that? Are he and Sullivan in this thing together? I thought Matthew was on your side."

"He said he was doing it for me. So the company would get the insurance money."

"I can't believe this," Ann says, sitting down again, rubbing her forehead.

"I'm the one who told the police about the bag," Manny says. "All this shows is that Matthew and Bobby Sullivan are both liars, because they want it all. And as I told Detective Moraski, people who lie about suicide will lie about murder."

"I don't know," Ann says. "This isn't good. This could screw up everything."

Manny walks around the front of the bed and sits next to Ann. "It'll be all right," she says.

Ann looks down. Her eyes run along the edge of the black cane, scuffed at the tip. She says, "If Matthew said Mrs. O'Neal just 'up and died' of natural causes, then he's given Sullivan an alibi, and you won't get a thing if we can't show that Sullivan killed her."

"I'm not worried," Manny says.

"You're not?"

"You're the lawyer; you said we had a strong argument."

"We do if we can show Sullivan killed her. Short of that you get nothing, and with Matthew lying for him—it just complicates everything."

"But Sullivan screwed him over. Matthew won't lie for him now."

"And who'll believe him? He lied once, and he's nuts on top of it!"

"But if I can convince the police that Sullivan did it?"

"Then we can do what we planned," Ann says.

"And I'll get the insurance money, too?"

"If we can prove Sullivan killed her."

"I can do that," Manny says.

"I hope so," Ann says.

"Trust me."

"I trust you, but you should have told me about this."

"About what?"

"About Matthew! Jesus, Manny!"

The two sit on the bed, a few inches from each other. The afternoon has gone dark and they're both tired.

Ann says, "You have to make the police believe Sullivan did it."

"He did do it."

"Well, somebody has to prove it."

Silence spreads through the room as they move their hands over the bedspread and touch fingers.

"Come here, baby," Manny says. At first Ann resists, then leans into Manny's embrace as Manny kisses her neck.

"Is there anything else you didn't tell me?" Ann asks.

"Yes, dear, there is."

"What?"

"That I love you, and if you help me we'll have more money than we'll know what to do with."

"You're sure of that."

"Most of it," Manny says. "The important part, anyway," and Ann knows that, like herself, Manny's talking about the money and not the love.

C. Coop Johnson, CFO, CEO, chairman of the board, lauded trustee of two hospitals and one university, Yale, B.A., Harvard Business School, New England Presbyterian, hard-knuckled pol, backroom king-maker, power wielder, Renaissance scholar, lover of Shakespeare, Tolstoy, Emerson, Twain, Grant, Eisenhower (the General), rowing, rugby, fine cuisine, and wines from the late Mrs. Simpson's orchards in southern France, entertains the few guests remaining in the Hunt Room with the bars and the walk-in fireplace. The mood is hushed, the gathering is respectful and relaxed. Johnson changed clothes when he returned home from the cemetery and wears the khakis, the ox-blood weejuns, the striped shirt with the white collar, and a navy blue sweater draped over his shoulders. He walks from friend to relative to friend, a glass of Scotch in one hand, his thick silver hair, perpetually damp and brushed in place with one wing tucked left-to-right behind his ear. His manner is social, controlled, a virtual handbook on how to keep emotions in check while contemplating the most onerous of days. His wife lies buried now. The nightmare that began three years ago when the doctors first diagnosed the cause of the weight loss is over. Money had helped with the personal care and the private nurses and the best treatments available. And Margaret Johnson had been strong, a reserved woman, as proud as her husband. No tears, she'd say: I won't give this disease a thing but a cold shoulder and my disdain. And yet, for all of it, she suffered, and when the end came, she'd been asleep for days. They called it palliative care. They took away the pain, and one afternoon when he left her bedside to take a call from Cal Stevens, she drifted away, like a boat drifting away from a dock.

She was peaceful in the end, he says to Tyler Bach, a friend from his

Harvard Business School days. Tyler's wife, Muffy, a petite woman with brilliant eyes, who looks younger than her age, who golfed with Johnson's wife (and who complained how Margaret Johnson cheated every round), looks up to Coop Johnson and touches his sleeve. "I'm so sorry, Coop. We all are. Margaret was a very special woman."

Officer Louis LaPorta, newly arrived and off duty, in a black suit from Bonds' Front Room, stands in the doorway to the Hunt Room with his hands behind his back. When a waiter stops by with a tray of finger food, Louis shakes his head and the waiter moves on. Louis often moonlights for Johnson as an all-around security expert and aide-de-camp. Louis has known Johnson for over a year and hopes to retire to a full-time position with the great man. Johnson often alludes to it, but he's yet to set forth any details.

Muffy Bach watches LaPorta from a distance. She notes the dark complexion, the straight nose, the heavy eyebrows, the large brown eyes, Mediterranean or "Zhivago's eyes," she thinks, almost black, hidden. The man's a kind of anti-Tyler, her husband, who's always been halfway to gay with the aristocratic foppery of his bow ties, soft skin, and the ballerina subtleties of an overweight movie critic.

LaPorta catches Muffy's eye as she steals another look and lowers her head, caught, blushing.

"Louis?" Mr. Johnson calls from a few feet away, inviting Louis to join him in another threesome of casual mourners. Louis approaches, and Johnson leans over and whispers in LaPorta's ear that he'd like Louis to look around the first floor to see if Cal Stevens has arrived. "I can't believe he wouldn't show," Mr. Johnson says, and Louis nods a military nod, and makes his way through the many and various rooms.

The rooms to the left of the central hallway are empty, and Louis marvels at the height of the ceilings and the huge paintings that hang on the walls. He stands in one of three libraries and steps before a painting of a Madonna and child. It's tall and there's gold flake in the Madonna's blue robe.

"Something, isn't it?" Muffy Bach says.

Louis turns and sees the petite blonde with the black hair band, holding a long-stemmed glass of white wine.

"Unbelievable," Louis says. "I used to think you'd only see this kind of thing in a museum."

"For the most part that's where you will see them, but Coop's got a thing for the Renaissance and when he got the price he was looking for, he bought it."

"Must have cost a fortune."

"It did, though he worked a deal. He had the appraiser identify it as being from Verrochio's workshop and not by Verrochio's hand."

"You're saying a workshop did this?"

"Actually, Verrochio painted it with the help of his apprentices, but labeling it that way kept the price down."

"I see."

"A little fraud, but the appraiser owed Coop big-time."

"I guess that's how it works sometimes."

"Do you know what makes Verrochio's workshop so intriguing, though?"

Louis looks from the painting to the small woman, standing so close he can smell the wine on her breath.

"I'm really not that up to speed on this sort of thing."

"One of his apprentices was Leonardo."

"Leonardo da Vinci? The *Mona Lisa* guy?"

"That's the one."

"Okay then," Louis says, standing there, looking at the painting and then at the woman standing at his elbow, having run out of small talk, not certain what to do with Mrs. Bach. "I guess I better get going then," he says.

"Are you leaving? I thought you'd just arrived."

"I'm not leaving. Mr. Johnson asked me to look for Mr. Stevens."

"Cal Stevens?"

"Yes."

"Oh, he's not here."

"He isn't?"

"No, no, no . . . Cal Stevens is probably home with a footbath and a Trollope novel."

"I don't know what that means."

"It means Cal Stevens is probably home with a footbath and a Trollope novel."

"I see."

"Look over here," she says, and she points to an Elizabethan wall cabinet with iron lace and cut glass. She opens the door to the shelves with several black-and-white photos in silver frames.

"There's Cal Stevens," she says, and she points to a photo where Mr. Johnson stands with his arm around a pretty woman while pointing to a taller man with a champagne bucket over his head.

"Under the bucket?" Louis asks.

"Cal's always been a little under the bucket," Muffy says.

"Okay."

"The three of them were like the three musketeers in their twenties."

"The three of them?"

"No, not her. I mean Cal, Coop, and John Somers, the father."

"Whose father?"

"The attorney general's."

"Oh, that Somers."

"Coop and Cal had their problems back whenever, but they made up and are still friends. Cal and Somers, though, they had a colossal falling out. Shut down their partnership."

"You mean like business partners?"

"A law firm. It was Stevens & Somers. Cal's family had money and Somers had the brains."

"Why did they . . . ?"

"Fall out with one another?"

"Yes."

"Well, there she is, right there."

"The woman in the picture?"

"You might have heard of her—Emma Kost, Emma O'Neal. The O'Neal Funeral Home."

LaPorta steps forward to look at the photo.

"Each one of those guys had their fling with her," Muffy says. "Coop Johnson and her." She pauses. "Well, enough said about that."

"Didn't work out, huh? Mr. Johnson and Mrs. O'Neal."

"Ended badly, for both of them. Nobody knows the whole story, but, let's just say they made their choices, and in the end she married this social climbing undertaker, and Coop married the late Margaret Portner Humes, of recent memory.

"It put a strain on things. Breaking engagements always does. Everybody blamed everybody else. And at that level whole families get involved. But you didn't see a word of it in print. Those folks know how to close ranks."

"So, she married Tommy O'Neal."

"Emma did. The late Emma."

"She's dead?"

"Last fall."

"Tommy O'Neal's widow," LaPorta says, as if he's just learned about it for the first time.

"So, you've heard of Tommy O'Neal?"

"There are stories all over town about Tommy O'Neal."

"I'm sure there are, and I bet all of them have something to do with booze, hookers, or both."

"He lived large; that's for sure."

Footsteps click down the hallway's parquet floor, and Tyler Bach enters the library.

"There you are," he says.

Muffy and LaPorta turn to look at a stout, soft man with an oversized yellow bow tie, white shirt, and blue blazer.

"Just showing Mr. . . . ?" she pauses.

"LaPorta. Louis LaPorta."

"Mr. LaPorta, here, a little history from Coop's days at Yale."

"How nice for you, Mr. LaPorta; and now, sir, if you don't mind, I will gather my lovely wife and escort her back to the Hunt Room."

LaPorta looks at the guy, takes offense, but doesn't let it show. "Nice to meet you both," LaPorta says, and starts to leave the library by the doorway that opens on to Mr. Johnson's study.

"Mr. LaPorta," Muffy Bach calls out.

LaPorta stops. "Yes, Mrs. Bach?"

"I enjoyed our talk about the Renaissance."

"I did, too," he says.

"Well, we must talk again sometime. Tyler here hates museums, but I can see you don't."

"I like them okay," LaPorta says, leaving the room with a little continental head bow, very Italian, very smooth.

Tyler steps back and grunts.

"Tyler?" his wife says.

"Muffy, sometimes you really piss me off."

"Do I, Tyler? How sad for you."

Mr. Johnson's study is immaculate. Two waiters prepare a tray for high tea with scones and biscuits, while a third waiter stokes the fire in the fireplace.

"Mr. Johnson has a meeting in this room in five minutes," one of the waiters tells LaPorta, and LaPorta nods. The front doorbell rings, and the second waiter leaves the room to answer the door. The sound of voices precede the attorney general and his brother Drew into the study.

"He's with some guests in the Hunt Room," the waiter says. "He asked that you make yourself comfortable and he'll be with you in a few minutes. Can I get you anything? Coffee, tea, a soft drink, mixed drink?"

Drew says he'll pour himself some coffee, and the attorney general eyes LaPorta standing in the doorway on the far side of the room.

"Good evening, officer," Thomas Somers says.

"Good evening, sir," LaPorta says.

"Here on official business?"

"I work for Mr. Johnson from time to time."

"That's good then," Somers says. "Always a place for good employees."

"Yes, sir."

"You're still on the force, though?"

"Yes, sir; I am."

"Detective?" Somers asks.

"Acting, right now," he says. "Hopefully next year."

"Good. The force needs good men. Maybe we can sit down and talk sometime. My campaign's going to need some good people to help with security issues."

"I'd like that, sir."

"Good then," and Somers sits and asks Drew to pour him a cup of coffee.

"I'll make sure Mr. Johnson knows you're here," LaPorta says, and he leaves the room, a little pleased with himself, entertaining thoughts of a campaign season and another ride on another set of coattails.

After two cups of coffee and a short conversation on his cell, the attorney general and his brother stand when Coop Johnson enters the room. They've known Mr. Johnson since they were young boys, and although the relationship never warmed to the "honorary uncle" status, they deem themselves members of the same tribe and act accordingly.

"Good to see you, Tom and Andrew," Mr. Johnson says, taking his seat, waving the two of them to the couch set perpendicular to the fireplace.

Drew offers his condolences, and Mr. Johnson dismisses the offer with a kind of pain, closing his eyes, raising three fingers to wipe them dry, as if the offer itself were sufficient to remind him of the funeral, to reopen a wound that had almost closed with the bustle of important guests and small talk.

"Thank you," Mr. Johnson says, and Tom tells him that their parents are in Madrid, that they send their condolences and will see him as soon as they return.

"I'll look forward to that," Mr. Johnson says, and he leans back in the chair and heaves a sigh, more sad than tired.

"This is a beautiful study," Drew says, sitting forward on the couch, full of eager warmth and easy compliments, the gilt-edged saucer balanced on one knee, the small cup in his little-boy's fingers.

"You think so?" Mr. Johnson asks.

"Yes, I do," Drew says. "Who was the decorator?"

"Margaret was," Coop Johnson says. "I'd hired the firm we'd used for our Manhattan offices, but Margaret took over and did the whole house, just as she wanted it."

"Well, she had marvelous taste, then," Tom says, not to be outdone.

"Do you think so?"

"Absolutely," Tom says, as Drew sips and nods. "Beautiful taste."

"The way things look . . ." Mr. Johnson begins to say, then backing off the statement.

"I'm sorry, sir?" Tom says.

"Nothing, it's just that I've been giving a lot of thought to all of that recently, with Margaret's illness and all."

"To what, sir?" Drew asks.

"The whole notion of appearance, good taste, form, the way things look."

"What about them, sir?"

"Frankly, Tom, and I admit this is probably due to my mood today, but I was thinking how useless they all are."

Tom and Drew stay quiet. They need more information before they can respond.

"I'm not saying one shouldn't concern himself with these things. They are important for a multiethnic polyglot like ours, but I do think some of us invest too much energy in the way things look, and we fool ourselves . . ." Again he stops, as if he were too tired to continue.

"How do we fool ourselves, sir?" Tom asks.

"We fool ourselves by believing in their power. Like some savage and his bracelet of fetishes, we start to believe that all of that can save us."

Drew and Tom exchange looks.

"You boys knew my wife."

"Yes, sir, she was very beautiful," Drew says.

"She was," Johnson says, "but you didn't see her during the last months of her life. It's a crime what the cancer did to her—to her looks."

"I'm really sorry, sir," Tom says.

"I've never been one to waste my time with philosophy," Johnson says. "Art? Yes. Sociology? Some. History? Yes. But not philosophy. And yet, now, tonight, after you lose someone who's been a part of you for so long, it sort of takes you down unfamiliar roads."

"I understand," Tom says.

"Do you?"

"Well, sir, of course I only have my own life to look back on, but I do understand how a loss can help us pose the bigger questions."

"When was the last time you suffered a loss, Tom, or failed at something? And how did you handle it?"

Tom Somers almost gulps for air. His story's been one of success after success, and no one's ever asked him about failure. But this is C. Coop Johnson, and Mr. Johnson doesn't ask questions or do anything else without reason. So Tom searches his memory for something from not so long ago, a dinner party with an unwanted guest and the memories of something they'd shared, something uncomfortable, awkward and, for Tom, embarrassing.

"My first year at college was not a success," he says. "I fell behind and then exams rolled around, and I had to ask some people I wouldn't have talked to otherwise for help. It was a humbling experience."

"How did you handle it, then?"

"It was a bad time, and I got through it. Transferred to another school. Did better there."

"And the people you wouldn't have talked to otherwise, what was their problem? Why did you feel that way about them?"

"It was one person in particular. He was smart, but he was—I don't know . . ."

"Was he crude?"

"Not particularly."

"Was he a bad person?"

"No."

"Was he a thief? Did he steal from you? Take your girlfriend?"

"No. None of that."

"Was he black?"

"He was white."

"Poor?"

"Middle class, I think."

"Was he gay?"

"I don't think so."

"Arrogant? Personality problem?"

"No. Maybe, he tried too hard."

"But there was something about him that really disturbed you."

"I suppose," Tom says, uncomfortable with the scrutiny and the staccato shots, short questions, like moves on a chessboard in a game of speed chess. "I mean I was young; I was intolerant. In some ways I suppose I still am. It's a failing."

"Is it?" Johnson asks, maddening, unable to let it go until he's chased down every thread.

"I think it's natural to want to be with your own," Tom says. "And I don't think there's anything wrong with that. Just look at country clubs and membership policies. This guy wasn't one of my own. We'll never belong to the same club. I don't think he even knows how to play golf or cares. He was the type of guy who'd look down on it. I guess he was arrogant, in his own way. It's just that you don't think of people like him as being arrogant. And he came from . . . I don't know . . . He came from someplace else."

Johnson sits back, old hands limp on the armrests, fingers wrinkled and tapping. He loves the give and take, the transparency of this audience. He remembers the two boys from their childhood when he and their father, an unrepentant snob, were closer than they are today. But he really doesn't know these kids, and for either to presume that kind of familiarity would be wrong. So he watches the ambitious young man with the capable manner, and it disturbs him that one so unresolved about everything except his intuitive sense of how to define "one's own" should think himself qualified, even as a Republican, to be the state's next governor.

"Let me be frank, Tom," Mr. Johnson says. "I'm not going to ask you why you want to be governor. That's the old Cronkite–Roger Mudd gambit."

"I remember that interview," Drew interrupts.

"Wasn't that before your time, Drew?"

"I saw it on the History Channel."

"I see."

Mr. Johnson takes a beat.

"But, Tom, I do want to know what you think about big business, as in the insurance industry."

"It's like this, Mr. Johnson," Tom Somers begins, warming to the question, calling up files, the answer he'd memorized. "I think liberals spout an ideology that they've never thought all the way through. If they had they would have bumped up against big business a long time ago, because it's business that creates the jobs they want and need, the goods they want and need, and even provides the services that work. Eighty years ago government might have helped out when business couldn't, but that was a rare phenomena, and it still took a world war and the military working with industry to get us back on our feet. To be honest I think we've had too many things ass-backward since Roosevelt's second term."

"Roosevelt was a long time ago."

"I think the country barely escaped a close call with him."

"Meaning?"

"Meaning his leftward bias, meaning the threat of a kind of social-ism."

"I remember some of it, Tom. And it was a very different country back then."

"I'm sure it was."

"So, you consider yourself a fiscal conservative?"

"If the vault's filled with other people's money, I am as conservative as they come. People have to have confidence that government will spend their money wisely."

"What you're saying, then, is you want the people's vote and busi-ness's money."

"Sounds like a politician to me," Drew says, trying for humor as the line falls flat.

"Tom?"

"What I want," Tom says, "and all I want, Mr. Johnson, is to be a good governor."

Coop Johnson stares at him, long enough to raise the shadow of uncertainty before the verdict.

"You know, Tom, you're preaching to the choir here."

"I figured as much, sir, though it flatters me to think so."

"Your opponent's a union stooge from Naugatuck who quotes Marx and John Lennon with that workingman-hero slogan of his."

"He's a little rough around the edges," Drew says, still trying, ever eager as he feels the wave of approval mount and roll just this side of the evening's horizon.

"So this needn't be a hard sell," Coop Johnson says. "We're going to back you. We'll contribute. We'll finance some TV and radio. I've got people at the *Courant,* and, given the tenor of the times, despite the obvious failures out of Washington, I think this state still remains predisposed to elect a fiscal conservative. You might have to soften some of your thinking on social policies to court some of the academics. It can be done. Massachusetts does it from time to time, and they're as left-leaning as they come. But whatever you do, don't get close to any of the national foreign affairs people. Right now they're all radioactive, so to speak."

Tom sits forward and Drew sits forward, the two of them like playful and obedient pups, lapping up the wisdom, the brilliance, the analysis and commentary, dying to please with damp-eyed gratitude when the sop of insincere gratitude becomes its own reluctant pat on the back.

"But Tom, one thing, and I'm asking this more on a personal level, if you will. It's something I need to hear from you."

"Yes, sir?"

"I need to know what you really think of the insurance industry."

"How do you mean, sir?"

"I mean are we good corporate citizens? Do we offer a benefit? Do we profit unduly from people's misery? Are we a force for moral good?" And with that, the crafty old man takes the conversation to a difficult place, like a trick question that begs for the wrong answer.

Tom leans so far forward he's in danger of falling off the couch. He posits the various avenues of approach from honesty to a kind of suck-up that doesn't show its smarmy, cloying, sentimental underside. He looks at the tip of his shoes, seeking an open floor of possibility where he might find a phrase that will drive the last thought home with the sound of a door closing on a dangerous room.

"Insurance saves lives, Mr. Johnson. It's as simple as that."

Johnson eyes the kid with quiet eyes. "Well said," he says, not caring one way or the other, the deal having been struck weeks before over dinner with a former governor, the kid's father, a money man out of New York, a senator and one of the wise men who flew in from D.C. to drip red wax over the whole thing.

Coop Johnson stands and the brothers stand. Coop and Tom shake hands and Coop watches as the young man stares into his eyes, doing the good-boy thing, the coming of age thing, the torch has been passed thing, as if this alone were necessary to communicate some bond between men of substance, men capable of something unspeakably strong and honorable inherited from ancestors who happened to be unspeakably strong and honorable.

"And none of it . . ." Coop says, not finishing the thought.

"I'm sorry?" Tom says.

"Oh," Coop says, as if coming to. "I can't help but think that in the end none of it will be enough when it's time to go."

Drew and Tom look at each other and wait.

Coop almost trembles with the swagger of the old hero, burdened more by wisdom than age.

They reach the front door and make a final parting, Tom Somers careful to withhold some, to eschew the appearance of fawning.

Drew leaves first, stepping out onto the porch, and Coop closes the door behind him, holding Tom by the arm. "A word," he says.

"Sure, Mr. Johnson, whatever."

"As you know my wife suffered terribly before she died. There were many times when the morphine wouldn't help. She asked for a way out, but I couldn't help her. I couldn't do it, and she couldn't help herself. She had to wait it out. She did and then she died."

"I'm sorry," Tom says, uncertain, unnerved.

"I only tell you this, Tom, because I'm an insurance man, and I believe in it, and I'm proud of it. And I know life insurance was never designed to pay for suicide, and I don't think an insurance company should be saddled with an obligation when the insured kills herself."

"I agree with that."

"You do?"

"Of course."

"Then why did you give the green light on the Emma Kost investigation?"

"I didn't know that I had. Jimmy Reis is handling that."

"At your direction."

"I have seen the file."

"Listen to me, Tom. Cal Stevens is a friend of mine. He used to be a good friend of your father's, too."

"I know, sir."

"Now Cal's had some rough years. His family's had some rough years and what used to be there isn't there anymore. Nonetheless, Emma Kost killed herself, and just because Cal's been screaming murder ever since, I don't think your office should promote an investigation unworthy of its reputation. Suicide is suicide. It's a kind of murder, but not the kind that requires an investigation that'll end up nowhere."

"Yes, sir, I understand."

"Do you?"

"Yes, sir, I do."

"I knew Emma Kost, Tom. Your father did. Cal did. We all did. But I knew her better than anyone, and I cared for her more than anyone. Now, she married an asshole, and that was her mistake. But we all loved her. Now, from what I understand she'd recently been diagnosed with something serious, and she was depressed and miserable about it."

"Yes, sir."

"So, it's not unlikely that she wanted out."

"No, sir. Not unlikely at all."

"So, if you would be kind enough then to let her rest in peace with her decision, I know that I, for one, would be very grateful."

"Yes, sir. I understand completely."

"Point is, when you get to be our age, some things are as bad as ever, but they become a little more understandable."

"Yes, sir."

"I'm talking about suicide, Tom."

"Yes, sir."

"Understandable, Tom, but not insurable."

In the hotel room with the wide mirror and the wide bed and windows on the dark city, Ann Dillon kisses Manny Whitman on the lips, says they'll meet next weekend at the bed-and-breakfast in Lenox, and leaves.

She walks down the hall, passing doors, takes the elevator to the garage, and starts across the lot. She steps without looking. A car screeches and rushes beside her. She steps back. The car stops with a skid. It takes a second to process. She's about to swear, and Mark Moraski gets out of the car.

"Get in," he says.

"Mark, what are you doing? You almost hit me."

"Get in, I said."

"Mark! What's the matter with you? Have you been following me?"

"I was curious."

"More like stalking."

"I've got a lot of questions. Now, please, get in."

Ann looks around, pouts, says something under her breath, and gets in.

Moraski drives out of the lot. The only sound is the static from the police band radio. After they drive through town, heading west, he asks her what she's up to.

"What do you mean?"

"What do you and Manny Whitman have to talk about?"

"That's none of your business, Mark."

"It is my business, Ann."

"Look, Mark, I don't have to talk about any of this. The fact that I know Manny Whitman is a personal matter."

"Personal?"

"Yes, personal."

"What do you mean—personal?"

"What do you think I mean?"

"As in, hello, how are you, and how do we get away with this?"

"That's beneath you, Mark. I don't need to get away with anything, because I've done nothing."

"Jesus, Ann, you know I like you; I've always liked you, but don't tell me you've got yourself mixed up in this thing."

"What thing?"

"What do you think—what thing?"

"Manny and I, we've been . . ."

"And don't tell me that, either."

"And what's it to you, Mark? You've got your life; you're a married man."

"Just don't, all right?"

The static goes loud with volume. The dispatcher's voice directs all units to an address on the border between West Hartford and Hartford.

"Look, Mark, my personal life doesn't have a thing to do with your investigation. When you asked, I told you I think the letter's a forgery."

"And then you go—whatever—with the girl you just accused?"

"She wrote a letter. At most it's attempted fraud by a confused, distraught orphan with a disability who just lost her last living relative. Oh, yeah, they'll throw away the key with that one."

"Quiet," Mark says, leaning into the sound. "That address," he says.

"What about it?"

Mark pulls a u-turn.

"Sounds familiar," he says.

They arrive at the O'Neal house. There's a black and white with two youngsters talking into their shoulders. The first kid with the baby fat and the acne on the chin walks up to Moraski and asks what he wants. Moraski flashes his badge, and the kid says a neighbor heard a commotion, saw lights, and called it in. He and Moraski start up the porch steps while the other cop goes around the back. Ann gets out of the car and starts to follow. Moraski tells her to stay where she is.

Moraski and Officer Delaney press against the front door. It's unlocked, unlatched. It swings open. The foyer is wide and empty except for a rocking chair that moves with the incoming breeze. The downstairs is almost Gothic in shadows with copper-white from one lamp near the staircase and the parabolas of light blooming up the walls.

Moraski takes the stairs slowly. Delaney follows until Moraski tells him to check the downstairs and the basement.

The darkness at the top of the stairs allows for the reflection of light from the end of the corridor, and when Moraski reaches the top step he hears noises from the bedroom. He starts down the hall and hears someone behind him. He turns and Ann Dillon stands there with a pale, open expression on her face.

He hisses, "I told you to wait behind."

"I think I know who's here," she says.

"Who?" he asks, and with that the breeze from the front door runs through the house and strikes the bedroom door. It swings open and Moraski and Ann see Cal Stevens on his knees beside Emma O'Neal's bed.

Ann rushes into the room.

"Mr. Stevens?" she says. "Are you all right? What are you doing here?"

He ignores her or doesn't hear her and continues to mumble words, racked with sobs, crying, asking, pleading. It sounds like a confession.

Moraski follows Ann into the bedroom, sees Stevens and a handgun with a silencer lying on the bedspread.

"I'm so sorry," Cal Stevens says, the words made broad with emotion and sounds Ann had never heard the old man make before. "He was going to get away with it," he says, and Ann looks to Moraski who looks to Cal as Delaney and his partner enter the room.

"We got a situation downstairs," Delaney says to Moraski, who's trying to figure out what Cal Stevens is saying.

"What situation?" Ann asks, as if she has standing, as if she's in authority.

"We got a guy down, shot in the chest," Delaney says.

"What?" Moraski yells, whipping his head around.

"In the kitchen," Delaney says. "And we got a little puppy down there shivering to death."

"A puppy?" Moraski says.

"That's right," Delaney says. "Puppy's okay, though. Just terrified—kinda made a mess. But the guy, I think he's gone."

"You think!" Moraski yells and then turns to Cal Stevens who's resting his elbows and forearms on the bed, crying with small gasps, admitting his guilt, calling out for somebody's forgiveness, crying for somebody's love.

"Jesus Christ," Moraski says, leaving the bedroom while Ann walks over to Mr. Stevens to rub his back, to help him to his feet.

In the television room of a lovely house on a lovely street in a quiet neighborhood of a small town, Mr. and Mrs. Wyman sit in their lounge chairs, foot rests up, prepared for flight. She's got the remote and switches channels until she settles on the Hartford station when the newscaster introduces the video of the young and handsome attorney general standing at a podium in the Senate caucus room, flanked by a younger brother and unknown members of his family, a priest with an Episcopal collar, and other supporters, as he announces his run for governor.

The sight of the young man on the TV stops Mrs. Wyman because he's so handsome with his hair falling in a full wave over his brow, left to right, unusual in most men, and the sad eyes, so blue, and the hard jaw, not square like some jarhead marine, but tapered with a touch of elegance, the line from cheekbone to chin.

"Isn't he handsome?" she says, and Mr. Wyman grunts and opens his eyes, sleepy now with time and whiskey and the last nod that took him someplace far away, gentle and kind, though out of reach, now gone, not to be remembered, as he looks at the skinny kid on the screen who's saying something about the return of integrity to state government, about how we all can do better, about some Greek poet who wrote a play. Mr. Wyman fingers the small glass on the side table and holds it and starts to nod again, wondering what it is he can do better since he's done the best he could for so long and has accomplished so little, leaving him bereft and tired, a visitor, a watcher, like many men approaching sixty, on the sidelines of a game he once played, a game that rewards propriety and manners and absolute devotion to the boss, the company, the rightness of a life lived correctly—a life for which Mr.

Wyman found a metaphor in columns of numbers and an arithmetic that seeks zero, as if seeking the grail, a magical and existential number, an unmoved and unmoving notation, a mystery and sometimes, if not a window on some other, better place, then a mirror of this place, the here and now, the unforgivable normal world, the unfortunate cipher his youngest, the gifted one, departs on occasion.

"Another drink, Henry?" Mrs. Wyman asks, and Mr. Wyman moves his glass a millimeter, which is all he has to do, and she gets up and crosses the room and fills it with rye whiskey, pouring another for herself, wiping the glass bottoms with a small towel to soak up the condensation, to make the glass cold again, to make it seem like the first and not the seventh drink of a short evening.

"I just think it'd be nice to have a handsome young man like that rise up in government," she says, handing Henry his drink, taking her seat, moving the remote, sitting back with those foggy eyes, uncertain whether they should flash with an ever-ready indignation, or just get pleasantly sleepy in the cocoon of medicinal drink.

"Who is he?" the accountant asks, having missed the beginning, which is deadly for accountants, having missed the name or the city or the reason why all the people on the TV are so serious until the skinny kid stops talking and they let loose with smiles and applaud as if somebody had actually done something worthwhile.

"He's Thomas Somers," she says, "the attorney general."

"He's a kid," Mr. Wyman grunts.

"He's Matthew's age," she says, defensive, defending Somers and not Matthew, which is her way of reminding her husband of failures and negation, of saying look at what this young Somers boy is doing and look at what your son's doing—next to nothing, reliant on the state and welfare to keep him in a room where he won't hurt himself.

"That's awfully young," Henry Wyman says, which is his way of telling his wife there's plenty of time for a man like Matthew, who has troubles, problems, but who's gifted, too, who will mature in his own time, at his own speed, in accordance with the Greek concept of *Kairos,* capable of great things, greater than empty and self-proclaimed integrity at a news conference called by oneself to further one's career.

"I think they even went to school together," Mrs. Wyman says, look-ing, seeking out some area of the bulky carb belly of the old man, dull with numbers, where she can plunge the short, wide blade of a Roman in Gaul.

"Matthew got all A's," Henry says, nodding again, the drink more than the conversation taking him down like a diver in cold water in a lake without a bottom, sinking in the all-forgiving, all-consuming wet green darkness, made pale here and there with broad beams of light from a sun that shines only at night, and he thinks how Matthew was never afraid, full of cocky brightness, a face that lit up, and how, even as a young boy, he'd sit on the edge of his father's chair and put his arm around his father's neck, breaking every rule in the house, seeking out, as lightning seeks the ground, the stability that follows change, something normal, his father's love, hidden, though not deeply hidden, under the glaze and shell of a man who'd placed his faith in obtaining a kind of certitude, settlement, equilibrium, balance, never wholly satis-factory, but workable—a kind of math that inferred greater realms of doubt and questions—realms desirous of more complex equations to re-flect other passages through higher levels of chaos, spun like so much marble in the broadcloth of God.

"Henry."

He hears his name from above the warm waters of sleep and wishes he could sink further to a realm of no-sight, no-sound, no-thought, but only vision and sense made perfect in an anesthetic heaven.

"Henry."

Again he hears his name and need not rise through water too quickly, his spirit in danger of crumbling with the bends, rendering his soul arthritic with oxygen, but merely look upward once to the shaft of yellow, now as pale as the yellow wall and the frames of photos of the family that came before, and he turns and coughs a dry cough, an in-flection, a breath, a gulp of air and looks at her, the woman he married almost forty years ago in a small church, three stoplights from the street with the oversized house on land his father owned and sold when things went badly, when things happened.

"What?" he says.

"Time for bed," she says, and already she's out of her chair, moving about the room, taking the glasses and setting them in the sink in the bar in an alcove, wiping things down, a white towel with blue stripes, determined, bossy, wearing her housecoat, a Monet print, the macadam of oils, oriental, the shogun's geisha with the little sticks in the tight bun and the failure of lace.

But this is not her, he thinks. She's grown short and fat and angry with herself, with me, with everyone. She disdains the world. She has failed at kindness.

"C'mon, Henry, please, now, it's time."

And he remembers his last class with a tall, bald teacher at a state school, who called him aside and told him that he had a special talent for numbers, for the rigorous detail of symbols as old as Mohammed, for the love of a metaphor unobtainable by most young romantics who seek their useless gods in grass and splashy rows of barley in a lake district.

"I'll put on the hall light," she says, moving out of the room, so that with the questionable strength of late middle age, he stands on legs that click and then find footing, his back about to spasm as he starts across the hard floor, following her, though he can't see her, only the lamps she's lit to light his way through several rooms running half the length of a house too large by a factor of seven—or whatever number of drinks she poured between eight and whenever. And she calls again from a dark distance to make sure he's up, her voice like an unhappy teacher from the fifties who prizes silence and order over everything, and he follows her like a pet, a man who's lost the will to assert his will except with the rare explosion of rage that marked and marred his life.

"Turn them off as you go," she says, and he hears her now, not through any web or veil of comforting sleep but in a dry and present reality he can't escape even when he does sleep, the unhappiness of company without love, the assault and intrusion of the other when love is absent and, being the vacuum it is, fails with its absence to make room for another.

He hears footsteps, his, perhaps hers, the sliding muffled sound of slippers on carpet as she ascends the stairs, one foot after the other, and he seeks out a rhythm, a repetitive percussive to mark the ascent, to count down the last moment of this all-too-painful consciousness when the sounds stop, the rhythm breaks, and she makes but one chirp of question and doubt and then, with a cascade of sound, as wild as any untamed utterance of jazz, resisting all call to normalcy and order, she falls backward, spinning like a wheel down the flight of stairs, landing at his feet in a heap of oriental myth, fabric, and twisted limbs, eyes open with a kind of innocent wonderment until they close and she breathes slowly with a different rhythm, with its own presentation and refusal to be anything other than what it is, the last gasps of a small woman who found life difficult, who found comfort in food, who drank, who smoked, who loved only her first son.

It's not a carnival or a circus or a sideshow. It's more like an old-fashioned church picnic with tables of pies and pastries and cakes and buckets filled with soda pop and bottled water. Two teams of nine play slow-pitch softball under lights. Behind the main podium, on a dais of old wood, the mayor and some councilmen and Bishop Ravezzi welcome everybody and talk about the changes taking place for the better in the community, while another crowd gathers under the bungee jumpers who fall from heights like a rite of passage.

Bishop Ravezzi stands at the podium and says that generosity is the keystone of community. The people applaud. They like the bishop who isn't a bishop or a minister or a priest or anything formal like that. He's the youngest son of Italian socialists from Buffalo, believers, who believed in the dignity of working men and the evils of greed. He tried the Catholic seminary in the eighties, but that didn't work for reasons better left unsaid. So he moved from western New York and settled in the North End of Hartford, where he married an African American woman named Leah and opened his own church in an abandoned used car lot, attracted a large following, and actually did some good.

The celebration on the green had been scheduled for late May when the weather would be warm, but there were problems with City Hall and permits and then there were problems hooking up with the Amazing Levon, which had almost strained Leah's friendship with Eddie Davis, the Amazing Levon's manager. After everybody got everything straightened out, they had to move the date up, and not back, to April, and they worried about the cold. But this night seems blessed. A warm front blew through about five and the air is mild and the crowd is large and people are being generous as kids pass through the crowd with buckets for donations and candies to give away.

Orpheus passes a plastic bucket near the outer edge of the crowd and holds it out for one guy who looks at him like he's a pest or crazy or something.

"What?" the guy says.

"We didn't charge no admission," Orph says, "but we still got to pay that motherfucker to fly his ass off."

"You talk to your parents like that?" the guy says, as he reaches into his pocket and pulls out his wallet. He opens it and a credit card falls to the ground. Orph picks it up and reads the name before he hands it back.

"And a' course we want you to have a good time, Mr. Brian Wyman, sir."

Brian looks at the kid and wishes he'd cut the shit, especially since other people are looking on.

"What are people giving?" Brian asks.

"About a hundred," Orph says.

Brian hesitates. He says, "Get real, kid."

"C'mon, man," Orph whispers, "You want these motherfuckers thinkin' you're some kinda cheap fuck?"

Brian grabs a twenty, holds it up for Orph to see, and drops it into the bucket.

"Thank you, Mr. Brian Wyman," Orph says, loud enough for everyone standing nearby to hear. "You are one generous son of a bitch."

"Get outta here," Brian says under his breath, and Orph leaves, spotting the next mark, thinking this might be too good to be true.

On the far side of the softball game a yellow cement mixer backs up, crosses the field, and stops play, making herky-jerk movements till it reaches the plot of land where a backhoe, parked against a fence, digs a four-by-seven-by-five grave. The cement mixer backs up to the hole and the workers attach the chute. About thirty yards from the grave there's a black tour bus like the country stars use, with THE AMAZING LEVON airbrushed on the side. Brian watches the crowd gather around the scene, pushing in and up to the yellow police tape and the space cordoned off for the Amazing Levon.

On the bandstand Bishop Ravezzi addresses the crowd, telling them that the Amazing Levon's in his trailer, preparing himself mentally and spiritually for the stunt of a lifetime, a stunt he's only tried once before, a stunt that will show the world that nothing, neither earth nor soil nor gravity, can keep the Amazing Levon from rising up and over the world.

After that Bishop Ravezzi jokes with a councilman about who's crazy enough to bungee jump. The people standing around the podium make catcalls and noise, egging them on until the bishop, who loves the celebrity and the stage, says he'll jump in his shorts if people will donate enough money to make it worthwhile.

Brian Wyman walks around the perimeter of the crowd and stands before a huge screen with a camera shot of the grave and workers carrying a Plexiglas coffin over their heads. They set it down next to the grave, and the camera swings away to the crane where the bishop, dressed in a red robe, climbs the ladder to the platform overhead. Brian watches the bishop mug for the camera, step up, and walk to the edge of the platform where he almost faints. Laughter and jeers follow and the bishop gets on his knees and puts his hands together in prayer. After that his wife, Leah, calls out that they'd collected another five hundred dollars, and the bishop arches one eyebrow, gives her a look, and starts down the ladder. The laughter continues. A few more people dig into their pockets, and the bishop returns to the platform. He walks a few steps, drops the robe, flexes his muscles, and waits while the bungee masters attach the bungee cord to his ankles and usher him to the edge.

As Brian watches it on the big screen hung between two trees, he's tapped on the shoulder.

"Louis," Brian says.

"Here it is," LaPorta says, taking a small yellow envelope from his jacket, handing it to Brian, who puts it in the space he'd carved out of the hardbound copy of *War and Peace*.

"Ten o'clock," Louis says.

"I know," Brian says.

"We're running a little late."

"I'll get on it."

"After you drop this off, meet me at Sabia's and I'll give you yours."

"Sure thing," Brian says, and he leaves to meet Clive at the bar on the near side of the north end.

LaPorta hangs around to watch the show. He's seen this Amazing asshole on TV, and he wonders what all the hype's about. The whole thing was an optical illusion or one of those computer-generated things, and he figures he'll watch it live to see how the guy pulls it off.

A roar goes up from the front of the crowd as the bishop falls from the platform and dangles like a puppet before they get him down. The whole thing's anticlimactic, though, the buildup having promised more than one second of free fall.

A few bishop lackeys, cleric groupies, clap and shout, though a new buzz and wave drowns them out when the Amazing Levon emerges from his tour bus and starts toward the grave.

LaPorta watches the guy on the screen. He's average-height, maybe five foot eleven at best, and he's fit with the muscles that show under the gold T-shirt with his name across the front. The guy's no kid, though. LaPorta figures he's in his forties and that he's done some serious work to make himself look younger, with the thick hair brushed back from his narrow forehead, with the way he walks, like a prince with a certain command of the event, a kind of theatrical dignity.

"He's a strange one," LaPorta says to himself, having seen this sort of thing before when he worked security at the Bushnell—meaning the way celebrities take on a look that's an inch off center, a touch exaggerated, a certain something in the features that draws the attention they want and hangs precariously on the edge of the grotesque.

When the Amazing Levon reaches the Plexiglas casket he looks around at everybody pressing in and appears a little disconnected. Except for the gold shirt, there's no Viva Las Vegas bullshit with a cape or showgirls prancing around. Except for the guy's strange look, there's no vaudeville or cheesy stage hype. There's just the guy, this Amazing Levon, stepping into a casket, lying down, folding his arms over his chest, and waiting as his handlers to close the lid, pick up the casket, and hand it to two other giants standing in the pit.

Louis watches all of this on the superwide screen. The cameraman, working with an off-the-shoulder video cam, has to squeeze through the crowd to get close to film the casket lying on the ground at the bottom of the grave. The camera peers over the edge and points down and closes on Levon's face, visible through the plastic glass. His eyes look black and are wide and vacant. He's still. He looks like a mummy.

At the bandstand Bishop Ravezzi, shaken from the fall, introduces Donny Kay, a radio personality, who'll describe Levon's stunt as it takes place before their eyes. Donny Kay says that it's almost time to pour the cement, and the cement mixer starts up and the cylinder turns and a gray-green slurry starts down the chute and pours into the space between the casket and the grave wall. Then the handlers move the chute and the cement pours over the casket and the last thing the camera shoots before it swings away to the mixer, spinning and coughing up its contents, are Levon's eyes, open and clear now, with a mixture of fear, foresight, and knowledge.

Donny Kay says: "This is it, ladies and gentlemen, this is what we've been waiting for . . ."

And then it happens. There's a shout, and then a murmur through the crowd. A pause follows as the crowd hesitates, trying to distinguish what's the show and what's not. The handlers are going crazy, but they could be acting, too. And then it's clear. With a crack and sickening thud, the cement cracks the top of the Plexiglas, pours into the casket, sinking to a deep and circular center.

One handler jumps into the pit and starts scooping with his hands, but the mixer continues to pour until another handler jumps into the truck's cab and grabs the driver by the shoulders. Two other handlers jump into the grave and try to help the first guy, who's begun to sink in the poured cement. They call for the backhoe, they call for help and continue to dig and scoop. A volunteer from the crowd jumps in, followed by another, but the additional bodies only crowd the space and do more harm than good.

LaPorta watches the screen and checks the second hand of his watch. The guy's been under for a minute and a half. One of the guys standing in the grave with cement up to his calves, thick, heavy, cold, beginning to harden in the night air, calls for a pipe or something to make a hole, to get air to Levon. But the idea's no better than it sounds.

Louis checks his watch again. Two and a half minutes. With normal lungs the guy's got about a minute. With extraordinary lungs, he doesn't have much more than that.

The big guys continue to dig and scoop, but they're not making enough progress.

At the bandstand Donny Kay gets word that the act's gone bad. He tells the crowd to step back, to give the handlers room, to cooperate. And then the lights around the stage begin to flicker and go out across the green and beyond, through office buildings and the city skyline and the homes and stores and places beyond that.

"Is this on?" Donny Kay yells into the microphone, but the PA system's down, too. The mayor rushes the stage and pulls Donny Kay aside with word of other disasters, new tragedies. There have been a series of new explosions in Manhattan.

Louis LaPorta stands back. He thinks he knows crowds, what they are, how they react, what they become. He takes the pulse of this one and knows something's happening. Panic is like the shadow the wind makes when it rolls through a field, moving from spot to spot, billowing out some, disappearing, only to be reborn as a larger, darker cell. Sometimes, midscream, at the tipping point, it will pull back and tendencies toward silence and order will prevail. And other times, some trigger, another word, rumor, sight, or sound will tip the whole thing and people will stampede and people will die.

Louis knows the Amazing Levon is gone, and that's sad, but that's not the news that's making this crowd move. Something else is going on, passing from person to person, like a virus, like seepage, like water through water.

Two kids run by and he hears the words "nuke" and "New York." He walks against the flow and hears more conversations and a few prayers. "They did it . . ." one guy says. And a woman says, "We waited how long for the other shoe to drop?" Then words almost become stories, and stories swallow stories, as news can swallow news, as people distinguish what's important, what affects them and what affects them vicariously. The passing crowd moves quickly now. They say nothing about the Amazing Levon, lying dead under a ton of cement. That was his death, something they'd paid for, something he'd almost asked for.

Louis checks the radium dial on his watch again and bumps into a gaggle of kids in their twenties with bottles in brown bags talking about going to war and what they'll do to those fucking-camel-jockey-towel-head bastards, and Louis knows Manhattan's been bombed, and that a bombing in Manhattan has swallowed a death in Hartford.

He moves diagonally against the onrushing crowd, the same way a swimmer swims against a riptide to get to shore, and when he reaches an empty place under some trees at the edge of the green, he looks at the black skyline, the black night.

"Look over there," a voice says.

LaPorta turns.

Matthew Wyman stands under the bare limbs of an old tree.

"What are you doing here?" LaPorta says.

"Came to see the miracle man, like everybody else."

"Yeah, well, you better move it along. This place needs to be cleared out," LaPorta says, invoking his authority, his badge, the power to make people move.

"Yeah, but look over there," Matthew says again, and Louis stops short and looks to the horizon.

"It's just a fuckin' cloud," Louis says as he moves away, anxious with the crowd that's begun to turn with the sound of shop windows breaking in the distance.

"Yeah, but it's still something to see," Matthew says to no one as he points to a place against the starless sky where the wayward cloud, a wisp of smoke, the exhaust of some small explosion, forms the shape of a man with arms crossed over his chest and rises like the effigy of young Elijah, levitating like the never-dead in the middle of the air.

MERITON

LaPorta was all set to bring Matthew in, cuff him, put a bag over his head, throw him in the back of a van with hookers and the wild men who were tossing trash cans through Bergman-Dorff-whatever windows. But even LaPorta had underestimated the power of a mob when word of the apocalypse sweeps through a place and resolves itself in movement—not directed movement, not purposeful movement—just movement, seeking its own boundaries with its own conformities to Fibonacci spirals and an architecture loosely grounded in the golden mean. Whatever it was, it wasn't military, it wasn't quality, it wasn't even early–German fascist. If anything it was late-empire Norse, Eurasian, Slavic, an invasion without source or terminus, and the danger was in the acceleration and the uncaring that accompanies speed.

It swept LaPorta away first, and Matthew became a mollusk, a clam, a crab, a burrowing thing, digging, burying himself by the exposed roots of an oak tree, placing himself so close to the base of the tree that he avoided feet and legs as the mob split like torn fabric to pass by. Some people yelled, some people screamed, some people whispered, but the words were subject to filters, and people heard what they wanted to hear, expected to hear. Crouching by the tree Matthew heard terrorism and dirty bomb, and rumors fed the panic, and panic spun through the park down main streets and side streets where it broke up and unraveled in the way hurricanes unravel when land scrapes the undersides of cloud banks, shreds eye walls, dissipates focus, dissolves momentum and force.

It was after midnight before the worst of the crisis passed and Matthew left the park and returned to Billy's. The house was empty, so he waited for somebody to show up. But nobody showed, not Billy, not Darren, not Orpheus. He ate some food from the fridge and felt things begin to slip again. It had been a while since he took his meds, and the absence of people became its own problem.

It's almost dawn and there's a band of light under a blanket of purple just visible beyond the yard by the house across the street where the old woman sweeps her porch every day. Matthew sits by the window and remembers that he's off the leash, AWOL, missing in action, because he escaped the hospital three days prior when he saw Billy drive up the hospital driveway in the O'Neal hearse. Billy was there to pick up a body from the far end of the complex where wealthy patients died from normal things. Matthew saw him through the window near the main entrance and waited for the temp receptionist to take one of her three hundred cigarette breaks. Then he walked out a side door and crossed the parking lot, all the time waiting for somebody to stop him. But nobody stopped him, Matthew walking the whole way like he owned the place, knowing people don't stop people who walk like they own the place.

When he got to the hearse he said: Hey, Billy, and Billy said, Hey, Professor, as if it were nothing. But it wasn't nothing, and Billy had to think about all of it. You sure you can just up and leave like this? Billy asked, and Matthew said he wasn't sure about anything. Then Billy said: Well, if I ask myself what's better, as regardin' you being locked up or not being locked up, I guess there's little contest between the two. So Billy told Matthew to get in the back of the hearse and lie down next to the coffin that housed the late Mrs. Johnson. Keep down till we get to my place, Billy said, and he started the hearse and drove back to Hartford.

The sun gleans the underside of morning clouds and breaks through. Matthew fingers the short stack of cassette tapes on the table by the window. The tapes are Billy's library, his oral history, scheduled, indexed, identified with his very own system of numbers and letters. Matthew picks up a cassette, slaps it in the Walkman and listens to

Billy talk about the day he and the Professor sat in the police station with the halogen lights. Matthew remembers Talmadge and how pissed off he was about everything, and how Moraski tried to be hard-nosed like Talmadge, but couldn't hide the fact that he liked Matthew, found him interesting and innocent, and rushed the interview because of it.

Matthew thinks: Something's impossible until it happens; then it's not impossible at all—then it's only the passage of time to reset the fulcrum, to obtain new balance, to gain purchase on the slope of possibility and the awful getting of wisdom. Some people adapt, accommodate, negotiate. Some people survive. Others don't. Either way, nobody lives long enough to register a hairline on any canyon wall.

Matthew walks down the stairs to Billy's basement and lies down on Billy's army cot. He sleeps and wakes midmorning and hears footsteps and voices overhead. He gets up, walks up the stairs, and listens by the doorway. He hears his brother ask Billy if the Caddy's ready. Billy says he replaced the plugs and changed the oil. He says: It's ready, enough, and Brian tells Billy that his mother (meaning Brian's and Matthew's mother) died the night before. He says: She fell down a flight of stairs and that fucking loser was too drunk to call an ambulance. Billy says he's sorry, and Brian says he's leaving for Meriton. He doesn't ask after Matthew. Officially speaking, neither he nor Billy knows where Matthew is; unofficially, they both know he's hiding out in Billy's basement. Either way, Brian's not going to wait around.

After he leaves, Billy goes to the basement where Matthew's sitting at a table, holding a Walkman recorder and writing in a notebook. Billy tells Matthew his mother's dead. He says he's sorry for his loss. He says he'll give him a ride to Meriton. Matthew takes the news without saying much. He says he'll get some things together. He says: Let's go, then.

Everything's on alert and shutting down at the same time. The night before, when they poured cement over the Amazing Levon, the second shoe dropped in New York—the shoe everybody knew would drop but had come to believe wouldn't drop. Already people were numb with it. They'd spent so much emotional capital on the first attack, there was little juice in the national reserves to spend on the second. There'd be fewer flags and yellow ribbons this time around. People would be pissed, and not just because of trouble and fear, but because so many stores threatened to close. Except for pharmacies and convenience stores, there'd be fewer places to shop.

Billy sticks to the back roads; the trip takes an hour. They listen to the radio. The commentators say how lucky everybody is because it could have been worse. Two subway lines are shut down, the upstate power grid's damaged, but not defeated, and the dirty bomb near the stock exchange failed to radiate the neighborhood. Matthew hears the news, but he doesn't feel lucky. He doubts if anybody feels lucky. When things are fucked up, Matthew prefers for people to say things are fucked up. To say things are better than they are only makes victims feel worse than they already feel, making them feel guilty, enervated with trauma and called upon to act like there is no trauma. Matthew figures that, in the end, no matter what happened in New York, positive thinking is a zero-sum game.

One time when Matthew was a kid he fell out of a tree and broke some ribs. Everybody told him how lucky he was. He didn't feel lucky then, either, and when he said so, people told him he was prone to self-pity. After that Matthew wondered if all the people who've fallen out of trees consider themselves lucky or prone to self-pity. Later on, when Matt was an adult and prone to crazy, the shrinks told him to open up. When he refused, they said he was being uncooperative. Then, when he did open up, they said he was prone to self-pity. That's when Matt knew he couldn't win with shrinks, and as Billy's wide car from Detroit's late empire descends the far side of Avon Mountain, Matthew wonders how many shrinks have fallen out of trees, how many shrinks consider themselves lucky, how many shrinks are prone to self-pity.

The traffic was heavy near Hartford, then light on the back roads and heavy again as they get close to Meriton. Given what's happened and threats of more to come, people want to know where safe is, and some of them keep driving, hoping to find it.

Matthew and Billy reach Meriton and drive down Main Street when Matthew asks Billy to drop him off. He thanks Billy for the ride and everything else. Billy tells the Professor to call whenever he wants a ride back to Hartford. Matthew thanks him again, and without wanting to, without asking for it, without anything, he almost starts to cry. Billy sees it and pats his hand and tells him things will be okay. Matthew coughs and says the same thing.

Main Street's empty and Matthew figures everybody's home watching TV. Garber's Pharmacy's the only place open. Old man Garber was a family friend, but he died years ago, and his son, Vinny, runs the place. Vinny and Matthew are about the same age. They went to high school together, but when Matthew stands at the end of the counter and coughs, Vinny acts like he doesn't recognize him. Can I help you? he asks, and Matthew says: How about something for the end of the world, and Vinny looks at Matthew like he's a wise guy, prone to bad taste. So Matthew says he's got some heartburn, and Vinny tosses a roll of antacids across the counter. The Garber girl works the register. Matthew says: Looks like you're the only place open, and Garber walks over and puts his arm around the girl's shoulder. He says: My daughter and I will be shutting down in a few minutes. We'll open tomorrow if they lower the threat level. Matthew asks: Do you know if the Madaux Funeral Home's open? Couldn't tell you, Vinny says. Matt says he's supposed to be there. He says: She was my mother. Vinny looks at him longer than necessary, and Matthew asks if he can use the store's phone. Doesn't work, Vinny says. Cell phone? Matt asks. No battery, Vinny says.

Matt finds the last pay phone in Connecticut and calls his father. His father says they'll probably have to wake his mother from the house. Madaux's people embalmed her and delivered the body that morning, carrying the casket to a guest bedroom on the second floor. Matthew asks how she died, and his father asks if he needs a ride. Matthew says: It's only a mile or two. I'll be there soon.

Matthew walks down South Main through the center of town, over the short bridge over the Naugatuck River. He bears left on Prospect and climbs Litchfield. The yards get bigger and the foothills of the Berkshires, thick with trees, rise up on the horizon. He crosses the narrow road that rings the duck pond on the near side of his father's house. The road's pale with old macadam, speckled with rocks and clusters of leaves that survived winter under old snow. The sunlight filters itself through new leaves and the branches of bare trees. The afternoon sun is almost warm, and the air is damp. Overhead, the sky's brilliant and deep, and the clouds are full of round white billows touched with shades of ochre, yellow, and rose.

Matthew sees the large Victorian in the distance, colonial yellow with gables, dark wood casings, slate shingles, trees growing on every side, and the wraparound porch set in deep-green shadows. It was his mother's house, passed down on her father's side, the side of the family with money. He starts down the walk lined with laurel bushes, turns once to the pond in the distance, quiet with the hint of ripples and the brush of cat's paws. Then he opens the back door and walks through the first floor. The place is immaculate with new drapes and window shades. The furniture's dusted and clean and the kitchen's polished and the pantry's full. Matthew passes through the dining room, a sitting room, and the main room with the fireplace. His father's on his knees in a space by the windows. He's scrubbing the parquet floor with an old rag and a can of polish. Matthew watches him and memories fill his chest with extraordinary sadness, completing his thoughts with the consequences of ordinary acts extending outward to some border between the here and there. He thinks: Nothing goes unnoticed here. Nothing will be measured in the old way. Little things will cause tidal waves.

I'm here, Dad, Matthew says, and his father drops the rag, grabs the side of a chair, and tries to stand. Matthew steps forward and helps him. His father says: Thank God you're home and hugs his son. Matthew says: Things will be okay, Dad, not believing a word of it, saying it as a comfort, finding courage in a situation that's larger than he is. Matthew knows it's easy to say things will be all right when there's not a chance, and that it's hard to say it when there is a chance. His father says: There won't be a wake after all. Matthew asks about Brian. His father says he called and said he was held up someplace. He asks: How did you get here? And Matthew tells him he and Billy took the back roads.

Matthew's not a primitive, and he doesn't pretend to be one. He never liked camping out, and he didn't like living in the shelter he made beneath two boulders at the edge of Hillside Cemetery. He'd never survive in a jungle, and he would have failed in the Left Bank salons of the twenties with their madness for primitive art, African warrior masks, all those almond eyes from Egypt, all those long narrow heads. And yet for all of that, he finds less comfort in this place, his home—the middle rank of the middle class in a country designed for that huge bubble of midlevel management—than the places he chose for shelter with the naïve romance of an imaginary Franciscan seeking conversion to soften the edge of indictment.

When Billy got him the job at O'Neal's, they said he'd be the yard man, and he cleaned leaves from a hedgerow behind the morgue. One day Mrs. O'Neal stopped by and asked if he was Billy's friend. She asked if he'd gone to school and where. And then without reason or precedent or anything, she asked if he'd studied the Romantics and whether Byron was ready for some revisionism. Matthew said he had, and didn't know. She asked about the Americans: Emerson, Whitman, Eliot, and Stevens, and Matthew held his own, and then she asked how an able-bodied, educated person like himself had ended up homeless and barely employable, and he told her he'd been prone to self-pity as a child. He told her all about the prone stuff, the diagnoses, the highs and the lows, the deprivations and the excesses, the failures of salt and lithium, the sins of pride, envy, sloth, and a chronic failure to get on board. He said: You know how when you start a new job they always say: Welcome aboard? She nodded. Well, I had a tough time getting on board. She nodded again, and he felt encouraged to say more. He said: The postwar, post-Depression groupthink of the fifties was the true darkness at the edge of the suburbs. He said: Those who belong only pretend to teach others how to belong and despise them when they try. He said: Tolerance and conformity are mutually exclusive remedies. He said: If your generation was such a great generation, how come all your kids are in recovery?

Mrs. O'Neal stood there in the pale sun, well-dressed in merino wool, flats, an Irish sweater, suede jacket, her hair, soft, full, straight, even, with a blunt cut, hair that had never suffered the indignity of a perm, a sister of the Seven Sisters, intelligent, informed, direct. She asked: Do you celebrate St. Patrick's Day, Mr. Wyman? And before he could tell her what he thought of Irish-Americans (being one himself, one who'd just enjoyed the mild bile of free-falling oration), she said her husband held a party every year. She said she did the same in his memory. She asked Matthew to attend, maybe to meet her niece, a woman named Manny. She said Manny liked angry young men.

The party was a ribald initiation. Bobby Sullivan was the master of ceremonies and introduced the Billy Dolan Irish Singers with guitars, a penny flute, a fiddle, and a chick-singer named Molly O'Something-or-other. They did the standards people die for, little baskets of grunt and pride, songs for the well oiled, songs to shed a tear, songs to take up and lay down the vague emotions of the dispossessed. The fiddle player's solo was like a drum solo with a rhythmic stomp that drove the crowd nuts until they gave the guy a standing ovation, which, to be honest, was their way of begging him to stop. There was booze and beer and from one window the unmistakable aroma of marijuana. There were speeches and declamations and impersonations of the Clancy Brothers singing "The Wild Colonial Boy." There were four green fields and all that Irish-American stuff, yellow-green, self-conscious, a little defensive, trumped up passion in search of a cause.

Matthew stood in the library next to a bookcase sipping apple cider and hoped no one would bother him. Mrs. O'Neal found him about three. She touched his elbow and whispered that she'd never fallen for all the lucky-charms nonsense, though her husband had been a charming man. Matthew said: I'm Irish and I'd like the Irish a lot more if Americans were a little less insistent about it. She asked if he read the Irish writers. He said he did when they wrote in English. Then she turned and introduced him to her blond niece with the frosted hair, who was pretty, walked with a limp, and carried a cane with a lion's head.

— ◆◆ —

After Matthew helps his father clean and tidy the place for the third time, his father sends out for pizza. They sit in a side room with the large TV, and Matthew offers to make him a drink. His father declines, saying he shouldn't, and Matthew asks why not. His father doesn't answer but punches the remote hoping to find something familiar and benign. Matthew sits on a couch and tries to get comfortable. The TV screen flips from channel to channel causing the light to pop like flashbulbs over the ceiling and walls. His father stops after one full turn and a newscaster on the local station replays footage from a helicopter flying over Manhattan. Matthew turns to the dark window behind him and looks across the field to the pine trees and woods where Matt's grandfather used to cut timber and shoot birds. Matthew remembers the old guy in a cloudy vision of white anger and bad temper and he wonders, as he wondered in the cold climate of cemeteries, whether he's confused the purity of the elemental with the incompatibility of the elements. Over the years he's read enough to know what lies at the bottom of the can't-go-home-again cliché, the black hole of sophomores insistent on declaring their independence from the very measure they'd used for nineteen years to define themselves. Matthew thinks: Several saints did their time in caves, but the revised histories only talk about the day they entered and the day they left. Matthew knows that reality is the fly-over banality in between and that stones lose their romance when the cold makes everything sharp and extra hard. What's wrong? his father asks, but Matthew just stares at the fading light. What's wrong? his father asks again, irritable with feelings he can't begin to identify. What's wrong? his father yells, and Matthew hears him for the first time and thinks how moments of insight are tissue thin, permeable walls that allow for the passage of ordinary and unremarkable earth.

The next day Matthew and his father wait on Brian and the guys from the Madaux Funeral Home. Matthew spends the day reading old newspapers and listening to the radio. His father watches the sports channel, old games, baseball, football, hockey, sports he doesn't even like, seasons replayed with outcomes determined. It's mindless stuff but his father doesn't care. He watches it through the afternoon when he falls asleep in the lounge chair, only to wake up, watch more TV, and then fall asleep again. It's a kind of anesthetic that drugs him and allows him to enter a parallel world without pain. Matthew's not sure if it's healthy, meaning normal people would tell him it's not healthy, but Matthew's got his own respect for the notion that progress is an illusion, that mental health is a kind of myth, and that all effort, no matter how small or great, flawed or successful, well intentioned or not, invariably comes to nothing, and usually causes more harm than good. So he checks the TV every couple of hours and changes the channel whenever they broadcast soccer in a foreign language.

The second night he's home, after he makes his father soup and a sandwich and serves it on a TV table, Matthew goes upstairs to the guest bedroom where his mother's casket sits at waist level on rollers by the side of the bed. The casket's closed, and when Matthew sees it he feels he's come upon something so intensely private that his presence is more than mere trespass. Just a few inches from where he sits, his mother's body lies within six walls of cherry wood. He touches the casket and from a paper bag removes a small clay sculpture of an angel, genuflecting, holding a pillar or candle stand. It's a flawed piece, but it's the only thing he's been able to finish. He thinks about leaving it in the casket until he realizes that he'd have to open the coffin to drop it inside. So he sets it on top and leans over, resting his elbows on his knees. It's impossible not to be self-conscious in a situation like this. The scene calls for so much drama he can't help feeling like an actor trying to remember lines. And because drama calls into question the whole conundrum of authenticity, all he can do is wait for some sense of moment, which doesn't come, like in the old days when he tried prayer as a means of coping, convincing himself that no matter how empty he felt when he was down, or how invincible he felt when he was high, the Holy Spirit was faithful and wouldn't fail to descend and comfort him just like Jesus said He would.

The lighting in the guest bedroom is natural twilight. There's no sound except for the quiet click of a clock. Matthew whispers something or other. He talks about love and forgiveness until his mind begins to wander and he notices the way the rug bulges under one of the castor wheels. Then he thinks about Billy, and then about his brother. He wonders if he'll ever learn how to make money. He wonders if there'll come a time when he'll enter a restaurant and buy a good meal in return for his good looks. After that his mind goes blank and he realizes that we keep the dead with us at our peril, that there are only three things we know about death: It's inevitable, it hurts those who remain behind, it's the source of that fear which has made humans one half of what they are.

—◆◆◆—

The summer Matthew worked at O'Neal's he repaired a stone wall marking the yard by the crematorium. He placed the flat stones where they fit, taking time to do it right. Mrs. O'Neal would visit and watch, and one time she asked if he'd seen Manny. He told her they'd been getting together for dinners and sometimes a movie. She said Manny had had a difficult life, and she hoped that they liked one another. Matthew was polite and circumspect and watched Mrs. O'Neal as she walked back and forth before the wall, checking it, placing her hand on a flat rock, then moving away. Mrs. O'Neal smoked menthol cigarettes. She said her generation was the last generation to smoke with impunity on buses, trains, and airplanes, in offices and restaurants and bars. People died, she said, but we didn't punish ourselves. We allowed some things and forbade others. Same as today, just different. All this craziness about health, she said. And for what—a few extra years of repetition and forgetfulness.

Over the summer Mrs. O'Neal invited Matthew to visit several times. They had similar interests. She encouraged him to read more. She valued his opinions. She was a vegetarian and extolled its virtues. She'd ask after Manny. She'd ask what he thought of Mr. Sullivan. She valued his insights. She didn't trust many people and neither did he. They had their reasons.

One Friday afternoon in August she asked Matthew to join her in the arbor behind her house. She asked if Manny had taken him to the lodge on Punter's Pond. No, Matthew said, what lodge? The one my husband built over my family's house. No, Matthew said, I don't even know where Punter's Pond is. Mrs. O'Neal said she knew Manny went there from time to time. She doesn't know I know, but I do. I'm thinking you must be careful with Manny. Careful? Matthew asked. How do you mean? I mean that she's a survivor and to survive she's learned how to tell truths that aren't true at all. Like what? Matthew asked. Like how she and I are related. I thought she was your great-niece, Matthew said. I suppose she is, Mrs. O'Neal said, at least for now. Has she lied to me? Matthew asked. It's like this, Matthew, when it comes to women and lies: All women tell their very own truths, and all men must decide if the truths they tell come close enough to their way of seeing things to make the whole thing workable. That sounds a little fuzzy around the edges, Matthew said. As is life, Mrs. O'Neal said, and you're old enough now, healthy enough, to let go of some of the rigidity that goes along with being a hero. I'm not a hero, obviously, Matthew said. You're an idealist, though, in a world that laughs at ideals because they cost too much. And you're an idealist in a world that only thinks about ideals after two cocktails and poor recall of imaginary pasts. Even before I married Tommy I'd become a realist, which makes my lies lies and not some word game. Realists have to guard against becoming cynical, but idealists have to guard against becoming bitter. She said: Something happened, Matthew. Something happened to me. A while ago now. I'm talking years and years, and I can't tell you what it was, but I wanted you to know that I'd been wounded, too, and that it made me cold and hard and practical, which is probably why I like you, because you're like the wounded romantic who can't help himself. You can't be wounded into realism. No, you remind me of what romanticism once was, the time before, I mean. So, I'll tell you what I would have told my son: Be careful with the ones who matter most to you because they're the only ones who can truly hurt you.

In September Mrs. O'Neal asked Matthew if he and Manny would join her for dinner. It was Cal Stevens's birthday and every year Mrs. O'Neal threw him a dinner party. It was a tradition because Mrs. O'Neal's birthday followed one week after, and Cal Stevens always threw a dinner party for her.

On the appointed evening, Matthew and Manny arrived at Mrs. O'Neal's house. Cal Stevens greeted them at the door and invited them to a sitting room where he served drinks and made small talk until Mrs. O'Neal entered and ushered everyone to the dinner table. There were settings for six and Mrs. O'Neal told Cal that Ann Dillon, his paralegal, had called to say that she and Tom Somers, the attorney general, would be late because Tom's meeting with the lieutenant governor had run over. Success has its price, Cal Stevens said, and Matthew asked Manny what they were talking about. I'll tell you later, Manny said, and everybody took their seats, and Mrs. O'Neal's maid served a thin soup from a silver tureen. Cal asked Matthew if he'd ever been to Rome and what he thought of Bernini. Cal was a professional dinner companion, schooled in the nuances of appropriate conversation. Cultured and precise, careful within limits, he was a man of repetition, of rehearsed and memorized quips. But he meant no harm. He seemed to like Manny, and he loved Mrs. O'Neal. Before they finished the first course the attorney general and Ann Dillon arrived. After apologies and introductions and a whimpering kind of happy sadness over the most important duties that can make important people late for dinner, the two of them took their seats—and Matthew recognized both of them. He and Ann had grown up in Meriton, and he and Tom Somers had shared some history, too. Don't I know you? Ann Dillon asked, after she and Tom settled themselves at the far end of the table. Wouldn't that be a coincidence? Mrs. O'Neal said, and Matthew waited for the attorney general to recognize him, to acknowledge him, to say something. But Tom Somers said nothing, perhaps hoping to scoot by, presuming it wasn't impolite because, if called upon, he could blame faulty memory and the passage of time. Matthew could have told the table a lot about Thomas Somers Jr., though. They'd known each other for years; they'd worked at the same summer camp; they'd even gone to the same college before Tom Somers transferred to a place where the kids were wealthier and dressed better. Matthew could have told the dinner guests that the handsome attorney general looked more capable than he was, and that one night, at the end of his freshman year, to his embarrassment, Thomas Somers Jr. had knocked on Matthew Wyman's door to ask for help with some calculus Matthew could solve in his head. Matthew could have told everyone present more than they'd want to know about the attorney general. But to what purpose? Tom Somers didn't need calculus to be successful, and Tom Somers was as successful as he'd always been, even when he failed, and Matthew was as envious as he'd always been, even when he succeeded.

The dinner lasted a few hours and Cal entertained everyone with stories of a friend of his from Yale who studied the paranormal activities of people who could perform all kinds of stunts and tricks. Like what? Ann Dillon asked. Well, Cal said, I've heard, and believe me now, I'm just telling you what my friend told me, and she is very credible, that one of her clients, or patients, or subjects, whatever she calls them, can speak with people who've passed over. Dead people? Ann Dillon said. That's crazy, Manny said, I don't believe in that sort of thing. Mrs.

O'Neal asked: Really, Cal? And Cal said, I'm only reporting what she told me. He's supposed to be like a modern day Houdini, with all that implies, but the thing that seems to be as impressive as his ability to speak with the dead is his ability to levitate. Off the ground. Wasn't Houdini a mama's boy? Ann Dillon asked. I read that somewhere, Tom Somers said. And what is this Houdini's name? Mrs. O'Neal asked. His stage name or his real name? Either, Mrs. O'Neal said, moving her chair, about to stand. Leavitt, Cal said. Deacon Leavitt, though he goes by the Amazing Something or Other. Mrs. O'Neal continued to stand, then paused with a slight hitch, before she straightened and stood at full height. Matthew saw it and Cal asked: Are you okay, Emma? thinking she might have pulled a muscle or something. What, Cal? No, I'm fine, just stood a little too quickly is all. Low blood pressure. Runs in the family. That's good, Cal said, low is better than high, I believe, as he stood with the others. I was thinking, though, Cal said, walking behind Emma to the library, wouldn't it be fun if we had Mr. Leavitt over sometime for a séance or something like that. Mrs. O'Neal stopped again and turned to Cal: Do you really think that's necessary? Well, maybe not necessary, but it might be fun. And just how old is this Amazing Mr. Leavitt? Mrs. O'Neal asked, and Cal said, I'm guessing somewhere in his forties. I don't know, Mrs. O'Neal said, it just seems . . . oh, I don't know, and she turned to her after-dinner escort, Thomas Somers Jr. as she rested her long fingers on the back of his hand: Tell me, Attorney Somers, what do you think about all of this paranormal stuff? Well, he said, I have to deal with hard evidence every day, so I think I'm a little too mired in the here and now to get very excited about the there and then. A good answer, Mrs. O'Neal said, a very good answer, and they led the way into the library for after-dinner drinks, cakes, and coffee.

Ann Dillon followed Matthew and joined him on a long couch while Manny started to pour coffee for Mr. Stevens and the others. Matthew almost gave Ann Dillon a heart attack when he told her that they'd grown up in the same town. She couldn't believe it until they talked about their respective pasts and how they overlapped. She talked about

Meriton where her father owned the biggest construction company in that part of the state, and she talked about the summers her family vacationed in a huge cottage on a lake and how strange it was they'd never met before. I spent summers on the same lake, Matthew said. At the camp where Tom worked? she asked. Yes, Matthew said, I worked there, too. Well, let me tell him, she said, and she was about to make the final connection in a triangle of coincidence and do-you-know when Matthew stopped her, telling her how he remembered her from high school when she and her friends returned from the cafeteria to the study hall in the math department. Why do you remember that? she asked. I don't know, Matthew said, though it wasn't true, because he remembered her for her looks, her face, her body, her clothes, her manner, her money, everything and all of that. But he lied a comfortable, white lie to bypass explanations and inquiries too sensitive for semiformal after-dinner conversation. And you even went to the same college as Tom? she asked, and Matthew said he had. But you two acted as if you didn't even know one another, she said. Isn't that odd, Matthew said, and to think Mr. Stevens knows a person who communicates with the dead. Now isn't that something, Ann said, and she stood to help Manny serve the cakes that were set out on small plates on a sideboard.

————◆◆◆————

Matthew wakes in his old room as the guys from Madaux's arrive to take the casket. They look harried, tired, and overworked, and Matthew and his father don't say anything as they watch the workers carry the casket down the stairs and out the door. There's some question about burial or cremation and Mr. Wyman says cremation. After that, one of the guys pulls Matthew aside and says: The crematorium's down, so we'll hold on to her till it's working again.

That afternoon Matthew takes a walk and sits on a bench by the edge of the duck pond. He remembers the Amazing Levon in the Plexiglas coffin and how they poured the cement and how the world almost ended, without ending at all, and how he and his father continue to wait for Brian. On the far side of the pond a young girl holds a little girl's hand. The little girl runs up to the edge of the water, bends down, and jumps up with a shriek as something, probably a toad, jumps from the bank into the water. Then the older girl takes the little girl by the hand, and they walk away, and Matthew watches them until the backs of their yellow slickers disappear like yellow stamps in the damp distance.

That night Matthew and his father sit in the television room with the TV off. Mr. Wyman says he's worried about Brian and can't understand where he is or why he hasn't shown up. Matthew pours his father drinks, and after a few, Mr. Wyman opens up and talks about his life and his parents and his brothers and sisters. He says he had an older brother who was a prick. He says that happens in families, that there's not much you can do about it. People aren't perfect, he says. They're barely competent. Then he asks about Mrs. O'Neal, the rich lady who owned the funeral home. Matthew tells him about how he found her that Sunday morning with the plastic bag over her head. He says: I really don't think the police care anymore. But how were you involved? his father asks, and Matthew says: I was the one who found her. That's all? his father asks. That was it, Matthew says. Well, how did you end up there in the first place, at the funeral home, I mean? Brian arranged it, Matthew says. What about Brian? his father asks, and Matthew tells him how a year ago or more, Brian introduced him to a cop named Louis LaPorta. LaPorta was a tough guy, Matthew says, and I couldn't figure if he lived his life perfecting the image or if the image was real. Either way, Brian took a lot of pride in calling himself LaPorta's friend because he thought it made him look tougher than he is. Things went along in a normal way until Brian told LaPorta that I'd scored the highest grade on some test, which was a crock and didn't impress LaPorta, the point of it being Brian never complimented me in public unless he wanted something. So I waited till LaPorta said he worked for a guy who wasn't your normal, run-of-the-mill employer. He said the guy was important, that he had all the money in the world, and that he needed some help. I asked what he needed, and LaPorta said: He needs someone on the inside at the O'Neal Funeral Home. On the inside of a funeral home? I said. What the hell's a funeral home got to do with anything? And Brian got pissed, wondering where I got off making fun of it, not taking the whole thing seriously, because it came from important people who were letting me in on important stuff. Then LaPorta said: Let's just say my boss has a personal fondness for the woman who owns the place, and he needs somebody to tell him what's going on there. I asked him: What does he want to know? He wants to know if somebody's taking her for a ride. He wants to know if she's okay or not. And why does he want to know that? I asked. Never mind why, Brian said, pissed, like he was going to smack me. I was just asking, I said, and LaPorta put his hand on Brian's arm and said: My boss has his own way of figuring things out. All he needs from me—all I need from you—is the information.

Matthew's father listens to the story, but Matthew's wordy, dragging it out, and Mr. Wyman feels drowsy after two drinks. Those guys today, Mr. Wyman says, interrupting Matthew, remembering how the guys from Madaux's looked when they carried the casket down the stairs and out the door. One guy had found the thing too heavy for an easy lift and looked as if he might drop his end. Then Matthew's father reminisces about his wife and how they'd met at a restaurant when she'd returned from Chesapeake Bay and had decided to make her home at the family homestead. She was thin then with a gorgeous figure and oval face, like the face of a cameo, or a woman-in-waiting painted by Watteau. He says: Your grandfather left her this house. I know, Matthew says, but now it's yours. It isn't, his father says. Your mother made a will; she left the house to Brian. I can live here till I die, at least that's what the lawyer said, but the house goes to your brother. Matthew watches his father fade and then helps him to bed. The next morning when Matthew tries to wake him, his father says: I'm sick, Matthew, and refuses to get out of bed.

Matthew sets up camp in the main room with the fireplace. He hopes to harvest some truth from the place, certain that, between time and space, space is the more difficult commodity to reconstruct, and that he'll only have to travel through time to witness what happened to the people who lived here to make them so despondent, cold, critical, cruel, and frightened. He's not a detective, and he suspects the scientific method ultimately fails for its linearity and obsession over ever-reducible things, nouns without life in an era of chaos, quantum, and the circular nature of verbs. So he won't look for evidence in the way they do on TV. Instead he'll seek something more precious, essential, and true, whatever he can intuit from the spirit of the place, that holy or unholy thing that floats (suspended as light sometimes suspends itself in air) and is without limits or the petty demands of the here and now. He will dream (as he was born to dream) scenarios of death.

He sleeps the entire day and wakes at night and checks on his father and listens to the old man snore. Then he goes to the kitchen and tries to make a homemade soup. The recipe's in a drawer by the stove. The ingredients are in the pantry. The soup starts to bubble when the back door opens, and Matt turns down the flame. He peeks around the corner and sees Brian's silhouette against the white door by the back staircase. The black figure moves and takes on color and volume as Brian shakes the rain from his coat, turns, and looks down the hallway. He sees Matthew and charges forward, a bull, the landed gent, the owner, usurper, elder brother, oldest son—home now to claim what's rightfully his.

——◆◆◆——

"It took me, I don't know how long to get here," Brian says.

"Yeah, Dad's been waiting."

Brian pushes past Matthew. He drops his bags and says he needs a drink of water. "I'm so hot, Matthew, I got people walking both sides of the street looking for me."

"Who's looking for you?"

"Jesus, Matthew, don't play stupid with me now."

"Who's looking for you?"

Brian barrels through the house, checking each room, taking inventory, getting a snapshot of the place. He returns to the kitchen and leans over the stove, smells the soup, stirs it with a wooden spoon, and sips some. Matthew waits for the verdict. Even Matthew admits his brother's a great cook, baker, everything. It's a natural ability. Brian always knew how to feed himself.

"Not too bad," he says. "Might need a little salt or something."

"I'm not the cook you are, Brian. Never was."

"So, where is he?"

"Upstairs. In bed."

"What's he doing in bed."

"He says he's sick."

"Is he?"

"He's grieving. Yeah, I guess he's sick."

Brian opens a cupboard, grabs a glass, runs water, pours, and drinks.

"Brian, tell me what's going on."

He drinks a second glass of water and rests against the counter.

"They take Mom?"

"Yesterday."

"Those useless fuckers, saying they can't do this or that. I told Madaux I'd have his license if he didn't get his boys in gear."

"You told them."

"Bet your ass, I told them."

"Well, they took her yesterday."

"They cremate her?"

"That's what Dad wanted."

"And what are you doing here? I thought you were in the hospital with all the crazies."

"I wasn't in the hospital."

"I thought you were."

"You knew where I was."

"I did?"

"I was at Billy's."

"Billy who?"

"Billy the Driver. Who do you think—Billy who?"

"Don't get pissed off with me, Matthew. I'm the one who took care of Madaux's."

"Yeah, well, Dad can't understand why you didn't show. He was worried about you."

"Bullshit, the only thing he's worried about is whether I'll let him live here."

"He can live here as long as he wants."

"So, what are you now? A lawyer or something?"

"I know she left you the house."

"Yeah, well, it's the least she could do. Remember, I didn't get to go to college. Won't change a thing though. Not with this fucked up family."

"What do you mean by that?"

"What do I mean? Here's what I mean: You love dad; dad loves you. You hated mom; mom hated you. Dad hates me; I hate him. Now mom's dead, he's useless, and we're left to fight over the crumbs."

Matthew sits and stares at the far wall. Brian waves his hand in front of his eyes. He doesn't like it when people ignore him; he especially doesn't like it when Matthew locks on to that thousand-yard stare.

"So what do you say, Matt?"

"What?"

"What do you say we bury the hatchet, all right?"

"Bury the hatchet."

"Yeah, you know, wipe the slate clean. Start again."

"If it's forgiveness we're talking about . . ."

"Don't worry about that, little brother, I forgive you."

"I wasn't thinking about you forgiving me."

Brian's eyes flash. He throws the glass against the wall. It smashes and pieces fall to the floor.

Matthew says, "Don't try to bully me, Brian. Those days are over."

"Then what are you so pissed about?"

"What do you think I'm pissed about?"

"I said I didn't know you were out of the hospital. I thought . . ."

"That's bullshit and you know it, but even if we forget about that, why don't you tell me what you were doing with Manny."

"Manny?"

"Yes, you and Manny at the lodge on Punter's Pond."

"Me and who, where?"

"Manny Whitman. I saw you through the front windows. That Monday night. The two of you."

"Jesus, Matthew, are you crazy?" and Brian sweeps shards of glass off the table with the rough part of his hand.

"I saw you, Brian; I heard you. Manny jumping around, screaming, 'Don't you understand?' And you saying how you'd get the old lady's money, and how if you needed a fall guy, you could pin it on me—your crazy brother."

"I don't know what you're talking about, Matthew, but if we're making up stories . . ."

"And if that wasn't enough, trying to set me up for murder, then the two of you dropped to the floor and you fucked her right there—legs in the air, moaning and yelling, the whole fucking show!"

"So that's what you think . . ."

"I saw it, Brian! Right there. She and I had been living together for Christ's sake. And you were fucking her the whole time."

"Don't be an idiot, Matthew. Manny Whitman's a con artist, and you're better off without her."

"That's not for you to say."

"Maybe not, but if you can't take the hint of what I'm trying to tell you here, obviously I did what I did to save your ass."

"You saved my ass?"

"I doubt the old lady died on her own, Matthew."

"You don't know that."

"I know you were the last one with her, and LaPorta says you had a bag in your pocket."

"Just stop it, will you? I can't take it when you just say whatever comes into your head—just to confuse people. And, anyway, what does fucking Manny have to do with saving my ass?"

"Jesus, Matthew, listen to you. Isn't it enough to know I sacrificed myself to save you, and now I'm the one who's in trouble?"

"You're not in trouble."

"I'm being set up, all right!"

"By who?"

"I don't know. Maybe LaPorta. He was in on some of this."

"So, now your friend LaPorta's after you."

"He works for Coop Johnson. He does whatever Johnson says."

"And Johnson's after you, too."

"Shut up, Matthew."

"It doesn't make sense, Brian. None of it."

"It doesn't have to make sense."

"The truth is, nobody's after you. You just can't live without being the center of attention, and if you've got nothing to lay on the table, you make your problems bigger than everybody else's so you won't have to deal with some other bullshit you don't want to deal with—like Dad, or Mom's death, or me."

"Why would I even listen to a fucking lunatic like you?"

"Nobody's chasing you, Brian. Nobody's chasing anybody. That stuff is over with. It's old stuff from another world. It's sort of like musical chairs. When the music stopped we ended up doing what we were doing."

"Yeah, well, when the music stopped for me I was halfway out of Hartford, and I was being chased." Brian slaps his hand on the tabletop. "You hear that, Matthew? That was sound. My hand felt it. This table's hard; it's real, and my hand's real. This isn't some made-up TV show in Matthew Wyman's fucking head. This is reality. This is real."

"So now everybody in Hartford thinks you killed Mrs. O'Neal."

"They know I didn't. But that doesn't matter."

"So who killed her, then?"

"How the hell am I supposed to know?"

"But you want to hide here."

"It's my house."

"Well, you got Dad upstairs, and he can't handle any trouble right now. So what do you plan on doing?"

"I own this house, Matthew, and I'll stay here as long as I want. Maybe you're the one who better start looking for a place to live."

"Don't worry about me," Matthew says.

"Yeah, right, I'm sure you got your cemetery all scoped out."

"I could do worse," Matthew says. "I could do a lot worse."

Matthew and Brian separate for a while. The fight's still hot and on-going, but they both need a breather, and both are hungry.

Matthew makes a supper of soup, bread and jam, a couple of baked po-tatoes, and brewed coffee. He brings a tray to his father and sets it on a side table. His father doesn't wake or move. The air in the room is heavy with sleep and darkness.

In the kitchen Matthew and Brian sit at the table in uneasy silence. Matthew ladles the soup and asks Brian how he takes his coffee. He knows already, but he needs to break the silence.

"Any meat in this meal?" Brian asks.

"I've taken up being a vegetarian."

"Since when?"

"I don't know. Since before."

"Like your friend, huh?"

"What friend?"

"Mrs. O'Neal."

"I guess."

"Even the night Cal Stevens had that dinner party for her birthday and that jerk-off psychic, he had to have a special plate prepared just for her."

"How do you know about that dinner party?"

"I know, all right?"

"I thought he hired a chef to come in that afternoon to cook every-thing."

"Cal Stevens was lucky if he knew what day it was."

"So, you did work for him."

"Cooking a meal for somebody ain't the same as working for some-body."

"You cooked for Cal Stevens?"

"Forget about it, Matthew. It doesn't matter anymore."

Brian finishes the soup, sips his coffee, fools with a cigarette, doesn't light it, and begins to talk about himself. Brian's monologue is the con-tinuation of the same fight by other means. The sum and substance of whatever Brian says is meant to stress his importance and Matthew's failures. He begins by telling Matthew how much money he has, how many bank accounts, how many cars he owns, how much property he owns, how important he is, and how he'd take over the world if he could just extricate himself from being the most wanted man in Connecticut.

Matthew listens as he's always listened. It might be better than yelling, though the low-level bombardments of Brian's voice are like body shots that make Matthew duck, cover up, and grow small in his brother's presence, reduced by the blunt force of a narcissist's unrelenting will, relegated to internal nitpicking defenses, noting inconsistencies and outright falsehoods, ever separating the small nuggets of fact from the airy froth of nothingness. Matthew's brother is the only person who can make him feel this way—like a haughty neoclassicist, a man of particularities and details, of pale taste, a man who favors function, restraint, and reason, a pettifogger, fact-checker. In Brian's presence Matthew feels the weight and gravity of normality, responsibility, of something like average, as Brian blows himself up like a blowfish, squeezing everything to the outer rim, proclaiming his genius, driving "very bright" from the room.

"So who's footing the bill here?" Brian asks.

"What do you mean?"

"Don't tell me that loser's giving you money. He's never given me a fucking cent."

"He doesn't have any money."

"Bullshit," Brian says. "She had money, and he squirreled that away over the years. The two of them lived pretty good around here."

Matthew clears the table and places the dishes in the sink.

"He doesn't have any money," Matthew says.

"Believe what you want," Brian says, standing, resting against the doorjamb. "So, you like it here, then."

"It's all right."

"It's as dull as a fucking waiting room. But dull can be good, too. I could use a little dull right about now."

Matthew starts to run water in the sink.

"I'm going to sell the place," Brian says.

"You are?"

"Soon as I find a lawyer who won't charge me. I've got a pigeon in Hartford. He'll do it for less than half."

"What about dad?"

"What about him?"

"Her lawyer said . . ."

"Forget her lawyer," Brian says. "And you just worry about yourself. You've got enough to take care of. LaPorta told me the attorney general wants to slap your ass in jail."

"I thought the attorney general was after you?"

"Don't get smart, Matthew."

"Thomas Somers Jr., candidate for governor."

"What did you do to piss him off?"

"Nothing."

"You must have done something."

"I helped him with a homework assignment."

"What?" Brian laughs. "You are one crazy motherfucker. I mean, okay, maybe you did a little I-spy work for LaPorta, and maybe you were the one who dropped her off, and maybe you were the one who found her and pulled the bag off her head, and, no, maybe you didn't kill her, but . . ."

"You're wrong, Brian."

"What do you mean I'm wrong?"

"You're wrong. You're the one who doesn't know what happened. You don't even know what's happening now."

"I don't, huh?"

"No, you don't."

"And I suppose you do."

"That's right."

"So, why don't you tell me then."

"You don't like to listen."

"This, Matthew, this I'm going to listen to," and he relaxes his shoulders, folds his arms, and takes his seat at the table. "Go ahead, Matthew Wyman. Tell me what I don't know. This will be good for me. It'll build character."

Matthew looks at him and above him and sits on a chair against the far wall of the kitchen, leaning back, his head brushing the underside of the calendar with photos of the Polish Pope. Then he draws breath and begins:

—◆◆◆—

"The afternoon before Cal Stevens's dinner party, the one for Mrs. O'Neal, she called the funeral home and asked Billy to drive me to her place. When I got there she was waiting for me. Her eyes were red, a little swollen. She held a handkerchief in her hand. She told me she'd been made a fool, taken in by someone who wasn't the person they'd claimed to be. She wouldn't tell me who the person was, only to say she had to rethink everything, that her health was failing, that she needed the help of someone she could trust. Then she asked if she could trust me. She said there'd be a difficult time ahead, that she needed the one thing she'd never allowed herself to give—unconditional and un-questioning loyalty and love. She said her marriage had not been per-fect, that Tommy had had his faults, and that there'd been more than one child. A boy who's a lawyer in Buffalo, a girl in San Francisco, and another girl who had red hair like her mother. She almost started to cry again but kept it together and offered me tea.

"She rang for her maid and asked me to wait behind. The maid served tea and cake and after a while Mrs. O'Neal came back with sev-eral hand-tailored suits. She said they'd belonged to her husband, that he and I were almost the same size. She asked me to get ready because I was going to escort her to the dinner party that night. It was her birth-day and the dinner was something Cal did every year. 'Do you want me to call Manny?' I asked. 'No,' she said. 'It'll just be you and me tonight.'

"The hours passed. I showered and shaved and put on her husband's clothes. I brushed my hair back and laid it down with water, parting it in the middle like they did back then, and when she saw me she let out a gasp because I must have looked a little like her husband.

"We arrived at Cal Stevens's house and met the woman from Yale who was studying the psychic. And then we met Houdini himself. His name was Deacon Leavitt. He was older than I expected, but he was in great shape and very handsome with the way he brushed his thick hair back from his forehead. He was wearing a tux, and he reminded me of what it might have been like to hang out with Peter Lawford and the Rat Pack when they were young and on top of the world and had that shining thing you can see in the films from that time. I mean, that's the impression he gave me, and Mrs. O'Neal picked up on it, too, and he was very solicitous of her, very cultured-like, witty without being cruel or too funny. Then there was Cal's paralegal, Ann Dillon, and your rabbi, Mr. C. Coop Johnson, who told me to call him Coop. The attorney general had been invited, too, but he was 'otherwise engaged,' at least that's what Ann Dillon said, and Deacon Leavitt said that was too bad, because he wanted to meet Thomas Somers Jr., Esq.

"The meal was a rack of lamb, mint jelly, all of that, though Mrs. O'Neal did have a special plate prepared. Coop Johnson chided her about being a vegetarian, and he and Cal reminisced about their days at Yale, about the fun they'd had when they were young and beautiful. Coop talked too much about Tommy O'Neal, though, and when he did, he spoke with this melodramatic and insincere reverence. It was obvious, even after all the years, that Coop Johnson was still jealous. He couldn't hide it. He knew Tommy O'Neal had been the better man, possessed of an energy and charisma everyone envied. Mrs. O'Neal just sat there with a bemused smile the whole night. She nodded from time to time, though when the conversation turned to her, she'd say, 'I'll let my escort speak for me this evening.' I'd start to say something, but then, sometimes, Deacon Leavitt would start in as if he were her escort. And he was a charmer and knew how to keep the words flowing without having to say a thing. It was a little practiced, and maybe some of it was memorized, but it was the surface stuff the table wanted. Nothing controversial. Nothing real, but as sincere as actors can make it feel when they've read the script a million times.

"After dinner we sat in a living room for coffee and dessert. Ann Dillon sat next to me and complimented me on my looks and clothes, trying to figure out who I really was, as in 'Are you really from my hometown?' and what my real story happened to be. I told her a second time that I remembered her when she and her friends would return from lunch in the cafeteria, and I probably sounded like a stalker, but she didn't take it that way, saying she'd been such a tiny little girl, that she'd worn all those big sweaters to make her look her age. She said, 'You know, I asked Tom if he remembered you, and he swore he didn't. He said he'd never have been so rude as to ignore you if he'd remembered you.' I told her being forgotten is probably better than being snubbed.

"Then Deacon Leavitt took over. He stood in the center of the room and slowly turned around looking at everybody, not so much staring as just looking. He stopped with me and said something about Bernini, and I said, 'The sculptor,' and he asked me not to talk, but to listen, as he continued to turn. Then he looked at Emma and said he was picking up an image of sheets of paper, stapled together, with tiny type. He said, 'Police—no, not police, a policy,' and Coop Johnson said, 'You mean an insurance policy.' 'Yes,' Deacon said, and then he changed subjects and asked who'd made the desserts set out on the server. Coop said he'd brought them, that he always brought the desserts for Emma's birthday party. Then the psychic said he was speaking with a strong personality, a charming guy with broad shoulders and a big smile. The guy was laughing, though he got serious when he said he wanted Emma to know he was very happy, but that she should be careful. Emma sat there. She didn't move, her face didn't change. Deacon Leavitt said, 'He's going, though he says something about your son,' and Emma said, 'Well, Mr. Leavitt, I'm afraid you've got that wrong. I've never had children.' And Deacon Leavitt, like he was listening to voices from beyond, just put up his hand and said her son was doing well, and this really pissed Coop off. He said, 'What does Emma have to be careful about, and what's this about a son? She told you she never had kids,' and Coop's anger changed things in the room. Deacon Leavitt said he was losing contact. He put his head on his chest and said that was it for the evening.

"Conversations followed, but they went nowhere. Deacon Leavitt might have been sharp, but he was no match for Coop when Coop got pissed, and all the energy had been sucked out of the party.

"Ann Dillon served dessert, and after Mrs. O'Neal finished hers she said it was time to go. Cal got her coat. Ann Dillon hugged me and handed me a piece of paper with her phone number. 'Call me,' she whispered, and Coop Johnson grabbed me by the shoulder and said, 'Now, you make sure you take good care of our Emma.' And that's when Deacon Leavitt darted across the room and extended his hand, saying how happy he'd been to make Emma's acquaintance. I'd never seen Mrs. O'Neal act the way she acted toward Deacon Leavitt. She didn't take his hand. She didn't smile or act gracious. She just looked at him and said, 'I'm not one for parlor tricks, Mr. Leavitt, and my husband's memory is very precious to me, so I take particular offense when someone uses his name to further their own agenda—whatever it might be.' And with that she turned on her heels and left the house.

"On the ride home Mrs. O'Neal began to cry again. Billy stopped at a red light and asked if she was okay. Mrs. O'Neal waved him off, said her stomach was upset, that it must have been something she ate. Then she just stared out the window where her reflection looked back on me.

"When we reached her house she dismissed Billy and asked me to come inside, to help her up the stairs. I took her by the arm and we stepped up slowly, one stair at a time. She stumbled once and grabbed my forearm and surprised me with the strength of her grip. When we reached the hallway that led to her bedroom she asked me to wait. I sat on one of the chairs with the spirals, grapes, and grape leaves carved on the armrests. I was as passive as a kid in a waiting room, obedient, uncertain, and then she called my name.

"She was propped up in bed, resting. 'I listened to them tonight,' she said. 'I listened to every one of them. And I heard their words and sometimes they made sense, but to be honest, for the most part I had no idea what they were talking about. And who was that awful man who kept talking about my son?'

"I told her about Deacon Leavitt, and how he was probably a charlatan, and that the others had talked about a lot of other things, stories from Yale, stories about her husband. 'And who was my husband?' she asked. 'You know,' I said, 'your husband, Tommy.' 'And who's Tommy?' she asked, and she took some tissues and started to cry again.

"I made up a bunch of stuff about Alzheimer's, about how they had miracle cures now, about some new medication that would bring her all the way back, but she waved her hand and pointed to the vanity table and asked me to bring her the small box sitting there.

" 'Can I trust you, Matthew?' she asked. And from the box she took a piece of paper that had gone yellow with age. She said, 'This is the deed to the property on Punter's Pond. I've signed it over to you.' I said, 'No, Mrs. O'Neal, you shouldn't have done that. I'm very grateful, but you don't know me that well. It's too much; I'm not deserving of such a gift.' 'You will be,' she said and from the box she took a bottle of pills and a plastic garment bag. 'These are barbiturates,' she said. 'I've already taken them, and when I fall asleep I want you to put this over my head and make sure I don't wake up again.'

"I stood up and stepped back. I started to gasp for air. I was having an asthma attack. 'I can't do that,' I said. 'How can you ask me to do such a thing?' And she said, 'I can, Matthew, and you will, because it is my last and most fervent request.' I shouted, 'What have you done?' and looked around for her cell phone to call 911. She reached under the covers and held it up. She said, 'Here it is, Matthew, but you won't call. You'll do me this favor and understand that it is a favor, something I want, something that must be done. If you knew what it's like to be lost within yourself, you wouldn't hesitate. You'd know that what I'm asking you to do is a kind and merciful thing.' I said, 'No, Mrs. O'Neal. Maybe you think it's kind and merciful because you're sick and despair of life right now, but I can't be made a party to this.' She said, 'Matthew, you are a party to this, and if you care for me as I believe you do, you will help me. Now, please, help me,' and with that her head fell to the side and her eyes closed and she began to breathe slow, shallow breaths.

"I stood there, overwhelmed. I tried to wake her, but she was too far gone. I said, 'Please, wake up,' and shook her, but of course she couldn't wake up. That's when I looked at the cell phone and wondered what I'd say to the ambulance people and the EMTs and the police and everybody else. I mean there I was, the yardboy, the handyman, the crazy loser, standing in her bedroom, wearing her husband's clothes with a deed to her property in my hand. What would Cal Stevens, Coop Johnson, or even Manny say about this? Then I looked at the plastic bag. It would only take three minutes—three minutes—and it wouldn't be as if I was killing her. She'd already taken the pills. She'd already made her decision. At most I was helping her do what she wanted. So I picked up the bag, opened it wide, and put it over her head. I held it there until, I swear, I saw something like smoke rise up and drift away. And then, at the last second, just before I removed it, she opened her eyes wide with fright and accusation and kicked her legs and raised her arms, her fingers digging into my forearms and hands. She didn't want to die after all, but what was I supposed to do? In one second I'd gone from being her loyal and obedient helper to being her murderer. All because she'd changed her mind. All because now she wanted to live, after I'd already committed the crime that would ruin my life. After I'd already committed the worst sin a person can commit. And the way she fought, her fingernails cutting my arms and hands. I just reacted. I pressed the bag around her neck. I drew it tight to make a vacuum and it collapsed about her features, distorting them as her eyes rolled white and her mouth opened and her tongue flicked about sucking in nothing. And I held her down, and I was so pissed that she'd seduced me into this fucking madness, only to turn on me when I was halfway through it.

"It didn't take long before her body went limp, and she fell back on the bed. I stood over her, gasping, sweat dripping from my forehead to the white quilt, making stains where the print of flowers lay against her breast.

" 'What have I done,' I asked myself, sitting in the chair before the vanity table, looking at myself in the mirror, debating whether I should kill myself, knowing I wouldn't, because although there was murder within me, I didn't have the courage to kill myself.

"After a while I changed clothes. I made sure to hang up Tommy O'Neal's suit without a wrinkle. Then I left her house and walked to Manny's apartment. 'Where have you been all night?' Manny asked. 'Out,' I said. 'Are you drinking again?' she asked. 'No,' I said. 'Well, come to bed then. We have to get up early to take my aunt to church in the morning.' 'Oh, that,' I said. 'I forgot all about that; I just forgot all about it.' "

Matthew finishes his tale and sits back, relieved that he'd confessed to something worthy of a man and not a boy.

Brian debates lighting a cigarette, lights a match instead, and tosses it into the sink where it goes out like a firefly.

"You sure got some imagination," he says.

"That's all you got to say?"

"What do you want me to say? That you tell a good story? Okay, you tell a good story. But that's all it is—a story. Just like the rest of your life, which isn't even a life, but just something inside your head. And that's the problem, Matthew. Everything's inside your head. It's always been inside your head."

Matthew slaps the wall behind him with the palm of his hand. He says, "You hear that, Brian? That was sound, too. My hand felt that. It's as real as anything you've ever done. So maybe you're the one who's being hunted, but I'm the one who killed her."

Brian stares at Matthew as something cloudy and mean-spirited descends over his eyes.

"Does he got any beer around here?" he asks.

"You're drinking again?"

"Might as well."

"He's got some rye, some bourbon, but he doesn't have any beer."

"They sell it in town."

"I guess."

"I'll be taking a ride then."

"Brian."

"What?"

"What if I stay here? You know, with you. We'll just live here, okay?"

Brian opens the back door and cool air rushes into the kitchen. He stands there and puts on his coat.

"Do you remember what you had for dessert that night?" he asks.

"What night?"

"The night at Cal Stevens's. The birthday party for the old lady."

"No, I don't remember."

"You had vanilla tarts," he says, and with that he turns and disappears out the door.

Matthew stays up all night waiting for Brian to come back, but he doesn't return. Around four, Matthew nods off and wakes with a start, gets up, and finds the couch in the TV room. When he wakes a second time it's almost noon, and he walks through the house and sees that Brian's bags are gone, that Brian's gone, too. There isn't any note or anything like that, just the absence and the distance that's always been between them.

———◆◆◆———

The kitchen's a mess. Matthew lights a burner and waits for the water to boil. He opens a jar of his father's instant coffee. He'll drink that and then try to set things right. He's never been neat, but now he requires that of himself. He must keep things in order within the space allotted. He imagines photos taken of others in dire circumstances and how the photos always show a place in chaos, as if chaos were the force (and not the resultant) that didn't steal lives, but stole reasons to live. Matthew figures a person will live as long as he's invested in his surroundings and that the first bond a person breaks on the final journey is the one between himself and the space he calls his own. After that it's a slow and painful free fall through weaker strands, made senseless with one's anesthetic of choice. A clean room can save the world, his mother had said once in a kind of poetry that was beyond her.

Outside the house Matthew hears the voices of good boys, company men, doctors, security guards, normal people, off to work, off to school, the walking dead. He thinks: All groups tend toward definitions of power, levels of authority wrapped about the hierarchy of needs stuffed in a lockbox of violence. And he listens as the sounds of voices narrow to a kind of cricket's buzz, like the sound of cell phones in a distant theater, like the sound of sleeping lovers on a distant train.

Matthew remembers there are only three things we know about death, and then he remembers the time he was put under for an operation and how he came to as if from a black and painless nothing and realized the pain of death is a mind contemplating nothing, but that death itself is nothing contemplating nothing and therefore painless.

All day the wind blows. All night the wind blows.

The universe is safe for souls, Matthew's father says the last day. It's something he'd heard and memorized from a Sunday morning TV service, realizing that in one way he'd never been safe, that in another way he'd always been safe, the realization freeing him to love as he'd wanted to love most of his life. Matthew holds him in his arms all day, feeling the ribs that are shadows beneath his chest, the bone skinny arms, the skin like baked paper. Matthew, he says, forgive your mother, and Matthew says he does. And forgive me, too, he says, I loved you, but I could have loved you and Brian so much more. His father moves a little, raises one arm, eyes clear, and Matthew feels energy pass through him. It's very beautiful, he says, and his body relaxes. He's warm, then still, and then cold.

All day the wind blows. All night the wind blows.

— ◆◆◆ —

Time later, no particular time, no particular measurement of time, just the sense of something new and different, Matthew walks to the duck pond and sits on the bench. In the distance the older girl with the yellow slicker walks around the pond. When she gets close, she says hello and Matthew says hello back.

"No more skating for another year," she says as she tosses a small stone into the water.

"We used to skate here when I was young," Matthew says. "It was one of my favorite things to do."

"Mine, too," she says, and she approaches the bench and sits on the far side with her hands in her pockets, her feet tucked up underneath.

"Are you one of the Wymans?" she asks.

"I'm Matthew," he says.

"We love your parents," she says. "All of us kids, they're so nice to us. When we skated, especially around the holidays, your mother and father would come down here with a huge thing of hot cocoa and muffins and cookies. And they were cool, too. Like fun, you know?"

"I know," Matthew says.

"And they were always talking about you and your brother. They'd tell us stories about how when you were young and your brother showed you how to skate and play hockey and things like that."

Matthew doesn't say anything. He just smiles.

"Well, tell your mom and dad I said hi. I'm Jennifer, by the way."

"I'll do that," Matthew says, and he watches as she gets up and walks to the edge of the pond and continues around to the far side and the trees and the narrow passage through the trees.

——◆◆◆——

Matthew returns home. The front door's open. He figures his brother's come back. He calls his name and hears a man's voice: It's me, Matthew. And Billy the Driver's sitting in the rocker in the middle of the front room. Matthew says it's good to see him and asks if there's anything he can do for him. I'm here for your father, Billy says, his eyes are dull and wide and damp and seem numb to fear. Then Matthew remembers what his brother said about LaPorta chasing him, and he starts for the stairs when Brian emerges from the kitchen and tells Matthew to stop, to stand where he is. What's going on? Matthew asks, and Brian says that if Matthew doesn't move things will be okay. Just stay relaxed, he says. Just settle down, he says. Matthew turns to Billy and asks what's going on. It'll be okay, Professor, Billy says, and the way he says it, and the way Brian approaches Matthew, cautious, like Matthew's a rabbit about to jump away, like he has to be careful, like his brother's afraid of him, makes Matthew want to run, and he would have run if the moment hadn't passed, because Brian's got Matthew by the shirt collar and Louis LaPorta's descending the staircase, having drawn his gun, saying: Matthew Wyman, you're under arrest for the murder of Emma Kost O'Neal.

SEASONAL COLDS

Occasionally the scapegoat is a man.
— SIR JAMES FRAZER, *THE GOLDEN BOUGH*

BILLY THE DRIVER

"Cell phones," Billy the Driver says as he drives his new boat east to Waterbury and then north to Meriton, because all the cars on the roads look like cell phones, and all the drivers in the cars look like cell phone drivers, and it confirms a suspicion he's been working on, that the longer this country hangs around, the more everybody's going to end up looking like everybody else with features coalescing, all the rough edges smoothed away, all the old-world character driven to some outer bank, leaving nothing but the anonymous nothing looks of robots, ad men, or the midlevel kind of loan officers who try not to look down their noses when they tell you you don't have the equity or the background or the future for the kind of money you want.

"Cell phones," Billy says, and he turns off the heater that rattles when it works, and he cracks the window with the sprits of rain striking the window's edge, raising a mist that dampens his cheek. He grabs a tissue from the box on the seat and blows his nose, feeling the itch in the back of his throat, and he remembers how he used to drink the common cold out of his system with a two- or three-day toot with two bottles of Jack, a bottle of Old Smuggler, and, at the end, a bottle of that Jewish Manny-something-or-other wine that tasted like cough syrup, oversweet, thick, good enough to knock him out so that when he woke he'd still be sick, but not in the way a cold makes you sick. "But those days are history," Billy says to himself and he thinks how he never suffered from much other than the drinking when he drank but has suffered all kinds of ailments since he got sober, the worst being the lung infection two years ago that landed him in the hospital and made him wonder how much karma he'd have to pay back for all the times he did what he wanted to do and only what he wanted to do.

The rain shower becomes a squall in the hills south of Meriton and he pushes the Buick he bought three months ago from the neighbor woman across the street, getting it for more than it was worth and paying her more than that because she was old and needed the money. The car didn't run well, hardly started three times out of ten, but he fixed it up in the garage with Darren and Orpheus, the two who were interested in mechanics and wanted to learn about cars. "Good kids," Billy says to himself, thinking how—in this day and age with hysteria running wild in the suburbs with all those SUV moms being certain from watching shrinks on TV that an older man who spends too much time with boys must be a pervert—a guy like himself, Billy the Driver, a bachelor, almost a loner, takes a risk spending as much time as he does with Darren and Orph. "Well, fuck that," Billy says to himself, because there are precious few places these days where youngsters can find the kind of guidance they'll need to get themselves through the minefield that's their lives with the gangs and the drugs and all of that.

"Darren and Orph are good kids and they're gonna learn cars," Billy says as he makes the turn off Route 8 down the ramp to one of the main streets that falls away into town. He pulls over to the side of the road and rolls down the passenger window and asks the first guy he sees where Saint Francis Cemetery might be, and the guy, wearing a toggle coat over one of those white lab coats, like a doctor or pharmacist, asks, "Which one, because there are two?" And Billy says, "The one where they're burying people today," and the guy looks down Main Street and says, "Drive about two miles down South Main past the Cemetery Ice Cream Shop and you'll see a low brick wall and the field and the headstones." Billy looks at his watch. He knows he's missed the church service; he figures he'll go straight to the cemetery and meet the funeral there.

He follows the directions and looks about the town, the old streets and buildings, the stores and the store fronts that are probably considered quaint, though Billy never could figure the difference between quaint and run-down, since "quaint and funky" is nothing but Realtor talk for "shabby and dangerous."

Billy's been here before, and he knows there aren't more than twelve or thirteen thousand people in the whole place. It's just another mill town with its history evident in the buildings themselves—the old ones made of brick with columns and pediments, the houses set on narrow streets with front porches and Victorian lattice work, and then the layers of prefab shit they call progress with the fast-food joints and a strip mall, made up of flat stores gouging the land the same way coal companies ruined Appalachia and places like that.

He drives past the low brick wall on his left and sees the field with old grass made gray with waiting. He turns into the cemetery and follows the narrow road that turns and curves and goes straight along the plots where headstones pop up like Chiclets.

He drives for several minutes before he retraces the way to the cemetery entrance and turns and starts again, this time taking a right where he'd taken a left, down a hill with a shallow slope to the place where two tents, separated by a hundred yards of nothing, stand in the passing storm.

One tent's crowded with mourners and the other tent's less crowded with people beginning to move about, their service at an end.

The rain stops and Billy drops his speed, approaching slowly, not sure whether the boat will sustain itself at a crawl. He stops this side of a second line of limos, hoping not to disturb either burial, hoping the one he'd come for is the one ongoing. He gets out of the car, stretches, and starts across the field toward the second tent farther down the hill from where, in the distance, like daubs of white oils that separate and move, several large birds step about the wet grass. With each beat of the minister's distant voice some energy gathers under them, passes through them, and they rise like a string of white beads, tracing the circumference of a circle, encompassing the whole field, meeting themselves, etching the underside of a dome, their flight more elaborate with each pass and ascent, invisible lines that remain, somehow, like the outer wall of a tunnel or the elaboration of nature's intermittent duty to remind the world of its holy source. Billy watches this and thinks he's the only one until he turns around and sees Officer LaPorta leaning against a car.

"Did you see that?" Billy asks, but LaPorta doesn't budge, and this time when Billy looks up, the birds are gone, having left a white sky full of rain waiting to fall.

Billy steps over damp grass and walks to the tent standing somber and wind touched in the cool air. The minister asks the people to hold hands for the Lord's Prayer. Billy watches the women dressed in black, the men in dark suits, one or two in pale trench coats, hold out their hands, one to the other, some of the guys in the back forgoing the request. They recite the Lord's Prayer, and Billy lowers his head and says the prayer, too, stressing the part where he asks for forgiveness and can expect it in the same measure he forgives others. Then people begin to disperse and through narrow spaces where men and women walk away, Billy sees Brian Wyman standing with his wife and kids. People come up to Brian, one at a time. They kiss him or shake his hand or pat him on the back. Brian's face is more serious than sad, as if he were working on something, like maybe a problem or something he's got to figure out, so that with each person saying good-bye or sorry or whatever, he seems startled out of one mood, brought to a civil and social surface, and then allowed to sink again as soon as they leave him to his thoughts.

Brian's second wife, Carol, bristles visibly when Brian's first wife appears out of the crowd and approaches and kisses Brian on the cheek. It's over in a second, but because Brian cheats all the time and Carol knows it, it's enough to cause trouble. So Carol pouts, ignores the woman she calls "the Bitch," grabs her kids, and hustles them away, making them walk faster than they want with the damp grass staining their shoes.

Brian stays behind and watches the cemetery boys lower the casket by hand. It's the kind of physical labor that returns all the pretty, sad words to earth, lessens the ritual's impact, makes the metaphysical physical and ordinary, because it's nothing more than people doing a job they've set for themselves, a job they're paid for. "We bury our dead," Billy thinks. "We just do. We got other ways, too, but when we think of the dead we think of burial first." And he knows it's as common as breathing, as everyday as eating, sleeping, and everything else. "Human stuff," Billy thinks. "Just human stuff."

Billy steps under the awning, scalloped at the edge of the overhang, the hard fabric brushing the top of his head. He crosses the space at the foot of the casket and circles the grave. He approaches Brian and holds out his hand. "I'm sorry I was late," Billy says, "but I wanted to extend my condolences." Brian takes Billy's hand, holds it, steps close, and gives Billy a man-hug—a press, a pat, and breakaway. He thanks Billy and means it, even as his eyes flicker and move up and over Billy's shoulder. "I need friends like you when God tosses the curve ball," Brian says, the words as sincere as ever, the eyes roaming, looking beyond Billy to someone in the distance. Billy turns and sees Manny Whitman, unmistakable in black, with her cane, with her hair, bright red, almost orange, full, and curly under a broad-brimmed hat. This is news for Billy, and he steps away. He needs space for all the questions and possible scenarios that pop up as quickly as a virus multiplies. There's some history here he knows nothing about, some dealings, even some intimacy, all of that, because that's what made Brian's eyes change as Manny came close and waited for Billy to step away. "I'll be going then," Billy says, nodding to Manny, not saying her name, not wanting to know about her, about where she's been or what she's been doing since she and the cops and everybody else all settled on Matthew Wyman as the one to take the fall. And Billy doesn't want to know why Manny's at the funeral, either—why Brian's never mentioned her in the way a person who knows another person will say so. And Billy tells himself the whole thing's old and settled and done for, meaning the investigations, the assessments and conclusions, and the deal that put Matthew where he is ("for his own good," Judge Nash said). It's old stuff and not to be looked at again, at least not by Billy the Driver, who knows only what he sees, and trusts no more than half of that, thinking what a shame it is the Professor wasn't even allowed to attend his own father's funeral.

Billy leaves the tent and, not wanting to listen, hears the argument begin with whispers. Manny says, "But what about me?" and Brian says, "It's over, all right? Just be glad about that." And Manny says, "It's not over, Brian. I got nothing to show for it," and that's the last thing Billy hears, walking quickly now, not wanting to know any more, passing some of the others who are walking slowly with that lateral "after church" sway people get when they don't focus on anything other than the conversation they're holding. He passes Brian's wife and her kids and stops just long enough to extend his condolences. Carol gives him a look and says, "Thank you," not sure who the middle-aged black man might be, though the kids know him and call him by name as she yanks them to the walkway that leads to the limousines.

Billy looks up and over the expanse of lawn to the far side of the field where the birds flew away, where the boat's parked, where LaPorta stands. Billy waves to him again, thinking it's the Christian thing to do, thinking cemeteries are the kind of places Christians should try to act like Christians. And LaPorta ignores him again, and Billy feels something strange go through him, something uncomfortable in the way some things can point to other things and little things can become heavy and hard with meaning.

"Well, to hell with all of them," Billy says to himself, reminding himself he's got nothing else to do for the whole weekend, thinking how maybe he'll drive south to Mystic and walk along the old streets and look at the old ships, or maybe drive into town and see if anything worthwhile is playing at the Bushnell.

"To hell with all of them," Billy says to himself, passing the son of a bitch, not looking at him, not giving him the chance to snub him again, wanting nothing to do with people who don't know about simple, civil manners, the very thing that keeps us from killing one another, if that's what they do. "Maybe I'll just go home and cook a steak and read a book," Billy says to himself, reminding himself the Celtics are playing on TV and that even though they're not the same team he grew up with, they're still his team. "And I've worked hard enough," Billy thinks. "I've done enough and don't have to do another thing," as if his life were on a table now with nothing else on it except the things he wants to put on it, one at a time, or all at once, so as to keep himself going, interested, really (which is what he means by "going"). "Though I sure do miss the old man," Billy says to himself, remembering Tommy O'Neal and the Sundays Billy drove him everywhere. "And I even miss the old lady," Billy says to himself, thinking about Mrs. O'Neal and how she came to her end because people are greedy and lie and have no consciences or moralities or whatever the gene is that makes some people so guilty over nothing, knowing he'll never know what really happened, except for what he's already pieced together, opening his car door now, getting in, breathing heavy breaths. "To hell with all of them," Billy says, starting the car, cursing it until the engine turns over.

CAL STEVENS, ESQ.

The nurse they assign to accompany Coop Johnson through the prison hospital is about forty, thick, angry, and uninformed as to the identity of her charge.

Coop Johnson takes it in stride as they pass through several segments of the complex with doors that open with a pop and close with a suck. They walk through wards past rows of beds with bad boys wearing nylon skullcaps, down corridors of cinder block painted GSA green. The nurse looks back to make sure the man in the expensive topcoat is following, prepared to scold him if he isn't, when Coop gives her the look he's used over the years, not to display his anger or frustration, but to let a person know he's got a fuse, it's not long, and there's power in the explosion.

The nurse picks up on it. It's instinct more than brains, and she knows to the centimeter just how far she can go with her attitude, so she softens some as she escorts Coop through an empty ward before he enters the last ward where the gravely ill sleep away their last days.

"Last bed on the left," the nurse says.

"Thank you," Coop says, overly formal, codifying the space between those who tell others what to do and those who do what they're told.

"And nurse," Coop says.

"Yes?"

"When I'm ready to leave, how do I notify you or whomever?"

"There's a call button by his bed. Just push that and wait. They'll send somebody."

Coop crosses the room to where Cal Stevens, barely recognizable, under covers, with his head back, his throat exercised and bare, breathes shallow breaths.

"Cal," Coop whispers, and he waits as Cal's eyes catch up with the brain that tells him to look to the side of the bed.

"Who is it?" Cal asks, not because he's blind, but because he doesn't have the will or the energy to remember anything.

"It's Coop."

"Coop," Cal says, tasting the name with a languor that accompanies unspeakable humiliation, wanting to be extinguished when every impression offers up a catastrophic reminder that it's not so easy to depart this world.

Cal drops his head to his chest, turns slightly, and watches Coop take a seat in a metal chair.

"We're going to get you out of here and into a hospital that'll do you some good."

"No," Cal says. "Don't."

"I've talked to the judge, Cal. I've taken care of the bond."

"Get your money back, then," Cal says. "I'm not leaving till I leave for good."

"Don't say that, Cal. I've got my lawyers on it now, and they're working with Mickey Trumble, you know him, out of Bridgeport. That's a guy who takes care of things."

Cal raises his hand and flicks his wrist, a semirhetorical flourish of disdain, as if Mickey Trumble weren't capable of anything when fate writes large the destiny of doomed men.

"I loved her, Coop. You know that."

"Of course, I know it, Cal. We both did."

"She was never the same after that summer. Something happened that summer."

"What summer?"

"Years ago," Cal says, and he coughs with a wheeze and hiccup before he covers his mouth with the back of his hand.

"That's ancient history, Cal."

"But it changed her."

"We've got more important things to attend to. Now, c'mon, friend. I don't want you slipping away on me."

"I don't believe some alcoholic Mick . . ." Cal begins and coughs again, the cough stretching then compressing the muscles of his chest as he appears to rise and bend at the waist. "I say," he begins again, "no Mick—Sullivan was going to get his hands on her money, not after he killed her."

"We don't know that, Cal. I never liked the guy, either, but that doesn't mean he killed anybody."

Cal looks down the length of the bed. He says, "I did what I did because I know he killed her. As well as I know anything, so, please do not," he coughs, "do not disabuse me of this final satisfaction."

"What satisfaction?"

"That I did for Emma what any lover would have done, I avenged her, Coop."

"Listen Cal, let's cut through this, all right? What you did is—you fucked up. You let this whole Emma Kost thing grow inside of you for so long that you didn't know which end was up anymore. God only knows where you got the gun and what you were doing at her house in the first place, kneeling by her bed, asking forgiveness, not for killing Sullivan, but for having failed to kill him before he killed Emma. Jesus, Cal!"

Cal begins to raise his head, coughs, falls back, and stops.

"No, Cal, you screwed the pooch, and now you're going to listen to me: I've paid the bond, and I've got a room for you at Saint Francis, and we're going to nurse you back to health and then take care of this nonsense with you and Bobby Sullivan."

"Leave me alone, Coop."

"And I'll do that, too, but we've business to attend to."

"I said leave me alone."

"Do you want Emma's foundation to fall apart? Do you want the one thing she cherished, her charitable trust—do you want that to dissolve because you lost your head?"

"No, I . . ."

"Then I want you to sign this."

"Leave me alone, Coop, I don't have more than—if I could I'd have willed myself gone by now."

"Just make a mark here," Coop says, and he takes his Mont Blanc and places it between Cal's fingers, setting the paper on his chest.

"What's this?"

"It's a resolution of the board appointing me trustee."

"What the . . . ?"

"I want you to appoint me trustee of Emma's foundation. You of all people don't want her fortune to go down the drain for lack of attention."

"What? No, Coop, I think I signed this."

"Not from me, you didn't, what you signed was your paralegal's appointment."

"Ann Dillon?"

"That's right. She must have had you looking the other way when she shoved her papers in front of you, probably hid it with correspondence and blue backs."

"I appointed Ann?"

"You did, Cal, and now I want you to appoint me. Emma deserves nothing less. She would have wanted professionals like ourselves to take care of that legacy."

Cal picks up the document, squints, and strains to read the heading. His wire-rimmed glasses are folded and resting on a side table near a glass of old water, stagnant with bubbles.

"Where?" he says, unable to see, unable to move. The pen hangs between the tips of his fingers.

"Jesus Christ," Coop says, fed up with Cal's absolute refusal to live, to engage, to take breath and responsibility for the time he's got left. "Here," he says, and he takes Cal's hand with the pen and forces it across the bottom of the page with a black slash over the signatory line next to the prenotarized seal.

"Then take it all," Cal says, and Coop looks down, reaches out, and touches Cal's shoulder.

"We'll be by tonight to pick you up," Coop says, but Cal doesn't respond, knowing in the way the nearly dead take on the talents of seers that he'll never leave this ward.

"I won't be here, Coop."

"Oh, really. And where will you be, then?"

"I loved her," Cal says, as Coop folds the document, places it in his suit pocket, presses the call button, pulls his coat tight, and buttons it more for protection than for warmth against the fetid air and ill humors blowing through the place.

"Good-bye, Cal," he says, and Cal doesn't answer, only to blink his eyes and keep them shut against everything that resides outside himself, nurturing for a time the self-sustaining notion that his love for Emma Kost, unrequited, sad, polite, proper, had afforded his life the architecture of something like meaning, a framework for something that almost rose to the level of purpose.

ANN DILLON

With the black minipuffball two inches from her lips and the razor line of shadow bisecting her smooth cheek, Ann Dillon walks about the well-appointed office and tells the vice consul to the Romanian ambassador that as trustee and chief executive officer of the Kost-O'Neal Charitable Trust, she will commit to the staffing and rehab of several orphanages dotting the Romanian countryside like the dark pebbles of bad memories. "We can do that," she says, her voice a whispering rasp, thick with a cold brought on by a virus wrapped in autumn's changeable weather. "I'll have to ask the board about those other items," she says, passing the second of four wall-size windows, her fingers touching the velvet face of one rose petal, the whole time knowing there is no board of trustees, except for her, because she is the board when she wears that hat and meets with herself in her office once every two months to do those things only the board can do, directing herself as the trust's CEO to do those things only the CEO can do. "I've come a long way," she says to herself, as she listens to the vice consul wrap up his part of the conversation, padding his closing remarks, maintaining a front, so serious and engaged, as indirect as *romanita*, old-world aristocracy, comfortable with approximations and evasions designed to draft the borders of intention, meant to express what isn't there, leaving for inference the implication of what is—a skill suited to children born last in large families who learn the value of never saying what they mean in order to get what they want.

"I've come a long way, indeed," Ann tells herself as the vice consul takes another side trip to Buffalo to get to Albany, and she edits him mercilessly, riding the sound, forgoing the sense, as she remembers the place from where she came—the air-conditioned auditorium with the halogen lights, the almost imperceptible buzzing, the screech of folding chairs, when she struggled to take the bar exam with a summer cold and the menthol-medicinal lemon lozenges with the almost bitter taste. She remembers the proctor, the awful man who decided to ruin her life, the sweaty tall guy with the comb-over and serial killer eyes embedded in many-layered lenses, correcting for some strange astigmatism. She remembers how he stared at her from the moment she entered the auditorium, staring at her legs with his up-and-down eyes, never still, never settled, but wanting to see every part of her and loathing himself for being the kind of loser who looks at a woman that way, knowing he can never have her, but wanting her all the same and then hating her for it.

His eyes, she thought that morning in late July, all those years ago, were furtive little beads popping snatches of look-see as she struggled with her sore throat and then the cough that started midmorning and bothered those around her. And yet she was so smart, so prepared, she sailed through it, her photographic memory scanning three years of law like turning the pages of a *Time* magazine, taking the exam to satisfy her divorced parents, the trade-off for having ruined their lives and expectations for grandchildren—the trade-off for not liking boys.

The morning session ended with a bell ringing, and they collected the tests and she stayed at her seat and ate the sandwich she'd brought for lunch when he crossed the floor and stared at her again, making her hurry, making her finish her sandwich too quickly, making her stand up and walk away, too quickly, leaving some things behind, feeling something come off of him as she passed him, something desirous and pathetic, misshapen, and he repulsed her and he knew it and felt it, and it pissed him off.

The afternoon session called for essays, and she wrote until the bell rang when she put her pen down and looked around, rubbing her neck, thinking only of cool sheets, a warm bed, and several weeks with nothing to do but rest and recuperate. The proctors collected the blue booklets and the guy walked down the other side of the room as Ann reached for the box of lozenges and put them in her purse. Then the guy crossed the room and told the woman collecting Ann's booklet to stop. The woman stepped back; they whispered. He pointed to Ann, approached her from behind, tapped her on the shoulder, and asked her to follow him. At first Ann refused until the woman proctor said it would be best if she just went along, and the three of them walked to a room behind a room behind a door in the far wall of the auditorium. The other proctors had gathered there and they were talking and laughing and drinking coffee from a huge coffee urn. Only one or two looked at Ann as she followed the awful man to another room where a little woman (couldn't have been more than four feet tall) sat on a raised chair behind a small desk, her hair pulled back in a bun, her mouth etched with a downward crease. She asked the guy what the problem was and the guy said he'd caught Ann cheating, and Ann protested and things began to spin out of control when the guy asked Ann to take the box of lozenges from her purse. Ann said he was crazy but placed the small box on the desk before the little person. Then the guy told the woman to take out the white paper inside the box, and she did so, and there, in the smallest possible script, they saw figures and numbers and letters, handwritten, something like a code, and the little woman looked at it, looked at Ann, and started to make phone calls.

"How could you?" Ann's parents asked her, having spent all that money on college and law school. "But I didn't," Ann said, and it was just like the time in college when Ann came home with her friend and told her parents why she and her friend had slept together in Ann's bed the night before Thanksgiving. "But you can't be," her mother had said. "But I am," Ann had said, "and there's nothing anybody can do about it," because "it's the way things are"—though these last words ("the way things are") were not Ann's words, but are the words of the vice consul on the other end of the phone, words that pull Ann back from her memory trip of faces, facts, dates, times, and weather. Now, sensate and present, immediate and solid, she gathers her extended self with the ease and energy of youth. She tells the vice consul that one must see things as they are and not as one might wish them to be, and the vice consul agrees and continues the long withdrawal preparatory to a simple good-bye.

Ann fingers another flower bright in the sunlight shred through silent blinds. Her personal assistant, Lorene, enters the office carrying a wide tray set for late morning tea. Ann smiles and thinks about the night before with Lorene, a tall, pretty young woman, Irish and Thai, and she points to the Hitchcock table by the long sofa under the Matisse print.

The vice consul finally signs off and Ann lifts the minipuffball with the invisible headgear and sits in one of the Louis XV chairs facing the table. "Jesus Christ," she says, as if talking on the phone were the same as digging a ditch, curing cancer, saving the world. But Lorene knows this part of the play and being young, ambitious, dependent on Ann's money (which is the trust's money) she knows how to exaggerate Ann's efforts and praise her accomplishments.

"What is it, honey?" she asks, sounding like the actress-comedian-model-whatever in the movie who tried to soothe Madonna when Madonna was bored and irritable, all presumption offered up in a sweet sop.

"Nothing," Ann says, as she picks up the phone messages on the tea tray—the pink leaves set in a square by the teapot and scones. "Did Mr. Johnson call?" Ann asks, and Lorene says no.

"And who's this?" Ann asks, pointing to a scribbled name.

"I'm sorry," Lorene says. "My penmanship is usually better than that, but the pot had begun to scream, and I was moving between my desk and the kitchen . . ."

"So who is it?" Ann asks, not mad, but busy, determined, the allowable bad manners of office life.

Lorene takes the slip of paper and prays she'll remember the name. "Emma," she says. "No, not Emma—Emmanuella. That's it: Emmanuella. I remember because it's such an unusual name," and she hands it back to Ann who puts it on the bottom of the stack.

"Did the people from Houston call?" Ann asks, but Ann doesn't care about the people from Houston. The question's just a transition, a way to ignore other things.

"I don't think so," Lorene says, playing along, pouring the tea, picking up a scone, careful not to get powdered sugar on her black sweater.

"They probably don't think the trust is up and running," Ann says.

"I think word's getting out, though," Lorene says, "and when these people realize you'll be the person running it now, they'll kill themselves to get in line."

"Place has a history, though," Ann says. "Disappointments, broken promises, whatever," and Ann pictures Cal Stevens, her old boss, the tall patrician with the bow ties, a good man, incompetent, fond of the very best things as long they were served up in a kind of Republican rectitude and understatement.

"I know Mr. Stevens let things go," Lorene says, like a question, still uncertain of her place, not wanting to provoke Ann to disagreement for the sake of disagreement.

"He did," Ann says, leaning forward. "I don't think he could bring himself to give away money he thought belonged to Emma. Everything he did was because of her."

"He loved her, you said."

"All his life."

"You went to his funeral."

"I paid for his funeral, or the trust did. His own family—Jesus, they're too old or dead and even the ones who could have been there were too embarrassed. People think he died from all of that, the scandal, the fact he couldn't raise the bond, the fact he went away. But he didn't die from any of that. None of that killed him. What killed him was a broken heart."

"I've heard about that," Lorene says, "how a couple can be together for years and then one dies and a month later the other one drops dead of a heart attack, even when there wasn't any history of heart trouble."

"Broken heart's more than just a word," Ann says, picking up the phone slips, going through them one more time.

"I hope that's not how it will be with us," Lorene says.

"What on earth do you mean?" Ann asks.

"What I mean is I want both of us to be 112 in a big bed in a nursing home and one afternoon we just drift off together."

"I don't know how romantic that sounds. Anyway, we can't be 112 together."

"Why not?"

"I'm twenty years older than you."

"Yes, but age doesn't matter after 110."

Lorene stands and rubs Ann's shoulders and Ann rewards herself with a sinking, momentary letting go. She tells herself she deserves a rest, because she works so hard; she does so much: She took over the trust; she's seeing it through probate; she out-conned a con artist; she keeps a beautiful young woman; she's impressed her parents who live in separate cities; she's made money, obtained position and the kind of power that comes with money. "Yes," she says to herself, "I deserve a rest."

The phone rings and Lorene crosses the office and picks it up. Ann, still warm, still sinking, turns in her chair and shakes her head to say she's not available to take calls. Lorene identifies the caller, mouthing the words, "Your mother," and then speaking into the phone, "Yes, Ann told me you planned to meet in New York sometime. That should be a fun trip for the both of you."

Ann settles back in her chair, grateful not to have to talk with her mother.

"I'll be sure to tell her as soon as she returns," Lorene says, and she picks up a letter from the desk, stationery from the French Embassy in New York, an invitation to a charity function for something or other, and she tells Ann's mother that her daughter's with the French ambassador.

Ann listens to all of this. She knows why her mother is calling. It's because Ann's high school class is holding a reunion in Meriton in a few weeks and Mr. Dillon's hopeful his successful daughter will choose to attend. But Ann wants nothing to do with Meriton or reunions. She wants nothing to do with the hometown people who made her feel inadequate, not because she was, but because they were envious, because she was so much better than they were—smart, wealthy, beautiful, and gay, and, because she was gay, doomed to downplay all of it in a mill town filled with dumb, shrewd, crafty, old-world people with an unwavering love for the kind of cruelty and sentimental nonsense that attends all mediocrity. No. Her father might want to show her off now—show the mean-spirited little town how the prodigal daughter turned out, but Ann wants nothing to do with the expenditure of all that energy just to be pleasant, to make nice with overweight fanny-pack women in stretch pants, greasers and their cars, rah-rahs with their small-town ambitions, the ones who made her feel small and not quite right. "Fuck them," she says to herself, worked up now, angry, wanting her mother off the phone.

"I'll tell her," Lorene continues, when Ann's cell phone rings and Lorene picks it up and hands it to Ann. "I have to take another call," Lorene says, and, "Yes, I will be sure to tell her," and she lowers the receiver as Ann answers her private line.

"Hello," Anne says, noncommittal, flat, the cold struggling to disguise the anger. "Then did you speak with the commissioner?" she asks, and Lorene knows enough to excuse herself.

"I already said I'd attend the dinner," Ann says, "but you said you'd take care of the other." Again there's a pause. "He's going to be the fucking governor, for Christ's sake. Are you telling me your brother can't twist a few arms at some second-rate commission?" She holds the phone and listens, and then explodes again. "Now listen, Drew, let's get a few things straight here, because maybe your brother's got a short memory." Drew tries to answer, but Ann interrupts, "No, Drew, I said you listen: Eight months ago he was down ten points and that was before the rumors started. My godfather asked me to do a favor, and I came forward and stood by his side and looked up at him with those lovey-dovey Nancy Reagan eyes, and now your brother is up six. But I haven't done it for nothing, and my godfather knows I haven't done it for nothing, and you assured both of us that you'd deliver. Now this deal isn't closed till that fucking commission scores my exam and admits me to the fucking bar." Again there's silence as Little Drew, Sweet Drew, backpedals and stammers, wondering what a Kennedy would do in a situation like this. He tells Ann he'll do what he can with the Bar Commission, but Ann says that's not good enough. She says, "You tell the attorney general I'm going to be a lawyer in this state or the *Hartford Courant*'s going to run an exposé that'll ruin his career before he gets a chance to ruin it himself."

Ann clicks off the phone and throws it against the far wall where it shatters and falls to the carpet.

Lorene looks in, tentative, uneasy. "Is everything all right?" she asks.

Ann stands with her back to Lorene. "Order me a new cell phone," she says, "and charge it to the trust."

Lorene makes a note.

"And try Coop Johnson again," Ann says. "It's about time his favorite little girl threw one of her favorite little tantrums."

DREW SOMERS

Columbus Day and the Victor Emmanuel Society gathers for its annual Citizens' Dinner in the ballroom of the Hotel Chevrie, after which they'll bestow on Mr. Coop Johnson their Honorary Italian-American Citizen of the Year Award.

Drew's cell phone vibrates three times before he checks the incoming number and takes the call in the coatroom behind the curtains behind the dais. His brother, the candidate, is midspeech, full blow, referencing again the idiocy of the Congress that changed "french fries" to "freedom fries" in the congressional cafeteria when France urged caution and more debate prior to the invasion of Iraq. He says the Italians wanted more debate, too, but the congressmen liked the pasta dishes too much to mess with that part of the menu. The comment sparks laughter and light applause, and Somers uses it to advance more substantial criticism of the administration's foreign policy. The speech might be a little heavy on the international news, but given the event and future considerations, Drew's convinced his brother to lace his speeches with more foreign policy to build a record as they look to future campaigns for the Senate and beyond.

Drew listens for the smattering of laughter and applause he'd hoped for and then answers the cell phone vibrating in the palm of his hand.

The caller's a reporter from the *Courant*. He's a young kid, unknown to Drew. The kid says he's going to run a story about the candidate that rehashes old rumors and something new that happened aboard a sailboat earlier that summer. The old rumors are a chronic threat, but Drew goes pale with the new stuff and feels the anxiety carve out a dome of air that becomes a vacuum and pulls him into himself. He steps two steps forward, heavy steps, deliberate, determined to maintain balance, to keep his composure. He's silent as the kid rambles on. He knows that everything will depend upon the tone of voice he's able to project, everything will depend upon the next thing he says.

"That is such utter nonsense. Is this for real or some kind of joke? C'mon, guys, we're at an awards ceremony here; he's talking with the crowd; we don't have time for the frat stuff."

"This is no joke, Mr. Somers. My source is very credible."

"Did you say 'your source'?"

"Yes, sir, I did."

"Your source," Drew says, and the disdain is palpable. "Now look, Cannava, Cannoli, whatever the fuck your name is, I'm going to assume that you're a young turk looking to make a name for yourself. I'm going to assume that you're too new to this city to comprehend the extent of the mistake you're about to make. I'm going to assume that you like working for the paper that pays your rent and everything else, and I'm going to assume that you want to keep your job. So, listen to me very carefully, son, because I'm about to give you the best advice you're ever going to get. You forget your source. We know who she is and we know what she's worth. You forget this story, because it will only hurt you, and you forget that you ever made this call, because it can only hurt you. You do that, and I'll forget it, too, and everything will go back to life as we know it around here. Otherwise, kid, you'll have to prepare yourself for the law of unintended consequences."

With that Drew slaps his cell shut and returns to his seat on the dais where his brother presents Mr. Coop Johnson with a lovely plaque etched with something in Latin.

———◆◆◆———

The after-dinner gathering in the Presidential Suite is packed with the best of Hartford's business and political community, all drawn together to remind themselves that power's nothing if it can't be enjoyed from time to time in the company of one another. The attorney general, running hard for governor, stands at one end of the room. He looks tired; the eyes are heavy and the brows descend as if he were sad. Drew can see it and with the phone call from the reporter he's concerned that his brother's career might have a built-in self-destruct button. Up till now there's been nothing but advance and hide, advance and cover up, advance and duck-and-cover, advance and retreat. Fifty years ago the boys had let everything slide with Kennedy, even liked most of the shit he pulled, but times are different. Clinton found out how things had changed, and after Clinton any public person has to be very pure or three times as careful.

The crowd mills about and power flows of its own accord from pod to pod. A light music filters through the room from speakers in the ceiling, something off a satellite channel or maybe a tape prepared by the hotel. The conversations create a low hum, and the men perfect the stance of one hand on chilly glass, undertouched with napkin, one hand in pocket, head bowed, the nods and whispers. This is the preferred stance of powerful men who converse with powerful men, as if nothing said has not been said before (the repetition understood and encouraged), the import coming not from the words but from the person who's saying them. These are the small moments of agreement and affirmation necessary for the turn and pull of the invisible gears and levers that make things work. Some matter's about to take shape with near silence. Some force is about to infuse an otherwise inert system and move it forward. A deal's about to be closed, a reputation's about to be made.

"Yes, I agree completely," Tyler Bach whispers to Judge Nash and some elderly gentlemen of Hartford Casualty when the door opens and Coop Johnson enters the room. The entrance is casual, but everyone feels it and the men with cocktail glasses and the remains of shrimp tail in the folds of damp napkins step back and make room. All smile. All greet him with a murmur of respect that mimics light applause. This is necessary and uncomfortable for Johnson. He need not be reminded of himself—true power always self-informs.

"Please, gentlemen," he says, "they must be serving very good booze to get a rise like that," and the wit's perfect and the laughter oversails the applause which tends to embarrass everyone.

Drew Somers crosses the room and waits by a small table near the end of an empty couch. He watches Coop Johnson move from man to man, group to group, shaking hands, laughing, promoting more complex banter.

Drew waits, torn by the opposing forces of concern and the supplicant's etiquette. Drew has no real power. And, except for a few perks of office, neither does his brother. At this stage of the attorney general's career, Tom and Drew Somers are merely the hired help with nice job titles. Ann Dillon, the dreaded "source," however, is Coop's goddaughter. He owns her and she'll do whatever he says. He owns her and because he owns her he'll underwrite just about everything she does. Drew knows why his entreaties to Coop to call her off have failed. Between a future Governor Somers and Ann Dillon there's no contest. Coop will back the girl, and yet he's hesitated to push her admission to the bar, the one thing she's demanded since early spring. "There's a reason," Drew says to himself. "Coop won't push it for his own reasons, but we're the ones catching hell for it."

"Mr. Johnson?" Drew calls out, having shadowed him across the room until they stand a few feet from where Tom Somers sips bottled water and tells stories from Trinity.

"Yes, Drew," Coop says, turning from Judge Nash to face Drew. "You've been busy tonight."

"Mr. Johnson, if you could give me a minute, we really have to talk about something."

"Of course, Drew, maybe you can come by the office tomorrow. Now let me think, yes, I'll be in tomorrow, late morning."

An overweight gentleman in a suit tailored by giants to fit his frame steps in front of the judge and interrupts the conversation. The guy leans forward, coughs into a napkin, excuses himself, and grabs Coop's hand with two huge hands, bowing and leaning forward as if he were about to kiss Coop's ring. He tells Coop how great he is and all of the praiseworthy nonsense that diminishes the big guy as he speaks. Coop cuts him short and introduces him to Judge Harry Nash, one of Coop's favorite judges, and Drew Somers. The guy puffs himself up, turns his head, sneezes, and takes off again, shaking the judge's hand and then telling Drew how great he is. Drew notices the perspiration and short breath of obesity. He can't wait for the guy to move on. But the guy keeps talking about the "new governor" and how great Tom Somers will be for Connecticut, and Drew watches as Coop slips away, quietly, engaging in conversations with other men, comparing golf scores and the make of certain clubs.

"Mr. Johnson," Drew calls out, his voice too loud for the company, the call too forward for the event.

Coop Johnson turns slowly and looks at Drew, more admonition than response.

"Tomorrow, Drew," Coop Johnson says, turning before he finishes the name, making it clear that he's putting off the governor and his brother, knowing the whole story from the kid reporter long before the kid reporter called Drew, knowing his goddaughter, the cheat, the source, still wants to be a lawyer and has decided to make the candidate's life miserable until she is, knowing it's in his best interest (Coop's best interest) to keep her from getting what she wants, knowing that his refusal to pull that lever makes her his weapon and check on the young and future governor's power—as important as anything in the game Coop Johnson plays.

JUDGE NASH

The limousine's too warm for the morning sun that rises over the line of pine trees near the edge of the field. Coop lowers the divider and tells his driver to lower the heat.

Outside the tinted window the sun continues to rise and strike the white marble stones measured like markers throughout the field. In the distance Coop sees the huge blue tarp that covers the block of marble he imported from Italy. It stands at the head of Emma's grave. Coop wants someone to sculpt a copy of Bernini's most famous work, the cupidlike angel about to pierce Teresa of Avila's heart. He even went to Florence to find an artist who said he could do it, but the Florentine wasted the whole summer making drawings, taking measurements, and accomplished nothing. Coop fired him and started looking closer to home. Money's no object, of course. The monument will be Coop's memorial to his love for Emma.

A cloud passes over the sun. Coop lowers the divider and asks the driver if he's seen anyone enter the cemetery. The driver tells him he saw a Pontiac drive through a few minutes ago, but it disappeared down the road on the far side where they've ordered the most recent burials.

"A Pontiac?" Coop Johnson asks, and Eddie says "a Pontiac," naming the make, color, and year. "That's him," Johnson says, and with that there's a small tapping on the tinted window, and Coop looks up and sees Judge Harry Nash standing in a gray topcoat, collar up, a white scarf wrapped around his throat.

"Get the door for him, Eddie," Johnson says, and Eddie jumps out of the car and walks to the back of the limousine and opens the door for His Honor.

The light from the partly cloudy morning fills the dark interior and then disappears as Eddie closes the door behind the judge.

Harry Nash, a big man, balding with a comb-over, shares the back seat with Coop Johnson.

"Thanks for coming, judge."

"No problem, Coop. Happy to do it."

"Looks like our boy's going to do well tomorrow."

"I haven't been following the polls much lately. Where does he stand?"

"Up eight among likely voters."

"Governor Thomas Somers Jr."

"Yes."

"And what about DelVecchio?" Judge Nash asks. "Our very own Connecticut socialist."

"Bishop Ravezzi's trying to get the vote out for him in the city, but eight points is a lot to make up in one day."

"America's Workers Party—like the rest us of don't work," the judge says.

"Democrats endorsed him. Held their nose, but they endorsed him."

"Well, God bless him, I hope he takes the whole Democrat party over the side with him."

"Tommy Somers will be a good boy for us."

"You sure of that, Coop?"

"Absolutely."

"He was a nondescript attorney general. I can't remember one thing he did."

"That's a good thing, don't you think?"

"In the end, less is always better. I just hope the power doesn't go to his head."

"What power?"

"Good point, Coop."

"Power's not a word I'm all that comfortable with, anyway."

"Really?"

"It's awfully close to pride, and pride can be a bitch."

"So, Coop, I take it you want to know what's what with . . ."

"I do, Harry. As you know, Emma and I were almost strangers near the end, and between you and me, ever since Tommy passed I think she went a little funny, but I do want to know what happened to her."

"Well, it's closed now," Judge Nash says. "It's over is what I mean, at least as far as my court's concerned. Now whether I dropped the gavel on the final disposition of the thing, well, you know as well as I there are more ways to appeal things than there are lawyers. But for purposes of your company, I did make a finding that there was insufficient evidence to contravene a finding of suicide. I take it your lawyers can run with that, depending on how you want to play it. If you pay out, probate's all but certain to rule everything should go to the trust."

"Who's the probate judge?"

"Judge Hart. You know her?"

"We've met."

"She knows what's what, Coop. You'll have no trouble there."

"I've got a good girl working at the trust for me now."

"Since Cal, you mean?"

"That's right."

"Ann Dillon?"

"That's her."

"Well, unfortunately, she brings me to issue number two. Now, I know she's been on Somers's agenda since last year, but I've already talked to the administrative judge and he's not going to budge on her application for reconsideration."

"That's no problem, Harry. I like her and she does good work for me, but I'm not sure she should be admitted to the bar. After all, cheating is cheating."

"That it is, Coop."

"But you committed that young man?"

"Matthew Wyman?"

"Yes, Matthew Wyman."

"Now, that is a story worth telling. The deal was pretty simple once you called off the D.A."

"I didn't call off anybody, Harry."

"Well, Somers called him off then."

"Maybe he did. I wouldn't know," and Coop lies as easily as he remembers the night when the Somers boys came to pay their respects, and Coop admonished the young attorney general about pursuing an investigation that would go nowhere.

"My point is," the judge says, "the deal was easy for several reasons: First, there was barely enough evidence to make it past a preliminary hearing. All we had was the older brother's statement and this officer's contradictory reports about a plastic bag in the kid's pocket. That might have been enough, except the same officer, this LaPorta guy, hadn't mentioned the bag in his first report and couldn't come up with any explanation as to why. I considered the indictment, but it would have been a waste of time. Any first-year defense attorney would've chewed it up."

"So, you all compromised?"

"Didn't need to, really. D.A. Reis . . ."

"He the one who stutters?"

"That's right. He was willing to drop charges, and the kid had already been committed by his family months ago. He was AWOL. He'd sneaked out last spring, so it was nothing to issue an order putting him back inside, and the irony is he's the one who's happiest about the outcome."

"What do you mean?"

"This guy's thrilled to be in a hospital."

"Doesn't sound right."

"He told me. He said, 'Judge, where else am I going to get three hots and a cot and all the time I need to do my artwork?' And I said to him—I said, 'Matthew, have you given any thought to living in a monastery or something like that?' And you know what he said, Coop?"

"What?"

"He said, 'A monastery!? Jesus Christ, Judge, I might have a few problems, but I'm not crazy!'"

Coop laughs a small laugh, an almost laugh, a cough.

"Have you ever met this guy, Coop? I mean have you ever talked with him?"

"I met him, once."

"Did he make an impression on you?"

"Not that I can remember."

"Well, I spent an hour with him in chambers, and he is one different guy, marching to one different drummer."

"How's he different?"

"Well, first, he's as sharp as they come. Very smart. He spent fifteen minutes going on about this and that."

"What is he, a professor or something? A scholar?"

"No, Coop, he's an artist."

"An artist?"

"A sculptor."

"Really."

"I had to send my clerk out to the hospital a few weeks ago for some paperwork on him, and she came back and couldn't stop talking about this guy's stuff."

"He's good?"

"Coop, you would love this guy. He makes sculptures like from the old times, classical stuff, Renaissance—it's just beautiful."

"You've seen it, too?"

"I went out there myself after my clerk couldn't stop talking about it."

"But how is he mentally? Is he sick?"

"Coop, he's different and sometimes not all that easy to understand, but I think it was easier for people to call him sick. And once a person gets tagged with that label, I mean, forget about it. You've got it for life. You know, it's virtually impossible for a sane person to prove that he's sane. It really is."

"But, Harry, are you sure he didn't kill Emma?"

"No evidence to support it."

"Forget the evidence, did he do it?"

"Coop, let me tell you, I was never a great lawyer, and God knows I've only been a fair to middlin' judge . . ."

"I wouldn't say that, Harry."

"No, Coop it's true. I've liked being a judge, and I've done the best I could with what I've got, and, all told, I think I've done an okay job. I don't think I killed anybody who was innocent, and I did my best not to ruin somebody's life when I thought the evidence or the law was an ass, no matter what the jury said. I know I got a reputation for being lenient, maybe even overly susceptible to outside influence, if you catch my drift. But you know better than anyone, that I wasn't, I'm not, and I've done my best."

"Jesus, Harry, all I asked was whether he killed her. What's the matter with you? Are you depressed or something? Do you need a vacation? I'll talk to Weaver and get you a sabbatical. You can stay at my place at Saint Bart's. Wherever you want to go, for as long as you want."

"Coop, you've always been more than generous, and Ida and I have appreciated your friendship over the years, but this Matthew Wyman, Jesus Christ—not only is he incapable of harming anybody, he's all too capable of taking the blame for somebody who did."

"Any idea who did it then?"

"As I said, there's insufficient evidence to contravene a finding of suicide."

Coop looks out the window to the blue tarp and the place where they buried his first love. He thinks about the impossibility of suicide, the cost of the marble, and the guy from Florence who couldn't produce. He says, "Thanks, Harry. And think about a vacation, will you? I'll set you and Ida up for as long as you want."

Harry looks at Coop, says nothing, shrugs, offers his hand, shakes hands, and leaves the limousine.

MANNY

Manny's changed her hair to its natural color, declarative red, and calls herself Emmanuella. She hopes the changes will herald a change of fortunes. She's never thought of herself as being superstitious, especially given the way she was raised with a mother who deemed practicality the realpolitik of hard lives lived in a material world. And yet, like many practical people, good with numbers, inventive with plots, Manny's mother—the original redhead with extraordinary legs—from time to time, did toy with the Tarot deck or the Ouija board, a name that defeated her any time she tried to spell it. So Manny inherited the practicality, the inventiveness, and a hint of superstition that surfaced when fortunes were low, when luck ran down, when she'd take up the bottle in a cycle of entreaty, disappointment, and blame.

She sits at a back table in the corner bar where she used to meet LaPorta. Clive, the bartender, waits on her with Brit politeness, and Manny tips him better than he deserves. She spends the extra dollar because it's nearing the holiday season and she's in one of her almost biblical modes, primarily New Testament, RSV, repeating scriptures to herself, believing in the giving-to-receive axiom as adjunct to the ill-defined spiritualism of tertiary alcoholism.

Manny's struggle with addiction might be uniquely personal, but it continues to trace the template of most alcoholic lives: Self-medication worked until it didn't work; she took from it what she could for as long as she could; she suffered from it when it offered nothing but pain and the compulsion to keep doing it.

She hit her first bottom when she was a secretary for a tool-and-die maker in Waterbury. Her boss was no stranger to similar troubles and he'd been kind enough to get her into rehab where it took a week before she realized she'd have to stop if she wanted to live. Her liver was swollen and almost cirrhotic.

Manny's mother was living outside of Bridgeport then. She hadn't aged well; she hadn't mellowed at all. The mean streets and fast life lived among men who couldn't care less evinced themselves in lines hardened as much by age as by the unkind indictment of one who'd played a game and lost, suffering the defeat of an inner self that bankrupts the starlet before the hair goes white and the body sags.

She wouldn't visit Manny in rehab. She figured the girl was making too much of nothing. People drank—that was the way it was: People drank and did crazy things, and then they woke up and went on about their lives; and none of it, not one headache, hangover, shiver in rough sheets in dull morning light, required doctors or hospitals or all those nosy communist social workers who had nothing better to do than to press themselves into places they didn't belong.

Manny cleared up some during the second week in rehab. She felt good enough to check herself out, but didn't do it after she made friends with a truck driver from Seymour who convinced her to stay. They spent their afternoons together and talked about everything, and one day he told her the new wing at the far end of the hospital complex had been named after some guy named Kost whose granddaughter gave away more money in a month than most people in Fairfield county made in a year.

"Kost," Manny said, and the guy said the lady's name was "Kost O'Something-or-other," because she'd married some Irish mortician in Hartford. It wasn't all the information Manny would need, but it was a beginning and more than enough to get her started.

She checked out of rehab after thirty days and moved to Simsbury and rented a room in a doctor's house. The house was huge and the doctor was old, semiretired and lonely, having lost his wife of forty years to throat cancer. He was a skinny guy with sun-browned skin. His name was Walker and he was generous and believed in AA and told Manny he'd forgive the rent, month to month, if she went to meetings and helped out around the place.

Manny spent most days reading and then she took up writing for therapy. She started a journal but turned to fiction when she discovered that she could lose herself in characters and stories and places she'd never been, making it all up as if she had the power to create people who wouldn't exist unless she gave them life. It was a heady experience and she developed a talent for dialogue and for writing letters in different characters' voices. She likened it to a kind of ventriloquism, and she wrote several lines of correspondence between imaginary lovers, burdened with the obsessions of romance while living at world-wide distances from one another.

She went to her AA meetings, and sometimes she'd travel as far as Middletown to make a women's discussion group. After a year in Simsbury, she became the doctor's housekeeper, home-health aide, all-around girl Friday, and the chairman of her home group. She ran great meetings and one Monday night in late winter she invited guest speakers from Hartford. That was the night she met Brian W. He wasn't tall, but he was broad with thick, muscular arms. His clothes were new, pressed, and clean, though they appeared to be one size too small. He wasn't her type (if you could say she had a type since she'd been pansexual for most of her life), but she watched him and was drawn to him despite herself, and after the meeting when he shook her hand and allowed his personality to overwhelm her, she felt herself taken in and gave herself to some unspoken promise of something, anything, that might continue after he and his friends left for Hartford.

Within days she learned that Brian W. was married to somebody named Carol, that he had kids, that he worked in a hospital, and although some of it mattered, most of it didn't, so that one night, weeks later, after the affair had lost some its spark, having been draped with the comfortable gown of routine, she asked him about some woman named Kost and about the charity that gave away money. Brian, who prided himself on knowing the inside story of every story told her all about Tommy O'Neal, the war hero, who'd inherited a mortuary and had married an heiress.

"He died a few years back," Brian said, "but he left a widow. I think she's the one you're talking about."

"I'm Tommy O'Neal's daughter," Manny said.

"You're what?" Brian asked.

"Tommy O'Neal was my father."

"No."

"He was. I guess you can say my mother was one of his girls."

"His mistress."

"That's right."

"But you didn't know about Mrs. O'Neal."

"I knew there was a Mrs. O'Neal; I didn't know she was Emma Kost O'Neal."

"The heiress."

"The very wealthy heiress."

"Well," Brian said. "Well . . ."

It's hard not to think about money when so much of it resides just one double helix away, and Manny and Brian plotted and schemed throughout the spring and summer as to how they could get their hands on it. With the end of autumn and the advent of the holidays, they finally settled on one of many proposed plans. It was a straightforward, moderate-risk, even-odds plan: The week before Christmas, Manny would arrive at Mrs. O'Neal's. She'd ask to meet with Mrs. O'Neal. They'd sit together. They'd have tea, or maybe not. Either way Manny would identify herself and declare her intentions. She'd say: "I'm Tommy O'Neal's daughter, and you're not my mother. I know how much you want to preserve Tommy's good name and memory, so I'll become your niece, and you'll provide me with an allowance and a modest inheritance."

Mrs. O'Neal would probably say, "Get out or I'll call the authorities."

And Manny would say, "Fine, and I'll call the papers with a lovely human interest story for the holidays."

"This is blackmail," Mrs. O'Neal would say.

"Of course it's blackmail," Manny would say, and Manny would get what she wanted or she'd get out of town. As Brian said before Manny put the plan into action, "It's one of those 'nothing ventured' things."

And it went better than anybody could have expected. Tommy's good name was precious to Emma Kost O'Neal, and Emma, having grown up among some very wealthy, very careless, and indiscreet people, was not unacquainted with cost-benefit analyses and ways of keeping things quiet—at least for a while, at least for a time. There was plenty of money to spend and Emma spent it. Manny became her niece, and things went along perfectly for Manny until the Sunday morning she learned that Emma had died and that she'd inherit nothing.

"Another?" Clive, the bartender, asks, interrupting Emmanuella's daydream.

"Yes, Clive," she says, as she moves the glass with the melting ice and amber water.

"I never see the gentlemen who used to accompany you," Clive says.

"Brian?" she asks.

"No, not Brian, I think he was Louis, a constable."

"Louis LaPorta," she says.

"That's the one."

"We don't call them constables."

"A police officer, then."

"That's right."

"So where's he been?"

"He gave up drinking."

"What a shame. He seemed like such a nice man."

"Did he?" Emmanuella asks.

"He did."

"I'm surprised you say that."

"Why is that?"

"Because he didn't like you very much."

"Really?"

"He thought you were spying on us."

"Me? Spying? You're kidding."

"You weren't spying on us, were you, Clive?"

"Of course not."

"You're saying Officer Louis is crazy?"

"No, I'm saying . . ."

"That he's paranoid?"

"Well, maybe that's the word . . ."

"I don't know if it is," Emmanuella says. "He told me about the man who hired you to find out what we were up to."

"Do you mean like as in an affair or something? Because to be honest, Emmanuella, with you and Officer Louis, it never looked like an affair to me."

"It wasn't an affair. It was more serious than that."

"What then?"

"What's more important than an affair?" she asks.

"I don't know," he says. "Money?"

"You are a bright one, aren't you?"

"Not really."

"Well, there are many ways to save the princess," she says.

"I'm sorry?"

"It's complicated."

"I should say."

"Make mine a double this time, Clive from Liverpool."

"Is it water or soda, then?"

"Water, Clive. The easy stuff I expect you to remember."

"Of course, Emmanuella. Scotch and water it is."

LOUIS LaPORTA

The kids on the skateboards look like rich white kids from the Upper East Side who'd clean up nice with a blazer and a club tie. But it's autumn and clear and bright in New York and everybody's out, and the kids with the studs-and-needles look, slaves to the seductive powers of self-mutilation, are full of juice and careless as they dare each other to try something on wheels that'll defy nature, gravity, or expectations.

The youngest kid's the wild man, taking chances, popping down steps, straddling the concrete collar of the circus maximus fountains. He's smaller than the other two so he tries harder, and when he almost plows into an old woman loping along with a walker, Officer Louis La-Porta, off-duty, a tourist in the Big Apple, grabs the kid by the collar and tells him and his buddies to get the hell out of there. They take off, screaming like Johnny Rebs, and give LaPorta the finger before they disappear down Fifth Avenue and into the park.

"Fuckin' kids," LaPorta says to nobody as the old woman continues on with the reach, set, step, and reach routine, inches at a time, oblivious, another New Yorker, unmoved by wild white kids or the tough-looking guy who intervened. LaPorta thinks that in Hartford this might have been a news story, but in New York it's not worthy of one word.

He shakes his arms as if dusting off the unpleasantness and looks north to Eighty-sixth Street and the stream of cabs that bears to the right as they pummel down the avenue, slowing, stopping before the plaza and the grand steps to the museum. He checks his watch and looks to the green light farther north and a second wave of cabs, certain she's on her way, that she will show up. He's not nervous or worried about it, more surprised than anything about her phone call and the invitation to spend the afternoon in New York. He figures she must really love art, or knows how to pretend to love art so as to make the whole thing seem proper and aboveboard, even if it carries the whiff of something clandestine and not quite right. LaPorta remembers her from the afternoon at Coop Johnson's house after Mrs. Johnson's funeral. He remembers her husband, too, Taylor or Tyler, and he remembers the talk they had about Mr. Johnson and Cal Stevens, the guy with the silver bucket on his head, the guy who died in jail. LaPorta's a cop and he's been trained to remember these kinds of things, though his memory fails to recall her looks other than an image that relies on the easy description of stock terms—short, petite, shapely, spirited, almost perky, and blond.

"Louis," she says, and he turns and sees her, surprised, startled that she'd approached from a different direction, catching breath as he takes her in and stock descriptions give way to other words, gathering himself, having lost the lead time he would have used to strike the pose of perfect composure.

"Mrs. Bach," he says.

"How polite," she says, "but we're in New York now, so let's do as the locals do and call me by my first name."

"Muffy," he says.

"Now, that wasn't so hard was it?"

"No, not hard at all."

They start up the steps and halfway to the entrance Muffy Bach turns and looks across Fifth Avenue. "I can't remember," she says.

"What's that?"

"Oh, nothing. It's just that when I was very young, I attended a debutante ball here and afterward we had a party in my roommate's friend's apartment. More than an apartment, really, it was a three-story mansion built into one of these buildings. Had its own elevator. I remember how much that impressed me. To think, a family that had their very own elevator. In one of these buildings. Oh, well, our past is made up of so many little tea bags of information, don't you think?"

Louis looks up and down Fifth Avenue. This kind of thing means nothing to him, and he doesn't want to look foolish with some bullshit smile, asking questions or making comments about something that's got nothing to do with him or his past.

"Where I grew up," Louis says, "frankly, Mrs. Bach, Muffy, we were happy if we had our own bathroom."

"Oh, I believe every family member should have his own," Muffy says.

"I was talking about my family."

She looks at him. Her lips move with an almost smile, wry, flirtatious, the kind of combative stance that presumes intimacy and flatters the opponent. Still, she's not about to be chastened by this populist from the hardscrabble schoolyard.

"Oh, please, Mr. LaPorta, let's not trade hardships."

"I didn't mean to," he says, and he asks himself whether he should call this a date and save himself the headache. But he hesitates and forgoes the quick exit, the proud indifference, because that's movie bullshit, and this is not a movie.

"Sure you did," she says, because she's won this exchange, and she's taken his measure, and she's seen the faint line of at least one boundary. "And I kind of liked it," she says, "but not too much," and she runs her arm through his and touches his hand as they enter the Great Hall.

She's familiar with the place and finds a ticket booth without a line. She shows her membership card and picks up two buttons and nods to the dark corridor to the left where the relics from the Middle Ages sit behind glass.

"Do you have a particular favorite?" she asks.

"What kind of favorite?"

"Artist? Sculptor? Era?"

LaPorta looks about the wood carvings of saints and warrior angels from northern Europe. He looks to the vaulted ceiling and to the hall on the right where knights wearing armor sit astride huge horses, draped with saddles and flags.

"Taxidermy," he says.

"I'm sorry."

"Look, Muffy, it's not that I don't like it, this, all of this," he says. "I mean I look at it, and I can see what must have gone into it, to make stuff like this. It's just that I never learned about it the way you did, or the way a person's supposed to know about it, so I—you know—I don't know enough to have a favorite."

"*Quel désastre, mon sauvage*," she says, laughing, a modification of the flirtatious challenge, a softening, a kindness, the first warmth of something like desire. Now Louis suspects that she is attracted to him, and although he's out of his depth, the waters are pleasant and almost warm.

Muffy takes him by the arm and they walk slowly through several galleries where she points out things and does her best to make it all interesting without patronizing him. By the time they hit the modern stuff with the lines and the colors going every which way, LaPorta begins to make his own judgments, saying, "What the hell?" and asking what people were thinking, paying good money for stuff that makes no sense.

"Is making sense important for you?" Muffy asks.

"What do you mean?"

"Could you enjoy something that doesn't make sense, that doesn't need to make sense?"

"Like what?"

"Feelings don't always make sense."

"No, I guess they don't," he says.

"It's modern art," she says, and he looks at her and tells her he's got names for things, too.

The afternoon carries on and the spark that enlivened things late morning when they stood in front of a Kandinsky has dulled some with the South American stuff in the Rockefeller wing. "What's this all about?" Louis asks himself, as they make their way through a dark room to the restaurant and cafeteria. He thinks, "This doesn't feel like the intro to an affair; it sure as hell isn't what I've been used to." And he remembers many motel rooms, each one looking like the other, the doors that barely lock, the bad lamplight, the mad grope, grab, and tussle on beds with pressed wood headboards.

He and Muffy stand in a short line for the restaurant, and he looks at her petite body with the narrow waist and the slim legs with a little heft about the ankles. She's wearing a country club outfit, with a denim skirt, a rose-colored shirt with the high collar and the alligator or the golfer or something over her left breast. She's got a sweater, cable stitched, the arms draped around her neck, tied in front, making a huge looping bow of long empty sleeves. Her hair is a young woman's hair. "All these rich women have young women's hair," LaPorta thinks, and he feels the old stirring, a softening, almost forgiveness for the distance between himself and others, a distance filled with bias and prejudice, fears, wounds, and then the giving way that comes when a person can envision himself in the embrace of another, when that first and most opaque veil of separation is breached with thoughts of something desirous if not transcendent. So LaPorta begins to like this woman, flirtatious and pretty, middle-aged (if she lives to be 108). The barbs that knocked him back a few hours before might have piqued his chronic misogyny, but they've worked a kind of seduction, too.

They take a table on the right wing near the small bar.

Muffy orders a Scotch and LaPorta drinks coffee. She looks about the dining area crowded with tables and patrons. Louis figures she's checking to see if she recognizes anybody, and only this brief perusal speaks to the clandestine nature of their meeting.

"So, Louis," she says, turning back, confident, pleased with herself, "tell me, then, just how did you come to work for Mr. Coop Johnson?"

"I moonlight from time to time. I was working security at Trinity one night. Some fundraiser or something. He was there. He came back to the kitchen to thank the help. He came over. He said, 'So here's the man in charge,' and he was nice about it, joking. We made small talk. He asked me a few questions, then told me to come by his office someday. I did, and he started hiring me for other things."

"Coop does that."

"What?"

"He finds a person, just comes upon them and takes an interest in them—takes them up."

"Takes them up?"

"You know what I mean, singles them out, pays attention to them, helps them along in what they're doing."

"I see."

"He prides himself on his ability to spot talent."

"Okay."

"He's taken up all kinds of people. One guy's a mechanic, one's a chef."

"A chef?"

"He's an amateur, works for some hospital—I don't know how, but Coop had some dessert the man made, and that was that."

"Sounds a little strange," Louis says.

"I suppose," Muffy says, "but powerful men like to dole out their power from time to time, just to show they can."

"I guess," Louis says.

"You should be flattered," she says, reaching across the table and touching his hand.

"I am," he says. "I mean, I guess I am."

"Believe me, being his friend is a million times better than being his enemy."

"Really?"

"Don't get me wrong, Louis. Coop's a great man and all of that, but he's got a mean streak, too. He covers it with all of that learning and charm and the way he carries himself, but he didn't get where he is by being the nicest guy in Hartford. There were stories about him in college."

"At Yale?"

"Yes, about his temper, about what he could be like when he didn't get his way. He'd go white-hot. It wasn't until he met his wife that he settled down some."

"She's the one who just died?"

"Yes, Margaret Portner Humes, the one who cheated at golf."

"They were married a long time."

"They were."

"He must have loved her, then."

"Loved her enough I think."

"What do you mean?"

"He had a true love once."

"Not his wife?"

"No. He met her when he was at Yale. They were going to be engaged, but there was a problem and she had to go away for a while. Then families got involved. Probably his one failure in life. Almost killed him. Drove him crazy. He even started drinking too much. Became very nasty. He pulled out of it though."

"What do you mean she had to go away?"

"In her day, Louis, that only meant one thing."

"Pregnant."

"And not by Coop Johnson, which is probably what drove him out of his mind."

"Successful men can do nasty things when they don't get their way. Maybe that's why they hire people like me."

"Louis, I find it very hard to think of you as being nasty."

LaPorta stares at the dark rim of his cup, the coffee going cold, the reflection of overhead lights.

Muffy looks over the heads of the patrons in the dining area. Time is passing and she must ask what she intends to ask. She doesn't know how Louis will take it. For an ill-defined moment she doesn't know what she's doing here, what she intends to do, and she thinks how honesty has the tendency to take us out of our depth.

"My daughter is Coop Johnson's goddaughter," she says. "Or maybe I should say Coop Johnson is my daughter's godfather. That sounds more like it."

"It's got to be a good thing to have Mr. Johnson for a godfather."

"Yes, and he's been wonderful to her. After his wife died he helped her start her own career."

"What does she do?"

"She's going to run a charitable foundation. She'll manage I don't know how many millions of dollars."

"She's gonna give away money."

"Well, after a fashion."

"Really?"

"Of course there's more to it than that, I mean, there are rules and regulations and all kinds of things that govern what she does, but she went to law school so she's capable of handling those things, too."

"She sounds very professional."

"Yes, she is. I mean, can you imagine a full-time job where your primary responsibility is to give away money?"

"Can't say as I can."

"She was supposed to join me on this trip, but she's busy. Always busy these days."

"You and Mr. Bach must be proud of her."

"Of course we are. I mean I am, and Tyler, too, though she's not Tyler's daughter. She's my daughter from my first marriage."

"Oh."

"I married Mr. Dillon when I was a wee girl, just out of Miss Porter's."

"Did you say Dylan? Like the singer?"

"No, more like the sheriff or marshal or whatever he was."

"What?"

"There was a TV show back then. Very popular, I can't remember . . . Anyway, Mr. Dillon's family was from Meriton. The Dillons of Meriton— the Meriton Dillons. We lived there while Ann was in high school."

"So you grew up in Meriton? That's a far cry from West Hartford."

"No, Mr. Dillon grew up there. But he wasn't your average blue-collar boy. His family owned the construction company that employed half the town. Italian and Irish. Second generation."

"So, what happened?"

"With what?"

"The marriage."

"We divorced. Many troubles. We're still—almost friendly."

"And Tyler Bach? What's his story?"

"What do you think?" she asks.

"It's not for me to say," he says.

"Why not?"

"It might offend you."

"Then do your worst. Believe me, I can take it."

"I'd rather not."

"It's a marriage of convenience," Muffy says. "That's the best I can say about it."

"Then we'll leave it at that."

"I guess so," she says, and she touches Louis LaPorta's fingers, reaching, looking to hold hands.

Louis takes her hand. Her skin is soft, almost smooth. He looks into her eyes that give way to hurt when they settle and give up the too-bright struggle. He holds her hand and feels her slipping away, the necessary dissociation precedent to hunger.

"Louis, I have to ask you something."

"It's all right," he says.

"I need . . ."

"It's okay, Muffy. I like you, too."

"Thank you, that makes this easier."

"I don't want it to be hard."

"Louis, I want to hire you."

LaPorta doesn't drop her hand, but he pulls back, mystified by the question.

"You want to hire me?"

"Yes."

"For what?"

"I need a private investigator I can trust."

Louis lets go of her hand and sits back. His skin feels warm and he has the need to stand up, though he remains seated.

"You want to hire me as a PI."

"My daughter, Louis, I think she's gotten herself into something very bad, I'm afraid. Very dangerous. She thinks she can handle anything, but this time I'm certain she's over her head."

"What do you mean—over her head?"

"I mean she could be in trouble."

"What kind of trouble?"

"My daughter's gay, Louis, and this has been a source of—what can I say?"

"It doesn't fit the picture?"

"It's led her into relationships from time to time. And recently she was seeing this woman who's nothing but a con artist."

"So what do you want me to do?"

"Find out what's going on. See who this Manny Whitman person is. See if Coop Johnson's pulling the strings—watching over Ann or not. Maybe he's using her. I don't know, whatever. Maybe, then, if I can find out what's really going on, and I warn her, maybe she'll believe me."

LaPorta looks over the dining area and tries to regain balance. He thinks of those motel rooms. He thinks how things are never the way they are in the movies. He thinks he'll take this woman for as much money as she can spend and become a double-agent in the process. He thinks how she'll be the one who gets in over her head if she gets too nosy with things that don't concern her. He thinks a lot of things, and he does it without letting on to anyone just how fucked up life can be.

OFFICER TALMADGE

Officer Talmadge enters the squad room with rumpled trench coat, hat, cigar, carrying a box with a cake. He sets the box down on Moraski's desk and lifts out the cake. The frosting's white and there's a turkey cast in brown icing with orange triangles for eyes, mouth, and feathers.

Talmadge tries to light the small candles with the tip of his cigar. Detective LaPorta walks by. "It ain't his birthday," LaPorta says, as he takes a lighter from his pocket and lights the candles. "And what's with the turkey?"

"Thanksgiving," Talmadge says.

"Thanksgiving?"

"The guy screwed up, so I took what I could get," Talmadge says, and he tosses the empty box and makes sure the cake is centered on the desk. The other detectives gather around and ask what's keeping Moraski. "It's a fucking exit interview," one of them says. "You tell the captain he's a genius and get the fuck out."

Then Moraski leaves the captain's office, carrying a cardboard box filled with personal items.

The guys start singing something that sounds like a cross between "For He's a Jolly Good Fellow" and "We Three Kings of Orient Are." Moraski stops and fumbles with the carton. The surprise isn't total, but it's not wholly expected. Moraski knows he never connected with the other detectives during his tenure. He figures they're happy to see him go.

Moraski's wrong, though, and Talmadge is about to tell him so. "I want to say a few words," Talmadge says. The guys make noise and laugh a little and Talmadge tries to get their attention. "Okay, okay," he says, "I know I'm not the best one to be standing here doing this kind of thing for our in-house lawyer and former marine. After all, it's no secret I did just about everything possible to get assigned someplace else last year when the captain told me what he wanted me to do. No offense, Mark, but you had one hell of a reputation before you even showed up here. Like one of those Elliot Ness boy scouts that nobody wants to get saddled with."

LaPorta calls out, "Now a Girl Scout, that might be another story."

"Shut up, newcomer." Talmadge calls out.

"Who you calling a newcomer?" LaPorta asks.

"You, ya stupid . . ."

"Don't say it," one of the old guys says, and everybody laughs.

"I might be a newcomer," LaPorta says, "but you're not even official yet."

"I'm as official as I want to be, Louie the Door, so shut the hell up so I can say what I want to say here before I forget it all."

The guys settle to silence, and Talmadge moves away from Moraski's desk. He's a little hunched over, looking up from under his eyebrows in his "curmudgeon with a warm heart" way. He says, "Mark, I'm serious here now. I've got to say that anybody who questions you or what you're about just doesn't know you at all because you're a fine detective, a good cop, and as good a human being as I've had the privilege to work with. Now, we're all pretty jaded around here. I don't think a person can do what we do, see what we see every day, and not get a little jaded, and after too many years on the force this job can become nothing more than a race to the finish line without getting yourself killed. Thing is, I watched you out there, and I'm here to say you're a rare bird because you actually give a shit. I mean it, fellas, this guy actually gives a shit. So from all of us to all of you, Attorney Moraski, we wish you good luck, and when you're making a million dollars a year don't forget who drove you around for the last year and a half."

"Kiss him," one of the wise guys yells, and everybody laughs again.

Mark Moraski and Officer Talmadge shake hands. Then, newly promoted Detective Louis LaPorta steps forward and shakes Moraski's hand. Some of the other guys follow after that, and the ones who don't just raise their paper cups filled with a sparkling grape drink and toast the guy, saying things like, "Way to go, Mark," and "Good luck, buddy."

Mark stands there, a little embarrassed, not certain what to say. His exit interview with the captain didn't go well, and it's left him with an uneasy feeling of false endings and failed closures. But he doesn't want that to darken his gratitude. He looks around the room, the several desks covered with papers and forms and notepads. He looks at the several detectives standing in a semicircle between him and the door. He says he doesn't know what to say except thanks, and that he'll remember his time here with quality people on a quality force, that he'll carry the memory with him forever. He says that even if he does forget, he knows Talmadge will pop up when least expected to remind him that a detective's job carries an awesome responsibility and that only the very best, like the guys in this room, are able to carry it off, day after day, year after year.

The speech ends on a high note, and the group feels the moment, and they applaud as Mark tells them to enjoy his holiday cake. Then, wiping his cheek with a finger, though he hasn't shed tears, he picks up his box and heads for the door.

After he's gone, Talmadge looks around the room and shrugs his shoulders. "I don't know," he says, "maybe he doesn't like cake."

Downstairs in the garage under the building Moraski beeps his key chain and pops his trunk. He places the box of personal items in the back. He slams the trunk shut, looks up, and sees Talmadge standing next to him.

"I really want to thank you," Mark says. "I appreciate what you said up there."

"I meant it," Talmadge says. "Wouldn't have said it otherwise."

"I know."

"You wouldn't cut some cake with the boys, though?"

"Yeah, well, I guess I just felt the need to leave. I hate good-byes and all of that."

"I understand. Only thing is, I was wondering whether it's got something to do with . . ."

"With what?"

"With the way we ended up."

"How do you mean? I thought we ended up pretty good."

"I mean, you know, with how they put the kid away."

"Matthew Wyman?"

"Yeah, him. I know it bothers you."

"Doesn't it bother you?"

"It does, but I'm not like you. I know when a fight's rigged."

"Well, I did want to fight."

"So, then it is the reason you decided to leave."

"Not the only reason," Moraski says.

"But a big reason," Talmadge says.

"It's like this," Moraski says. "You and I both know that kid didn't do it. Even Judge Nash knows the kid didn't do it, which means somebody else did, which means the case is open no matter what everybody says. I think we both know his brother set him up, and the deal they made to call him crazy and put him away was cooked up by people we don't know and couldn't get to if we did."

"That's what I'm saying, Mark. There's no reason to kill yourself when the judge himself is following orders. Anyway, the kid did confess."

"You believe that brother of his?"

Talmadge looks around the parking garage, looking for words, looking for something. He says, "Well, it's over now, whether we like it or not."

"Yeah, I guess so."

"You're a good man," Talmadge says. "I mean that, but you're the type of guy who makes other people nervous as hell. You remind me of one those kamikaze guys who'll run a one-man sub into the side of a battleship just to prove he's right. Doesn't make you any less right—just shortens your career some."

"I don't know," Moraski says, laughing some, "maybe I'm just Polish stubborn, maybe it's the marine thing, maybe it's the Catholic in me."

"Polish stubborn," Talmadge says. "I vote for that. Not that it's a bad thing, but it shouldn't kill you, either."

———◆◆◆——

It's past five and a few guys from the day shift are waiting by the elevator as Talmadge returns to the squad room. Talmadge slaps the back of his folding chair and sits at his desk with his coat on, hat over his forehead, cigar between his teeth. He stares across desktops to his new partner, Detective Louis LaPorta.

"So?" LaPorta asks.

"So what?"

"Is he okay?"

"He's okay."

"It's still buggin' him, though."

"Hell, yeah."

"That kid said what he said."

"To his brother."

"And all I did was turn it in," LaPorta says.

"You arrested him," Talmadge says.

"I had probable cause. I mean, I did see that bag in his pocket. I swear."

"Nobody's sayin' you didn't do the right thing."

"His brother gave me the confession and I made a decision."

"I said, nobody's sayin' . . ."

"So, what are we supposed to do now, keep looking for somebody else?"

"Louie the Door, we're supposed to go after the bad guys."

"And the kid was crazy. At least now they got him where he won't hurt himself."

"There are plenty of bad guys out there, Lou. More than enough to keep us busy."

"So, what are you saying?"

"I'm saying it doesn't do us any good to be holier than the Pope. The Kost O'Neal case is closed."

"You mean that?"

"I mean there's no percentage in disagreeing with everybody else in this corrupt little city."

"Okay then," LaPorta says.

"Okay then," Talmadge says.

"Tell me, though . . ."

"What?"

"Why won't you make this appointment permanent? Everybody else figures it's permanent."

"What appointment?"

"This temporary detective thing you got goin' here. They're begging you to take it on for good."

"I don't know," Talmadge says. "No reason."

"There's got to be a reason."

"Maybe it's because it's best not to take everything they put in front of you. Maybe it's my way of keeping my postage stamp of a life less cluttered with all the payback bullshit."

LaPorta stares at the guy. His phone rings. Talmadge stands and starts for the door. He slaps LaPorta on the shoulder.

"If it's a bad guy, I'm not here," Talmadge says.

"Detective LaPorta," LaPorta says into the phone, thinking how it sounds, liking the sound of it.

BRIAN WYMAN

The news bunny from the local CBS affiliate wraps the long black cord from around her legs and lets it fall behind her. She snaps her compact and looks in the mirror and checks her teeth, her lipstick, and the eye shadow. She asks her cameraman if her suit with the fine herringbone weave will strobe, and before he can answer she switches the microphone from hand to hand, feeling for balance and weight.

Jennifer Munch, the "Good Time Correspondent," is standing in the center of Brian's Bakery and Coffee Shop, an establishment that was financed in July, built in August, opened to rave reviews in September, and has been packed with customers ever since.

The TV station didn't see any need to report on it when the grand opening took place on Labor Day, until Ms. Munch's boss received word from on high that the station had been remiss in its duty to inform the public of Brian Wyman's fabulous baked goods. So today's the day for lights, camera, action, and Brian, shaking hands with customers who stand in line and stretch and peek to put themselves in the shot, asks Jennifer if he'll need more make up for the on-camera interview.

Jennifer answers and ignores him at the same time. She mumbles something about his make up being fine, though he should wipe the perspiration from his forehead.

"Too much shine?" he asks, feeling like a celebrity, talking celebrity talk.

"Maybe a little," she says as she takes some index cards from her pocket.

The camera guy's a kid from U of H, on sabbatical for the semester with an internship at the station. He's been working with Jennifer since August, traveling around the greater metropolitan area, lugging the equipment, and dealing with the high-maintenance newslady. Jennifer's a bitch, but she's been worse than usual because she's frustrated with her boss and the station. She's eager to do hard news, breaking news, investigative reporting, and every week she makes a request for more substantive assignments—and every week the station sends her off on one more puff piece. She's losing respect for all of it. She feels stuck and wants to make a change. But first she has to interview this baker about muffins and cakes and sweetness and light.

She takes a deep breath and bows her head. She tells herself there are no small stories, only small correspondents. She tries to center herself. She thinks: "energy" and "focus." She flips through the index cards one more time. She makes a mental outline: Brian Wyman's the good kid who made good. He used to work in a hospital doing something she needn't get into. He became famous among friends and relatives for his culinary skills. He's self-taught. The talent appears to be God-given. His desserts have caught the eyes of some of the best chefs in the city. However, nothing exciting happened for Brian until one day when Mr. Coop Johnson, president of everything and CEO of everything else, had the opportunity to taste one of Mr. Wyman's vanilla tarts. After that things began to happen. Mr. Johnson secured the financing for the new bakery, and Mr. Wyman promised to build it on site where Mr. Johnson and all the insurance company employees could avail themselves of Brian's genius. "Things happen fast when good people get behind something," Brian was quoted in the *Courant* as saying, and, indeed, things had happened very fast for Brian Wyman.

"Well, tell me, Mr. Wyman," Jennifer begins, on camera, film at eleven.

"Please, call me Brian."

"Okay, Brian, tell me if this feels like overnight success for you?"

"Well, it was always a dream of my mother's that maybe someday I'd have a place where I could cook and bake for people."

"She must be very proud of you then."

"I'm sure she's looking down from heaven, and I hope she's proud."

"Now, tell us, what's the story with Mr. Coop Johnson and your vanilla tarts. I heard that he's your number one fan and prime mover behind this endeavor of yours."

"I can't thank him enough," Brian says. "A friend of mine worked for him last year, and Mr. Johnson had something come up and needed some catering done right away. My friend asked if I'd do it. I dropped everything, catered the event, and that was the beginning of that."

"I hear he tasted one of your desserts, and you won him over forever."

"Like I say, he's a great man with great taste."

Jennifer steps to the side of a table with three separate displays. The camera kid follows along, moving in to get close-up shots of the food, coffees, and teas.

"Now let's see what you've set out for the viewers at home."

"What I've set out here is a potpourri of what we offer our customers every day." Brian points to the first display of muffins, donuts, and croissants. "In the morning before work we specialize in extra-large muffins . . ."

"Everybody tells me the cranberry muffins are wonderful."

"They are, though I especially like the pumpkin-cheesecake muffins."

"Stop it, my mouth is watering."

They move along past the donuts and the croissants. Brian points to the second display of breads and a large stone crock of soup. He says, "For lunch we like to offer a soup, salad, and sandwich combo. I'd like to think we've got the best soup man in Hartford with us now . . ."

"He's not the Soup Nazi, is he?"

Brian's smile goes blank with incomprehension. "The what?" he asks.

"The Soup Nazi," Jennifer says, unable to leave it alone. "Didn't you watch *Seinfeld?*"

"I guess I missed that one."

"I thought everybody knew about the Soup Nazi. Anyway, what do we have here?"

Brian moves to the third display with steaming pots of tea, scones, and various small pastries and cakes. He says, "This is the late-afternoon or after-work special. We liken it to Irish tea. Now it might not be for everyone, but for those who work late and need a little sugar pick-me-up at the end of the day, we'll deliver to their desk an assortment of pastries, cakes, and tarts and a pot of hot tea in the winter, or iced tea or coffee in the summer."

"Sounds wonderful."

"Thanks, we try hard."

"Very Continental, too."

"Yes, I guess it is."

"European," I mean.

"Yes."

"And looking around I can see you're not without customers." Jennifer waves her arm around the room and the camera follows the people lined up for service.

"We've been very lucky," Brian says, "and we only want to serve the downtown workers as best as we can."

"Sounds great, Brian of Brian's Bakery in downtown Hartford. And this is Jennifer Munch, Action News 7, inviting all of you to join me for a muffin and a cup of tea."

She smiles into the camera as the lights fade and Brian wipes his eyes.

"How did I do?" he asks.

"Fine," Jennifer says, "Except for the *Seinfeld* thing."

"Can you edit that out?" he asks, though she's moved on, slapping her cell phone open, dialing, checking in with the station, arranging transportation for the next piece of airy nothing.

"What I mean is, did I do okay?" Brian asks, and Jennifer looks at him and mouths the word "fine."

"It's just that it's important," Brian says and Jennifer snaps the phone shut, takes out a small notebook, and while writing something with a ball point pen, tells him not to worry about it because it's only filler and the station will run it if they need to stretch a broadcast.

She looks around the store again. She says, "It's not like you need the free advertising."

"What do you mean by that?"

"What do you think I mean? Look at this place. It's packed. I talked to a few of these people earlier. Sounds like they've almost been ordered to buy here."

"I wouldn't say that."

"Hey, if the boss says Brian's the muffin man, guess what, Brian, you're the muffin man. And you better hope you never piss off the boss."

"People like my food, I don't need anybody telling them to come here."

"Suit yourself, but one thing I'd like to know is what did you do for him?"

"For who?"

"Coop Johnson, who do you think?"

"I told you, I catered some desserts for him."

"I know that, but from what I know about Mr. Johnson, he doesn't put himself out like this unless he's taken back double up front. So what did you do for him? Maybe it was something from when you worked at the hospital. Free autopsy or something?"

"Look," Brian says, trying to control his temper, trying to walk away. "Thanks for coming, but we're done here, right?"

"And what about your brother?"

Brian turns to face her.

"What about him?"

"I don't know—something about him being put away for no reason. Something about a funeral home, an heiress, and a lot of things being swept under the rug."

"You don't know what you're talking about."

"Yes, I do, and if the station did what it's supposed to do I'd be reporting that story and not this happy-happy crap."

She orders the camera kid out the door. She follows and turns back with the door open and cold air blowing the hem of her topcoat. She says, "You know, Mr. Wyman, you might as well enjoy this while it lasts, but sooner or later, muffins are muffins and tastes change."

LYLE BRANDO

The hermit has little choice: He's an object of margins, a subject of certain phobias, hatreds frozen in place, made silent with nonjudgment born of self-service, a husbanding of those energies too easily spent in anger, resentments that need go unresolved because he's moved beyond the anger attendant to judgment, having judged everything (including himself), having damned everything (including himself).

The hermit's closure is the closed door, the dark cabin, the sleeping dog, the tin can of cold food.

Lyle sits in the autumn cold in the cabin he built years before in a stretch of woods several miles north of Punter's Pond. The cabin's nothing, just four walls and the aluminum siding he fashioned to make a cylinder that went through the ceiling, wide at the bottom, narrow at the top, a makeshift chimney for fires he'd make on a bed of rocks underneath. He sits there now, stoking a small one, two potatoes pierced and hung over it. He's got his winter coat on and his hat and he watches the fire, cursing the scratch in his throat that was there when he woke up. Lyle never gets colds like this, and this time the cold was more than a thing he could ignore because it made him colder than the air outside and tired and warned him off doing normal things.

He has a new dog. He calls him Truck, just like the old one, the one who stayed behind with Lilly, and he never thinks of that dog, never thinks of his wife, either, since the only thing they'd shared, really, was time, and not much to show for it, except what had been a warm place, a warm bed, some good meals, all the things that are normal for two people. He wonders if people figured that he and Lilly must have been in true love to have stayed together all those years, and he admits, sitting there, leaning forward to move a shard of yellow log from the center where it's too much for the small flame, that they did have something like that in the beginning, though after that night on the porch with Tommy O'Neal and the redheaded bitch, he and Lilly didn't share love so much as a common and deadening sense of shame, so strong that if they ever split apart, the shame would have been strong enough to kill one or both of them, maybe not in the physical sense, but in the sense that they'd feel it every minute, reminding them, especially when things seemed okay, that things would never be okay, because at the bottom and source of their being there was something defective and wrong.

Lyle grew up on Punter's Pond and he'd known the Kost house since he was a boy, long before Tommy O'Neal tore it down and built it up again. He knew Emma Kost O'Neal, too, when she was just Emma Kost, a tall, beautiful girl with hair so pretty it almost pissed him off, made him wonder why some people get all and some people get shit. But he couldn't stay pissed because everything he'd assumed about Emma Kost was wrong. He'd figured a pretty girl from the city with money, from a family who owned all the land around the pond, would have to be a stuck-up bitch. But she wasn't. Emma Kost was nice to Lyle, his senior by how many years, he never knew exactly, but old enough that she could look at Lyle and see the boy and the man implied there in the burgeoning height, growth, and subsequent maturity. The first summer they met, she'd sit on a rock by the pond, and he'd throw his line out, and she'd ask if he ever caught anything, and he'd just look at her and point to the bucket by his feet, and she'd say, "You bought them at the store," and he'd get all excited telling her she knew nothing about fishing. And then, the next summer she'd sit on the same rock and she'd tell him how college had prepared her for just about nothing and asked him if he'd teach her how to fish so that before the summer was over she'd be able to acquire at least one skill. And Lyle, a teenager, going crazy with his teenage self, taught her how to cast, holding her arm, touching her waist to direct the swing of her hips, almost losing it, almost embarrassing himself. And what made it so great and so awful all at the same time were Lyle's suspicions that Emma Kost was nice to him because at the end of the day—at the end of that particular summer—he didn't matter,

not to her, not really, not in the ways of passion and romance that de-
mand more of a game or a dance or displays of temperament, reticence,
and confusion. And then the next summer, when he was taller, darker,
and his voice had changed again, Lyle learned that what he'd suspected
was true—Emma Kost had let herself be nice to him as long as he was a
boy but couldn't afford to be nice to him (couldn't afford to acknowledge him) once he'd become a man. And that summer Lyle would walk
three miles from the far side of the pond and set up his fishing gear and
cast a line and wait for her to join him, but she never came down to the
pond, except for the one time she drove by in a Cadillac convertible
with a scarf around her head like Grace Kelly and the big dark glasses
like a movie star.

And then there was the next summer, the hottest summer of all,
when the Kost house was empty and nobody came to open it up or air it
out and Lyle watched it, June, July, August, not telling himself that's
what he was doing since he'd taught himself not to care about the
people who came in the summer and, after that, hardly at all.

It was a bad day, the absolute hottest day, and Lyle was down the
road, walking with his dog, when he saw that the front door of the Kost
house was open and the curtains in the bay windows were drawn back.
Lyle thought about crossing the road to see what was happening inside,
though he didn't want anybody to see him do that. He'd need a good
reason to cross the road, something better than curiosity about a woman
who couldn't care less, so he called his dog and thought maybe if the
dog went after something near the Kost house, it'd be okay to cross, because then he wouldn't be doing it just to catch sight of some woman,
but because he'd be minding his dog, which was what he was supposed
to do. And then, sure as he'd hoped for it, his dog shot across the road
after something so serious it took the dog over and made him one sleek
muscle of instinct and intent.

Lyle started to where the dog turned, pivoting in a small explosion of
dust and leaves, disappearing into the brush a ball field away. Lyle
hitched a short skip and ran over the dry grass, pressed down and bare
where the Kost people usually parked their Cadillacs. He ran by the
back of the house with the kitchen windows and the door for deliveries

and thinking there had to be somebody inside, looked to see what he could see through the windows. But there was nobody there as he ran to the brush along the back end of the property, conscious the whole way of how he might look to someone who might be watching, running so fast, strong, with good arms and legs and broad shoulders.

The sweat poured down and he breathed hard when he got to the place where his dog had disappeared behind weeds as tall as trees and behind pine bushes and laurel bushes and the leaves that had yet to break down and become dust. He heard the dog whine and watched him jump back and forth with the curious movements of instinct at war with itself, from curiosity to caution and back again, and the first thing Lyle figured was "snake," though when he got close he saw it wasn't a snake, but a black hunk of steel, a trap fashioned in the shape of a horseshoe or his grandfather's plate. It had snapped shut on a small brown rabbit, caught by its tail and some of its backside. The rabbit wasn't moving, except for the way it shivered and looked at Lyle with dumb comprehension. Lyle had no special regard for critters one way or the other. They were good; they were from God, and some had been put here for a reason, which was to give themselves up for food, though that didn't mean you killed every damn thing you came across. It meant you did it when you had to eat. That was the way of it, the way nature and God and everybody else intended it to be. So Lyle stepped forward and stood over the rabbit and figured the trap belonged to old man Fuchs, who'd never been friendly to Lyle or anybody else. But then Lyle examined the trap and saw that it was brand new and expensive, and Lyle knew Fuchs didn't have the money for something like that, especially when he was supposed to have a collection of traps that filled the inside of a small shed.

Lyle bent over and stroked the rabbit's back. It was soft and his hands were gentle and the rabbit shivered and trembled. He put both hands on the bars with the teeth and pulled, but the trap was new, the spring overly taut, and the bite was too much for him, so he struggled to get the mouth open wide enough for the rabbit to run away. The rabbit wouldn't move, though, and Lyle had to shout at it because he couldn't hold the trap much longer. Then something did move over his shoulder, not his dog, not the rabbit, but something or someone he hadn't counted on, and his dog leapt up and struck his arm, causing Lyle's hand to slip over the black teeth, damp with rabbit's blood, as the trap shut and cut his wrist to the bone.

The pain shot through him and then became something separate from Lyle, something that didn't rise up from within, but mugged him like an intruder. And the pain didn't give up all of itself right away. Some of it waited and doled itself out like there was cruelty in it, as Lyle's brain tried to take in what had happened. He looked down and saw his arm from his elbow to his wrist, and then, on the other side of the trap he saw his hand hanging by a patch of skin, the bones visible, the blood pouring out. Fear went through him and competed with the pain so that his system overloaded and Lyle opened his mouth to scream and uttered nothing but hot breath. He knew that this could be it because people who killed themselves cut their wrists, which meant there must be the kind of veins and arteries there that go straight to the heart.

As the full impact of the pain landed whole, he heard the rustle of branches and the crack of twigs and hoped there might be somebody nearby who could help. He called out, wanting his voice to sound like a man's voice no matter what, and he saw her, a girl, a woman, as tall as he was, as beautiful as ever, moving, her back moving, her legs moving, as the sweat stung his eyes and dimmed his vision, making him wonder what he'd seen, certain he'd seen someone, hoping he'd seen the woman he'd wanted to see all along. And he called her name, and prayed she'd come back and help him, because if she didn't, nothing would matter, not love or hate or fear or anything as the blood poured out and things went cloudy, as the pain rose and hit a ceiling of white-light torture, when something inside broke away, and he dropped to the side, senses unable to accommodate the imminent cessation of everything.

He woke in a hospital, not certain how he'd gotten there, aware only of images that floated like dreams of young Fuchs and a truck and the doors that spun and made a whooshing sound, little wheels that needed oil. He looked down the blanket and saw where his hand should have been, how short his arm looked without his hand. He didn't let himself cry, he just held it in, promised himself never to cry, to remember who'd been there, who'd watched from a distance, who'd walked away.

Lyle sits back and watches the embers go white with the dust that means there's more fire than wood, the way it beats, almost like a heart, glowing, subsiding, and he thinks about the redhead, not the mother, but the mother's daughter, the illegitimate one. "The cunt," Lyle thinks, because it's the ugliest word he can think of, and he applies it to all of them, man or woman, mother or daughter. He remembers the first time he saw the daughter, sitting on the porch of the abandoned house a year or more before she moved there with that useless coward from the city when Lilly made the mistake of inviting the two of them for dinner. The redhead called herself Manny, and Lyle knew right off she was a fraud, a con artist, born of a whore who sold her body and a man who thought himself superior to everybody else. He was walking with Truck that day, and seeing her in the distance, he crossed the road and stood in the place he hadn't stood since the night he'd been told to take his lovely little woman and move on. He introduced himself and saw that she wasn't as young as he'd first thought. She was pretty enough, her face was regular, but her eyes were like an old person's eyes, having seen too much to remain very bright or expressive. She had a broad back and overly broad shoulders, and when she leaned back in the lawn chair with her feet up on the banister, he saw that one leg was too heavy and one leg was too thin.

It wasn't like Lyle to make any kind of effort to be normal or neighborly, especially with women, but he did it regardless, having caught sight of her with her red hair and the memory of her mother, and he wasn't going to let it pass without some kind of back and forth.

She acted friendly with her bird eyes, like a bird of prey, cold eyes, wary, watching, never smiling no matter what her mouth did, moving most of the time since she liked to talk, the way bad liars talk too much. They exchanged all the old pleasantries, Lyle playing one of those idiots Hollywood cooks up once in a while to portray men like himself, though he knew he wasn't fooling her, either, and the two of them talked, as if talking were surfing, riding the top of something muscular and moving, all the while underneath the currents rising and subsiding. She asked him what had happened to his hand, and he told her, the whole story, and she told him what had happened to her leg, and they shared this strange insubstantial telepathy of the species that, given everything, she was more of his kind than she wasn't, and he took to her in the way members of an angry species can withhold judgment until they assess the potential benefits and drawbacks of being civil.

"That was a lousy thing for that woman to do," Manny said, talking about Emma Kost O'Neal.

"Surely was," Lyle said, pleased that he'd told the story he never told, realizing that people like himself and the redhead might want the same thing for different reasons.

Lyle was no fool, no gap-toothed hillbilly without a brain. He was shrewd, ambitious, desirous of money, a kind of justice that resembled balance, and he was patient. He'd been patient for all the years he'd sported one hand and a hook. He'd been patient all the years since the last weekend of the last summer Emma Kost showed her face on Punter's Pond.

It was a Saturday afternoon when Lyle followed Emma Kost from the local store to the Kost house and entered the house, nobody to stop him, the door, half open, careless, as she carried bags of whatever and dropped them in a chair in the front room. That's when she heard him and turned and saw him and said, "Lyle Brando, how are you? I've been worried about you. How has it healed? Fortunately for both of us young Fuchs was driving by that day just as I reached the road, otherwise you might have lost too much blood." And Lyle just looked at her, taking in the first few things she said, not hearing anything else but a kind of buzz as he stepped closer, and she stepped back, and he stepped again, and with the second step caused her to stop talking because he wasn't there to thank her or talk to her or be nice to her or anything like that. That's when he lunged for her, grabbing her, turning her, throwing her to the floor, pinning her, straddling her, placing the tip of his hook in the soft skin under her chin. "You gonna be still and take what you got comin'?" he asked, and she said nothing, her face a mask as she turned her head and stared at nothing, the fear having turned her into somebody else, a martyr who'd take it for her. And he pushed the tip in, pressing the white skin with a brush of down, so delicate, daring to break skin, to cause her to bleed, and she went catatonic like a possum, so that with his good hand he was able to unzip himself and pull at her skirt and panties, fumbling all about, trying to get hard enough to put himself inside, wondering why anger and revenge weren't enough to make him as hard as the stupid photos in magazines off the back rack, which is when he used his fingers to put it where it belonged, all the time awkward, with the hook under her throat, with Emma Kost lying underneath him like she was already dead—and he did it to her, pushing, pumping, shoving, causing her to bleed down there, an angry tearing like a slap across the face, but so much worse than that, and when he was done, he rolled off her and lay on his back, catching his breath as she folded up, like a baby in a crib, knees up, arms around herself, crying, softly crying tears, her shoulders trembling, a gasp and a cough, as she allowed herself to breathe again.

Lyle was someplace else in his head and had to travel some distance to get back to where he was in his body, on the floor, lying there, out of breath. He rolled over on his side and took his hand and touched her back, lightly, a soft touch, moving down her spine, shoulder to waist, and her skin was cold and something went dark inside and grabbed him around the heart, until it dropped like a stone or something heavier, like lead, the weight of something inert and dirty.

He got up, pulled up his pants, and ran out of there. That was all he could do at the moment to clean himself—compelled to clean himself—so, he ran one mile, two miles without stopping and then two more miles, trying to lose himself in the woods on the northern end of the pond, so that when he got to a place in the woods where there was no sound but for a few crickets and some birds overhead, he screamed as if someone had torn something from his gut, and he screamed a second time and collapsed on the ground and tried to hold his breath, thinking if he could stop his life and start over again, he'd be able to flush this thing from inside of himself. But it didn't work, nothing worked, and he made a bed of leaves and lay there for longer than he thought possible, that day, that night, another day, until the weight inside coalesced into a bitter silence, grew hard, and allowed him to stand again and walk away.

The fire pops and the potatoes begin to sizzle over the flames that meet and lick the undersides of the brown skins. Lyle remembers everything and only self-preservation makes him draw the curtains on it, knowing that part of being a man is living with things that happen, things that go too far, things that don't work out, things that take energy when there's no energy left, asking no mercy, no forgiveness, because asking would mean he'd done something wrong when he'd none nothing wrong, no more than what nature does when it removes some things and adds others to make a balance.

He coughs and spits into the fire and leans back, his chest sore from all the coughing. He damns the cold and the autumn and wonders why this time of year doesn't do for him what it used to since he can't find anything special in the rain or the way the rain hits the leaves that are yellow and doomed to fall and make a blanket of sorts. He remembers the blankets of leaves. He remembers the pillows he'd make of leaves. He especially remembers the pillows he'd make of leaves.

PROBATE

STATE OF CONNECTICUT
PROBATE COURT

* *

IN RE: ESTATE OF   JUDGE HART
EMMA KOST O'NEAL   PC—CV—07-0613

* *

TRANSCRIPT OF STATUS CONFERENCE

JUDGE HART: I asked my clerk—you know Nancy Talbot—

MS. DILLON: Yes, Your Honor.

JUDGE HART: I asked Nancy to set this down for today . . .

MS. DILLON: Yes . . .

JUDGE HART: And call you in for a status conference on the Kost-O'Neal Estate.

MS. DILLON: Thank you, Your Honor, this will help.

JUDGE HART: You and Nancy met earlier.

MS. TALBOT: Yes, Judge, we went over some details.

JUDGE HART: Good, then. I thought maybe an informal setting—in chambers—might be appropriate, though I do want to make a record, so Ms. Horvath will be our Court Reporter this morning. Now, Ann—it's Ann, right?

MS. DILLON: Ann Dillon, Your Honor.

JUDGE HART: And you're here on behalf of Mr. Stevens?

MS. DILLON: That's correct.

JUDGE HART: He's the one who—

MS. DILLON: He shot and killed Mr. Sullivan.

JUDGE HART: The same Mr. Sullivan who's named in the will?

MS. DILLON: That's right, Your Honor.

JUDGE HART: Well, this is something, then—perhaps a little more drama than we're used to in Probate Court.

MS. DILLON:	Yes, Your Honor.
JUDGE HART:	And what is Mr. Stevens's current status?
MS. DILLON:	He's dead, Your Honor.
JUDGE HART:	Dead?
MS. DILLON:	Yes. After he was arraigned and remanded for trial . . .
JUDGE HART:	No bail?
MS. DILLON:	No—yes, I mean the Court did set a figure, but Mr. Stevens was unable to pay the bond.
JUDGE HART:	That doesn't sound right—a successful lawyer, well connected, well known . . .
MS. DILLON:	Mr. Stevens had been in financial difficulty for some time, and his family, the ones still living, are either distant relatives or chose not to help.
JUDGE HART:	And now he's dead.
MS. DILLON:	He suffered a heart attack and a stroke the night after he was arraigned. He was a broken man, Judge.
JUDGE HART:	I see.
MS. DILLON:	He was my boss for years. He was always good to me, and the whole thing was such an aberration . . .
JUDGE HART:	And a capital crime.
MS. DILLON:	Yes, Your Honor.
JUDGE HART:	Now, Ann, I understand that you are not a lawyer.
MS. DILLON:	No, Your Honor, I'm not. I attended law school but was never admitted to the bar.
JUDGE HART:	Chose not to sit for the bar exam?
MS. DILLON:	Something like that.
JUDGE HART:	This is a bit unusual, then. As a rule I don't allow paralegals to appear on behalf of their firm's clients; however, given the circumstances, why don't we push ahead.
MS. DILLON:	Thank you, Your Honor.
JUDGE HART:	Now Nancy's read all the papers and has filled me in on the high points, and it appears that the lawyer who drafted the will . . .
MS. DILLON:	Mr. Stevens.

JUDGE HART:	Mr. Stevens might have made some matters more complicated than they need be. In addition we have to deal with the murder of Mr. Sullivan, Mr. Stevens's passing, the letter that's in the file from . . . Do you have the file, Nancy?
MS. TALBOT:	Right here, Judge.
JUDGE HART:	And the letter?
MS. TALBOT:	From Mrs. O'Neal to Manny Whitman.
JUDGE HART:	Because all of these matters might bear on the disposition of the estate. But first things, first—who's the executor of the will?
MS. DILLON:	Mr. Stevens was.
JUDGE HART:	Any alternate?
MS. DILLON:	He was the only one named.
JUDGE HART:	No first runner-up, then?
MS. DILLON:	No, Your Honor.
JUDGE HART:	Well, I'll have to look into that, maybe appoint one of my clerks so we don't get held up with a lot signatory problems.
MS. DILLON:	Yes, Your Honor.
JUDGE HART:	I say that because Mr. Stevens appointed you trustee of the Kost-O'Neal Charitable Trust.
MS. DILLON:	Yes, Your Honor.
JUDGE HART:	And when was that?
MS. DILLON:	Last April.
JUDGE HART:	Right around the time he shot Mr. Sullivan.
MS. DILLON:	Actually, it was the same day, Your Honor.
JUDGE HART:	Should the Court draw any inference from that, Ms. Dillon?
MS. DILLON:	I believe it's clear on its face, Judge. He knew what he was going to do and wanted to take care of some housekeeping before he did it.
JUDGE HART:	Housekeeping.
MS. DILLON:	I mean details . . .

JUDGE HART: I know what you mean, and I gather Mr. Stevens knew what he was about, too. Anyway, insofar as the Trust is a beneficiary under the will, you know you can't be named executrix.

MS. DILLON: Of course, Your Honor.

JUDGE HART: So, in your capacity as Trustee, then, why don't you outline for me how the Trust argues for the disposition of the property.

MS. DILLON: Yes, Your Honor. At your clerk's request, I did draft a memorandum on this.

JUDGE HART: Nancy?

MS. TALBOT: I have it right here, Judge.

JUDGE HART: So fill me in then, Ms. Dillon.

MS. DILLON: Under the will, Mrs. Kost O'Neal sought to pass all of her property, real and personal, to the Kost-O'Neal Charitable Trust, except for the shares in the company that owns the funeral business, which she'd agreed to leave to Robert Sullivan in accordance with the wishes of her late husband.

JUDGE HART: Just a second—Nancy? Would you please ask Terry if we could have some more coffee in here? (Off the record at 10:45 A.M., back on the record 10:47 A.M.) Go ahead, Ann.

MS. DILLON: The late Robert Sullivan.

JUDGE HART: All right then, everything to the trust except for the shares in the funeral business, which go to Robert Sullivan, deceased.

MS. DILLON: Yes, Your Honor.

JUDGE HART: So the shares now pass to his estate.

MS. DILLON: No, Your Honor, that's the wrinkle in all of this. Mrs. O'Neal was very specific about the bequest to Mr. Sullivan. She wanted to leave the shares to him, personally, in memory of her late husband's express wishes; however, should Robert Sullivan predecease her, or for any other reason be unable to carry on the business of the O'Neal Funeral

Home, then she wanted her shares in the funeral business to go to the Trust for purposes of sale and liquidation.

JUDGE HART: I take it Mr. Sullivan had a particular relationship with Mr. O'Neal and his wife.

MS. DILLON: Tommy O'Neal loved Bobby Sullivan like a son. Mrs. O'Neal allowed for it, but she and Robert Sullivan didn't get along. In any case, she agreed to give him the shares in the funeral business, because that's what her husband would have wanted, but she was not willing to enrich his estate. The bequest was specific to the person. After that it falls under the remainder clause and passes to the Trust.

JUDGE HART: You and Nancy seem to have come to the same conclusion. Is that right, Nancy?

MS. TALBOT: Yes, Judge.

JUDGE HART: But tell me, Ann, what was all of this noise, then, about a criminal investigation holding up probate. Nancy, what was the name?

MS. TALBOT: Wyman, Judge. Matthew Wyman.

JUDGE HART: With charges brought against this Wyman character. I understand he was arrested for Mrs. O'Neal's death?

MS. DILLON: Yes, he was.

JUDGE HART: I take it he confessed to it.

MS. DILLON: He confessed to his brother, and from what little I know his brother's not the most reliable witness.

JUDGE HART: Do they have any other evidence?

MS. DILLON: Nothing credible.

JUDGE HART: So, who's hearing the case?

MS. DILLON: It was before Judge Nash.

JUDGE HART: Was?

MS. DILLON: Yes, Your Honor, the district attorney dropped the charges.

JUDGE HART: And this was before Harry Nash.

MS. DILLON: Yes, Your Honor.

JUDGE HART: Enough said, then. There are hanging judges and judges who cut the rope—Harry cuts the rope.

MS. TALBOT: It's moot now, Judge.

JUDGE HART: Tell me then, Nancy? Ann? How is it moot?

MS. TALBOT: You go ahead.

MS. DILLON: Well, Your Honor, before Mr. Sullivan's murder the criminal investigation, which was also a determination as to how Mrs. O'Neal died, had a direct impact on the probate of the estate. When Mr. Sullivan was alive there was the issue of whether shares in the funeral business could pass to the prime suspect in Mrs. O'Neal's death.

JUDGE HART: And the prime suspect was?

MS. DILLON: Robert Sullivan.

JUDGE HART: Of course.

MS. DILLON: After that there was the issue of whether the insurance company would pay out on a policy while the cause of death remained in question. And finally there was the O'Neal–Manny Whitman letter to complicate everything else.

JUDGE HART: It seems to me that all of it begs the question: Just how did Mrs. O'Neal die?

MS. DILLON: I don't mean to sound flippant, Judge, but it depends on who you talk to.

JUDGE HART: I don't mind flippancy if it clears this up for me.

MS. DILLON: Mrs. O'Neal died either of natural causes, murder, or suicide. Those are the three possibilities. Robert Sullivan and the Coroner said natural causes. Manny Whitman and Mr. Stevens, independently of one another and for their own reasons, said Sullivan murdered Mrs. O'Neal. Louis LaPorta, the first officer on the scene, filed two reports which contradict one another, and, finally, the insurance company with the key-man policy argues for suicide and refuses to pay.

JUDGE HART: Obviously each have or had their reasons.

MS. DILLON: Yes, Your Honor. In the end it was all about the money.

JUDGE HART: What do you think happened to Mrs. O'Neal, then?

MS. DILLON: Do you mean what is my personal opinion?

JUDGE HART: Yes, Ann, your personal opinion.

MS. DILLON: Well, I don't know. I guess I suspected Robert Sullivan, too. He seemed to be the person who had the most to gain.

JUDGE HART: And you said he was the prime suspect.

MS. DILLON: Absolutely. But they never gathered enough evidence to indict.

JUDGE HART: Was that why Mr. Stevens killed Robert Sullivan?

MS. DILLON: Yes, Your Honor, by his own admission.

JUDGE HART: And this Manny Whitman? What's her story? Nancy?

MS. TALBOT: Yes, Judge.

JUDGE HART: Do you have that letter?

MS. TALBOT: Right here, Judge.

JUDGE HART: We have this beautiful letter from Mrs. O'Neal to Manny Whitman.

MS. DILLON: It's a forgery, Your Honor.

JUDGE HART: It's a forgery?

MS. DILLON: Yes, Your Honor.

JUDGE HART: Can you prove it's a forgery?

MS. DILLON: Yes, Your Honor. The letter asserts that Manny Whitman is Mrs. O'Neal's great-niece and sole living relative. I've done some research into the Kost family, and I've found birth records for Emma O'Neal and an older sister named Elizabeth. Elizabeth did have a daughter, married-name Margaret Mannion, and this Margaret Mannion had a daughter named Theresa Mannion. Theresa was single, lived in Phoenix, and died from breast cancer at the age of twenty-nine.

JUDGE HART: So Manny Whitman stole this young woman's identity?

MS. DILLON: Not exactly. You see, Mrs. O'Neal was very much aware that her husband, Tommy, was a . . . let me find the word . . .

JUDGE HART: Philanderer?

MS. DILLON: Exactly. He'd fathered at least three children with three mistresses, the last being Manny Whitman. Before he died he asked his wife to do what she could for them, his children, so to speak, if any of them came knocking—looking for help.

JUDGE HART: Help?

MS. DILLON: Money.

JUDGE HART: And she went along with that?

MS. DILLON: She loved Tommy and circled the wagons. Over the years Mrs. O'Neal authorized payments to a woman in San Francisco, a man in Buffalo, and finally to Manny Whitman. The fact that she called Manny her great-niece was cosmetic, a fiction, and, except for Mr. Sullivan, nobody cared or was the wiser.

JUDGE HART: Very careless, for such a worldly woman. Mrs. O'Neal, I mean. But I guess the heart has its reasons.

MS. DILLON: It does, Your Honor.

JUDGE HART: So when Mrs. O'Neal passed, however she passed . . .

MS. DILLON: Manny Whitman knew she was out of luck. Her allowance had come to an end. So she forged the letter and jumped on the bandwagon claiming Mr. Sullivan had killed her great-aunt. I believe she thought that if she could prove Sullivan was the murderer, then she might be able to persuade this court to recognize her as a beneficiary in accord with Mrs. O'Neal's last wishes.

JUDGE HART: Is she a lawyer?

MS. DILLON: No, Your Honor.

JUDGE HART: Then she must have had someone advising her. These are fairly complex issues, even for a lawyer.

MS. DILLON: Yes, they are.

JUDGE HART: Any idea who was talking to her?

MS. DILLON: No, Your Honor.

JUDGE HART: And a letter? Even if it was genuine, it isn't a will. What did she expect?

MS. DILLON: I don't know, Your Honor. Obviously she was desperate. Though I do have one possible theory.

JUDGE HART: Please, enlighten me.

MS. DILLON: After Mrs. O'Neal's death, Manny's only hope to recover anything was dependent upon her ability to convince the authorities that Sullivan had murdered her great-aunt. I think maybe she wrote the letter, not just to muddy the waters, but to make it look like Sullivan had a motive to kill Mrs. O'Neal before she changed her will.

JUDGE HART: But Mrs. O'Neal had no intention of changing her will.

MS. DILLON: In fact, she didn't, and the letter is a forgery, but as long as Manny Whitman got away with it, it made Sullivan look very guilty.

JUDGE HART: And then he was killed.

MS. DILLON: He was.

JUDGE HART: Has anybody notified the District Attorney about this fraud?

MS. DILLON: Your Honor, I had to deal with Manny Whitman after Mrs. O'Neal's death, and all I can say is that she's a damaged woman who's lived a hard life without much support. She has a disability from a childhood illness, and, as the Court's noted, whoever was advising her obviously led her down a primrose path of false expectations. I can say on behalf of the Trust that it has no interest in seeing her prosecuted. Given everything, with Mr. Sullivan's death, Mr. Stevens's passing, the potential for future litigation with the insurance company, my feeling, as Trustee, is that Ms. Whitman be left to herself.

JUDGE HART: You're very kind, Ms. Dillon. Very forgiving.

MS. DILLON: It's not that, Your Honor. I just want to turn the page on all of this so the Trust can get about its charitable business.

JUDGE HART: So where does all of this leave us then?

MS. TALBOT: Judge?

JUDGE HART: Yes, Nancy.

MS. TALBOT: If I might summarize?

JUDGE HART: Please do.

MS. TALBOT: The good news for this Court is that given Mr. Sullivan's death, the Probate Court need not concern itself with how Mrs. O'Neal died or issues concerning the insurance policy. With Mr. Sullivan's death the impediment to probating the estate's gone. No matter how Mrs. O'Neal

died, and no matter what the insurance company decides
to do, there remains only one beneficiary, identified and
uncontested.

JUDGE HART: The Charitable Trust.

MS. DILLON: Yes, Your Honor.

JUDGE HART: Which you've been running since Mrs. O'Neal's death?

MS. DILLON: Since Mr. Stevens appointed me Trustee.

JUDGE HART: Acting Trustee.

MS. DILLON: Yes, Your Honor, though I hope with the probate of the
estate the appointment will become permanent.

JUDGE HART: I see. (pause) All right then, why don't I take all of this
under advisement and set a date for a formal hearing.

MS. DILLON: That would be great, Judge.

JUDGE HART: Now, I've reviewed the Trust's balance sheet, and I see
that it is a very significant Trust.

MS. DILLON: We hope to do a lot of good, Judge.

JUDGE HART: I'm referring to its size, its assets, and income.

MS. DILLON: The Kost family was very wealthy, Your Honor.

JUDGE HART: It makes me wonder whether or not you might feel
the need for some help with this whole thing, someone
schooled in the ways of high finance and large
numbers.

MS. DILLON: Your Honor?

JUDGE HART: I'm asking if you might feel the need for some assistance
in managing this Trust, perhaps a Co-Trustee, someone
who could play a role in an advisory or even a supervisory
capacity.

MS. DILLON: No, Your Honor, I don't think so. I did attend law school,
and I'm familiar with the laws governing foundations like
this. I believe I'm qualified to fill the position.

JUDGE HART: I'm not questioning your abilities, Ms. Dillon, I'm thinking in terms of size and complexities.

MS. DILLON: Of course, Your Honor, if you'd like for me to report on a
quarterly or monthly basis as to . . .

JUDGE HART: No, Ms. Dillon, I'm not a school teacher and I don't like grading papers. I'm getting the impression that you're missing the thrust of my concerns here.

MS. DILLON: No, Your Honor, I . . .

JUDGE HART: Now, you're not a lawyer, is that right?

MS. DILLON: No, I'm not.

JUDGE HART: I'm curious, then. Why didn't you take the bar exam? You're obviously bright enough.

MS. DILLON: It's a long story, Judge, I really don't want to burden the Court with all of that.

JUDGE HART: All right, then, but these are serious matters we're discussing here. And if the monies from the insurance policy ultimately pass to the Trust, then we are talking about a very, very well-endowed charity, and I believe the appointment of a second Trustee would be in the best interest of the Trust and the wishes of the deceased.

MS. DILLON: A second Trustee.

JUDGE HART: Yes, two pairs of eyes, so to speak.

MS. DILLON: I see, Your Honor.

JUDGE HART: Nancy? Do you have the red file?

MS. TALBOT: Right here, Judge.

JUDGE HART: As Nancy would say, the good news is . . . The good news is we don't have to look very far for a suitable candidate. I have here an executed and notarized document appointing Coop Johnson as Trustee.

MS. DILLON: That's imposs—

JUDGE HART: I'm sorry?

MS. DILLON: I had no idea that Mr. Stevens had signed a document like this.

JUDGE HART: He signed one to appoint you.

MS. DILLON: I didn't know he'd also appointed Mr. Johnson.

JUDGE HART: Well, it appears that he did. Do you know Mr. Johnson?

MS. DILLON: Yes, Your Honor.

JUDGE HART: Do you know him well?

MS. DILLON: Very well, Your Honor. Mr. Johnson happens to be my godfather.

JUDGE HART: Your godfather!

MS. DILLON: Yes, Your Honor.

JUDGE HART: Well, that's excellent, then. The Court's satisfied that the two of you will do a wonderful job working together, and, given no further impediments to probate, I'm confident we can wrap this up. Nancy, what's the calendar look like?

MS. TALBOT: We're staring at the holidays and then we have the second week of January.

JUDGE HART: Let's mark it down for that Tuesday. 10:00 A.M. Is that all right with you, Ms. Dillon?

MS. DILLON: Yes, Your Honor.

JUDGE HART: Good, then . . . Oh, one last thing. Do you have Manny Whitman's address?

MS. DILLON: What?

JUDGE HART: Ms. Whitman. Do you have any contact information for her?

MS. DILLON: No, Your Honor. Why do you need . . .

JUDGE HART: Ms. Dillon, it's very simple. I've been made aware of a fraud perpetrated on this Court. Obviously Manny Whitman was involved, but there must have been somebody else advising her, somebody conversant in the law. Whoever that might be, the two of them conspired to commit a crime. Now, I might admire your forgiving nature, but I have a duty to . . .

MS. DILLON: With all due respect, Your Honor . . .

JUDGE HART: And I appreciate your offer of all due respect, but fraud is fraud, Ms. Dillon. Certainly you would agree that it must be investigated.

MS. DILLON: Well, I . . .

JUDGE HART: And that's exactly what a district attorney is charged to do.

MS. DILLON: Yes, Judge.

JUDGE HART: Nancy? Get me District Attorney Reis's number.

ms. talbot: Yes, Your Honor.

judge hart: All right, then. So, I guess we'll see you in January, then.

ms. dillon: Thank you, Your Honor.

Status Conference ends at 11:42 A.M.

NAM

—◆—

Former Detective Mark Moraski wakes early on New Year's Day, the Sunday morning after the New Year's Eve he and his wife partied with the partners and associates from the firm he'll join in two weeks. The night went well, the mine field of booze, bosses, and bullshit offered up no victims of consequence as Mark and his wife dodged and weaved and charmed and smiled their way through four hours of "welcome aboard" and "we could use a detective on staff."

His wife stays in bed, sleeping off the one rum and tonic that was more than enough to remind her why she never drinks liquor. Mark rubs his head, feeling the four drinks, especially the last one that unsettled him, loosened his tongue, and allowed him to laugh a genuine laugh, the kind of laugh that rings ten times louder the next morning when a person dissects the prior night's activities and their potential impact on his career, salary, and future.

"Fuck it," Mark says as his bare foot steps on a small toy made of rubber as hard as a diamond bit. He falls to the side and lands with legs spread on the couch. The Christmas tree looks tired in the morning light. His head aches a little, but he writes it off to a head cold that's been plaguing him since Thanksgiving. Barney, the bulldog, saunters into the room, his thick tongue folded like the petal of a red flower, panting as if he'd run a mile, looking at Mark the way dogs look, offering whatever they offer, waiting on whatever is offered in return.

"Come here, Barney," Mark says, and Barney leaps twice before his short legs hoist him onto the couch where he snuggles by Mark's side. "Have a good New Year's Eve?" Mark asks, and the dog yawns. Mark looks over the packages, some in piles, all opened with the wrapping paper torn in strips, and the little cardboard village from his childhood set up under the green tree, a real tree, because it would always be a real tree.

"Are we going today, Dad?" It's Mark's daughter, Celia, his youngest, and Mark watches as she steps into the room avoiding all the toys and dolls and everything else strewn across the floor, as if she has a sixth sense about toys and where they belong.

"Good morning, my lovely daughter," Mark says, as Barney raises and lowers his head, debating whether to jump off the couch and join Celia by the tree.

"I told Marnie we probably were," Celia says.

"Were what?" Mark asks.

"Going to see the kids. It's Sunday. They'll be waiting," and Mark remembers his promise to bring puppies every Sunday for the kids at the Children's Hospital. He wonders whether New Year's Day qualifies or relieves him of his promise, and realizing it doesn't, pulls himself together, makes mental notes about calling the rescue pound, getting the puppies, driving the car, doing what he promised to do.

"I guess we're going then," Mark says, and Celia tells him she can't wait, that it's her favorite thing to do, that it makes Sundays better because she doesn't spend the whole day worrying about going to school on Monday.

"Why do you worry about going to school?" Mark asks.

"I don't really," Celia says. "It's just because I'd rather stay home and play."

"School's no fun?" Mark asks.

"Dad," Celia says. "It's school."

Mark leans back and ponders the wisdom of children.

———◆◆◆———

It's late morning and Mary-Ellen Moraski's in the kitchen scrambling eggs and making waffles. The two girls are seated at the kitchen table playing with the new dolls Santa brought for Christmas. Mary-Ellen's talking to Mark about the people she met the night before, and Mark leans against the counter.

"I thought he was particularly nice to you," Mary-Ellen says, and she's referring to Mr. Forbes, the octogenarian partner, the grand presence, who oversees the workings of the firm he helped found sixty years ago.

"I don't think he heard a word I said," Mark says.

"Of course he did," Mary-Ellen says.

"He's deaf as a post," Mark says. "Everybody knows that."

"He may be, but he noticed you, and men like him don't get to where they are without a certain sense about people, and I'm telling you that old man knows you're something special."

The compliment, seductive and almost true, embarrasses Mark. "Oh, I'm special all right," Mark says to himself.

"Daddy," Celia calls out, disturbing him, bringing him back, the special man, the good father, the good husband, the good boy.

"What is it honey?"

"Did you call the rescue pound?"

"Sure did," he says.

"You're going today?" Mary-Ellen asks, a hitch in the question.

"Yeah, we promised," Mark says. "Why don't you come with us?"

"No," Mary-Ellen says, pouring the scrambled eggs onto a platter, placing waffles around the outer edge, dodging the dog as she sets the food on the table. "I thought we'd watch football today," she says, the southern girl brought up on the Southern Conference with tales of the Bulldogs, the Hurricanes, the Gators, the Tide, and the Bear.

"We'll be back by the second game," Mark says, taking a seat next to Celia, helping her with the platter and the large spoon, serving the eggs and a waffle with extra syrup.

"I like football," Marnie, the older daughter, says as she flips through the newspaper looking for the funnies, and Mary-Ellen asks if maybe she'd like to stay home on this frozen day and watch TV with her.

Marnie looks around, looks at the ceiling, looks at her sister, Celia, looks at her father, and shakes her head no; she'll go to the hospital like she said she would.

"Well, I guess it's just me again," Mary-Ellen says, and this time the southern accent is so broad, it makes the girls smile.

———◆◆◆———

The puppies are housed in small carrying cases set on the backseat. Celia talks to them the whole way, putting her fingers up to the screen windows.

They arrive at the hospital, and the girls get out of the car. Mark grabs the carrying cases, and Marnie lets Barney jump down on the cold asphalt where he shivers and waddles across the lot to the hospital's front doors. "Barney," Marnie calls out, but the dog keeps walking, knowing in his dog brain that he'll get warm again as soon as he gets himself behind those doors.

The nurse on duty welcomes Mark and the girls and tells them it's a light day because most of the kids are visiting with parents and Santa's still around.

"Santa?" Celia asks.

"He stays an extra day or two for the sick kids," the nurse says, and Mark gathers his brood and starts down the corridor to Lounge B where seven kids are sitting in wheelchairs. As soon as they see the Moraski family and the puppies, their faces brighten and Celia and Marnie walk among them, as comfortable as children can be with one another.

Karen, a candy striper, enters soon after and helps unload the puppies. Mark oversees the operation and when he's sure things are under control and everybody's busy with the dogs, he tells Karen he has to run an errand that will take him an hour or two. "Will you be okay here?" he asks, and Karen says she'll be fine, that the kids will be fine, and Mark tells his daughters to be good, that he'll be back soon. They wave without looking at him, rolling on the floor with one of the dogs they've named Midget.

———◆◆◆———

Mark leaves the hospital and walks to the car, clicks the key ring, opens the trunk, and takes out a brown-paper package. He closes the trunk, looks around the white horizon, and starts across the parking lot to a row of pine trees at the edge of the lot. He steps over an old drift and through a small thicket of pine bushes, picking up the walkway that circles the narrow end of a frozen pond fed by the runoff from the reservoir situated on the other side of the hospital complex.

In the distance he sees the low building, a cinder-block bunker attached to an older blond building with the nineteenth-century frieze of neo-Greek Americana, something borrowed and meant to signify power, excellence, honor, and good medicine.

Mark walks the hundred yards along the path to the bunker, slipping once, almost causing a muscle spasm, an admonition to watch his step.

He enters the hospital through a side door in the bunker building. The security desk is empty, and Mark looks around and listens to the sound of a football game on a small TV on the edge of the desk. "Hello," he calls, but there's no answer until a door opens and an old guy in a rented uniform pulls his pants tight around his waist and hooks his belt.

"Help you, sir?" he says.

"I'm here to see a friend," Mark says.

"Who would that be?" the guard asks.

"Matthew Wyman."

The security guard looks at Mark, says nothing, his eyes going over him, stopping on the brown package and then moving on. He flips a few dog-eared pages in a three-ring binder. "You here to see Michelangelo," the guard says.

"I'm sorry?"

"We call him Michelangelo. I tell you that boy's got a way with making statues. You know he could do all that?"

"Yes, I did, I mean, I do," Mark says, and he takes his wallet from his back pocket, flips it open, and shows the badge he kept from his early days on the force. "I've been working with him for a long time now," Mark says.

The guard sees the badge and his shoulders relax. He takes his seat and turns down the audio on the TV.

"Yes, sir, I expect you have," the guard says.

"So where can I find him?" Mark asks.

"Where he always is these days—down that hall there, in the artsy crafts room. If he's not sleeping in his room he's down there and sometimes he even sleeps down there. They let him. Everybody round here

likes him. Fact is everybody round here wonders what the hell he's doing here."

"I wonder, too," Mark says, and he asks the guard who's winning the
game and the guard tells him Oklahoma's up by three.

"Sooners," Mark says.

"Sooners better than Laters," the guard says.

"Yes, sir," Mark says.

"Yes, sir," the old guy says.

———◆◆◆———

The crafts room is wide and long with windows on one side, netted and
meshed, narrow little mail slots set nine feet high in ten-foot walls. The
lights in the ceiling are long and bright and the walls are yellow and the
crafts tables are clean except for the one at the end where there's a box
with several clay sculptures.

Behind the table Matthew and his friend Charlie, the orderly, sit
and drink tea while overhead the TV flickers and football players run
about the field.

"Here he is," Charlie says, and Matthew looks up.

"These your latest?" Mark Moraski asks, pointing to the box of
sculptures.

"Happy New Year, Detective," Matthew says.

"Same to you, Matt and Charlie, and I'm not a detective anymore."

"So you did it then," Charlie says.

"Right after Thanksgiving. Gave notice and they gave me a cake."

"So it's on to a law firm," Matthew says.

"How bad can it be?" Mark Moraski asks.

"I expect it can be pretty bad," Charlie says. "But then again I bet
those boys downtown pay pretty good. I got a cousin, he was the one
with all the brains in our family, they even sent that boy to Princeton in
New Jersey, if you can believe that, he started in a law firm in New York
City and first year he's making more than my entire family's ever made."

"Well, money's money," Mark says, one of those wisdom statements
that mean nothing. "So this is interesting," he says, looking over the
clay figures in the box.

"He's been down here fourteen days and nights straight doin' them," Charlie says. "Not to mention the one he's workin' on now."

"What one?" Mark asks, and Charlie pulls a huge sculpture draped in a gray sheet from behind a partition.

"Can I?" Mark asks Matthew.

Matthew nods and Mark pulls the sheet off the large figure of a young woman, draped in a nun's habit, semireclining, one arm limp by her side, her face turned and made beautiful in passion, ecstasy, or both.

"Oh my God," Mark says.

"Told ya," Charlie says.

"This is unbelievable."

"He's gettin' good, huh?"

"Thank you," Matthew says, turning back to the TV.

"No, really, what is this?" Mark asks.

"It's Bernini's Teresa of Avila."

"I thought I'd seen this somewhere, on a card or something."

"Michelangelo or what?" Charlie says. "I told ya."

Mark can't take his eyes from the sculpture. He steps up to it, close enough to breathe on it, and follows the many folds of drapery down the woman's long body. Then he stands straight, looks at Matthew, and shakes his head. "Jesus," he says, and Matthew continues to watch the football game.

"Oh," Mark says, "I almost forgot," and he holds up the brown-paper package.

"What?" Matthew asks.

"These are for you," and he hands the package to Matthew.

"How much was it?" Matthew asks.

"Never mind about that. Merry Christmas."

"No, I've got money," Matthew says.

"He's got a benefactor is what he's got," Charlie says, and Matthew gives Charlie a look.

"I got money, too," Mark says, "but this is a present."

"Thank you," Matthew says, and he rips the paper and takes the three books in hand. "You even got the Schopenhauer."

"Shope and who?" Charlie asks.

"Schopenhauer," Matthew says.

"Wasn't he some kind of musician or something, like Beethoven?" Charlie asks.

"Philosopher," Matthew says. "A pessimist."

"Now what the hell you want to go readin' some pess'mist for? You're already in a nut house, don't need no other reason to get down on things."

Matthew turns the pages. The book's old and battered, the pages thumbed and brown.

"That was the hard one," Mark says. "I had to go online and find one of those old book Web sites."

"There is a paperback," Matthew says. "But I guess there's not much call for him these days."

A bell sounds and a voice wrapped in cotton announces three names, Charlie's being the third.

"Now what the hell is that?" Charlie asks, taking a look at the football game and the scores in the crawl line. He tells Matthew not to miss the halftime scores on two channels and then leaves the crafts room, saying he'll be back when he's back.

Mark circles the room, looking at the patient art taped to the walls. Then he sits in the chair near the hot plate. He looks from Matthew's sculpture to Matthew and back again. The whole time Matthew doesn't move.

"Well?" Mark asks.

"Well," Matthew says.

"Did you think about what we talked about?"

"I thought about it," Matthew says, "but I don't think I've got any information that would help. Anyway, you're not a detective anymore."

"That's right, Matt, I'm not. Now I'm just a lawyer with a big firm that takes on all kinds of cases, pro bono and all of that, and I'll have a staff of paralegals and as many investigators as I need to straighten this thing out."

"Leave it alone," Matthew says.

"No, Matthew. I won't. You know I won't, and you know you don't belong here, and the only reason you're stonewalling me is because you got this crazy idea in your head that you do belong here, that you're guilty for something, and this is the only way you can pay it off."

"I like it here," Matthew says. "It's a good place for me. I got a friend. I got all the art supplies I need. I got a bed, food, a roof, health benefits. It's not so bad. The only fucked-up thing about it is it's better than what I could do for myself out there."

"No, Matthew, I won't accept that. You're too sane, and you've got too much talent to spend your life in a psych ward."

"It's not like it's voluntary," Matthew says. "The judge ordered it. He's the one who put me here."

"Don't even get me started on that trumped-up deal," Mark says. "The whole thing was bullshit out of the A.G.'s office from the get-go."

"And now he's the governor."

"He is what he is."

Matthew looks at the TV screen. He grabs a pen and piece of paper. There's ten seconds left in the first half of one game. He writes down the score, stands, reaches, changes the channel, and writes down the second. He says, "Charlie's got so many ways of betting these things, up and unders and overs and halves and quarters. Guy's a maniac."

"Charlie says you got a benefactor?"

"Anonymous. I don't even know how he came upon my situation here."

"What does he do? Give you money for supplies?"

"A little spending money for the commissary, and every two weeks I give the head nurse a list of what I need. Art stuff. Two days later they deliver it. Whatever I ask for."

"That's a good deal."

"I think it is," Matthew says.

"Matthew," Mark says, rubbing his hands.

"What, Detective Moraski?"

"Please, just tell me what you saw that night—who was there, what you heard."

"What night are we talking about?"

"The night you went back to Punter's Pond. The night you got sick."

"I really can't remember."

"I know Manny was there."

"I figure she was. We lived there."

"But there was somebody else there, too."

"Yes, I guess there was."

"Well, who was it?"

"I can't remember."

"I'll tell you what I think."

"What?"

"Your brother was there."

"You think he was involved?"

"I do."

"What makes you think that?"

"Because he's the only person who'd make you keep silent this long."

"He's the only family I got."

"Yeah, well, how many times has 'the-only-family-you-got' come to visit you since you been here?"

"He's a busy guy."

"Bullshit, Matthew. He hates you; he fucked you; he can't help himself. He'll always fuck you." Moraski inhales deeply and blows it out with a sigh of almost surrender.

"Mark, don't think I'm not grateful. I am. I know you want to help me. I know you're a good man, and I am very grateful for your visits and the books you bring me, but really, look at me, I had a lot of chances out there, more than most, and the best I could do was to end up here."

Mark and Matthew say nothing for a long time. Then the sound of the TV strikes the room with the sound of a marching band, and Matthew checks to see if he's got the scores right.

"I'm not giving up on this," Mark says. "I'm going to find out how to prove what I know, and I'm going to get you out of here, whether you like it or not."

"And then what?" Matthew asks. "Where will I go? What will I do? Live in a cemetery again?"

"You can work for me," Mark says. "You can sculpt things, you can do legal research and make a few bucks and get your own place and have your own studio and go out to dinner and walk around the park and meet girls and normal stuff—just normal stuff, and what the fuck is wrong with normal stuff?"

The speech makes Matthew smile, and then Mark Moraski smiles, and they both begin to laugh.

"I like that," Matthew says. "'What the fuck is wrong with normal stuff?'"

Moraski stands and stretches. He's tired now. It was a long night and this has been a long day. He tells Matthew he'll see him next month, to wait on it, to pencil it in, to plan on it, normal stuff, and he'll bring the book on Stevens if he can find it.

Matthew stands and takes a small box wrapped in Christmas paper from under his chair. He hands it to Moraski.

"What's this?" Moraski asks.

"It's nothing," Matthew says.

Moraski starts to open it.

"Don't open it here," Matthew says. "It's a gift—like, so maybe it'll be best if you open it at home."

Moraski stops and holds the little box. "Jesus, Matthew, you're giving me a Christmas present?"

"Yeah, kinda. I mean it's New Year's so maybe it's like a present for the new year. New beginnings and all of that."

"But it's a present?"

"Yeah, it is."

Moraski shakes his head, and he and Matthew embrace. "So you mean it when you say you're gonna help me with all that normal stuff?" Matthew asks.

"I will," Moraski says, "you can count on it. Marines don't leave their wounded behind."

"I'm not a marine," Matthew says.

"No, but you're fucked up enough to be one," Mark says, and he waves once and leaves.

━━━◆◆◆━━━

Moraski pulls into his driveway. The girls and Barney get out and run over the sidewalk and the snow to the front door where their mother waits for them.

Mark drives to the back of the house and parks the car in the tool-shed that's big enough to double as a garage. He puts on the light inside the car and picks up the little box off the seat. He opens it and pulls back the tissue paper. It's a tiny sculpture of something, though at first he can't make it out. He moves it about with his fingers and then sees it, two walls that meet at the focal point of a wide angle. The walls are deepest in the center where they meet and then recede in height, rising to the flat line at the top, equal to the horizon and the ground behind. It's painted black and polished and there are faint markings on the flat walls. It's a miniature sculpture of the Vietnam Memorial.

Moraski holds it up to the light and marvels at the precision of the angles, the manner in which Matthew made the whole thing on such a small scale. "Vietnam," Moraski thinks, the place he didn't have to go. He sets the piece back in the box and remembers Billy the Driver. "Two tours," Billy told him that day in April when they sat on Billy's front porch. There was the gold chain around Billy's neck with the little gold cross and something else, a gold charm in the shape of the war memorial, cast in gold like the cross, hung on the same chain.

"Billy James," Moraski says, his breath fogging the inside of the windshield. He checks his watch and dials the kitchen on his cell. His wife picks up. Moraski tells her he has to run an errand. He asks if there's anything she needs at the store, the offer made to soften the unexpected change in plans.

"What about dinner?" she asks.

"You and the girls go ahead," he says. "I'll grab something while I'm out."

Moraski drives across town, takes a wrong turn, rights himself, and finds Billy's street. He makes the slow house-to-house crawl and tries to visualize Billy's front porch or the neighbor's house across the street. It's dark and two street lights are out and it's hard to make out one house from another. Then, as he nears the end of the street, he sees the silhouette of a man's head in a front window backlit by yellow light. He looks to the left and sees the neighbor's front porch. He turns to the right and sees the driveway and the garage where the kids sat at the folding table, counting money for the Amazing Levon.

Moraski parks. He grabs the little box, leaves the car, and steps onto Billy's porch. Before he rings the bell, Billy opens the front door.

"Yes, sir," Billy says.

"Hi, Billy, maybe you remember me. I'm . . ."

"Detective Moraski."

"Well, you're partly right. I'm not a detective anymore. Now I'm just a small-town lawyer."

"Is that good or bad?" Billy asks.

"Too soon to tell," Moraski says. "Mind if I come in for a minute?"

Billy hesitates a moment, then opens the door.

Moraski walks into the hallway and wipes his shoes on the carpet laid to the side, cluttered with a row of work boots.

"Ever wonder why we live in such a harsh climate?" Moraski asks.

"Yeah, sometimes I wonder," Billy says.

Billy leads Moraski to the front room where Moraski takes a seat on the other side of the table where Billy's piled books, a Walkman, and a stack of cassette tapes.

"You like to listen to music?" Moraski asks.

"Not so much anymore," Billy says. "Thing is I've got these cataracts in my eyes, so when my eyes tire, I get into them talking books."

Moraski nods. He says his father had cataracts. He says there's surgery for that.

"I know," Billy says. "So, what can I do for you, Detective?"

"If I'm not way off on this," Moraski says, "I'm guessing you might already know."

Billy just stares at Moraski. His face is unmoved. He says nothing.

"What I mean," Moraski says, "is that I visited a friend of ours today."

"Of ours?"

"Matthew Wyman."

"The Professor. How is he?"

"He's good, Billy. I mean, you and I both know he's no crazier than half the people we deal with every day, and his health is good. He's put on some weight, and he's got a friend out there—this guy, Charlie.

Seems like a good guy, and as Matthew says, where else is he going to get three hots and a cot, benefits, art supplies, and a friend?"

"Probably the army if they ever got into the art business," Billy says.

Moraski laughs, recalls Paris Island and the blunt aesthetic of sargent bodybuilders with pop eyes and impossible voices.

"So, what's up, Detective?" Billy asks, leaning forward, wanting to move it along.

"What's up is this, Billy. Matthew gave me this present before I left today, and I got home and opened it up and thought maybe you'd like to see it."

"What is it?"

Moraski opens the box and pulls back the tissue paper. He pulls out the small sculpture and hands it to Billy. Billy takes it in his fingers and holds it up to the light on the table.

"This what I think it is?" Billy asks.

"Think so."

"To be honest I always put up with the Professor talkin' about him being an artist, but I never thought he had the talent for it. Though I gotta say this here's a pretty good piece of work."

"You should see the other things he's been doing out there."

"Oh, yeah?"

"Unbelievable. I mean, really, unbelievable."

"I hope to visit sometime."

"Anyway," Mark says, pointing to the piece in Billy's hands, "when I saw that, I thought of you."

"You did, huh?"

"Well, yeah, two tours and all, and you got a sweater on now, but last spring when we were sitting outside . . ."

"You mean this," Billy says, and he reaches in and pulls out the gold chain around his neck with the little cross and the charm-sized model of the war memorial."

"That's what I mean."

"We got these from this colonel we served with in '71. Second tour. He had 'em made special for three of us. Said we'd saved his life, which we had. Though one of the guys never made it all the way back."

"I'm sorry, Billy."

"Ancient history now."

"Yeah, but," Moraski pauses, "just sayin' I'm sorry is all."

"Thank you, sir."

"So, Billy . . ."

"So?"

"Maybe nothing, I just had this idea that maybe Matthew, being as clever as he is, might have left some information with you that would, you know, help his situation or something like that."

"Information about what, Mr. Moraski?"

"Call me, Mark, please. I'm just a bullshit lawyer now."

"They got them in Hartford, too?" Billy asks, and he starts to laugh, and Moraski laughs, this time for real, and the ice melts some, and Billy leans forward in his seat and starts to finger the cassettes on the table. "It's like this, Mark. I won't do anything that hurts Matthew, and I won't do anything that hurts me, either. I know Matthew pretty well by now, and I know what staying at that place means to him, even though it doesn't make a bit of sense to me or you. I figure you've got to give a man the benefit of the doubt sometimes. Anyway, he's always told me he's got a way out anytime he feels the need."

"A way out?"

"That's right."

"It's just hard to believe he wouldn't have shown it to me by now. Or to somebody. He knows we're for him."

"Like his family was for him?"

"Good point," Moraski says, and he begins to stand. Billy stands, too, and they start to shake hands when Billy pulls back and rubs his forehead.

"You okay?" Mark asks.

"Yeah, yeah," Billy says. "But there is one thing."

"What's that?"

"Wait here." Billy walks to the end of the hallway and opens a tool-box sitting on a shelf near the kitchen. He takes out a hammer and walks back.

"Could I see that thing again?"

"What?"

"The sculpture Matthew gave you."

Moraski hesitates and then hands it to Billy.

Billy holds it in his hands, shakes it once, sets it on the floor, swings the hammer, and smashes it to bits.

"What the hell did you do that for?"

Billy holds up his hand, bends over, and rummages through the shards of clay. He picks up a paper, yellowed at the folds.

"This is for you," he says, and he hands the paper to Moraski.

"What's this?"

"Looks like a phone bill."

"I don't understand."

"Can't say as I do, either. All I know is Matthew told me if you ever came by here with a clay thing like you brought tonight, I was supposed to do what I just did, and give you whatever I found inside."

"Matthew was behind this."

"He was."

Moraski takes the phone bill and examines it.

"This is a bill from last September."

"All right, then."

"He's highlighted some things. September 29."

"Whose bill is it?"

"Manny Whitman's."

"Well, that's something."

"Matthew," Moraski says.

"The Professor," Billy says.

"He's a funny one."

"Now maybe you got what you were lookin' for."

"Yes, Billy, maybe I do."

MATTHEW'S CATALOGUE

Moraski left the hospital around five and Charlie's still on call. Matthew takes a broom and sweeps dried chips of clay in the corner of the crafts room where he works on his Bernini. Then he unloads the pieces from the cardboard box—clay sculptures of everyday people doing everyday things. He lines them up and considers them a company, a troop, an ensemble. He places them on a shelf in accord with a chronology known only to himself, and he imagines that someday, maybe a hundred years from now, when this empire's a subject for history and the Chinese rule the world, somewhere in Taiwan or Hong Kong or Beijing, at a new Christie's or Sotheby's, they'll take out his little sculptures and raise their Ping-Pong paddles and bid outrageous prices in their decadence as we've paid outrageous prices for bottled water ostensibly drawn from melting ice shelves in the Antarctic. He imagines how there will be a full-color catalogue with four-color separation and a short biography of America's Utrillo, all of it designed to confirm the escapade, to affirm the prices paid, to salve buyer's remorse.

LOT 1, ITEM 1: "Untitled"—Clay sculpture, baked, hardened, shellacked: Two men sitting in a booth in a diner; one holds a coffee cup, one holds a fork.

And Matthew remembers:

Yes, Mrs. O'Neal was upset after her birthday party. Yes, she cried on the ride home. Yes, the Amazing Levon, Mr. Deacon Leavitt, only made it worse, waltzing about, telling people's secrets, talking about children who've never been born, a dead husband, and the divergence between

383

the way things are and the way things are supposed to be. And, yes, I walked her to her door while Billy the Driver stayed behind in the car, and it was painful when she shed her armor, when her sadness made her a person and not a type of person, the pleasant aristocrat, the often generous, but always guarded, character I'd known for months.

Billy and I drove around for a while. He asked if I wanted to go for coffee and I said that would be good. We stopped off at a diner and sat in a booth and ordered coffees, and Billy had a piece of pie. The lights inside were bright enough to turn the windows into mirrors, and I saw myself, clearly, the face I'd always wanted—thin, drawn, with that cowboy squint and the heroic grimace of the drifter riding forever into a sun that will never set.

What are you starin' at? Billy asked, and I said nothing and watched him as he cut the pie with the edge of his fork and ate it. Then he held the fork in his fingers and poked the air with it.

Who was this psychic guy? he asked.

I don't know, some guy. Deacon somebody.

He was a deacon?

That was his name.

I thought his name was Levon.

That's his stage name.

Stage name.

That's right.

You know who he is?

No, yeah. I mean, what do you mean?

Who invited him to the party?

I don't know.

What's he doin' in New Haven?

Some paranormal shrink's been studying his brain. She's at Yale.

So you don't know, then.

Know what?

How they're connected.

Who?

This Deacon-Levon and Mrs. O'Neal.

What do you mean they're connected?

Never mind what I mean.

Okay.

But that's why Mrs. O'Neal was crying.

Why?

I had to drive her downtown couple of weeks ago, state offices. She went in and came out, and she was not a happy woman.

So what are you telling me, Billy?

Never mind what I'm telling you; I ain't telling you nothin'.

Yeah, okay, but you are.

Nothin'.

She once told me that she had a son.

You forget about that, Billy said. Now, you want some pie?

No, thanks, I said, and he finished and paid the bill and drove me to Manny's place.

When I got inside I took off Tommy O'Neal's suit, stuffed it in a bag, and put the bag in the hall closet. If Manny had seen me wearing the suit, she would have peppered me with a thousand questions, and I didn't want to get into the whole thing about Mrs. O'Neal not inviting her to her birthday party. Then I went into the bedroom, got into bed, rolled over, and waited.

Where have you been? she asked.

I was out.

Out where?

I browsed a bookstore and then sat in a diner for a while.

All night?

Time got away from me. I was thinking.

You should have called me.

I didn't have my phone.

I got the package deal for both of us. You should keep the phone with you.

I will, I said.

What were you thinking about? she asked.

I was thinking about how TV's fucked us all up.

Oh god, one of those nights.

Yeah, one of those.

Well, get to sleep; we have to get up early.

What for?

We're taking my aunt to church in the morning.

Oh, right, I forgot about that. I just forgot.

I'll wake you.

Thanks.

> LOT 2, ITEM 1: "Untitled"—Clay sculpture, baked, hardened, shellacked: Young woman descending a staircase, holding a cane and a cell phone.

The next morning we drove to Mrs. O'Neal's house. It looked different in the sunlight, like any big house in a clean and well-tended neighborhood, like a postcard from another time when everybody was supposed to have lived in clean houses in well-tended neighborhoods.

Manny asked if I had any cash.

Some.

Get some bagels, then.

What?

Why don't you drive down to that deli we went to before and get my aunt some bagels and a small tub of cream cheese. She loves that in the morning.

Why don't I go after church?

Just go now, she said, and I watched her lean on her cane, shaking her bad leg once, twice, before she swung it out of the car and found her footing. Then she turned and leaned into the open window: Get two kinds of cream cheese, she said. One plain and the other with onions or garlic.

I hate that kind, I said, and she said the plain will be for you.

So I drove to the deli with no license, no right or privilege to drive, but driving nonetheless, having gotten used to it, because Manny hated to drive.

The deli was open and almost empty except for the guy behind the counter and the two women standing there. The first woman paid and left, but the second woman took forever. She was old and anxious and began the long nightmare as she ordered, looked again, changed her order, questioned the guy, changed her order, argued, changed her order, complained, and changed her order.

And you, sir? the guy said, as the old woman grabbed her bag, stopped, and was about to ask for something else.

Please, madam, the guy said, I have another customer, and she turned, saw me, shrank a little, and looked down, almost shamefaced, apologizing for having caused trouble, for being almost blind, for being old.

I ordered the bagels and the cream cheese and drove back to Mrs. O'Neal's house.

The parlor was dark and it took a moment for my eyes to adjust when I saw Manny stepping down the stairs, unsteady, her cane in the same hand she used to grab the railing, her cell phone pressed to her ear.

Are you sure? she asked and slapped the phone shut when she saw me.

What's going on? I asked, and she stood there, her face pale, her eyes wide and dark.

What is it? I asked. Did something happen upstairs? What happened, Manny?

She crossed the room and took a seat. My aunt, she said, and we went back and forth with it until I climbed the stairs and saw the strip of light outlining the door to Mrs. O'Neal's bedroom.

What do you want me to do? I asked. What's going on, Manny? Tell me what happened here. And she told me to keep going, to continue on. So I walked down the hall and opened the door and the first thing was the silence, more than the absence of sound, more like a fluid or medium, the kind of balmy air in which one moves slowly, in which one might look over his shoulder to see if somebody's nearby, to see if somebody might feel the same presence of something ineffable described by the borders of what's there and the inference of what's not.

Mrs. O'Neal, I said, and the sound of my voice bounced off nothing and I was hyperaware of everything, as if someone had put the world in high definition.

I entered the room.

There was the carpet, the bed, the white and powder-blue bedding, rumpled, and pulled a little, the topography of tiny Alps, and then the plastic garment bag, draped over her head, with her hands at her side, palms down, her face peaceful, her eyes closed, her skin smooth with the hint of a smile on her closed lips.

My first thought was to remove the bag, to fix things, to get her air as soon as possible. But I stopped when I realized it was too late for that, that the best thing I could do would be to leave everything as I'd found it.

Jesus, I said, an exclamation and a kind of prayer, because there was energy in the room to be lapped up in the way some psychics and seers say they acquired their gifts. But this energy wasn't the postlife cry of an undeserving victim, this was the energy of something else—of questions, worry, anxiety, inquiry, too much thought, something dark and all too recent.

I left the room, walked down the hall, and looked down on Manny who was sitting in a chair in the middle of the parlor, head down, forehead in hand, that thinker pose, made doubly intense with concern that mimicked sadness.

Call the police, I said. Call Bobby Sullivan.

She looked up, her frosted hair falling back over her pale face, her fingers trembling, then drumming the arm of the chair.

Call the police, I said. I'll call Bobby Sullivan, thinking if I divided the labors maybe she'd do something. But she just sat there and stared at me.

I went back to the room and called Bobby Sullivan. He called Louis LaPorta and within an hour the place was noisy with people and arguments.

Who did this? was the first thing Bobby Sullivan asked me, and I realized he was thinking something other than suicide.

Who did what? I asked.

Who put that bag over her head?

I don't know, I said. You're making assumptions, here. Maybe she did it to herself.

Bullshit, he said. Look at her hands, look at her face. She died a peaceful death, natural causes. If she'd done it to herself, or someone had done it to her, she wouldn't look so peaceful. Believe me, I've seen too many suicides over the years and more than a few murders. Her hands wouldn't be down by her side like that; they'd be grabbing the edge of this thing. It's not easy to suffocate yourself.

That's a stretch, Bobby, Louis LaPorta said, and Sullivan turned on him, invoking reason, experience, history, friendship, and anything else to keep Louis LaPorta on board, calling him Louie, reminding him that he'd know him since he was a kid, that they went back, that loyalty trumps everything.

Billy appeared at the top of the stairs and craned his neck to see what was going on. Sullivan slammed the door in his face and then turned on me, pointing his finger at my chest, telling me this whole thing must have been staged and that I better get on board with the way things went down, because the truth of what really happened was the only thing that mattered.

Then he took the bag off her head and handed it to me.

Get rid of this, he said.

I looked at LaPorta, who shrugged his shoulders and looked away.

Ten minutes later, the coroner arrived.

LOT 3, ITEM 1: "Mail"—Clay sculpture, baked, hardened, shellacked: Man perusing envelopes in hand, standing next to a door with a mail slot and several items of mail strewn about the floor.

That same day, Sunday, they cremated her body and later that week they buried the ashes in a coffin in the family plot with a full-blown, Anglican high-church funeral. The O'Neal Funeral Home spared no expense. Bobby threw his Irish wake, and I picked up a drink and drank a little and then a lot. Manny got crazy about it. She was in the program and looked on slips with a judgment as harsh as her fear of drinking again.

That afternoon, late, almost dusk, the bartender told Sullivan he'd run out of Scotch. Bobby Sullivan grabbed me by the shoulder and told me to accompany him to his place where we could pick up a few bottles for the party. His apartment was with in walking distance, so we started down the street with that fast overenergized purposeful attack that fuels drinkers in the middle of a great drunk, especially when they embark on that most sacred mission to obtain more liquor.

Slow down, he said, as I walked past the front door of the luxury apartment complex. He took out his key, unlocked the door, entered, punched the elevator, and the whole thing was a blur until I entered the apartment that looked like a Rock Hudson–Doris Day movie when early-generation Technicolor gave everything a neat, clean, insubstantial, disposable look—pop contemporary with Saarinen curves and a minimalist flair derived from mistaken thoughts of what a future in space might look like.

C'mon, he said.

I stood at the edge of the sunken living room, thinking of Barbarella and Jack Paar, and imagined Tommy O'Neal at the wet bar on the far wall, the war-vet-hero-glib-Mick entertaining any number of girls in this fuck pad, his fuck pad, Bobby's fuck pad, probably one of many.

C'mon, Sullivan said, what's the matter with you?

I shook my head and grabbed two bottles from a box in a broom closet off the kitchen.

When do you see Moraski? he asked.

Who?

Moraski, the detective.

This week sometime.

Billy going, too?

I don't know. I guess.

Moraski talk to Manny yet?

Yeah, they talked yesterday, I think.

I know Moraski's partner, Talmadge.

Okay.

He's a good guy, he won't fuck you. Moraski I don't know so well. He's a marine so that can cut either way.

What do you mean?

He can be a Boy Scout or a fuckin' serial killer or both.

Oh.

What do you plan on saying to him?

That when I entered the room there was no bag.

You got any problems with that?

Yeah.

What?

When I entered the room there was a bag.

Yeah, but the question is who put it there and why.

I didn't.

I know you didn't. I wasn't thinking about you. I was thinking about that girl who's got a ring through your nose.

You think Manny did it?

Of course she did it.

I don't think so. She loved her aunt.

They weren't even related. Manny was Tommy's kid from this Bridgeport redhead he was fuckin' years ago. Tommy had three or four kids scattered around the country. Mrs. O'Neal knew all about it. But she was a stand-up woman. She wasn't about to screw anybody if they kept things looking good.

I don't believe it, I said.

True, he said.

So you think that gives Manny some kind of motive, then?

Of course it does.

To kill her aunt?

No.

What then?

To make it look like somebody else killed her—preferably me.

You think that's what happened?

Listen, kid, you and I aren't friends. Nothing against you, but we don't know each other. I run into your brother now and then, and, frankly, he's an asshole, so it's not like you come highly recommended— though Billy says you're okay. Thing is I've been around this place longer than anybody, and not much happens that I don't know about.

So keep your nose clean with this one. Don't go swimming upstream, is what I'm saying. LaPorta's on board. The M.E.'s on board. You get on board and they won't get edgy, pointing fingers all over town.

Okay, I said.

Okay, then?

Yeah, okay.

Let's go, he said, and we walked back to the party and I drank the day away, the next day, and crashed the day after that.

The investigation started off pretty hot and then cooled after a week or two. They held interviews with everybody who'd ever known Mrs. O'Neal. They even got Manny to write out a report, which she amended a few times because she kept on thinking up new stuff to help her cause.

She convinced herself that Bobby Sullivan had killed her aunt, and every night she'd feed me with all of this bullshit about Bobby Sullivan—how evil he was, how he'd killed Emma, how he'd probably kill her if he got the chance. I'd listen and look to see if her features could have derived from the same family that had endowed Emma Kost O'Neal with such a regal bone structure, and I remembered something Mrs. O'Neal had said about Manny being her niece—at least for now.

At the end of October Manny said we should move to Punter's Pond. She said she'd be safe there, and she made it sound good with the country feel and the lake and the country roads and the woods. I probably should have thought better of it, but I didn't have anyplace else to go, and I needed my meds, and Manny used money from her allowance to help me with those. So I agreed and waited and entered this altered state of institutional sloth, suspending disbelief, taking Manny's side in the struggle for Emma's estate, spending too many hours in bed each day, unable to eat, wanting to go outside but unable to bring myself to do so.

And then one afternoon, while Manny was off somewhere, the mail came with a cell phone bill addressed to both of us. I ripped it open and searched for the date of that Sunday morning in September. I scrolled down the list of numbers and found what I was looking for—two calls to one number, made while I was at the deli.

I picked up my phone and dialed the number.

This is Ann, after the beep you know what to do.

I dialed a second time: This is Ann, after the beep you know what to do.

I dialed a third time: This is Ann, after the beep you know what to do.

LOT 4, ITEM 1: "Ann"—Clay sculpture, baked, hardened, shellacked: Woman standing in front of desk, pointing and reaching for phone on desktop; man in uniform standing with notepad, taking notes.

We moved to Punter's Pond in late November. After we got settled I told Manny I needed some money to pay for my meds. Without them I couldn't rely on myself to remain in touch with everything going on around me. She said she'd take care of it, but she kept forgetting.

After the holidays, the winter, and that season between seasons, neither winter nor spring, with the first strains of paranoia playing in the sound of the wind scraping Punter's Pond, I fell in a sinkhole and was as fragile then as I was the night we went to the Brandos for dinner when Lyle did what he could to frighten me, like in one of those one-star movies with the chain saws, sheds, and hooks.

The envelope from Bobby Sullivan had arrived and I was naïve enough to think he'd send the money, even though the truth had gotten the better of me when I finally met with Talmadge and Moraski.

By the time I drove to Hartford with twenty bucks and Sullivan's note telling me what a drunk's worth, my adrenaline was pumping, and I was ready for trouble. I arrived at the funeral home late Sunday or Monday night, I can't remember which. I'd kept a key from when I'd worked there, so I let myself in. The place was empty and dark with a few nightlights and shadows going every which way, and I figured there was a good chance Bobby Sullivan might be there since he was famous for drinking a jug and making midnight commando raids on the morgue to go through the employees' desks and lockers.

I thought I heard movement, a door opening, and stepped down the back stairs to the morgue. The overhead nightlight was on, the steel drainage tables were empty. All the bodies had been placed on pallets with runners and locked away in temperature-controlled vaults.

I was tired, inside tired, desperate tired. I took a duffel bag filled with lab coats and towels from the linen room and curled up on the floor. I figured I'd sleep a while, wake up, freshen up, and wait upstairs for Sullivan.

It blew up the next morning when little Heinrich Himmler from Troy caught me sleeping in the morgue and treated me like a rodent that should have been exterminated the last time they'd had the place sprayed. Then the other guy came in, the guy from New Haven, and he'd always been decent, and he tried to calm things down and let it slip that Sullivan was meeting with his lawyer.

So I left the place with the Nazi screaming at me the whole way out the door, and I drove across town to the football building and took the elevator to Cal Stevens's office.

It wasn't much of an office. The front was all glass with his name in gold leaf on the door. Ann Dillon was sitting in the reception area making notes on a phone pad. When she saw me she caught her breath and refashioned her imperturbable front, the prerogative of a vastly superior person.

Hello, Matthew, how can I help you?

Is Bobby Sullivan here?

He is, but I'm afraid they're both in conference right now—he and Mr. Stevens.

So, why are you afraid?

What?

You said you were afraid.

I'm not afraid.

You just said you were.

That's a figure of speech. Jesus, Matthew, what's gotten into you?

I started toward the back of the office when she grabbed my arm. She's a petite, youthful woman, but her hands are an older person's hands, fully articulated and strong.

Please, Matthew, I can't allow you to break in on their meeting.

Then I'll wait here.

And I can't allow that, either. You're not stable, and I'm afraid Mr. Stevens wouldn't want you sitting around his office.

There you go, being afraid again.

Please, Matthew.

And how do you know I'm not stable. What does not stable mean? That I want to talk to somebody who doesn't want to talk to me? That's not not-stable; that's life.

No, Matthew. It's because of what Manny's told me about you, the drinking and the medications and how you can lose it from time to time.

Manny told you that?

She did, and I'm not comfortable with you being here without an appointment or anything.

Ann, what happened to you? We grew up together. We're from that same bullshit little town. You gave me your phone number. You said we had a lot to talk about.

I'm sorry, but I must ask you to leave.

I took out my wallet, opened it up, and showed her the phone bill.

And what's that supposed to be? she asked.

It's Manny's phone bill from that Sunday morning. You know what it's supposed to be. Manny made two calls. One for ten minutes and one for twelve minutes. Both calls to your home phone. As in: This is Ann, after the beep you know what to do.

So?

So, why was Manny calling you before she dialed 911 or the police or Bobby Sullivan or me? Why you?

I don't know.

What did you talk about?

I don't remember.

Yes, you do. Don't lie to me. What did you talk about? Was Mrs. O'Neal dead already or were you helping Manny work up the courage to kill her?

Now that is crazy.

People use that word a lot lately, especially when something's not crazy. So why did Manny call you? What did you talk about? Everything comes down to that phone call, Ann.

She reached for the phone bill, and I pulled away and told her I had plenty of copies and that maybe she'd better brush up on the best evidence rule since it was a rapidly developing area of law.

That's when the security guards entered the office. Two of them. Central casting. The conversation went something like this: What's the problem? Let's go. No trouble, now, and host of other peacekeeper sayings to get me out of there.

> LOT 5, ITEM 1: "Untitled"—Clay sculpture, baked, hardened, shellacked: Man standing on porch, on tip-toes, straining to look through tall bay window of country home.

I drove around Hartford with the twenty bucks and tried to find a pharmacy that would front me some pills. I'd already gone through the insomnia-hyposomnia phase that usually precedes a crash, and stress was wreaking havoc on my biochemistry; so I started to feel the high-pitched anxiety when the stomach gets hollow and heavy, about to give way, an inner self about to collapse, the most personal shrinkage, a need to withdraw with no place to go, and deep vertigo to make passage impossible.

I started to drive back to Punter's Pond and had to stop in a rest area to run around the edge of it to work off the adrenaline that was making me want to shed my skin, tear at my face. It was like the all-consuming itch, irritation, and swelling of an allergic reaction precedent to anaphylactic shock.

When I reached Punter's Pond it was nighttime and dark and cold. In the distance I saw lights in the bay windows and the silhouette of two people moving back and forth. I parked down the road so they wouldn't hear me, walked back, and stepped up and across the porch to the window and looked in.

And there they were, the two of them: Manny and Brian, going at it, yelling at one another.

And who the hell told you to put that fuckin' bag over her head? Brian asked.

Somebody a lot smarter than you.

Shut up, Manny. I'm not stupid, and I don't do stupid things. Now who told you to do that?

Ann did.

Ann who?

Ann Dillon.

The lawyer?

Whatever.

Why? I mean why would you get yourself involved in such a bullshit scheme? You had a good run. You got a few bucks for nothing.

Ann's got a plan so I won't be cut out of everything. All I had to do was make it look like she'd been murdered.

Murdered?

Yes, murdered.

By who?

Robert Sullivan.

Bobby Sullivan? You're trying to set up Bobby Sullivan for a murder he didn't commit?

He's a bastard.

Jesus Christ, Manny, he's the fuckin' Prince of Darkness. He'll kill you.

No, he won't. I've got this thing covered.

This is unbelievable. You're out of your mind.

I don't think so, she said, and after that they settled down some, as Manny started to flirt with him, doing her Fred Astaire thing with her cane, telling him not to worry, that he'd been a big help, but that this was something else altogether, that it wasn't his problem, that she'd even set it up so that his little brother would take the fall if they couldn't nail Bobby Sullivan.

My brother?

Yes, your brother.

Matthew.

He's your brother, isn't he?

And Brian shook his head, one of those what-am-I-going-to-do-with-you exasperated looks, as she took him by the hand, pulled him up, and tried to make him dance.

My brother, he said.

What about him?

My brother is so fucked, he said. He's just a fucking embarrassment.

LOT 6, ITEM I: "Break"—Clay sculpture, baked, hardened, shellacked: Left side—Young man in fetal position lying in tall grass next to bear trap, circular, open, about to snap. Right side—Old woman, bent at the waist, walking through tall grass, searching for young man.

What happens is this: After the long buildup, like a buzzing in the head, there's this cessation of effort, pain, and sense. It lasts a second or two, and makes an impression by nature and not by duration. Then something slides, gives way, a bolt breaks, something pops, a nut cracks, clarity and confusion mix, what's real and what's imagined merge, separate and merge. There's the need to urinate and a fear based in manners and propriety that soon gives way to a fear that's got nothing to do with manners or propriety. It's like a fear of falling, an acrophobia absent the element of height, an immeasurable descent from dust to darkness. You're about to be swallowed and want to get it over with, as self-recrimination encounters no defense and the vicious bastard who is the ground of your very being rips up the person you once believed yourself to be. When it ends you find yourself wet and humiliated, clawing the earth, capable of nothing but little chirps, a bird's song, broken, not quite human, a voice that would speak of the acid arrow, the burning wire, the mad snake, poised and ready, the inconstant spinning when nothing holds.

Some think it's because Brian fucked her right there, on the floor, her legs in the air, but it wasn't that. It was all of it, the certitude of evil born within the soul and how death is the necessary and unwanted heir of those who lie and by lying create worlds in which they think they will not die.

I told myself lies, too, after that, and I didn't care who believed me, as long as I could make another world in which I was valued, esteemed, loved, in which women found me attractive, in which I'd be strong and not a coward, in which I might promote the agon of the gifted child. And so I entered this other world, not unknown to me, and I stayed there until borne back on the waters of that genius that requires only one irreducible element—the clay of this forgivable earth, the offal of generations made clean with time, gifts given and received, the burial of the dead.

LOVE

Clive flips the lights twice as if intermission were over, as if there were a second act for the last three drinkers left behind by others, life, or what had passed for their holidays.

Let's go, fellas, time to close up now.

What the hell are you sayin'? Time to close? It's New Year's Eve. You don't close on New Year's Eve.

It's time for closin', Mr. Bucket, so you might want to notify your friend there that it's time to wake up and go.

But how can it be time? It's a national holiday, says Bucket, with his sunken growl and dark glasses set in tarnished circular rims, elbow-wise poking his drinking companion, Mr. Tubbs, till Tubbs raises his head, snorts, looks around with damp, rheumy eyes.

Bucket and Tubbs, Clive says, the two of ya, like somebody's *Miami Vice* nightmare.

What the hell's he sayin'? Tubbs asks Bucket.

Says it's time to close.

So, close, what's that got to do with me?

Bucket turns to Clive: He's right, Clive. You can't close on New Year's Eve; it's not right.

Wouldn't be right if it were New Year's Eve. Problem is, it's not even New Year's Day. You fellows missed a day. It's two January and all the old rules apply.

Clive wipes the bar, sets bottles in their places, taps Bucket's glass, noting the inch of bourbon remaining.

C'mon now, Mr. Bucket, drink up before I have to toss it, and Bucket, reluctant, puffed up with litigator shock, raises his chin and stares straight ahead, eyes almost blind behind black lenses.

I would like another, he says, and Clive reaches for the glass, and Bucket grabs it and downs the bourbon.

Good, Clive says, now if I'm not mistaken you've only got twelve hours till I serve you again.

Let's go, Dwight, Bucket says, jostling the heavy guy who holds the end of the bar with one hand and waves to nobody with the other.

It seems, Bucket says, that the gendarme here's not about to serve his most loyal customers on New Year's Eve.

Shut up, Tubbs says, it's not New Year's. It was New Year's, but it's not now.

The two guys grab each other by the shoulders until Tubbs's feet start to move, and he rushes forward in the desperate hope of aligning his feet with an ever-moving center of gravity.

Stand up, now, Bucket yells, and he grabs Tubbs's arm and opens the door as they disappear into the cold night, though not before Bucket turns once to wave to Clive, to say goodnight.

Clive turns off the low overheads, and the bottles behind the bar shine in the bar's mirror. He grabs a bottle of brandy and two small glasses and crosses the room and sits in the booth with Manny Whitman.

We are officially after hours now, Manny.

Crockett and Tubbs are gone?

Those two are a three-act play in a two-act theater.

Too much month at the end of the paycheck.

What? Clive asks.

I don't know. Just one of those too much x for too little y sayings.

Right, like a five-dollar bird in a ten-dollar suit.

There you go, Clive.

Thank you, Ms. Whitman.

You Brits are so formal.

We're not really, love, it just sounds that way. A Mersey-side river rat with marbles sounds like quality to the average Yank.

I guess. Just like all you English think we're all cowboys or hoodlums or spoiled children with too much money and no taste.

Not true, love.

It's not?

That's what we think of Germans.

What time is it, Clive?

Twelve something.

Closing early?

A little.

I'd better be going then.

Have one brandy with me, Ms. Whitman.

He pours her two fingers and she drinks it.

Do you have your car? Clive asks.

Of course.

Well, I'm driving you tonight.

No, Clive, I'm fine.

Don't even start with me, Manny. This ain't the seventies and the cops and those MADD mothers out there are just waiting for people like you.

Like me?

You know what I'm saying, love.

I'll be fine.

Manny, this is what they call an executive decision. No appeals, no digressions, no amendments to the Constitution.

You're an odd one, Clive.

I am, mum. As odd as a round-trip ticket on a one-way bus.

What? I like that.

Clive stands and takes Manny by the elbow as she tries to stand, resting at the edge of the seat, pressing her hand, palm down, standing and almost falling when she turns too quickly to grab her cane.

All right, then, Clive says, taking her by the arm.

They exit the bar and cross the lot on the side of the building.

That yours? he asks, pointing to the BMW.

What did you do to me, Clive?

What do you mean, Ms. Whitman?

Yes, it's mine, but I'm so dizzy; I never get this dizzy.

You drank a quart and a half, Manny. You're lucky to be dizzy.

Don't say that.

What?

That I'm lucky. I'm not lucky. I'm the most unlucky woman who ever lived.

Oh, that's not true, love, you're just having a bad patch is all.

No, Clive, you don't understand.

Understand what, Manny?

I wanted—I want things to be different.

Clive holds her, supports her, as he takes her keys and opens the door.

Get in, love, and I'll drive you home.

Manny eases herself into the car, placing her cane down the length of one leg.

Clive gets in on the driver's side and starts the car.

Did you hear me, Clive?

I believe I did, Ms. Whitman.

And call me, Manny. Not Ms. Whitman, not Emmanuella, but Manny.

Manny, of course.

I said I want things to be different.

And what is it that you want, then? Clive asks, as the engine revs and the car warms.

My heart is broken, Clive.

I'm sorry, Manny, but I told you I never liked the look of that Louis character.

Not Louis.

No? Then what was his name?

His name was Louis, but it wasn't him.

It wasn't.

No. And it wasn't Brian either.

I never met Brian.

It wasn't any man.

So, he was special then?

Please, Clive, I'm not kidding. My heart is broken.

I'm sorry, Manny. I just thought a lighter touch—you know what I mean.

Clive slips the car into drive and accelerates out of the lot.

Jesus, isn't this a beautiful car, he says.

It wasn't a man at all, Manny says.

No, love, I figured as much.

I fell in love with a woman, Clive, a beautiful, delicate, classy, brilliant woman who treated me so well and was kind to me. Why can't people be kind to one another, Clive. People should be a lot kinder, you know.

Yes, they should, Clive says, eyeing the rearview mirror. So, tell me what happened, Manny. It sounds like you really loved her.

I did, Clive. I do, and things have got to be different than they are, but I don't know how to change them. I don't know how to do anything anymore, and she begins to sob, a drunk sob, a full-breath exhalation, a virile expulsion of something damp and sad as the liquor breaks down the last walls of decorum and Manny falls through herself to an empty plain of tender vulnerability.

I loved her, Clive. I love her. I know I've been a bitch, but I've had to do things to survive and I've had to make myself hard, but I'm not different than other people—I've got a heart, no matter what I did to myself or anybody else, but I never thought a person like me, who's never known love, Clive, never, not ever, could feel what I feel for her and I do feel it, right here, and I want her and that's that, and what else can I say—I want her because I love her.

Manny cries and her shoulders shake; Clive pulls the car down a quiet street and parks.

It'll be all right, he says, barely affecting the old accent from Merseyside. He reaches for her, one arm, soft-like, a comfort, a support, humanity shared, sorrows shared, and Manny, on the verge of collapse, falls into his arms, her body trembling with the kind of pain that seeks release in liquor, only to suffer its betrayal, the haunting emptiness.

Aw, c'mon, now, love, you're a survivor, just like you said.

I'm a mess, she says, trying to catch her breath, and I have fucked up everything.

Now, now, sweetness, don't be so hard on yourself. We all have our times; everybody's chipped a tea cup now and then.

This is more than a tea cup, Clive.

I know, hon, I'm not trying to make light of it. I know you're suffering.

Manny buries her face in the crook of his elbow and continues to cry, a low, simple maintenance cry that can go on for hours with eyes more damp than tearful.

Clive rubs his cheek over the soft billow of red hair. He whispers soft, bedtime talk as she relaxes some. He reaches into his coat pocket and takes out a leather eyeglass case and sets it on his thigh. Manny raises her head, and he holds her tighter, and she rests her head against his chest. He looks down and finds the white slope of her pale neck where arteries run to the brain. He fingers the leather case, snaps the button, and takes out a syringe filled with amber fluid. Manny's white neck is a field half-hidden in shadow, and he imagines pathways of blood and plunges the needle into her neck—an inch, a stop, another inch. She shakes her shoulders and tries to snap her head back, but his arms are strong, and the drug works as fast as they said it would. Manny's eyes roll once and the lids almost close, leaving slivers of blue-white moons waning.

Clive waits several minutes. Then he pushes the body, raises it, and sets it up in the passenger seat where it sits, a lifeless hulk miming sleep.

He takes out his phone. He taps the numbers. It rings.

Yes?

It's done, Clive says.

Where are you?

He tells her.

Wait there. Louis will be by in a few minutes.

Then what?

He'll take the car.

What's he going to do with it?

Not for you to worry about.

So, what about me?

Take his car, drive home, and make sure you park where we said.

He's okay with that?

He'll have your money.

All right then.

Make sure you don't leave anything behind.

Yes, Ms. Dillon.

There's a click, and it's over, but for the waiting and the scratch a memory can make on a conscience yet to be salved with the balm of money.

ICE

Charlie's on his cell phone with his bookie. He won one and lost one and is trying to work out the differential. Matthew stares at his Bernini. He sees the progress, but wonders how difficult it will be to carve it in marble.

Charlie gets off the phone and curses something and sits on the edge of the table.

"You never explain nothin' but you gotta explain this one," Charlie says, as Matthew stands and moves some of the other figures about.

"Explain what?" Matthew asks.

"You know what I mean, this is the first time I seen you make something that wasn't an angel or a Jesus or a Moses or one of them Bible people. These people look almost normal with their clothes. So tell me, what's the story with them?"

"No story," Matthew says. "They're just people."

"You mean to tell me you spent the last fourteen days in here every day and night working like a mad man to make jes' people?"

"I was working on the Bernini over there."

"You were working on all of them, Matthew."

"I was working mostly on the Bernini. I've got a patron now, Charlie. I'm in business. This is real stuff. I get paid for this now."

"I know you get paid, Matthew, I was just wondering is all . . ."

Matthew pauses. The seduction's begun. He gets paid for this now, and the first effect has been to blunt the fine filaments at the outer edge of kindness. He looks at Charlie and stops moving the figures about.

"Okay," he says, "what do you want to know?"

"I wanna know who this one here is," and Charlie points to the guy in the fetal position, lying down in tall grass.

"That's the lost sheep," Matthew says.

"The what?"

"The lost sheep, you know, like in the Bible where the good shepherd goes out looking for the lost sheep."

"But that's an old woman, that ain't no Jesus."

"That's creative license."

"Yeah, right, so then who's this?"

Charlie points to the woman standing by the desk.

"That's Ann," Matthew says.

"Ann who?"

"Just Ann."

"Yeah, but who is she?"

"I just told you."

"And who's with her?"

"That's a security guard."

"What's his name?"

"I don't have a name for him."

"Okay, so then who's this woman on the stairs."

"She's the one who thinks she's a con artist, but she's really just a pawn. She gets by in life with a pout and a kiss. I guess you could say she's the seductress."

"She don't look like no seductress to me."

"A seductress doesn't have to be the most beautiful woman in the room," Matthew says. "She just has to have this thing where she can look at you and make you feel a certain way."

"Don't go tellin' me about women, Matthew. I know all about women," Charlie says, "and, anyway, how do you get all of that jes' outta some woman stepping down stairs."

"It's the backstory," Matthew says.

"Backstory, my ass. I still don't see where you get all of it."

"Don't worry about it, Charlie. We've got nothing to worry about."

"Who said I got something to worry about?" Charlie asks, and Matthew goes blank, having hit the wall of revelation, having come too close to telling a story he's promised himself he'd never tell.

"Well?" Charlie asks.

"What?" Matthew asks, his eyes locked on something far away.

"Jesus Christ, Matthew don't do this to me; don't tell me we got to put you back on the ward with a fucking drip again."

Matthew blinks, comes to, and pats Charlie on the back. He says, "C'mon Charlie, it's just clay. It's nothing; it's like dirt. We let it stand here long enough, it'll dry up, turn to dust, and we can bury it with everybody else."

"Matthew Wyman, you know there's a story you're not tellin'."

"I've said enough."

"You've said jack-shit."

"Maybe I have," Matthew says.

Charlie stands in the center of the room, having had enough of Matthew's back-and-forth. "You ready then?" he asks.

"Ready," Matthew says, as he runs his hand under the tap, wipes his fingers on a towel, grabs his jacket with the lamb's wool lining, and follows Charlie out the door down the back corridor to the stairwell, where they descend to the lowest level and walk through another corridor and up three steps to a door. Charlie looks around to see if anybody's watching. He presses the keypad four times, waits for the click, and opens the door.

They step out into the cold. The air is immense and foreign and intimate all at the same time, containing the future and the past, playing with time and memories of people lost in time.

They step up a flight of concrete stairs and trudge through snow with a lacy wash of newly formed ice over the top. They make sounds with each step, and Charlie looks to see if any lights have come on, if anybody on the first floor is watching, thinking how they can't see out if their lights are on, reminding himself that it's Sunday night, that given everything in a state-run place with state-run employees, nobody will really care.

They step over a frozen drift onto a plowed walkway. They walk over black grass and stones that shine when the moonlight strikes the quartz or the mica or whatever mirror flakes make simple rocks shine in moonlight.

They come to a chain-link fence, and behind three pine bushes

Charlie pushes the fence all the way out so Matthew can squeeze through. Then Matthew holds the fence so Charlie can squeeze through.

It's quiet with only a little wind up above, so the cold feels okay as they start through the woods, along a path they've made with several trips on similar nights.

They come to a small rise and then look down over a short space that gives way to a flat space raked clean before the frozen water. The reservoir is huge, tapered to a point at this end, but expanding outward for miles, so wide and long neither Matthew nor Charlie have ever made it all the way around.

They step down off the rise and stumble some as they reach the octagon of logs set around the place where a long time ago kids made fires and made out and drank beer and all of that. Charlie takes his Swiss Army knife and scratches at a pile of leaves pressed up against the base of one of the logs. He reaches in and pulls out two pairs of men's skates. "Here you go," he says, tossing one pair to Matthew who catches them and feels how cold they are.

"C'mon, Matthew," Charlie says, the guy in charge, the guy who runs the show, the guy who makes the decisions, and Matthew sits on a log and removes his boots and puts on the skates. "Now we don't got much time tonight," Charlie says, "cuz I gotta be back there time Molly shows up, and she's been working the extra early shift since her old man spent her into debt with all his bullshit."

Matthew finishes tying the laces, stands, and walks to the edge of the ice. He looks up overhead to the immense sky and moves slowly at first, little circles and then larger circles. He's good at this. He knows how to skate; he's got great balance, and for a guy who's never been comfortable with movement and the physicality of it, having preferred to describe it with numbers, figures, and equations on a whiteboard, measuring the force of a man moving through space, Matthew's found the one pastime that works for him, this seasonal endeavor of white steel on ice made almost blue at midnight.

"Now don't go so far this time," Charlie calls out, stumbling some to get to the ice, tentative, slow, in charge but unable to move like Matthew, as Matthew skates backward now in a looping arc, moving around Charlie, circling him, and Charlie says, "You just wait, white boy, the brothers are gonna learn how to do this thing and then we are gonna kick your National Hockey League ass," and Matthew skates away again, spinning once and then returning to where Charlie makes his first attempt of the night to make a circle as grand as Matthew's, only to bend at the waist, overcorrecting for the imbalance that almost makes him fall.

"Keep your weight toward the front," Matthew says, instructing Charlie, telling him how to do it, with Charlie needing the instruction, but not necessarily wanting to hear it from one of the crazies.

And then Matthew lets loose with a power that would have surprised so many people, that would have shocked his physical brother and his cold mother and perhaps his father, his legs so strong, his thighs like pile drivers as they propel him over the ice, perfect and smooth, not so much human movement as a kind of flight, the minimal coefficient of friction as white steel barely touches blue ice while overhead the sky is too much to comprehend. He looks back once to the place where the reservoir tapers to nothing, the kiddie pond where Charlie continues to stop and go, bending too much, sway back and gravity a constant threat, and from that distance Matthew hears Charlie call his name, telling him he's going too far. And tonight Matthew is going too far, but he can't help it because he's caught up in something, like that tunnel they talk about, so wide and open, his arms wide and open, as infinite as the sky above and the dark distance in front of him, as he moves with the grace of a spirit, having visited this poor dumb earth, tired in its relentless struggle toward the infinite middle, having accomplished nothing, though that's what he'd been sent to do, and having done it so well, moves on now with a speed that can't be measured, a lightness that can't be felt, a heart beating, taking flight, beating . . .